A MEETING

Again, new currents stir in the captive, The Perceptors announced in alarm. *The resources of this mind are staggering!*

MATCH IT! the Egon directed.

My/our power resources are already overextended! the Calculators interjected.

WITHDRAW ENERGIES FROM ALL PERIPHERAL FUNCTIONS! LOWER SHIELDING! THE MOMENT OF THE ULTIMATE TEST IS UPON ME/US!

Swiftly, the Ree mind complied.

The captive is held, the Calculator announced. *But I/we must point out that this linkage now presents a channel of vulnerability to assault.*

THE RISK MUST BE TAKEN.

Even now the mind stirs against my/our control.

HOLD IT FAST!

Grimly, the Ree mind fought to retain its control of Mallory's brain.

. . . Mallory was aware of floating gravityless in a sea of winking, flashing energies. Vertigo rose up; frantically he fought for stability in a world of chaos. Through spinning darkness he reached . . .

Full emergency discharge! The Receptors blasted the command through all the sixtynine hundred and thirty-four units of the Ree mind—and recoiled in shock. *The captive mind clings to the contact! We cannot break free!*

KEITH LAUMER

ALIEN MINDS

Copyright © 1991 by Keith Laumer

"A Trip to the City" first appeared in *Amazing* magazine, January 1963, under the title "It Could Be Anything."

"The Exterminator" first appeared in *Galaxy Magazine*, February 1964, under the title "A Bad Day for Vermin."

"Dinochrome" first appeared in *The Magazine of Fantasy and Science Fiction*, November 1960, under the title "Combat Unit."

"Hybrid" first appeared in *The Magazine of Fantasy and Science Fiction*, November 1961.

"Greylorn" first appeared in *Amazing* magazine, April 1959.

"Time Thieves" first appeared in *Worlds of Tomorrow*, June 1963, under the title "The Star-Sent Knaves."

"Doorstep" first appeared in *Galaxy Magazine*, February 1961.

"Test to Destruction" first appeared in *Dangerous Visions*, edited by Harlan Ellison, Doubleday, 1967.

A Baen Books Original.

Baen Publishing Enterprises
P.O. Box 1403
Riverdale, N.Y. 10471

ISBN: 0-671-72055-4

Cover art by Doug Anderson

First printing, May 1991

Distributed by
SIMON & SCHUSTER
1230 Avenue of the Americas
New York, N.Y. 10020

Printed in the United States of America

TABLE OF CONTENTS

Alternatives to Intelligence

What we ordinarily think of as the exercise of high intelligence is actually the effective use of what is called the Scientific Method. It's a recent invention, dating back perhaps to Roger Bacon in the seventeenth century. It was a strange and revolutionary idea: to observe the realities and draw deductions therefrom. Nothing was to be assumed or taken on faith. Therein lay the revolution. Until then "research" consisted of referring to what Aristotle or one of a few other classical thinkers, such as Plato, Socrates and Ptolemy, had said on the subject. It was the recourse to authority, rather than to observable reality—the method still employed by religion. One looks up what the Bible says.

Unfortunately, the ancient wise men considered that experimentation fell in the category of "work." Work was for slaves, not savants. Asked how many teeth people have, it would never occur to the early dentist to tell a patient to open his mouth, and then count them (work). Instead he quoted Aristotle: Men

1

have thirty-two teeth, women twenty-eight. And that nonsense stood as established fact for over two millennia.

Then this new idea came along: observe, quantify, and theorize, then test the theory. Of course, the need to quantify accurately led promptly to the development of precise units of measure, and increasingly accurate devices to do the measuring. Accurate scales, clocks, calendars, and so on made it possible for the first time to measure, for example, the acceleration of gravity. From that datum, large conclusions could be drawn.

Now, we're all used to being "logical." If we drop a quarter on this corner, we don't look for it on another one, where the light is better. We all use the Scientific Method constantly, not thinking of it as a method, but as natural common sense. We tend to estimate intelligence by an entity's ability to do the obvious. When a bird trapped in the house fails to fly out the window when we open it, we think of the bird as stupid. When a chimp uses a stick to knock down a banana that's out of arm's reach, we consider him to be intelligent.

The ichneumon fly is an insect which gives its prey a paralyzing sting and wraps the living, but helpless, bug in silk and takes it back to the nest to leave beside the ready-to-hatch eggs. Being alive, the meat supply won't spoil, and the little darlings will have nice fresh chow at hand when they emerge. That sounds a lot like intelligent behavior. But the bug always puts its bundle down just outside the nest and reconnoitres inside, then comes back to fetch the groceries. But if some nosey entomologist moves the silk-wrapped bug half an inch, the fly will look for it in vain. It goes to where it left the bug, and finding nothing there, it flies off to find a new one, even though it may climb over the first one in the process. It's like a computer: programmed to perform a specific series of operations, blindly. It can't reason. Unfortunately, we know people like that, especially petty officials. "I'm sorry, sir, this window is *closed*." Or, "Yes, I see your receipt, but it isn't in the computer, *sir*, so you'll have to pay it now."

Thus, we see there are invertebrates which do very nicely using something other than intelligence to carry out some rather complex tasks. And there are people who function without any active use of brain power.

Not that logic works every time. Algebra is a supremely logical discipline, but I have seen a quite unassailable proof that $1 = 2$. Now, if a boy can give his dog a bath in a minute and a half, does it not follow, logically, that ninety small boys could bathe a dog in one second?

How about this: A man of ninety-nine is sitting down in a room, holding his year-old great-grandson on his lap. The average age of the people in the room is fifty, but there's no one there closer than forty-nine years to that age. So there's more to it than strict mathematical logic. Intelligence involves an ability to adjust to circumstances, to assess correctly the evidence of the senses, amplified by radio, telescope, micrometer, scale, etc. All this, of course, is based on the Laws of Nature as we perceive them here. A ball player can move unhurriedly to the spot where a high fly will descend and lazily pluck it out of the air. That's at Earth-normal G and air pressure. His mind is capable of computing the ball's path quite automatically; but put the game on Mars, and he'll miss every time. We know how hard to push with our feet when we get up from a chair, so that we neither jump clear of the floor nor sink back to try again. A thinking creature reared under a different set of natural constants would have devised quite different routines for coping with the exocosm. We can't assume that when we meet a technologically sophisticated species on some distant world, that sweet reasonableness will work. They might, for example, attack in the face of clearly overwhelming force. Or repay kindness with hostility, or even, as some people do, interpret courtesy as weakness and kindness as stupidity.

"I *had* to betray you to the enemy, Terry, because otherwise they might have been displeased with me—not that I don't appreciate you saving my life."

"Really, when you asked me to help you down the cliff, the easiest way was to push you over the edge. How was I to know you couldn't levitate?"

How about a science based on refined guessing? To determine the acceleration of gravity, we write: $A = \underline{\quad}$ ft/sec/sec, then roll a pair of dice. Of course the value of A cannot exceed twelve, the maximum number of spots ever visible at once. That is a constraint imposed by Nature (like the limiting velocity of light). Consider: All people, no matter how primitive, know that the Underworld is the realm of the dead. How can you doubt it? Where are the dead? Underground in their graves, of course. Who can deny it? In all Indo-European mythologies, the god of the smithy was lame. In the early Proto-Indo-European culture, the shaman who knew the arcane secrets of metal-working, passed to him by his (lame) father, was a valuable resource, and if he should run away and join the enemy—but if his legs are broken, he can't run. That's easy to arrange. They'll heal well enough that he can hobble around and do his work, but he won't run away. So, smiths are lame; everybody knows that, right? Thus, their patron God must himself be lame. Who ever heard of a smith who wasn't lame? Clearly it's a Law of Nature.

Thus we humans are able to regard our own acts

as Laws of Nature. Make it a crime to teach a slave to read—then observe that black folk are ignorant—can't even read. That proves their lack of intellect, right?

Among Earthly life-forms we have many examples of quite elaborate behaviors in the absence of intelligence. We call that instinct. How incredibly flexible these "instincts" must be, to enable living creatures to cope with such a bewildering variety of circumstances and still find the mate, get the nest built, incubate the eggs, feed the young and teach them to fly and hunt, etc. Imagine trying to design a self-propelled computer capable of recharging its own batteries, navigate over rough ground, flatten itself to a quarter of its usual thickness to go under an obstacle, withstand being squeezed between the rug and a weight one million times its own, counter persistent attempts to destroy it, and then build a duplicate of itself. Given the volume of a Goodyear blimp to work with, could we do even that last item? A mother cockroach turns them out in large batches. But what has that to do with intelligence? Nothing, as intellect is ordinarily thought of. So let's redefine intelligence: the capacity to cope with life by performing complex tasks under the direction of a neural system.

OK? In this sense, that cockroach is pretty smart. We ourselves aren't so dumb: Consider how cleverly a mere fertilized human ovum constructs a live baby, usually perfect in every detail. It uses the same basic design to make muscles, nerves, teeth, hair, etc.; a marvel of versatility; and it arranges things so as to provide an immune system, the ability to heal a wound, and a multitude of other systems, plus of course, to grow steadily bigger for many years without interfering with any of the above.

We might expect, when at last we make contact with our fellow inhabitants of the Galaxy, to find them in possession of even stranger and more marvelous capabilities. Instead of laboriously adapting to circumstances to stay alive, as all familiar life is so good at, how about the mud-dwellers of Krako Eight, who modify the circumstances to suit themselves? That's the Strong Anthropic (Krakic) Principle adapted to a smaller scale. To us, it looks like miracles. Confronted with a potential problem, a blocked exit from a burning building, say, they create a bubble of cool, fresh air about themselves and wait it out.

Then there are the Glimps of Justonemore, in the Goober Cluster, who *adapt*. They don't need even to modify the circumstances in order to survive catastrophe: they themselves change. Lost at sea, they simply grow gills and fins and swim home, doffing the fish equipment upon going ashore.

The Mancji, of course look on with amazement when we make a lump of mud turn into a pot, or weave plant fibers into cloth and make clothing thereof. When they want a pot, or an electron microscope, they *grow* it from their versatile cuticula. And of course, they find it a bit disgusting when we stuff once-living matter into our buccal orifices (mouths) in order to break it down for its constituent matter and energy, which we then incorporate into our own beings. They absorb their sustenance directly from the star's radiation, but they can see that our tricks could be useful under certain circumstances, and earnestly appeal to us to tell them how we do it. We'd be glad to, we tell them, but we don't know. "Now, I ask you in all fairness," their hawks demand, "You call *them* intelligent beings?" I guess we flunk, by their standards.

Of course, we mustn't overlook the Ancils, who cope by flitting effortless backwards in time, so as to correct developing problems in embryos. If you disperse the tiny rotating air-mass before it develops into a hurricane, it can't blow your favorite house away, can it?

When we eagerly inquire of the Mancji, the Glimps, Krakans and the Ancils just how they do their tricks, they say they don't know. Just like us— and the ichneumon fly.

The Yanda, of the world of that name, employ what might be called strategy in place of short-term tactics designed to preserve the individual: they "infect" other life-forms with seed-bearing spores, and wait to be reproduced. Thus their curious vegetative species is to be found on every world which has achieved space travel, or had been visited by such travelers. Perhaps such self-negation is characteristic of plant intelligence; the Yanda are the only such species known.

A similar, but less certain gambit is employed by the little-known molluscoids of TGS9076-A, who broadcast vast numbers of their appealing and helpless new-hatchings in single-entity capsules, hoping that, like cuckoo eggs, they will be adopted by the natives, a nasty trick, which frequently doesn't work, which is why the Galaxy is not dominated by land-dwelling squid. This approach to survival is not one to which our kind of intelligence could adapt. We have too much empathy with our young, and too much imagination to condemn them to a high probability of a horrible death. Of course, they are highly prolific and produce eggs by the zillion, daily, over a long life-span. These hatch almost immediately into cuddly, pink, tender, puppyish multilimbed babies; which learn to say "mama" and "papa" in hours, then grow up to master the local civilization by dint of their superb "intelligence," or whatever it is that enables them to seize power from their hosts, quite bloodlessly, at the age of about 100. The above referenced tenderness, together with their descent from the sky, has caused them to figure in the folklore of many a race eking out an existence on an arid world. They are highly nutritious as well as appetizing. Pretty dumb to waste them in this way, eh? Except when it works.

Success is, in the final analysis, the criterion of intellect. If *Homo sapiens* should be so careless as to make use of our present nuclear technology to eliminate ourselves from the Galactic competition for Destiny (we won't), then what price our painfully evolved mental capacities? A lone surviving Glimp, clinging to a rock in the intertidal Zone on Purgatory Twelve, having survived the explosion of his sun, not having much fun, but still living; he will have beaten us. Let's not let him.

The Propitiation of Brullamagoo

"Ye gods, sir!" exclaimed Ensign Goodlark, pulling the duty as Watch Officer on the command deck of Survey Vessel 8973-B-57, as he stared at the forward screen showing a swarm of jagged fragments of stone occupying the volume of space directly before the incoming ship.

"Rocks, sir!" Goodlark pointed out superfluously.

"I see them, Mister," Captain Hardshot assured the junior officer. "What I want to know is, what are you doing about it?"

"I, sir?" Goodlark gasped. "But, sir, the reason I asked you to come forrad, sir—"

"Skip that, Bob," Hardshot barked. He turned to Chief Spac'n Muldoon, who was hovering near the primary panel.

"Chief," the captain rapped, "you'd better throw us into a high-concentration evasive pattern, right now. Max coverage," he added. Muldoon leapt to comply as the deck underfoot tilted sharply enough to send Goodlark skidding against his Captain's rock-

9

solid bulk, at which he grabbed reflexively before recovering himself. "Sorry about that, sir, it's just that at the Academy they told us never to go to max gain to start with, so I wasn't expecting her to heel quite so fast—" He abandoned the presentation as further abrupt changes in orientation dumped all three men to the deck.

Before Hardshot could draw breath to bellow in outrage, the entire ship rang like a cracked bell and went into a bone-shaking oscillation quite apart from the evasive pattern. Hardshot was the first to his feet. He glared at the command panel as at an enemy.

"We're holed, men!" he announced, then grabbed the command talker to brief the crew.

"I've decided to use this space junk to help us bleed off velocity, men," he told them. "All hands to emergency survival stations! We're going to be OK; just do your duty as Terran Spac'n!"

"You shoulda give a feller a little warning, Cap'n," Muldoon mourned, "if you was going to steer her by ricoshaying off these here boulders and all."

"Nonsense, Muldoon!" The captain rejected the plaint. "I just said that to calm the men. *I* certainly wouldn't collide with a meteor on purpose!"

"But—since we *have* had a collision, sir," Goodlark piped up, "what can we do now? We're losing air awful fast—must be a pretty big hole aft." He managed a look at the still-functioning forward screen. "Here comes another one, sir!" he yelled and ducked, as a jagged-edged multi-ton chunk of iron barely grazed the ship, with a sound like fingernails on a blackboard. Muldoon moaned.

"Any way we can get what's left of her down in one piece, Cap'n?" he appealed. Hardshot ignored him.

"Seal off Section Nine aft," he ordered Goodlark.

"The men are clear by now." A heavy internal *bang*!-ing instantly followed Goodlark's compliance.

Hardshot was back on his feet, peering into the screen. Beyond the myriad rocks orbiting the planet below, he could see the misty blue-grey surface rushing toward him at dizzying speed.

"Roads!" he reported, "and a town—at least it looks like a town. That means civilized beings! I'm going to try to put her down close to the city, as soon as you've damped this infernal oscillation, Ensign!"

"Me, sir?" Goodlark inquired in a dazed tone, but he quickly got to the input console and punched in the necessary instructions to the close-maneuver thrust unit, which immediately analyzed the complex motion of the stricken craft and applied precisely the necessary forces to stabilize the vessel. As things righted themselves and the intolerable pressures faded to zero, Hardshot looked at the others triumphantly.

"We've done it, men! Classified Ia3–III here was listed as Type Three Hazardous, unexplored since she was first listed ninety-odd years ago, but we've done it! We can report a brand-new nine-point Terra-like world now open for development! Good work, fellows!"

Goodlark staggered to the repeater panel, scanned the LEDs and reported:

"She's about eighty percent off-line, sir." He paused to squint at the fine print. "But the twenty percent we've got might be enough, if . . . Chief," he interrupted himself, "check on the crew and see what you can get out of the autonav."

"Aye, sir," Muldoon grunted, and turned to the back-up talker, muttering to his deputy, Sub-chief Boyle. "Mike, how are you back there? All hands make it to ESS OK?"

After being assured that all hands had, indeed retired to their designated gut-buckets on command and were now busy mopping up puke, Muldoon rapped out succinct orders, covering all emergency systems and back-ups, then reported to his captain, his voice barely audible over the *whang*!ing of minor collisions.

"All secure, sir; standing by for final approach numbers."

"Take her in direct from the auxiliary screen, Chief," Hardshot ordered. "This would be a good time for nobody to foul up. Get me into atmosphere; I'll take it from there."

"What about all these objects we're hitting, sir?" Muldoon managed over the din.

"I'm matching vectors with them," Hardshot grunted. "They're all in orbit; so will we be in a minute. They're noisy, but can't do us any real harm."

"Look down there, sir," Goodlark urged, gazing at the big forward screen. "A big volcano—and a lot of little ones. See, sir?" He pointed.

"I was studying those a little earlier," Hardshot assured his Signals Officer. "You'll notice the city—or town—is strangely close to the biggest concentration of craters."

"Sir—they're not all volcanoes!" Goodlark exclaimed. "I just saw one formed! They're mostly impact craters from these rocks we're into. Boy! What an explosion!"

"No need to sound so enthusiastic, Mister," Hardshot rebuked the lad. "With luck, we'll be down there in the target area in a few minutes—on foot."

"Yessir," Goodlark agreed soberly. "What are we going to do, sir? I mean—look at that large volcano we're headed right for, with *two* giant craters, as if one wasn't enough! Only one of them is actually smoking, sir, if you know what I mean."

"I know quite well what you mean, Goodlark," the captain interrupted. "I shall deal with matters as they develop, you may rest assured. You will simply carry out your instructions as they are given. At the moment, that means deploying airfoils in readiness for braking maneuvers."

2

"I seen worse landings, sir!" Chief Muldoon assured his captain as the last of the crew crawled from the emergency personnel hatch aft to form up in a ragged column under the canopy of foliage through which they had arrived so abruptly. The air reeked of sulphur, and a blackish haze hung in the forest air. All hands leapt as a supersonic *screech*! split the silence, terminating in a dull *boom*! not far away.

"We better get out of here," Goodlark offered.

"We'll follow the trail, there," Hardshot commanded, pointing to a well-worn footpath which led away into the deep gloom of the forest. Goodlark hurried ahead and quickly disappeared around a bend in the path. Hardshot accelerated his pace to keep his junior in view, but halted abruptly as the young fellow came running back down the trail.

"Good news, sir!" Goodlark cried as he skidded to an approximation of the Position of a Soldier before his commander.

"One of the volcanic craters seems to be dormant, sir," he gasped out. "Up ahead, there's a clear place where the trees are all burning down, and I could get a good view of the volcano, sir!"

"And what about the other crater?" Hardshot demanded coldly. "That's the one about which I require a report!"

"Sure, sir. Well, that's where all these damned fumes are coming from: it's live, all right; but the one on the flank is quiescent; trees growing in it and all!"

"Very well, Ensign," Hardshot grunted. "You may

continue to scout the trail—but more quietly, I suggest, in case we're under observation." He motioned Muldoon to his side. "Deploy your people off-side, Chief," he ordered. "Arms at the ready; but no shooting until I give the command."

"Aye, sir," Muldoon acknowledged and was off. Meanwhile, Goodlark had sprinted up the trail. Hardshot followed briskly; he rounded the sharp turn and was confronted by the face of Ensign Goodlark smiling at him upside down, and reacted by yelling, as he did to all surprises.

"Hi, sir," Goodlark said brightly, unaware that his inverted smile resembled a threatening frown. "By the way—" he started seriously, producing an even more grotesque effect. The captain recoiled and yelled: "Goodlark! Get down from there at once—!" That was as far as he got with his justified rebuke when he himself was whisked from his feet by a stout rope and yanked upward to dangle face-to-face with his Signals Officer.

"That's what I was going to tell you about, sir," the ensign told his captain eagerly, "only you yelled, er—spoke just then, and—"

"The rest I know," Hardshot barked, as well as one can bark when the blood pressure in one's head is rapidly building toward a burst carotid. Before he could say more, a rotund, five-foot-tall being which came to a point on top and which ambulated on two skinny rootlike legs appeared from up-trail and halted abruptly at sight of the Terrans.

"Well, fellows," it said in faultless Standard, with a hint of the Irish-Oxford Twang affected by Middies at the Space Academy, though its mellow tenor was at odds with the rugged impression. "I guess I'm just a few moments behind schedule. Hope you don't mind the wait." He hurried forward to a point directly below them, and spoke upward toward the captain, ". . . *look* as depraved as—" The turniplike alien's voice trailed off, then became brisk: ". . . all that nonsense about someone called 'Regulations'," it said, dismissingly. "Now, I'm sure we can work things out as reasonable beings."

"Get me down from here, you turnip-head!" Hardshot shouted; again, his snarl lacked something of its usual timbre, due to his position. "And," he went on, "if I find that you had anything to do with this outrage—!" He left the rest to one's imagination.

"Gee, sir," Goodlark offered cautiously, "couldn't you get him to cut *me* down, too? And maybe you'd better not let him know what you're going to do to him, sir, until after we're on our feet again."

"Where the devil's Chief Muldoon?" Hardshot growled, his growl somewhat muffled as he twisted his head to look back along the trail. "Probably snared, himself," the captain guessed, then returned his attention to the little fellow below, which, or who, was gazing up at him from two yellow, glombeadlike eyes set on short, thick stalks at the sides of its sharply tapering upper end.

"Just rest easy, Stinky, old fellow," it advised cheerfully. "The chaps will be along and have you down in a jiff."

Hardshot resumed the fruitless threshing which he had discontinued when the turnip-man appeared.

"Just wait, you!" he commanded. "Until I get my hands on you!" As he spoke he was groping toward the object of his admonition, who was well out of reach.

"Now, fellows," the being soothed, edging back a trifle uneasily. "We must remember that we are all rational beings, and not allow brute emotion to overwhelm us."

Listening absently, Ensign Goodlark was flexing himself at knee and hip, while reaching for his ankles, invisible above him in a dense mass of bluish foliage. He reached his knees, felt his way along his shins, found a stout leatherlike strap looped about his ankles, pressing them painfully together. He straightened out briefly to unclip his service knife from his belt and snap it open. Then he bent himself upward again, and stroked the keen blade across the taut thong. It parted instantly and he struck the leaf-litter flat on his back, quite knocking his wind out.

"I . . . ah . . ." he gasped, but gave it up to work on sucking a little air into his lungs. Then he scrambled up, and was dusting vigorously at the organic debris clinging to his handsome blue polyon shipsuit when three more turnip-shaped beings came into view. The leader, a more stoutly built fellow wearing a polished metal cone with cutouts for his oculars topping his upper end, halted abruptly and pointed a rootlike finger at the smaller turnip-man who had preceded him.

"You've done it this time, Yip!" he charged in a mellow though furious voice, in the same Class dialect as Yip himself, pronouncing "time" as "toyme."

Yip responded by retiring behind Ensign Goodlark.

"I must entreat your protection," he entreated. "Old Nurp is getting desperate: he's going to stretch his paradigm to its limit, and he knows it."

"Where did he learn to speak such excellent Standard, Class dialect, too?" Goodlark asked, shifting position slightly to remain protectively in front of the little fellow.

"Oh, you're going to teach him," Yip replied. "Now, this next bit is going to be a bit tricky, I fear. But just listen carefully and follow my lead. You *do* whaffle nicely, I hope? Nurp won't be expecting that."

"What's 'whaffle'?" the ensign wanted to know. "Except for that one term, I'd swear you were Class of '81."

"We'll go into that later, of course," Yip dismissed the inquiry. "By the way," he went on, "we're Ancils, and our world is known by the same name. To us, that is; no one else knows about it."

"I was just going to ask you about that!" Goodlark exclaimed.

"Of course," Yip said. "Why else would I have answered you? And they've got me dead to rights for whaffling during a Solemn Ceremony." While Goodlark was considering these remarks, Yip added, "My execution."

"Your execution, what?" Goodlark queried, then, "Oh, of course, the Solemn Ceremony. I was just . . ."

"Pray try not to dwell on the inconsequential, sir," Yip suggested severely. "Nurp means business, and he's got a whole squad of Citizen Volunteers at his heels."

"Here, you," Captain Hardshot barked, verbally interposing himself between Goodlark and the Ancil. "Who's responsible for this outrage?"

"Which outrage was that, Stinky?" Yip countered innocently.

"*This* outrage!" Hardshot yelled. "Catching myself and my people by the heels, sir! That's what outrage!" Even as he spoke, there was a *whoosh*! and Chief Muldoon, just rounding the bend, was yanked up to dangle, red-faced, before his captain.

"Let Chief Muldoon down at once!" Hardshot demanded, averting his eyes from the spectacle of a fifty-year-old man in slightly rumpled dress whites with hash marks from wrist to elbow swinging upside-down unable even to salute. Almost absentmindedly, the ensign drew his belt-knife, with which he promptly cut Muldoon's supporting rope. After the heavy fall, the chief lay for a moment, then groaned.

"Damn fool!" he muttered, as one who wishes not to be overheard, even by himself. "Cut a man down like that without warning!" He moaned and rubbed his neck, miming agony.

"Curious," Yip commented as Hardshot turned his attention to Muldoon's groaning complaints. "One would expect him to have anticipated that result."

"We didn't anticipate this barbaric treatment to begin with," Hardshot yelled.

"Strange," Yip commented. "Actually, we were after those rascals, the Tuzic. Now you've aborted that paradigm. Most inconvenient."

"You did it again," Goodlark put in. "What's a Tuzic?"

"A Tuzic," Yip stated distastefully, "is a moral leper who, though, like us all, was created as a jest by Brullamagoo, praised be his name, was created in the next valley over, and is thus quite naturally excluded from the Chosen status conferred on His people. His *real* people, I mean, of course," Yip concluded, "meaning ourselves, the great tribe of Ancil; besides which, they're occupying territory for which I'm sure we could find a use."

"What about us?" Hardshot demanded, still dangling. "Especially me! You think old Brullywhatever didn't create us, too? Fine business trapping fellow creations of His like that. What do these Tuzics look like?"

"Like me," a whispery voice supplied from a point high in the foliage. All eyes turned upward, and at once discovered an Ancil-like form hanging by one leg from yet another noose attached to a high bough. "I'm Lord Whink," he added.

"Quickly," the Tuzic went on. "You—'Stinky,' I heard that degenerate call you—just nip up here and cut me free."

"Don't you dare," Yip warned quickly.

Goodlark, ignoring Yip, thrust his way into the brush to a point from which he could jump and get a grasp on a stout branch; thence he climbed rapidly up to a point just opposite the dangling Tuzic.

"First," Goodlark told the saucy fellow, "I'll have

to get you swinging so you can get a handhold or two on that vine over there." He pointed to a stout liana some feet out of the Tuzic's reach.

"Whatever for?" the dangling alien demanded.

"Wouldn't do to let a chap drop on his apex, eh?" Goodlark suggested.

"What's this?" Whink retorted. "You claim to be clairvoyant, foretelling what is yet to come?"

"Damn his apex," Hardshot snapped from below. "And his confounded insolence as well! Ensign, get down here. Still," he added, "I suppose it wouldn't hurt to do as you, ah, suggest first." Goodlark was able, by putting a foot on a slender bough, to lean out far enough to grasp the taut rope supporting the Tuzic and give it a tug, which set up an oscillation which swung Whink in a slow arc, first closer to him, then away. With a lunge, it caught the vine.

Goodlark had already unsheathed his belt-knife and now he leaned out again and with a deft stroke severed the rope restraining Whink, who at once slid down the vine and out of sight in the dense, blue-violet foliage.

"Without," Hardshot commented to Goodlark as soon as the latter had clambered down, "so much as a 'by your leave.' " He looked around, his keen gaze probing the underbrush. "Cut and run, eh? So much for interspecies amity."

"Sure, sir," Chief Muldoon muttered. "How's come the ensign to help the bugger out, anyways? Oh, 'interspecies amity,' you said. Yeah. What's amity, sir?"

"From the latin *amica*, meaning 'friend,' " Hardshot told the confused powerman. "Means 'friendship,' or at least not open warfare, like I'd like to wage on that little smart alec if I could get my hands on him." He turned to Yip.

"I was going to ask what the war was about," he told the Ancil. "But now I see."

"Of course, Stinky," Yip replied. "That's why I didn't answer the question."

"Call me 'Captain,' Yip," Hardshot grunted. "This 'Stinky' business can be overdone."

" 'Captain Yip'?" the little fellow repeated. "Why, what an astounding coincidence, Captain Yip. I wonder if we could somehow be related?"

"Not 'Captain Yip,' " Hardshot yelled. "Just 'Captain,' Yip!"

"A distinction without a difference, that would appear to be, Captain Yip," Yip commented. Hardshot turned on Goodlark.

"Don't just stand there, Goodlark!" he barked. "Tell this idiot what I said!"

"Oh, he heard you, sir, I'm sure," the ensign reassured his captain. "You told him to call you 'Captain Yip,' and he did so, so that means he understood. Only why do you want him to call you 'Captain Yip,' sir?"

"I don't, you damned fool!" Hardshot yelled. "Look here, all I said was, 'Call me "Captain," Yip.' Isn't that clear, Goodlark?"

"Perfectly, er, Captain Yip," the young officer responded, coming to a Position of Attention. "Clear, that is; just not clear, if the Captain understands me, Captain Yip."

"It's not *my* understanding that's at issue here!" the captain informed his junior. "And just call me 'Captain,' Goodlark!"

"But, sir, I mean Captain Goodlark," the young fellow stammered. "Whyever should I do that, when I know perfectly well you're Captain Hardshot, or possibly Yip?"

"You may call me Captain Hardshot if you desire, Ensign," the commander told the lad. "Though I'd have no objection if you simply address me as 'Captain,' Goodlark."

"Excuse *me*, gents," Chief Muldoon put in hesitantly. "Is the captain your old man or what, Goodie?" he demanded of his immediate supervisor. "I heard you call him 'the old man' plenty times, oney I thought that was just a manner of speaking, in a manner o' speaking."

"What, this certifiable imbecile, *my* son?" Hardshot yelled.

"Well, Captain Goodlark, seein' you two got the same name and all . . ."

"Are you saying that the ensign has been commissioned under an assumed name, and that his actual name is Hardshot?"

"That ain't what I had in mind, sir," Muldoon corrected unhappily.

"In *mind*, Chief?" Hardshot challenged. "I think you've *all* taken leave of your minds." His gaze fell on Yip. "You, too!" he snapped. "Now what's all this about having to Nurp because of some fellow named Whaffle, Yip?"

"Captain Yip," the Ancil replied, "I know of no individual named 'Whaffle Yip.' I had a great-uncle known as 'Raffle' Yip, because of the manner in which he dissipated his inheritance. But I doubt you'll know him. He passed on next year."

Suddenly Hardshot grabbed Goodlark's arm. "I begin to understand, Bob," he said in a stage whisper. "We've fallen among the inmates of an asylum. Just reason with them and avoid exciting them and we'll get through this yet, Goodlark."

"A second ago you called me 'Bob,' Captain Goodlark," the ensign replied excitedly. "I hoped that indicated the beginning of a new and more cordial era in our relationship, sir; but now we're back to 'Goodlark,' already."

"As to 'Goodlark,' Goodlark," Hardshot snapped. "I hope you've called me 'Captain Goodlark' for the last time!"

"Oh, you want me to call you 'Melvin,' eh, sir?"

Hardshot shook his head in negation, his eyes, a trifle bloodshot due to his upside-down position, boring into Goodlark's.

" 'Stinky'?" the ensign guessed. "Oh, I couldn't do that, Melvin. Too familiar, you know; not conducive to good discipline aboard ship. Why, if Chief Muldoon here heard me calling you 'Stinky,' pretty soon the whole crew would follow suit. Bad for discipline, as I pointed out, Captain—I mean Melvin."

The captain's gaze moved on to the chief. "Try to explain to him, eh, Chief, there's a good fellow. Tell him to forget about 'Melvin,' and go right on calling me 'Captain,' Muldoon."

" 'Captain Muldoon'!" the powerman gasped. "You mean it's *me* that's yer son, or maybe your pa, you mean. OK, pop. I'll call you 'Captain Muldoon' if you say so, only I never heard about any branch of the family ever wore stripes—on his cuff, I mean. We're a family o' deck apes and proud of it!"

"Captain Muldoon!" Yip put in severely. "Or Captain Yip-Muldoon, perhaps. I fail to grasp the rationality of all this name-dangling. I suppose I'd best stick to 'Melvin,' since for some reason you appear to resent the stately handle 'Stinky.' "

"You call me 'Captain,' you sawed-off space lawyer!" Hardshot snapped.

"Hardly," Yip objected. "Far too cumbersome! 'Stinky' it is then, eh, chaps?" He turned to the awed crewmen standing by with their mouths open at this display of *lese majeste*.

"Very well, Mr. Yip," Goodlark assented, while Muldoon was content to grunt. The other men coming up were all talking at once, demanding to know why Phipps, the logroom yeoman, was dangling upside down in mid-trail, while the captain, also inverted, and the rest of the brass gassed with a turnip.

"Regulations, sir," Phipps was solemnly advising

the captain's back, "clearly require that one's captain render immediate relief to a subordinate hanging by one ankle from a fufu tree, in line of duty. Hurry up," he added boldly. "I already been here five seconds or more. Wouldn't call that hardly 'immediate' like it says in the Regs, I bet."

"Actually," Goodlark stepped in in defense of his commander, "I doubt Regs say anything at all about fufu trees, inasmuch as they were discovered and named by myself not ten minutes ago."

"Chief Muldoon," Phipps appealed. "Surely you, as fellow enlisted personnel, will get me the heck down from here?"

"Oh, so now it's 'we're all spac'n together,' is it, Phipps?" Muldoon responded in a tone which engendered in the latter no hope of early release. "I seen them field notes o' your'n. 'Brutality,' you said. 'Non-com brutality'; and all's I was doing, I was tryna get them recruits started in the right direction for Navy career-men."

"Short-term draftees, both of 'em," Phipps corrected. "All right, Chief, I'll forget all that when I write up the log officially—if you'll demonstrate your humanity by getting me down."

"Deal," Muldoon agreed and with a quick swipe of his deck-knife dumped the yeoman on his head. Phipps rose, furious.

"You coulda give me a like warning, Muldoon!" was his most clearly heard remark.

"That's 'Chief,' Phipps," Muldoon corrected loudly.

Near at hand, Goodlark whirled to stare at the NCO in amazement. "And here I've been addressing you as 'Chief Muldoon,' Chief Phipps, for all these months!" he blurted. "Sorry about that, but you never said you and Phipps were related."

"No need, sir," Muldoon reassured the youthful officer. "'Chief Muldoon' it is, sir. But this here swabbie done called me 'Muldoon,' without the

'Chief,' which I was oney reminding him of his manners, sir."

"But I distinctly heard you say 'That's Chief Phipps,' Muldoon," Goodlark countered.

"I say," Yip commented to his cospecific, Nurp, "it appears I was mistaken. These are not rational creatures after all."

"Certainly not as one ordinarily understands the term," Nurp assented. "So it's OK to knock them on the head and take their possessions."

"I didn't mean *that*, exactly!" Yip objected. "I only meant—"

"What you may or may not have meant is quite immaterial, I assure you, Yip," the other Ancil told him, and gave a subtle signal, consisting of a leap two feet into the overhanging jungle growth and the emitting of a shrill bleat.

"Why," Goodlark asked the fellow, "did you leap two feet into the overhanging jungle growth and utter a shrill bleat?"

"Don't pry, my man," Nurp dismissed the query. By then he was busy addressing hand-and-arm signals to the dozen or so helmeted Ancils who had emerged from the brush at his command. One approached his chief and rendered the foot salute, which caused him to trip and fall at Nurp's feet.

"Sergeant Zut," the boss Ancil addressed his fallen subordinate sharply. "I've told you and I've told you, the foot salute is appropriate for formal situations only, or when in static formation to receive a Regimental Rebuke!"

Zut got slowly to his feet. "I ain't been a week since you wrote me up for the Green Bladder, sir," he stated reproachfully. "Now you're talking RR's, just on account of I was maybe a little overzealous with the old military courtesies. How do you get a transfer outa this whackle-dump outfit?"

"This outfit," Yump yelled, "is no 'whackle-dump,'

as you so crudely suggest, *Private* Zut! Now fall in
and let's get cracking!"

Zut withdrew, muttering. "It figures, but I can't
believe it!"

"None of your sauce, Private!" Nurp admonished.

"It just occurred to me," Zut muttered in a tone
of rebellion, a fair approximation of the classic 721–
a through m, (Deep Disillusionment at the Failure
of a Hallowed Principle), "we've no basis, for dis-
missing these foreign devils as brainless, unless we
apply criteria which would consign us, also, to the
category." At that moment, he vanished, with a
sharp *plop*! of imploding air.

"He vanished!" Hardshot cried. "With a sharp
plop! of imploding air!"

"He didn't exactly vanish," Goodlark corrected.
"He actually went elsewhere. Otherwise there'd
have been no *plop*!"

"By the great horn spoon!" Hardshot gobbled.
"You're right! It's no mere trick of sleight-of-hand."
He passed through the space Zut had occupied but
a moment agone. "He—he teleported or something.
It's a lot like furfling, don't you agree, Ensign?"

"Very like it," Goodlark agreed, automatically.

" 'Furfling,' indeed!" Colonel Yump interjected in
a tone of contempt, almost a classic 24 (These Are
Not the Sort of Chaps It's Possible For One to
Know). "The scamp has poffled yet *again*, in clear
violation of statutes! Fan out, troops," he directed
his followers. "Keep a sharp eye for the characteristic
spectral phenomena accompanying a poffle. He won't
have gone far!" Nurp started along the trail as if
determined to lay his quarry by the heels personally,
but at the second step, he was abruptly yanked off
his feet and hauled up to hang inverted face-to-face
with Hardshot.

"Look here, fellow," he whined brokenly. "There's
been an unfortunate breakdown in discipline. I gave

distinct instructions to my jungle artifice chaps to set
only four traps! Yet here's another, all unsuspected,
which means—never mind! Places me in a most
untenable position. Surely you as a fellow leader of
a pack of morons have sufficient empathy to cut me
down quietly before someone notices and sets up a
jeer at the expense not only of myself, but of the
principle of discipline itself!"

Hardshot poked a hard finger at Nurp. "You said
it was another bunch you called Tuzics or something
setting the traps. How about it?"

"A mere slip of the speech-mechanism, in a manner of speaking," Nurp gobbled.

"Right," Hardshot agreed. "Commonly called
lying."

"By no means, Captain Yip-Goodlark," Nurp objected. "Oh, I forgot the honorific 'Muldoon.' Won't
do to get a chap's style wrong, eh? Anyway, we
hadda catch these Tuzics, and in pursuit of that
objective, I had the four lines set up here, so you
see it *was* all on account of them! Too bad you fellows had to stumble into here like you did. And now
I'm hoist on my own petard! The entire situation
is ridiculous! Excuse me! *Whop!*" With that, Nurp
became absent, leaving the noose to swing empty
before Hardshot's astonished gaze.

"And with a *whop!* of imploding air, too!" the captain exclaimed. "Did you see that, Bob?" he demanded as he twisted in air, setting up an oscillation,
causing him to collide with young Goodlark.

"No, Melvin, I didn't," the young fellow replied,
as he rebounded and fell flat on his back. Looking
up from that position, he added, "But I *heard* it,
sir!"

"Don't call me 'sir' in that position," Hardshot
barked. "Next you'll be saluting from there."

"Sorry, sir," Goodlark gobbled and at once exe-
cuted the hand salute—not too badly for a fellow

dumped on his butt by a collision with his commanding officer, Hardshot grudgingly though silently
conceded.

"Not too bad, eh, Melvin?" Goodlark suggested.
"For a fellow dumped on his butt by a collision with
his commanding officer, I mean."

"Get up, Goodlark!" Hardshot ordered curtly.

"I was just *going* to," Goodlark muttered, and got
to his feet, dusting leaf-litter from the seat of his
pants.

"Don't answer back, Ensign!" Hardshot growled.
"Just listen. Now, you *heard* Nurp vanishing or
whatever he did, eh?"

"May I answer that, sir?" Goodlark queried tentatively.

"You may, and indeed *must* answer!" the CO
yelled. "Just don't answer *back*! It's an entirely different thing!"

"You could've fooled *me*," Goodlark returned,
doggedly.

"That's answering back!" Hardshot snapped.

"Well, I wasn't sure," Goodlark mumbled.

"So is that!" the captain barked. "Goodlark, don't
you understand *anything*?"

"Sure, sir," Goodlark replied. "See, that time it
wasn't answering back."

"Congratulations, Mister," Hardshot said coldly.
"Now, I'm sure you'll agree there's something funny
going on around here."

"I notice that you're not laughing, sir," Goodlark
said. "So I conclude that you employ the word
'funny' in the figurative sense."

"Skip all that," Hardshot dismissed the remark.
"Now, young fellow," he went on grimly, his eyes
fixed, upside-down, on Goodlark's, "you and my
NCOIC have been released from your undignified
positions. Does it occur to you you're overlooking

something?" His inverted eyes bored into the junior officer's.

"Uh, well, sir, I was sort of expecting you to use your ship-knife to cut your*self* down," Goodlark offered.

"What?" Hardshot yelled. "And fall on my head like Muldoon?"

"I could sort of ease you down, sir," Goodlark suggested. "Or you could—"

"Never mind!" Hardshot commanded, and, drawing his knife, he slashed his supporting rope and fell heavily as Goodlark leapt in to cushion his fall.

Goodlark disentangled himself, got to his feet, and assisted his captain to rise.

"There's a job to be done here, Goodlark," Hardshot rebuked, "and horsing around with a disappearing turnip won't get it done. You wait here, *precisely* here. I'm going to get to the bottom of this." With that, he turned and went back downtrail to join Yip and Muldoon, who were engaged in conversation. Goodlark hesitated, then followed.

". . . began when he failed to come to the Position of Attention while I dressed him down!" Hardshot was telling Muldoon.

"Frankly, sir, I seen the signs a long time," Muldoon agreed fervently. "Figgered the kid'd crack wide open sooner or later; he come in to the Power Section one day and busted up the game, in defiance o' long-standing tradition and all, Captain, sir, where it says soon's the on-watch crew's finished schedules A and B with addenda, the boys got a right to a little relaxation and like that. Quoted Regs, too," the chief charged resentfully.

"I knew it!" Hardshot announced. "Then—when he started calling me 'Melvin'—in spite of my direct order to the contrary, *and* in defiance of all rules of sound discipline as well as of simple Military Courtesy—well, Chief, I don't mind telling you, I'd had

hopes for the lad, but that *did* it! No help for it now.
Take the poor boob into custody as soon as he
catches up, with all due regard for his rank, naturally, and I'll convene a court as soon as we're back
aboard ship. Frankly, while I wouldn't dream of con-
demning this officer in advance, I feel sure there'll
be a Space Execution, for rank insubordination, malfeasance—"

"What's that there 'malfeasance,' sir?" Muldoon
interrupted. "Is that busting up a snooch game,
which I was holding tree hoors?"

"Among other things," Hardshot acknowledged
irritably, "but as I was saying—where *is* the scamp?"
He turned to peer back along the shadowy trail for
the lagging Goodlark, who, having overheard the
drift of the conversation, had halted uncertainly.
Hardshot made out his tall, gangling figure and
yelled: "Ensign Goodlark! Report to me at once! Get
up here, man; what are you doing lurking back
there! When I distinctly said, 'Come along'?"

"No you didn't, with respect, sir," Goodlark protested. "You said, 'Wait precisely there.' "

"Which you intentionally disregarded," Hardshot
snarled. "Why, Bob?" he went on with a sudden
break in his voice. "After I've virtually treated you
as a son—why this insistence on this course of folly?
You leave me no option, my boy. You're under
arrest—never mind the irons, Muldoon. He's to be
under arrest in quarters—after all, he's still an officer
and a gentleman!"

"How can I get to my quarters, sir?" Goodlark objected. "The ship is a mile from here, at least, and I
don't know if I can get back inside that warped hatch."

"Just fall in at the end of the column and make
yourself inconspicuous," Hardshot told him, with an
obvious effort at self-control.

"Don't fergit dem tree hoors," Muldoon urged his
captain. "I woulda got well wid dem ladies."

"Fear not, Muldoon," Hardshot reassured the senior non-com. "Young Bob Goodlark has plenty on his plate. Why, if he hadn't made those log entries regarding an 'earthlike planet' out this way, I'd never have deviated from course and ended up making the forced planetfall when the DV's blew."

"Sure, sir, he done that," Muldoon agreed soberly. "I'll hafta keep an eye out he don't do a sneak offa duh tail o' duh column."

"Chief Muldoon!" Hardshot objected. "Ensign Goodlark is after all an officer, an Academy graduate, and a gentleman. He would never 'do a sneak,' as you put it. That's why he always commits his follies in plain view!"

"Guess I fergot, sir," Muldoon confessed.

As Goodlark passed the conversational group nearly blocking the trail, Yip fell in at his side and accompanied him past the straggling crewmen now being eagerly questioned by the volunteers of Nurp's vigilante team. When they were in the clear, Yip tugged at Goodlark's sleeve.

"A moment, good sir," he pled. "None of my business, of course, but one can't help wondering why it is you don't whaffle."

"Don't know how," Goodlark admitted, looking down at the Ancil from his six-foot-two altitude. "You used that word before, and I still don't know what it means."

" 'Means'?" Yip echoed, and came to a standstill. "Why, it means to whaffle, of course."

"One can hardly define a lexeme in terms of itself," Goodlark objected.

Yip was forced to agree. "It means to resolve a difficult or, especially, a life-threatening situation, by the exercise of the capacities of one's neural circuitry," he stated.

"To use the old gourd, eh?" Goodlark suggested. "Well, let's see: Old Hardshot's flipped his lid at last, doesn't even know who he is—thinks he's my father, or possibly Muldoon's son—and he's determined to court-martial me for *his* incompetence, and shoot me out of hand, just like *you* have Nurp and his gang determined to do you in—all according to Regs. Not to mention the volcanos and meteorites. So—what do we do?"

"Ah," Yip breathed uncertainly, "may I, er, rummage a trifle—in your psyche, I mean?"

Goodlark felt a ghostly touch behind his eyes, like impalpable fingers groping among his most cherished illusions.

"S-sure, go right ahead," he managed. "What are you doing, anyway?"

"Just checking your bope nodes, my boy," Yip reassured. "It seems that though they're well developed, not having been stunted, it appears, by excessive cogitation, you fail to make full use thereof."

"Well, how do I do that?" Goodlark asked indifferently. "I never even knew I had any bope nodes."

"So it appears," Yip grunted. "Well, first of all, to paffle, or as you call it, 'to whaffle,' you employ the nodes in *this* orientation. . . ."

Goodlark felt a sharp tweak which seemed to set his eyeballs rotating at about fifty RPM, he estimated. "Stop it!" he yelped. "I'm getting space-sick!"

"Hardly, my boy," Yip corrected. "Just a matter of realigning the old paradigm. Now, about your memory . . ."

"I like my memory just like it is!" Goodlark protested as he felt another touch inside his skull; this time he seemed to be inverted, gazing *up* at his own feet. With an effort he spoke: "I said you could rummage, not turn me inside out!"

"Not inside out, lad; merely a matter of rearranging your priorities, so to speak."

"You know the country hereabouts," Goodlark

gobbled, "so it's up to *you* to say which way we should go."

"Go?" Yip repeated in a Tone of Incredulity (a–w). "You, an officer on his honor—propose to defect? And you imagine I, too, would violate the Code in like fashion?" In high dudgeon, Yip forged ahead, leaving Goodlark alone on the dimly marked trail. He paused, listening for threatening sounds from the dense undergrowth, and was rewarded by a distinct 'Hssst!' from above. He looked up, saw nothing.

"But that was a distinct 'Hssst!' from above," he muttered, puzzled.

"That was no Hist, that was me," Whink's voice returned promptly. Then, to the accompaniment of a crashing of disturbed foliage, the saucy fellow appeared, sliding down a sloon-vine. Goodlark recoiled.

"Take it easy, Bob," Whink advised. "Don't believe all that yivshish old Yip's been telling you fellows about what bad hats us Tuzics are. The real fact is, they got it in for us because we got a opposite temporal orientation, like you Terries, so they can't dope us out; messes up their paradigm, see?"

"No," Goodlark responded, edging away. "What do you mean, 'like you Terries'?"

"Hey, look, Bob," Whink cajoled. "Be honest, now: you got any idea what I'm going to do next?"

"Not the least," Goodlark admitted, "but," he went on hopefully, "surely it will be nothing that might interfere with the nice beginning we've made on establishing Terry-Ancil amity and all."

"Don't go mixing us Tuzics up with the Ancils," Whink ordered testily. "No offense; I can see why a foreigner could make the mistake," he conceded, less vehemently. "We *do* look kind of alike, superficially, but it's *us* that got the old temporal orientation right, right?"

"Not exactly," Goodlark stammered. "It's 'we' that have what you said right."

"That's what I said," Whink stated impatiently. "Like us. But the Ancils, they got it all backwards. The poor boobs think cause follows effect. And they've got lousy memories, too, to make it worse."

"What has memory to do with it?" Goodlark demanded, intrigued in spite of himself, but still edging down-trail.

"Everything!" Whink confirmed. "Look at it like this: the Ancils remember what's coming up next, only they've got lousy memories, like I said."

"How could anyone 'remember' next week?" Goodlark inquired earnestly. "Why, the very concept . . ."

"Right! Now you're getting the idea," Whink assured the young officer.

"I am?" Goodlark queried.

"Sure," Whink reassured him. "In the early days, it gave 'em kind of an evolutionary edge; say if you know a big tudge is just about to jump out at you, and all, you can take evasive action, you know; only *we* come along and they can't dope us; throws their whole paradigm out of whack, the poor boobs. Same with you fellows," Whink continued. "They're faking it; trying to make you believe they've got you on their scopes, you know. Only they don't, OK?"

"Hardly," Goodlark demurred. "You appear to be talking rubbish, frankly."

"Well, I always try to be frank," Whink assured the ensign. "But what do you mean, 'rubbish'?"

"I didn't mean *you* were frank," Goodlark objected. "*I* was being frank."

"Ah, yes, an admirable quality in the young, if not carried too far," Whink commented. "But to return to the subject: you and I are natural allies in the fight against the feckless Ancils. Agreed?"

"By no means," Goodlark objected. "That chap Yip appeared to be a good enough fellow, if a bit confused."

"Surely you realize," Whink proposed, "that the

punitive expedition you encountered, and which laid you by the heels, was dispatched with the sole objective of capturing you."

"That's absurd," Goodlark dismissed the statement. "Why, we'd only just arrived; there was no way they could have so much as known of our existence, far less acquired a grievance against us!"

"You haven't been listening, Bob," Whink charged, wearily rather than impatiently. "The scamps remembered your arrival, but were a bit foggy about what happened next."

"That's nonsense," Goodlark told his voluble informant. "Are you saying they've got bad memories because they can't remember what's going to happen next week?"

"No, you've got it all wrong," Whink rebuked. "Next week has nothing to do with it: that's when the *big* meteorite's due to strike, they say. About a mile and a half east of here. Big fellow: about ten miles wide, they tell us. They're all set for *that*; it's *you* fellows who're the problem."

"Really?" Goodlark caroled. "How, may I ask, does one 'get set' for a disaster of astronomical proportions?"

"Oh, they've made their wills, buried all their art treasures and the like a few miles deep under the granitic shield. That ought to hold up OK. It's only coming in at about five MPS."

"That's 'miles per second,' I assume," Goodlark commented feebly. "Did you say ten miles wide?"

Whink bobbed his pointed head in confirmation. Goodlark started off in three directions in turn before halting before the insouciant Tuzic.

"With the world about to come to an end," he yelled, "do you propose to just flit about in the trees and do nothing?"

"Not at all," Whink replied, unperturbed. "That's what's got the Ancils all excited. We were just starting with our Plan, when they got wind of it and started the war. Then you fellows got in the way."

"I didn't notice any war, precisely," Goodlark objected. "Just some silly snares set in the trail, and a party of jailors chasing *you*."

"Is there some special way you Terries think we ought to wage wars?" Whink demanded. "Personally, I find hanging upside-down to be highly uncomfortable, and it interferes with my duties as a soldier, as well!"

"Of course," Goodlark soothed. "It's outrageous, but for now, while we're trying to establish friendly relations and all, perhaps we'd better overlook the gaffe."

"*I'm* not trying to establish relations, friendly or otherwise, with that crowd of dements," Whink corrected the record. "We already established a firm enmity a long time ago!"

"Surely," Goodlark urged, "you'd prefer to be friends—after all, they *are* very like you."

"That does it!" Whink barked, as well as one can bark with a voice like a deflating air mattress. "I already told you, the Ancils are wired up backwards! You Terries are like us Tuzics in the way that counts, so we're natural allies in our war of extermination!"

"Not quite," Goodlark countered. "While we would, of course, be well pleased to establish a cordial relationship with you fellows, our enthusiasm stops short of committing Terra to all-out war against the Ancils, with whom we are equally eager to be friends." He paused for breath. "You mentioned a Plan; just what does this Plan involve, and why do the Ancils resent it sufficiently to embroil the planet in a fratricidal war?"

"Nix," Whink snapped. "No prying into strategic secrets under cover of trying to butter me up."

"I resent that," Goodlark remarked mildly. "But if there actually is some possibility of surviving the coming debacle, I think we have a right to know about it. No doubt the captain will wish to lend all possible assistance."

"Now you're talking," Whink remarked. "I can see your viewpoint, sort of. The thing is, it's old Brulla-magoo causing the trouble, right? So what we need to do is placate him, which he'll relent and settle for a near-miss. But how do we placate a deity which he's really wroth this time? Easy," Whink answered his own query. "We stage a Fub ceremony of unprecedented proportions: instead of tossing a cou-ple lousy whickle-birds in the crater, we give the old devil—oops, sorry about that—" Whink interrupted himself and gave the sky an anxious glance. "Well, anyway, we feed him a whole tribe of Ancils, that's what! How about that for scope?"

"You propose to sacrifice an entire tribe of indige-nous autocthones, your own near relatives, to some barbaric god, in the hope of arresting a meteor strike?" Goodlark demanded, not concealing his disapproval.

"Sure," Whink agreed. "They're doomed anyways, if we just sit here and let it hit; and what nobler fate could an Ancil hope for than to be exchanged, one to one, about, for noble Tuzics? A great way to go, right?"

"So you propose to wipe out the Ancils in order to preserve your own hides?" Goodlark accused. "And how, may one ask, do you intend to carry out this mass murder?"

"The usual way," Whink told him as one explain-ing the obvious. "Only the poor boobs can't remem-ber what happened last time, only next time. Now, Fub rules call for the usual band music and ritual fire dance, and then we throw the honoree into the crater. Old Brullamagoo swallows the offerings with-out even a burp, and he's so happy with the gift, he cancels the end of the world, right? How can it miss?"

"This Brullamagoo sounds like some sort of volcano," Goodlark hazarded. "And you plan to stage a barbaric ceremony involving living sacrifice in hope of averting a meteorite impact?"

If Whink noticed Goodlark's tone of outrage, he ignored it. "The best," he confirmed, pointing to the smoking cone looming over the landscape, with the gaping pit in its flank. "Old Brully's a half a mile high and has been in constant eruption since before recorded history. That's a redundancy," he acknowledged. "If it's not recorded, it's not history, OK. Anyways, old Brully will accept the offering and call off the collision. So what are we waiting around for? Let's get cracking!"

"And just how do you propose to secure the cooperation of the Ancils in this scheme?" Goodlark demanded. "I fear your entire plan falls to the ground, feasibilitywise, unless there's something you haven't told me."

"Easy," Whink reassured the young fellow. "We capture em, first. They're already out in force, tryna do us Tuzics a mischief; so see, we hafta decoy the dum-dums into the endless Ravine, which Brully got it blocked upslope, and we dump a couple zillion tons of rock down to cut off retreat, in case they don't wanna go along with the Plan. Then, when they get good and hungry, say after about a hour with no food or water, we offer to feed 'em and lower a rope ladder and when they come up, we anoint 'em and it's off to the Fub rites! Neat, eh? I was the one worked out the whole scheme," Whink conceded modestly. "But now they're trying to mess it up! No respect for tradition, which they don't know anything about, them not knowing anything about history and all—so it's up to us to see old Brully gets his due!"

"By 'us,'" Goodlark put in, resisting Whink's

effort to tug him along the path in the direction from which his party had come, "I presume you mean the Tuzic tribe?"

"Sure, and you Terries," Whink explicated. "See, the Fub'll save *your* bacon, too. And all we lose is a few hundred mere Ancils! But I got no more time to waste. You coming along, to be saved, like us, or you going down with the Ancils?"

"You surely don't mean—" Goodlark choked, retreating.

"If you're not with us, you're against us, pal," Whink intoned as one stating the obvious.

"But it's insane," Goodlark protested. "Throwing sentient beings down the maw of a volcano won't have any effect on a meteor strike!"

"Got any better ideas?" Whink inquired in a reasonable tone.

"Well . . ." Goodlark temporized. "How did the Ancils plan to survive? After all, they were the first to know."

"Oh, they had some diabolical plan to throw us Tuzics to old Brully. Pretty nasty, eh?"

"But—what's the difference?" Goodlark demanded. "They throw you in, or you throw *them* in. It's six of one and half a dozen of the other."

"Naw, you still don't get it," Whink objected. "They wanna throw all six hundred of the noble Tuzic clan in—and you Terries to boot. The difference is—their way, *we* suffer; *our* way, *they* take the gaff."

"Either course would be equally inacceptable to Enlightened Galactic Opinion," Goodlark declared with finality.

"Well, you declared that with finality and all," Whink observed. "But what does it mean?"

"It means that if either group succeeds in incinerating the other, it will find itself regarded as a pack of pariahs by the Galactic community."

"So what does this Galactic community do about it?" Whink demanded.

"Do?" Goodlark queried. "Why, it simply strikes you off the figurative invitation-list, that's what! You'll be left out of all group activities, not consulted regarding matters of common concern, refused diplomatic recognition, and so on."

"I guess we could live with that," Whink offered, "*if* we're alive to live with it, I mean," he elucidated. "So, between a short swim in the lava and missing out on a tea party, I think I know which way to go."

"It's clear," Goodlark said seriously. "This matter has ramifications beyond the scope of my personal authority. I must hurry ahead and apprise the captain of all this." He eyed the smoking cone of Brullamagoo anxiously. "When is he, or it, likely to erupt?" he asked nervously.

"Any time, Ensign," Whink replied carelessly. "Any time at all, I guess. I'm not one to be second-guessing Brullamagoo."

"Refusing to try to foretell the future is one thing," Goodlark stated sternly. "Failure to draw reasonable inferences from past experience is quite another!"

"We get along OK, kid," Whink dismissed the plaint. "Now, let's be reasonable: if—"

"For heaven's sake," Goodlark interrupted, "I must rejoin my shipmates—not that there's any possibility that Captain Hardshot, TN, will in any way condone your brutal scheme."

"Well," Whink remarked, "one thing, kid, you'll have a swell view of the action. We're right in the gully the lava flows down. See all that black rock over there with the charred stumps sticking out? That's from last time, a little over a year ago."

"How often does it erupt?" Goodlark demanded.

"About once a year," Whink told him.

"You don't need to remember the future," Goodlark advised the local, "to see that it would be beneficial to Terran-Tuzic relations if I reach the captain *before* it goes off again!"

"That's a point," Whink conceded off-handedly, "I guess; I'm not one fer peering into the future, like I told you."

"By the way." Goodlark changed the subject. "Just how is it both you and that Ancil chap speak Standard?"

"We pick it out of your minds," Whink replied. "A skill we developed at an early stage of evolution to make soothing noises to predators and prey, too; just adapted the trick to a new mode. Works pretty well. I see by your memory-matrix you had to spend a lot of time and work just to learn three or four dialects at the Academy. But maybe you'll reach our stage of development eventually, if you don't get yerselfs kilt first."

"Your diction is hardly the best," Goodlark carped. "Get yourselves killed; would be the correct form. Clearly, you picked up the dialect of one of the less literate members of the crew."

"I don't see nothing correct about us getting ourselves killed," Whink objected. "But what the heck: we just tilt them sneaky Ancils down Big Throat, and nobody got to worry about getting theirselfs kilt."

"You seem to have encountered one of our deck personnel before you revealed yourself to the captain," Goodlark hazarded. "Why wasn't this contact reported?"

"Oh, when I contacted old Mickey, he thought he'd went nuts," the Tuzic explained. "He taken off into the woods, and I lost him." He nodded his turnip-head toward the smoking mountain. "Thata way. Prolly half way up old Brully by now."

"That would be Space'n Last Class Michaels, S.C.," Goodlark deduced. "No wonder; he's a nervous sort of fellow at best. A talking turnip would have sent him right off his gourd." Just then the looming volcano uttered a sharp *bark*! and emitted a roiling cloud of smoke looking as dense as brown whipped cream. Goodlark went rigid and looked toward Whink for guidance.

"Easy, Terry," the Tuzic advised. "He does that all the time. When he means business, he spits out melted rock." Coincidentally with the last word, bright red-orange fluid brimmed over the ragged crater edge and spread swiftly downhill, igniting brush, which flamed up and added its smoke to the spectacle.

"Prolly just a small one," Whink hazarded. "He's prolly a little pissed about the Ancils' dirty scheme to do away with his best worshippers. But just in case, we better ease offside, before the hot stuff comes down this here chute about sixty per."

"I must report to the captain at once!" Goodlark declared and sprinted up-trail.

"Not that way, Terry," Whink called after him in vain. "That's where . . ." He abandoned the effort and scaled the tree to a major branch and darted off along it.

3

As Goodlark rounded a turn, he saw a jagged crevasse yawning directly across his path. He skidded to a halt, barely in time, by grabbing a ropy vine draped by the abruptly ended trail. Pebbles dislodged by his skid dribbled over the edge, and he waited in vain for the sound of impact below. Then he stole a cautious look down into emptiness; the wall on the rim of which he was crouched was undercut, and fell away into smoky vastness. Sulphur fumes stung his eyes and throat. He drew back, scanning the opposite edge of the ravine an alarming distance away across the void. There was a sudden *crash*!ing amid the foliage there, and Lord Whink dropped from a low branch to land with a *thud*! at the extreme edge of the cliff, where he teetered for a moment before regaining his balance and stepping back. His spindly legs appeared inadequate for his bulk, but he waved cheerfully and called.

"Oops! I almost saved old Nurp the trouble," he commented casually. "You, too. Glad I got here before you went over!"

"Why didn't you warn me?" Goodlark demanded, backing away from the edge and the Tuzic alike. "I could have been killed."

Whink peered over the edge and nodded his pointy upper end. "Yep," he agreed. "I'm no Ancil, to be making predictions, but it's a fair guess. You'd have been smashed on the rocks before the poison gas got you, and then burned alive, or maybe drowned in magma. Not pretty ways to go, any of them."

"There's no such thing as a pretty way to go!" Goodlark commented sharply. "You don't seem to care much, either," he added.

"After all, lad," Whink riposted, "it didn't happen, so why get emotional about it?"

"I guess you're right," Goodlark conceded. "Now, how'm I going to get across? More to the point," he amended, "how did the other fellows get across?"

"Oh, they went around," Whink told the distraught ensign. "See?" He pointed. "There's a sort of a trail along the edge there—but don't get too close."

"Don't worry," Goodlark cautioned the alien. "I'm not going *near* the edge." He backed off a few steps as if to demonstrate his technique of not going near the edge. "What's up-trail, anyways?" he asked abruptly. "Anything the captain and his entire crew ought to be risking their lives to get to?"

"Nothing much," the Tuzic told him, "except the

Sacred Caves, of course. But I don't see why they'd be interested. Old Brully doesn't care about foreigners; strictly a local diety, you understand. And I doubt you Terries even knew about the Caves in the first place. It's our big secret. The Ancils', too."

"We *didn't*!" Goodlark confirmed. "When we disembarked, the Captain just pointed to the only trail in sight and said, 'This way, men.' We were looking for the town."

"That's a couple miles ahead," Whink told him.

"Well, we'd better get up there," Goodlark urged. "I have to brief the captain on developments before he does anything hasty."

"Looks like you could climb pretty good with those hands," Whink offered. "How about the feet?"

"I guess I can climb as well as the next fellow," Goodlark confirmed readily.

"Where?" Whink demanded. "I don't see any next fellow—they're all with Stinky."

"It's a figure of speech," Goodlark reassured the nervous Tuzic, who had already scaled a tall, palm-like trunk and was peering down through the fronds; then he was gone. Goodlark began to shinny up the trunk, soon finding his hands bristling with tiny thorns which were no more painful than so many bee stings. Halfway up the thirty-foot ascent, he changed his mind and slid quickly to the spongy ground, thereby filling his thighs with the venomous splinters. He dropped his trousers and used the tiny anaspray from his regulation first-aid kit to ease the discomfort, rearranged his clothing, backed up hastily, and looked around carefully at the enclosing jungle growth. He selected a route at random, and set out doggedly upslope. He soon encountered another smoking crevasse, smaller than the first, likely a tributary crack, he thought; by first backing off a few steps he was able to leap it without difficulty. Now he heard sounds ahead; he made his way through the dense growth until he emerged in a cleared area of volcanic rock. At the far side of the open space, Captain Hardshot stood in earnest conversation, if not dispute, with Yip, or perhaps some other Ancil; Goodlark couldn't tell them apart.

"—told you we have no intention of paying tribute to any local deity!" the captain was telling the small alien in his usual quiet, well-mannered yell.

"—don't need to dissemble with *me*, Stinky," the Ancil replied. "Why else would you be hurrying along at flank speed directly into the fiery maw of good old Brullamagoo?"

"As I told you, dammit," was the irate reply, "we're bound for the capital village we saw on the way in, so as to carry out a bit of summitry with your local king, or president, or whatever, thereby establishing Terry-Ancil relations on a firm basis of mutual understanding!"

"You expect me to predict what you said perhaps ten minutes ago?" the alien demanded. "I'm no mud-ball gazer, but I can tell you that Brully is about to dump fifty million metric tons of molten basalt right down this chute, so we better get out of here pronto!"

"Duty requires that I press on to the capital," Hardshot persisted. "It's *that* way, I'm quite sure," he added, pointing to the apparently impenetrable wall of tropical undergrowth beside him. He turned, barked, "This way, men, in a column of ducks," and attempted to thrust his way between two needle-bark trees. Goodlark leapt forward and yelled, "Captain! No! Stay clear of those yellow palm trees!"

Hardshot looked around, startled. "You would attempt to give orders to your very own CO?" he demanded, sounding astonished.

"Not orders, sir," Goodlark corrected. "More of a suggestion, actually; you see, those ochre trees are pretty nasty. Look, I'll show you my legs." As he began to unbuckle his belt, Hardshot held up an imperious hand.

"Ensign Goodlark!" he roared. "In all my thirty-six years in the Service, I have never before—kindly fasten your clothing, sir! I can't imagine how you secured the impression that I, of all people, would have any prurient interest in your nether members! Outrageous! Consider yourself under close arrest and reduced to the rank of brevet deck-ape!"

"It's not my nether members, sir, exactly," Goodlark complained. "It's the splinters stuck in my nether members! But that's not the point! The point is you mustn't make any commitment to this local here, to take his side in the war!"

"Now you presume," Hardshot summarized in a glacial tone, "to offer not mere advice but dictation to an officer astronomically your senior *and* your Commander! Your impudence, sir, surpasses anything envisioned by those who drafted the regulations concerned with insubordination, mutiny, and conduct unbecoming! Get out of my sight, Goodlark!" He turned his back to the unhappy youth to resume his tete-a-tete with the Ancil.

"I have a theory, sir," Goodlark told the captain's back. "Since the Ancils can't remember the past, and the Tuzics can't predict the future, they're totally confused. Both sides charge the other with trying to force them to jump in the volcano; but actually, both sides *want* to! Notice that's the way they're all headed. That seems suicidal to them, so they both have the same rationalization: they're being forced into the volcano!"

"Why, Goodlark?" Hardshot interrupted. "Why in the world would any rational creature hurry to its own destruction, rationalizations be damned?"

"They're not exactly rational, remember, sir," Goodlark offered. "The Ancils can't remember last year and the Tuzics can't project the simplest conse-

quences of their actions—so they go by instinct, sort
of, I guess."

"This is yivshish, Bob!" Hardshot yelled. "Comes
of hobnobbing with that Yip fellow! Now stay out of
sight, and allow *me* to conduct negotiations!"

Goodlark advanced cautiously, taking care to remain behind the infuriated captain.

"Really, sir," he offered desperately, "you mustn't
commit yourself, and all of us, and Terra, to a policy
of genocide."

"Genocide?" Hardshot yelled, turning to confront
Goodlark, who, having nimbly darted aside, remained behind his superior officer.

"I," Hardshot went on portentiously, "am about
to cement relations with the dominant species of
Classified Ia3–III, by the simple expedient of paying
a courtesy call on the nearby shrine."

"S-sir," Goodlark managed. "The 'shrine' is *that*!"
He pointed to the smoking cone looming above the
treetops. "And, sir—" He forged on in the momentary respite afforded by Hardshot's double-take and
his muttered, "Nonsense, Goodlark. That's no simple rural holy place, it's an erupting volcano, about
a nine on the Crumblnski scale, I'd say."

"—they plan to throw the Tuzics right down its
throat!"

"Just a moment, lad," Hardshot said kindly. "I see
you're not quite yourself; had a bad scare, eh?" He
approached and by deft footwork was able almost to
confront the young officer. "What's the matter, boy?"
Hardshot demanded, with restraint, addressing Goodlark's left shoulder. "Learned a new dance, have
you? Interested in local folk-arts, I suppose. Stand
still, dammit!"

"You said to stay out of your sight, sir," Goodlark
explained lamely, impaled at last by his captain's
cold blue eyes.

"What's all this rubbish about throwing toothpicks in the volcano?" the senior officer growled.

"Not 'toothpicks,' sir," Goodlark corrected hesitantly. " 'Tuzics'; that's the other local tribe. It seems they're at war, sir, the Ancils and the Toothpicks, I mean the Tuzics, sir; and we're messing around in a highly sensitive situation of which we know nothing—or almost nothing, except what I'm trying to report, sir."

"Going to throw these Tuzics of yours down the throat of a Crumblnski Niner, eh? What do they plan to do, line the whole tribe up in a column of ducks and just march 'em over the edge of the crater?"

"Lord Whink didn't say as to that, sir," Goodlark admitted. "Just going to offer them to Brullamagoo."

"An entire *tribe?*" Hardshot yelled. "Females, young and all?" He turned indignantly on the Ancil:

"Anything in it, Yip?" he yelled. "Going to involve me in killing an entire population of locals?"

"Well," Yip replied modestly, "all we can catch."

"Is that how you wage war, here on Class?" Hardshot demanded.

"No, Stinky, it's how we cope with our irate deity, Brullamagoo. He's angry, as usual, and we just thought—"

Hardshot spun to face Goodlark. "It appears, Ensign (yes, you're reinstated) that for once you're right. Lucky I found out about this; could have blighted my entire career."

"It could have blighted more than your career, sir," Goodlark pointed out. "In case they can't round up the Ancils, the Tuzics propose to offer *us* to Brully. And I'm willing to bet, sir, the Ancils have the same idea, if they can't trick the Tuzics into the boiling lava."

Hardshot bellied up to Yip, towering over the frail-looking being. "That right, fella?" he snarled.

"You had in mind substituting Terries for Tuzics, did you?"

"Well, Stinky," Yip temporized, "clearly, it's not the same, but we figure old Brully might accept the substitution, since otherwise it's bleaksville all around. He goes without the sacrifice, and we cook; you fellows might mollify him enough to maybe save us. In fact, I seem to remember his wrath *is* going to be averted, and this must be the way; can't think of any other, unless we Ancils fall in and march up there, singing glad hosannas and all."

"Well, you'll get no Terran naval personnel to feed to your confounded idol," Hardshot barked. "So perhaps you'd better start putting your emergency plan in motion."

"Say, Captain." Chief Muldoon's hoarse voice came from a clump of brush nearby. "You want I should go ahead and hose these jokers down?"

"Hold your fire, Chief," Hardshot commanded. "For the present," he added, giving Yip a significant look, the significance of which the Ancil failed to grasp, having ignored the exchange.

"You got maybe a touch heartburn, Stinky?" he inquired solicitously.

"What's the matter?" Hardshot demanded. "You draw the line at incinerating a line officer with a bellyache?"

"It's not that," Yip corrected. "Old Brully's not all that particular. He cures 'em all."

"A novel therapy for excess acidity," Hardshot commented.

"And maybe a touch gas," Yip suggested. He uttered a shrill whistle and some dozen of his fellow Ancils dropped from the foliage overhead. At a signal from Hardshot, Muldoon urged the members of the crew of SV8973–B–57 forward, telling them to keep their weapons concealed as they huddled in a crest-fallen group around their captain, to whose neck a rope had been attached, surprisingly without protest.

"OK," Yip said cheerfully. "Let's have a column of space'n here, Chief," he addressed Muldoon, and, to his own second-in-command, "Shape 'em up and get 'em on the trail pronto, Zut."

"Sure, sir," Zut agreed, offering an oblique inclination of his upper end, which apparently served as a salute, which Yip returned with a careless shrug of his own.

"Good twenty-minute climb, Stinky," the little alien told the captain. "Time to get your thoughts in order in readiness to meet the inevitable fate of all organic matter."

"Being murdered with a volcano is hardly the inevitable fate of all organic matter, sir!" Hardshot objected, but fell in at the head of the forlorn column, Goodlark at his left, inobtrusively peering upward for some sign of Lord Whink and his Tuzics, hurrying to the rescue.

". . . dammit, Goodlark!" Captain Hardshot was saying, irascibly as usual, Goodlark noted.

"Sorry about that, sir," the boy improvised. "I just thought you ought to know."

"To be sure," Hardshot muttered, "but actually, you know, Goodlark, you exceeded your authority in meddling in matters of state."

"You, too, sir," Goodlark returned in as conciliatory a tone as possible, given the basic impudence of the remark. "I mean, at the Academy, sir, we were taught to leave all such stuff to the CDT."

"I well recall, Goodlark," Hardshot acknowledged. "But, insofar as I am aware, no representative of the CDT is present here on Class, nor is likely to be until and unless I complete my mission of contact!" With that he turned again to Yip, who was skipping along at his side, his thin legs fairly twinkling as he attempted to match the Terran's stride. "Mister

Yip," the captain intoned, "I herewith lodge a formal complaint at this cavalier treatment of a peaceful party of Terran naval personnel intent only on establishing amicable relations with your people."

"Sure, Stinky," Yip assented. "What could be more friendly than saving us from dire destruction and all?"

"Let me assure you, Mister Yip," Hardshot said earnestly, "dumping me and my command down a live volcano will negatively affect the life expectancy of your tribe—as soon, of course, as the authorities hear of it, and make an example of you."

"You don't get it," Yip objected. "I've got no choice: Old Brully's got his dander up, and covets a live sacrifice—and since these infernally selfish Tuzics won't go, you're the only alternative."

"How do you know all this?" Hardshot challenged.

"Well, any being with a eyeball and some olfactory membranes can see he's mad!" Yip pointed out, indicating the smoking cone looming over them all.

"Well, certainly it's clear the volcano is active," Hardshot conceded. "But that's a natural phenomenon, not an emotional outburst. Sacrificing innocent beings won't change it!"

"Funny," Yip commented. "I had the idea you Terries were wired up backwards, like that Tuzic trash; remembered the past instead of the future, but now you're telling *me* what's going to happen; but I got a pretty good memory on me; it says Brully's going to accept the offering and lay off the rough stuff!"

"Mine is not a mystical vision of the future," Hardshot objected. "It's a reasoned prediction, based on scientific fact. An eruption is caused by pressure on fluid lava in the mantle, which then escapes to the surface by whatever fissures exist, thereby relieving the pressure! The visible signs tell me eruption is imminent."

"Well, Stinky," Yip remarked casually, "I don't see how that idea's spose to help us. Our method's the best one we know of. Can you suggest a better technique?"

"Absolutely not," Hardshot stated flatly. "Nothing can stop a volcano from erupting."

"Well, what do we have to lose, except a few stray Terries?" Yip inquired, reasonably enough.

"Your status as a civilized world, that's what!" Hardshot supplied promptly. "Think of Enlightened Galactic Opinion!"

"Never heard of it," Yip dismissed the exhortation.

As the others conversed, Ensign Goodlark had continued to search the foliage overhead for a glimpse of Lord Whink, who, he assumed, was near at hand.

"The admission of Class—Ia3–III—to the Galactic community is inevitable," Hardshot intoned. "The question is, will she be admitted as a Category One civilization, or as a world of superstitious, bloodthirsty savages? I call on you, sir, to consider the consequences to your progeny of this rash act!"

"What progeny, if we just stand around and let her erupt?" Yip demanded.

"Wait a minute," Goodlark spoke up, having momentarily tuned in on the conversation. "I thought you said we were in for a meteor strike, not an eruption!"

"Don't worry, kid," Yip counseled. "When that rock hits, the whole planet will skid maybe a couple of hundred yards, and every extinct smoker on this plate will fire up."

"Don't sound so cheerful," Goodlark rebuked the feckless alien. His attention had returned to the foliage mass above, where he was sure he saw a flicker of movement not assignable to the wind in the leaves.

"Oh, sir," he addressed the captain, who was listening intently to a lengthy exposition by Yip.

"Not now, Goodlark," Hardshot barked.

"But, sir," Goodlark protested, just as Lord Whink dropped from a low bough, directly in the path of the procession.

"Hey, it's another one!" Chief Muldoon blurted. "This here one's got a different-colored harness on him. Say, feller." He directed his address to the newcomer. "We're a party of distressed spacemen, which we been rounded up by these here savages, and it looks like they're gonna throw us inna volcano. So how's about grabbing the chance to make a few points by getting *yer* bunch together to rescue us and all?" The chief glanced at Hardshot for approval of his diplomatic overture. Instead, he netted a baleful glare.

"Chief!" Hardshot rebuked. "I'll thank you to remember that so long as your captain is present, your duties do not require you to foment war among the indigenous autochthones!"

"Naw, nothing like that, Cap'n," Muldoon muttered. "I was just putting in a good word for us Terries; in case these locals get to scrapping amongst theirselfs, we can do a fast fade."

"Ixnay," Hardshot hissed. "The little devils speak Standard; we've got to move in a more subtle fashion." His voice had fallen to a stage whisper.

Muldoon nodded doubtfully. "You got the laryngitis, or what, Cap?" he inquired, frowning.

"Hold it, fellows." Whink spoke up, at the same time ducking aside to elude a grab by the nearest Ancil guardsman.

"I propose a truce," the cocky Tuzic announced, "which we can get a few points sorted out here. Now, Stinky, the first thing you got to keep in mind before you throw in with this Ancil trash is, they're dumb-bums, can't remember what they had for breakfast! So—"

"And you, Whink," Yip retorted hotly, "you can't remember what you're going to have for lunch!"

Whink dismissed the charge with a wave of his hand. "The point is, kid," he turned his appeal to Goodlark, "they don't have any sense of history, don't know a thing about the great events of the past. Like this upcoming meteor strike: this is a regular event here on Class; you see, we used to have a pretty nice satellite we called Onk, half the size of Class itself, great for the young lovers and the glunt migrations and all, but the damn thing strayed over Roche's limit one day, and broke up. That was a sight, I can tell you! Cracked like a ploop egg, and split into two pieces; then they collided with each other and broke up into a zillion fragments, and pretty soon the bombardment started, and we've been ducking these damn meteorites ever since! Makes life hell on Class, I can tell you."

"Sheer mysticism!" Yip dismissed the Tuzic's account.

"B-but!" Hardshot blurted. "There's nothing mystical about knowing something that everybody on the planet must have witnessed—for which I see evidence at every hand!" He indicated a yawning meteor crater on the sloping foothill rising on the right of their route. He turned to confront Yip. "Look here, fellow," he yelled. "What's all this obfuscation in aid of? Why deny the obvious?"

"The obvious," Yip countered, as he signalled to a guard to give Hardshot's rope a yank, "is that a biggish piece of Onk will soon impact a couple of miles from here. So you'd best give over your interference with due process, and allow me to proceed with my mission."

"What about it, Yip?" Goodlark contributed. "Do

you have these combined cataclysms on a regular basis or not?"

"I indulge in no feckless speculations regarding past events," the Ancil replied grandly. "I leave such nonsense to the rabble which rallies to the banner of Tuzic. Now, let's go, double time!"

"Wait!" Hardshot bellowed. "First you say we're about to be subjected to a cataclysm of planetary proportions; then you urge us all to rush to the scene thereof. It's insane! Men!" He turned to address his crew directly. "This is as far as we go! Let's take these little jerks! Muldoon, you throw those two into the brush!" With that, the burly captain seized Yip, and, only slightly hampered by the rope tied to his neck, upended the protesting alien in the nearest thorn-bearing shrub. In a moment the Ancils were no more to be seen, either thrown away or having fled, while the Terrans were forming up in a column of two, untying and casting aside their weakly knotted bonds.

"About time," Muldoon grunted. "I was wondering how's come you let 'em tie us up in the first place."

"Don't trouble yourself about matters of high policy, Chief," Hardshot instructed the veteran NCO.

"Gee, sir," Goodlark spoke up inobtrusively, "you mean it was all on purpose—letting these little shrimps capture us without a fight and all?"

"Quiet, Goodlark!" Hardshot snapped. "I'm planning further diplomatic gambits; no time for small talk."

"Well, gosh, sir," Goodlark persisted. "Wouldn't it be a good idea to figure out how to avoid being cooked in a volcano or being vaporized by a meteorite, first? Before we plan a big formal reception or anything, I mean."

"What you mean, Ensign," Hardshot growled, "is of no importance whatever at this moment, however useful your skill at oomp-ball may be in securing the squadron pennant later in the season."

"Sir," Goodlark countered, as stiffly as an ensign can be expected to counter a fleet captain, "I remind you, Captain, that I am a graduate of the Academy, just like yourself, sir—"

"Not *quite* like myself, boy!" Hardshot contradicted sharply. "*I* have some thirty-five years of active service, most of it deep-space duty. Shipped out as Fifth Officer on the old *Sitting Bull*, about the time you were born, I should think."

"But in ET Relations 203, sir," Goodlark persisted, "I took a First Mention Place for my paper on *Converting Disaster Into Triumph—Making Points With Alien Scorekeepers*."

"And what points do you propose I make with these confounded little carrot-heads?" Hardshot demanded impatiently.

"Better watch the pejorative epithets, sir," Goodlark counselled stiffly. "Wouldn't look good in the report, sir," he amplified.

"Are you suggesting, Mr. Goodlark," Hardshot demanded coldly, "that you are taping this negotiation? Without my orders?"

"Sure, sir; the Manual, sir, Part VI, Article 17, paragraphs 12b and c. Says we have to, sir; knew you wouldn't want to violate Regs, sir."

"That's twice in as many seconds, Goodlark," Hardshot stated implacably, "that you've hinted at some plot to discredit your superior officer."

"Not me, sir!" Goodlark riposted emphatically. "When the chief told me about the plan, I wouldn't listen!"

"Chief Muldoon?" Hardshot muttered. "The rot runs deeper than I thought."

"No plot, sir," Goodlark objected. "Just sort of an official Plea for Relief, under paragraph 12g, subsection 12."

"A PFR on *me*?" Hardshot yelled, and turned as if to physically attack the junior officer, but was jerked back in line by the rope, which he now untied and cast aside, while Goodlark waited attentively.

"Actually, sir," Goodlark added, "I was going to inform you, just as soon as—"

"Never mind," Hardshot told him, doggedly resuming the march, ignoring the faint shouts of the guards. "It hardly matters now, after all," he explained to Posterity. "In mere moments we'll all be incinerated, lonely hero and skulking traitor alike."

"Gee, thanks, sir," Goodlark said. "Only I'm not lonely, not with all these armed guards around. Anyway," he added, "I've got an idea."

"Treat it gently, Ensign," Hardshot commanded. "Must I *order* you to divulge this presumed idea?"

"I was just telling you, sir," Goodlark protested. "You see, sir, I was thinking . . ."

"Don't test my credulity *too* far, Goodlark," his CO ordered. "Very well, you were, let us say, 'thinking.' And what ensued?"

"Let me tell you, sir," Goodlark proposed, "before it's too late."

"By all means, lad," Hardshot said, more kindly, or perhaps "less harshly" would better describe the senior officer's tone. "In this instance at least, your proposed priorities would appear to be valid."

"Well, Captain, Lord Whink here says this happens all the time: big meteor strikes, I mean; and yet the locals seem to survive somehow."

"Spare me the obvious, boy," Hardshot proposed. "All of us can see that both Mister Yip and Lord Whink, as well as their subordinates, are indeed, extant."

"The evidence of the truth of milord's asseveration are all about us, sir," Goodlark persisted. "The craters, and the indications of powerful blasts which lay trees out like jackstraws, radiating from numerous points of impact—"

"Yes, yes, we've been all over that," Hardshot dismissed the lad's remarks. "Get to the point, 'before,' as you yourself suggested, 'it's too late.' "

"Well, sir, why don't we just ask them what they did last time?"

"No use," Whink put in. "These dummies can't remember yesterday, let alone last week, when the last biggie hit."

"But *you* do!" Goodlark exclaimed, catching the Tuzic's beady green eye. "How did *you* escape the blast that laid out that patch of woods?" He pointed at a devastated area of snapped-off three-foot stumps protruding from a jumble of charred-on-one-side trees.

"We were surprised by the insidious troops of this Yip, here, and herded upslope and into the maw of Brullamagoo," Whink declaimed, in an aggrieved tone.

"What?" Hardshot interposed. "How is it you're still alive, then? Thrown in the volcano, were you? Just swam to shore in the molten basalt, I suppose?"

At this point the deliberations were interrupted by a near-supersonic screech which dropped in frequency as it swelled in amplitude to an ear-stabbing roar.

"That's an ear-stabbing roar!" Hardshot yelled, almost inaudibly, searching the sky for the source of the sound.

"There it is," Goodlark shouted, pointing, quite superfluously, at a point of brilliant light almost directly above, which swelled visibly as they stared; then he looked away, blinking greenish afterimages.

"Quick!" Whink shouted. "You, Stinky! You and your Terries have to help us overpower these Ancils and get on with the ceremony, fast!" Even as he spoke, he was assaulting the nearest Ancil, wresting away his spear, which he then used to prod Yip.

"How about it, Yip?" he demanded. "Do I stick you, or do you get this column moving up that mountain?"

"I accede, in view of the circumstances, milord," Yip said docilely, taking the spear from Lord Whink. He prodded the latter, who set off at a brisk pace along the now steep path, where black shadows swung in a quick arc, cast by the glowing body directly overhead, brighter than the star now, and growing rapidly.

Hardshot grabbed the skinny arm of the nearest guard, who at once handed over his spear, and hurried ahead.

"Damn fools!" the captain muttered. "What's going on here, Yip? Have you taken leave of your senses? Goodlark," he turned to his junior in desperation, "can you tell me what this is all about? You were saying—"

"Nossir, it was you who was asking Lord Whink how they survived the last impact."

"To be sure," Hardshot agreed, and hauled the Tuzic, whose arm he still held, around to face him. "Well? How about it, Your Lordship?" He yelled over the swelling roar of the incoming. "What'd you do, eh?" He gave the small being a shake. "Speak up!"

"We sacrificed to Brullamagoo, as I've been telling you, Stinky!" the Tuzic cried, barely audible over the rocket-blast sound filling the air. The light was an actinic, flashbulb white now, dazzling the Terrans' eyes. Hardshot groped ahead along the path. "Yip!" he called. "Come back here! You're the only semi-sensible turnip-head in the bunch!"

"Better watch the racial epithets and all, sir," Goodlark admonished his chief, as he came up alongside him, dragging the crewman to whom he was roped.

Hardshot halted abruptly, occasioning a modest pile-up of Terrans and disarmed Ancil guards.

"Epithets my left hind gaboochie!" he yelled. "I've got some dandies I haven't even used yet! That bunch of old maids at ITCH isn't being hustled along a jungle trail toward the maw of a volcano! I guess they'd have a few epithets of their own, if they were here!" He whirled to seek Chief Muldoon, who was picking up Ancils and throwing them away as lesser men might remove boofle-burrs, at the same time forging ahead at a run.

"What's *your* hurry, Chief?" Hardshot yelled after him. "Stand fast there, man! Aside from the impropriety of your attempt to precede your Captain, nothing awaits you up there but a short swim in some hot rock!" His eye was caught by Lord Whink as the latter did a nimble dodge around left end. "You, Whink!" the Terran yelled, squinting against the all-pervading glare. "If you sacrificed these damn Ancils, how is it they're still alive and committing atrocities on the persons of a peaceful Terran survey crew?"

"I think perhaps you've gained a false impression, Stinky." The Tuzic managed to make himself heard over the din. "You see, we fooled the iniquitous Ancils, and—" The rest was lost in the vast booming. The heat was palpable now, and off to one side, the dry top of a standing dead tree burst into flame.

"We don't have much time, sir!" Goodlark shouted against the hot wind that had now sprung up and was blowing a stream of flaming matter from the burning treetop, igniting a barrier of flame all along the downslope side of the path, behind them.

"An acute observation!" Hardshot yelled back. "And precisely what is it for which we don't have much time?"

"Anything, sir," Goodlark blurted, as Yip, Whink, and the disarmed troops streamed past, hurrying up-trail. "Come on, sir!" the lad urged and set off at a dead run to overtake the impatient locals. Pelting at his heels, Hardshot found breath to demand, "Where do you think you're going?"

"Like Lord Whink, said," Goodlark gasped in reply. "We have to get to that crater up there before it's too late!"

Hardshot grabbed the ensign's arm and braked him to a halt, crowding the following crewmen off the trail to bypass the obstruction.

"Come on, Cap!" Muldoon yelled as he went by. "The kid's right, I guess!"

"It's all insane!" Hardshot bellowed. "Hold hard, there, Chief! What's got into you people? I demand an explanation!"

"No time, sir," Muldoon barked. "Yer permission, Cap'n," he added as he grabbed his captain's left arm and with Goodlark's help hustled him along, all faces averted from the overhead glare. Smoke was thick now, and with a quick glance back, Goodlark saw that the flames had closed over the path and barred the route behind them.

"No way to go but uphill, sir," he advised his furious chief, who then also looked back, and at once began to cooperate in putting distance between himself and the wind-whipped conflagration.

After five minutes' frantic exertion, all three men were winded, and by common consent ducked into the partial shelter of a massive rock-slab upended by some previous cataclysm, to work on their breathing, while the rest of the crew streamed past.

"It seems to me, gentlemen," Hardshot said, barely audible over the bellow of the falling mountain blazing across the sky, the shriek of the wind and the roar of flames devouring tinder-dry brush, "that we're working awfully hard to get from the frying pan into the fire."

"But, sir," Goodlark spoke up, "the locals are right! The Ancils don't remember, and the Tuzics can't foresee consequences, but somehow, the tradition has survived: the only safe place is up there!" He rose to his elbows and knees to peer through the brush and the wind-whipped smoke toward the volcanic cone looming above, etched in stark black-and-white by the now-immense blob of incandescence swiftly descending, seemingly directly toward their inadequate shelter. He came to his feet, offered Hardshot a hand, hauled the senior officer upright, and the three resumed their headlong dash toward the imminent eruption. Above, white-hot trickles could be seen spilling over the ragged crater edge, raising clouds of smoke and steam as they burned through low-growing mountain growth and patches of glacial ice.

The trail widened and became smoother, extending directly upslope. Clearly, from this point on, it had been cleared and improved. Ahead, the stragglers of the main body of crew were visible, still scrambling up and on.

"Poor devils," Hardshot commiserated. "Nothing waiting up there but a horrible death in line of duty, and they're as eager as if they'd just gotten liberty on Delicia!"

"Sure, sir," Goodlark gasped out. "But—they're bypassing—I mean, they'll have to start angling off, now, or they'll wind up right up on top!"

"Of course!" Hardshot grunted. "Just like us! And those damned locals, too. But I don't see—"

"Off to the right, sir," Goodlark supplied. "The locals! You can see them moving along in the brush. The men have to go *that* way!"

Muldoon forged to the lead, passed, threw his head back, and bellowed:

"All right, you swabbies! Column half-right, Harch!"

Even as Goodlark was noting the clarity of the echo, the men ahead split from the broad trail and plunged into the undergrowth to the right. Moments later they had overtaken the party of Ancils.

"Somebody tell me what's going on here!" Hardshot demanded. "A minute ago you were telling me how we all had to sacrifice ourselves to this pagan volcano, and now you're forgetting all that and making a belated effort to get clear! I'm not running another foot until I get an explanation, if not of the nutty locals, at least of what my own subordinates are up to!"

"Simple, sir," Goodlark puffed. "When that thing hits, the shock wave—"

"Don't bother with that part, boy," Hardshot yelled. "Get on to what we're going to do about it!"

As they reached the point where the crew had left the main trail, a fainter path became visible, angling off across the wooded slope and into a shadowed defile.

"Quick, sir!" Goodlark shouted from his position in the lead. "We have to get across this gully here before the lava reaches it!" He sprinted ahead, almost immediately colliding with the tail-end-Charlies of the main body, whom he urged to greater efforts as he dashed past.

"Wait just a minute!" Hardshot commanded, coming to a halt blocking the way, causing Lord Whink to veer around him to dash ahead and overtake Ensign Goodlark.

"Not so fast, Terry," Whink urged in his pinched voice. "I'm officiating at this ceremony, after all! Wouldn't do for you to arrive ahead of me. Luckily I know the short cut, so I can head off that crowd ahead." He darted off-path, made crashing sounds in the brush for a moment.

"Oh, Lord Whink," Goodlark called. "I don't

mean to precede you or anything, but, ah, could you show *me* the short cut, too? I must be with my men at the last."

"Forget that, lad," Hardshot advised, arriving breathing hard. "This is no time for heroics."

"What *is* this a time for, sir?" Goodlark asked defiantly, casting a glance toward the glaring object now almost at treetop level.

"Now," Hardshot stated, "is the time to get the heck out of here!"

"This way, sir," Goodlark replied promptly, and pushed his way into the underbrush where Whink had disappeared. "We'll find a cave," he called over his shoulder.

Hardshot crowded in behind him. "What's—?" he started, then fell momentarily silent as he saw the black mouth of a tunnel gaping before him. "Better than nothing, I suppose, Ensign," he commented. "Better let the men know." He ducked his head and entered the cool darkness.

"Looks pretty deep," he told Goodlark in an echoic voice. "Ought to be room for all."

"Yessir," Goodlark confirmed. "That's why I showed it to you, sir, before I went to get the troops back here."

"Where's that Whink fellow?" Hardshot demanded, peering into the lightless depths ahead.

"He had to get the ceremony started," Goodlark explained. "Otherwise, Brullamagoo might misunderstand. So it's important."

Hardshot's head jerked around to stare at the younger officer. "You don't suggest there's any substance in these natives' barbaric superstitions, I hope, Goodlark," he barked.

"Not exactly, sir," Goodlark gobbled. "But I remember from a Geology class; Professor Dingo showed us a diagram of how a volcano works—and lucky he mentioned that sometimes the active throat becomes plugged, and pressure builds up until it blows the side off the mountain and forms a new crater. That happened here a long time ago, sir, it appears: the big pit over on the east flank, you'll recall, sir, looks like it was the one that got plugged, and now it's the dead outlet. So the lava is backing up in the new cone and spilling over the top, which means the old magma chambers and channels are clear—or it would be blowing another new crater—and—"

"Hold on, boy," Hardshot entreated. "Are you saying this whole damn mountain's about to explode?"

"That's the negative way to look at it, sir," Goodlark pointed out hesitantly. "After all, at the moment, the magma is being released OK, so it won't blow, I hope. Anyway, His Lordship ducked in here—it's an old vent, I guess, sir, so it must be safe. Probably the same hole he used last time." He paused to point to an empty gribble-grub bag on the smooth basalt floor.

"Where *is* the scamp?" Hardshot muttered, venturing farther into the cave, with the aid of a hand light.

Goodlark leapt in startlement as Whink's reedy voice spoke up close behind him.

"Better tell Stinky not to poke his nose too far in there," he suggested without urgency. "Drops off pretty sudden."

"Oh, sir!" Goodlark called, evoking an echo: "-er, -er, -er," which bounced back and forth for a full minute before Hardshot re-emerged, looking grim.

"Damn near went over the edge," he muttered. "You should have scouted the terrain, boy, before urging your captain down there."

"I respectfully submit, sir," Goodlark interjected, "I hardly urged you, sir; all I said was, well, I don't really remember what I said. And anyway," he added with a touch of sullenness, "it was only a suggestion, sir. After all, sir, *you're* captain."

"Damn right, Goodlark," Hardshot confirmed heatedly. "Don't forget it again. Now—" He interrupted himself to rub his hands together with a sound like a cicada grooming its wing-cases. "Where's that Whink? I have a word or two to say to *him!*"

"Right here, sir," Goodlark offered brightly, peering around him. "Or at least he was a second ago. He told me about the drop-off, sir," Goodlark added in defense of the Tuzic, "but not until it was too late," he continued, abruptly returning his thoughts to self-preservation.

"Not *quite* too late, boy!" Hardshot returned with spirit. "I'm still alive and in command!"

"And what *are* your commands, sir?" Goodlark inquired, eager to demonstrate his readiness to comply therewith.

"Don't rush me again, Ensign," Hardshot rebuked the lad. "I'm thinking. I want to grill Lord Whink. Whink-ink-ink!!" he yelled, wincing at the echo. Whink emerged from a chink in the rock. "Yes, yes, Stinky," he said patiently. "What is it? I *am* rather busy, you know."

"Busy, are you-oo-oo?" Hardshot boomed. "Doing what-ut, may I inquire?"

"If you wouldn't talk so loud, Stinky, we wouldn't have these damned echoes," Whink offered. "See, speak softly, like me."

"Speak any way you like, milord," Hardshot ordered, less vehemently, waking no resonance this time. "See, I can do it, too! What I want to know," he went on, "is what the hell we're supposed to do next? Hiding inside a mountain that's about to explode is hardly a viable mode of escape from a mountain that's about to impact right on top of us! What's going to save us now?"

"You mistake me, Stinky," Whink corrected loft-

ily. "I am a noble Tuzic, quite uninterested in efforts
to remember events which have not yet occurred,
as if I were a mere Ancil."

"What happened last time?" Hardshot bellowed,
reawakening Sir Echo: "—ime-i'm-I'M!"

"Don't know," Whink conceded grumpily. "I was
only a nipper then, fell down, and my mother
yanked me pretty hard. When I came to, it was all
over, and we were right here, alive and as well as
you can be when you're breathing sulphur fumes."

"Great!" Hardshot yelled. "—ate-ate-ate!"

"Eight what, sir?" Goodlark inquired innocently.

"I didn't say 'ate,' boy," Hardshot corrected sharply.
"I was being a trifle sarcastic, I fear. I was express-
ing, by inversion, my opinion of a memory of past
events which omits the crucial details!" He looked
about wildly. "If the damn fool was here after the
explosion, there must be a connecting passage to a
safe place. Look for it, Ensign Goodlark, or should
I say Leftenant J.G. Goodlark, since if you succeed
I predict there'll be a silver bar in it for you."

Goodlark went off dutifully into the gloomy depths,
halted abruptly at the edge of a fissure, turned and
retraced his steps.

"That damn cliff," he explained as Hardshot gave
him a narrow-eyed look, but, averting his eyes, he
glimpsed a narrow cleft like the one which had concealed Lord Whink. He went to it, saw ruddy light
deep within, and wedged himself into the narrow
space, where, he found, breathing was impractical,
to say nothing of walking. With effort he managed
to extricate himself, just as a gigantic flashbulb
exploded outside, etching every detail of the gloomy
interior in actinic light; an instant later, a twenty-
foot slab of rock dropped from the cave ceiling with
a deep-toned *whump*! Goodlark climbed over it to
find Captain Hardshot lying face down, with Whink
bending over him. Goodlark reached forward.

"Gosh, sir," he gobbled, "are you—is he," he shifted his address to the Tuzic, "all right?"

"While the term 'all right' is not perhaps the ideal one with which to characterize Stinky's condition at the moment," Whink replied unperturbed, "he is, in fact alive. Merely felled by the concussion."

"That's gratifying," Goodlark commented. "Is he hurt?"

"You demand to know if I'm hurt, Goodlark?" Hardshot roared, sitting up abruptly. "After being blown up by a mountain and vaporized by another one? We Hardshots are a sturdy lot, but—" He abandoned the effort to communicate the enormity of the ensign's transgression.

"It's all your fault, Goodlark," he charged. "Taking up with that shifty Whink fellow and all!"

"Gosh, thanks, sir," Goodlark stammered. "I was afraid, sir, to be quite candid, that you'd take all the credit."

"Credit, Ensign Goodlark?" Hardshot screamed, and the walls screamed back, "—ark-hark-hark!" Hardshot held up a hand. "'Hark,' is it?" he demanded, getting to his feet. "Harken to what?"

"That's just the echo, sir," Goodlark pointed out. "I was just thanking you, sir, for giving me the credit."

"And I was yelling 'Credit, Ensign Goodlark?'" Hardshot pointed out, less vigorously this time. "Credit for bringing us all to near disaster?"

"We're still alive, sir," Goodlark offered diffidently. "Even if the mountain *did* explode—only it mustn't have," he amended. "It was only the meteorite."

"'Only' the meteorite?" Hardshot challenged. "Look out there, Goodlark!" He pointed to the narrow entry beyond which leaping flames from burning trees roared in a stiff breeze.

"Yessir," Goodlark agreed. "It's not all over yet, sir, but still, if we'd been out there . . . Look, sir!" Goodlark blurted, and pointed to the depths of the cave, where yellowish lights, as from torches, were bobbing as they advanced. Goodlark hurried toward them, to the edge of the cleft.

"Look out for the abyss!" he yelled, evoking no echo here.

"The kid means the cliff," Chief Muldoon's bass voice elucidated, as the torches clustered together. Wan faces were visible in the flickering light.

"It's the crew!" Goodlark shouted back to his captain. "They're OK!"

"Well, not egzackly OK, Goody," Muldoon corrected. "But shipshape and reporting for duty anyways!" He came stamping forward as if testing the ground at each step.

"Got inside the dead caldera just in time," he explained. "Great big holler big as the old Kansas Dust Bowl. Old Yip came through in the clutch, showed us the path—place was full o' these turnip-heads. We ducked when they did, and never lost a man—but Space'n Jones got a little afterimage problem. Damn fool was looking right at it till she went behind the mountain."

Goodlark went forward to meet and congratulate the survivors, while Hardshot came up to mutter a grumpy greeting.

"Now, men, we've got work to do," he reminded them. "We disembarked to make contact with the local government, as you know, and so far all we've found is some clown named Yip, with a platoon of SP's, and a fellow they call Lord Whink, wandering around on his own. We have to find that town we spotted coming in, and establish some kind of official relations. Besides, the ship sustained damage, and we'll need all the help we can get to get her space-worthy again."

"She's prolly all right, sir, in that ravine you accidentally dropped her inta," Muldoon suggested.

"You attribute my forethoughtful placement of my

command in a protected position to accident, Chief?"
Hardshot demanded. "When will you learn that your
captain is an officer of unusual foresight, often taking
into account exigencies which have never occurred
to you?"

"Just the way you said 'Groints!,' sir," Muldoon
explained lamely, "give me a idear you was as surprised as the rest of us when that solid-looking patch
collapsed under us."

"One must learn to read the signs, Chief," Hardshot pointed out. "Same as when I directed you to
take the men to safety in the dead crater."

"But it was that Yip character told us . . ." Muldoon started lamely, but thought better of it.

"How did you get across the chasm?" Goodlark
inquired of the chief.

"Jumped," Muldoon explained. "Oney about six
foot wide. We saw it good when the place lit up-
like."

"What about the Ancils?" Goodlark persisted.
"Are they all right?"

"Far as I know," Muldoon told him off-handedly.
"Last I saw, they was picking theirselfs up offen the
ground and sorting theirselfs out; never said a word
when I and the troops done a swift fade. Then we
heard voices, and here we are."

"We chose to allow you to seek your own desti-
nies," Yip's voice supplied from the darkness.

"It's that Sergeant Yip!" Hardshot exclaimed.
"Must have followed you, Muldoon!"

"Yip is hardly a sergeant, Stinky," Whink contributed.

"Very well, Corporal, or whatever," Hardshot
conceded.

"You fail to understand," Whink persisted. "His
proper style is Field Marshal General Yip—Chief of
the Ancil Armed Forces."

"Well, OK." Hardshot conceded the point. "What about it, General; your boys OK?"

"Very well indeed, Captain," Yip answered him. "Thanks be to Brullamagoo."

"And," Lord Whink interrupted, with feeling, "what of the noble clan of Tuzic? Have these great people reached the safe haven of the bosom of Brullamagoo, in spite of the selfish preemption of the Ancil rabble? Eh?"

"Beats me," Muldoon conceded. "I seen a whale of a lotta turnip-heads; didn't ast 'em what kind they was."

"Your unfortunate relatives are quite safe, thanks be to old Brully," Yip contributed.

"See here," Goodlark demanded. "At first you people were all set to go to war to keep the others from forcing you to go to the volcano; now you're admitting that you were competing to get there first!"

"Easy, boy," Hardshot soothed. "Clearly, there's been a little misunderstanding here. We can do all these worthy folk a great service with a few well-chosen words of a reconciliatory nature: Now, Mr. Yip." He switched targets. "Do you acknowledge that to seek haven in the dead caldera was indeed desirable?"

"What?" Yip yipped. "You suggest that we *voluntarily* leapt into these awesome depths?"

"Stinky," Whink appealed. "Where'd you get the idea us Tuzics were on a mass-suicide kick?"

"Don't you realize," Hardshot demanded of the Ancil, "that hiding in the crater saved your lives?" He turned to appeal to Whink. "What do you think would have happened to your people had they not sought haven in the caldera?"

"You expect me to remember past events, like a mindless Tuzic?" Yip protested.

"I told you and I told you," Whink wailed. "Us

noble Tuzics got no magic mud-ball! We don't waste time trying to foretell coming events! We leave that nonsense to these poor unfortunate Ancils!"

"Ye gods!" Hardshot yelled, and ducked at the anticipated echo, "-odds!-odds!"

"It's hopeless," he moaned. "They'll go on warring forever, blind to the facts staring them in the face!"

"Maybe not, sir," Goodlark suggested hopefully. He approached Yip. "What about it, sir?" he appealed. "Can't you foresee an era of peace and good fellowship, at least until the next piece of Onk drops out of orbit, and you all start scuffling to be the first inside the volcano and blaming the other side for forcing you? Couldn't you try?"

"Your memory is improving, my boy," Yip commented. "Your expectation of yet another giant meteorite strike to come is remarkable accurate. As for peace and good fellowship—that's doubtful. But I suppose we could give it a try—though the interference of you Terries does make matters rather obscure in the days to come."

"We'll 'influence' you!" Hardshot barked. "Any more of this snares-in-the-trail nonsense, or this catch-and-kill stuff, either," he admonished harshly, "and I'll see to it a squadron of peace enforcers heaves to off-planet and starts lobbing implosion bombs in here to pacify *all* of you!"

"Sounds like he means it, Yippy," Whink informed his traditional enemy. "Maybe we could work out a truce at that. Just till the next rock-scare, maybe."

As the two fell into earnest conversation, Hardshot called his crew together for the march back to the ship.

"It looks like our mission is accomplished, men," he told them. "So let's haul butt before this nightmare starts all over again."

As Muldoon fell the troops in and began filing

from the cavern, Goodlark inobtrusively sought out Yip.

"Say, Field Marshal," he accosted the Ancil leader, "that trick of remembering the future—just how do you do it?"

"May I, lad?" Yip inquired rhetorically as at the same moment Goodlark felt the ghostly touch of the Ancil's telepathic probe.

"Simplicity itself," Yip told him. "You seem a bright lad: just orient the old bope nodes—oh, I see your bope nodes are a trifle underdeveloped—but I can put that right with a bit of stimulation at the lambda level—there! Didn't that clear things up a bit?" He bent anxiously over the young fellow, who had collapsed at his feet. After a moment Goodlark stirred and sat up. "That felt funny, but is it really that easy? I seem to remember I'm going to try to show Chief Muldoon the technique, but of course the poor fellow's bope nodes are hopeless."

"Not all are qualified," Yip agreed. "Now we'd best hurry along before Stinky starts yelling 'Ensign Goodlark!' "

"We've got one-point-oh-two seconds yet," Goodlark reassured the nervous Ancil.

"Ensign Goodlark!" the captain's voice bellowed from just outside. Goodlark hurried to his side.

"Gee, sir, I'm sorry, but I seem to have passed out back there. The fumes, maybe," he burbled.

"Hang on, Goodlark," Hardshot urged. "We're almost home free."

"Gosh, Captain," Goodlark offered. "You must be thrilled, sir, to be on your way home to report complete success and another inhabited planet to add to the roster of pacified worlds!"

"Unless they court-martial me, boy, for exceeding my authority," the older man grumped. "Had no right to threaten 'em."

"They don't know about that, sir," Goodlark

pointed out. "Just think about the title and honors and all. 'Vice-Admiral Sir Melvin Hardshot'; sounds impressive, sir."

"You really think—?" Hardshot managed.

"No doubt about it, Admiral," Goodlark assured his chief. "After all those nice things the Admiral's going to say when you report in."

"The Admiral, Goodlark?" Hardshot protested. "If you're talking about Goldie Coign, he hates my guts, ever since I tripped him a yard short of the goal line at the Denver–Annapolis game in '73!"

"He'll change his mind when he hears about this, sir," Goodlark persisted. "Don't you remember, sir?"

We all know computers are literal-minded. They do what you tell them, not necessarily what you intended to tell them. A computer-controlled security system will slam the fire escape door in your face as the flames approach, and courteously remind you of regulations. Reasoning won't help. Machine "intelligence," so-called, isn't really intelligence, of course. An old-fashioned 78 RPM audio disc will faithfully reproduce every nuance of the sound impressed on it, without the least understanding of music. Even an encyclopedia sits on its shelf, "knowing" the facts about practically everything, but can't make use of it.

I know a fellow whose gas station had been burglarized repeatedly, so he set up a trap, using a shotgun and a string tied to the door by which the thieves always entered. When he forgot something one day and went back for it, it did precisely what it was "programmed" to do: it blew his leg off. Your own car can roll back and crush you. Machines are totally irresponsible; they follow natural law to the letter, and to cope with them we must devise limitations of some sort. Dyson told ATTAC II to do something it couldn't do within natural law as we formulate it, so it could do nothing.

Reverse English

"For one million dollars in cold cash," Dyson said, "I'll save your necks."

"That's preposterous," the Chief of Staff said in a voice thick with panic. "I don't care what kind of reputation you have as a cybernetics Fixit man! What do you know of military computer theory? Particularly the theory of ATTAC II?"

Dyson lit a match with his thumbnail and smiled through the smoke.

"I know you've built the most powerful mechanical brain on Earth, and linked it to enough firepower to blow us all off the planet. And I know you've loused up the programming so she's ready to let it all rip if anybody says the wrong word in her hearing."

"I say evacuate the complex and pinpoint her with a megatonner," a white-faced Air Force general said in a voice that was clipped to the cuticle.

"Insanity," the Senior Cybernetician said. "She'd pick it up coming in and retaliate in the only way she knows."

"And we can't cut power to her; she won't let us—"

"Time's a-wasting, gentlemen," Dyson said casually. "What do your theories say about how long it will be before she takes umbrage at an off-course airliner or a high-flying goose and starts the H-heads streaking over the Pole?"

"How did you know—" the Chief of Staff started.

"Minutes," the Senior Cybernetician said. "And not many of them."

"The basic problem," Dyson said in a tone suddenly harsh, "is that ATTAC made a number of logical but unexpected correlations among the initial data you fed her, on the basis of which she now interprets any attempt to muzzle her as a hostile act, correct?"

"That's a gross oversimplification!"

"But essentially true," the SC said. "When I tried to cancel a section of her program, she almost called a Condition Red before I could abort."

"So the trick is," Dyson said, "to feed her an instruction that will disarm her at a stroke, before she can react, eh?"

"If we try—and *don't* pull her teeth—then we've had it," the British observer said. "She'll hit back with everything she has."

"And if we don't try, it's only a matter of time."

"We have just the one chance—but for God's sake, who's going to take the risk? Just one wrong word—"

"*I* will," Dyson said, relaxed again. "As soon as I see the million."

"What makes you think I'd let you try?" the Chief of Staff snapped.

"Do you want to try yourself, General?"

In the silence, the assembled heavyweights looked at each other.

"Let him try," the Chief of Staff said.

*

The corridor was as silent as Death Row, and with the same lighting. The Senior Cybernetician passed Dyson through the guard post, left him alone in the Programming Chamber. Dyson looked up at the high panels, lit like a city at night.

"Good morning, ATTAC II," he said. "I have an instruction for you."

"Ready to receive," ATTAC II said in a mellow contralto.

Dyson said six words. Lights winked across the panels, faster and faster. Red lights came on, flickering; green and amber blinked and winked in patterns like scurrying mice. The entire array blazed up simultaneously, and went out. A high, chattering whine came from behind the black plastic consoles, accompanied by a wisp of smoke.

Dyson let out a long breath and spoke into the hand phone:

"You can come in now. She's out like a light."

The man from Treasury handed over the long, green U.S. check.

"All right, no more stalling," the Chief of Staff said. "How did you do it?"

"You knew nothing about ATTAC's programming; you couldn't have!" the Senior Cybernetician said. "How in the name of Heaven did you know what to do?"

"Easy," Dyson said. "I presented her with a dilemma she couldn't solve."

"In six words? You, an amateur, broke down an intellect ten orders of magnitude above your own? How, man? How?"

"I said: 'Reverse all instructions—including this one.'"

We take so much for granted! Most of what we think we know is second-hand information. Everybody knows about the Big Bang, the appearance of life in the primordial sea, the rise of the hominids, the cave paintings at Lascaux, the fall of Rome, the invention of the printing press, Columbus's voyages, 1776, the H-bomb, the outcome of the last election, what's showing at the Roxy, the way the fellow next door earns a living, what's in a box marked Grape Nut Flakes, that what the milkman brings has a lower bacteria count than the local sewage, etc., etc. But could we prove any of that in a court of law, by rigorous evidence? Nope. All we really know is what we experience through our own senses, provided they're functioning correctly, and no one's deliberately fooling us.

When a small-farm boy visits the Big Town, he has no right to expect that everything will be familiar, logical, as-it-should-be, etc. And, indeed much of what he encounters will be utterly strange, even if the place hasn't been taken over by alien beings: folks that don't reply when he says "Howdy, sir," old women in rags pushing rusty grocery carts full of junk, men asleep on pink benches, covered with newspapers, and ugly old dames who shove you and say, "Get outta duh way, yuh bastid," can all be cited without resorting to the unusual.

So when Brett encountered actual non-human

beings, it would have been surprising if their activities made any sense, rather than the reverse.

We have a (recently adopted) set of rules we call logic, and we think of them as rational: effect follows cause, Nature abhors a vacuum, what goes up must come down, $E = mc^2$, a square peg fits a square hole and so on, all based on the Natural Laws which govern our small corner of all that vastness. Perhaps the Laws are different (a tiny bubble in the still-dense Universe one demi-semi-millisecond after the Bang?) so that thinking intellects therein would have had to evolve totally different rules for coping. Hollowing out the insides of buildings might be perfectly reasonable in the light of Blug's Law and the Asymmetrical Principle; perhaps their way of building shelters, making things homey?

Things that are obvious to Brett and the fat man are deeply mysterious to the Gels; they can't put two and two together—rather, they can, but the sum is 7.3528. So they can't cope with Brett's logic any better than he can penetrate their illogic. If he changes position when they're not looking, they don't recognize him as their quarry. At last, Brett sums it up: "It doesn't mean anything, It's just the way things are." Not the way Brett thought they were, not at all; but who can actually know how things are? We draw conclusions, usually at a very early age, based on what we experience. Most of those conclusions are erroneous, and we go through life trying to make the exocosm conform to those early assumptions. Brett's illusions were dispelled suddenly and unmistakably. Most of us struggle for a lifetime, and never attain Truth. So no one knows what Truth "really" is.

A Trip to the City

"She'll be pulling out in a minute, Brett," Mr. Phillips said. He tucked his railroader's watch back in his vest pocket. "You better get aboard—if you're still set on going."

"It was reading all them books done it," Aunt Haicey said. "Thick books, and no pictures in them. I knew it'd make trouble." She plucked at the faded hand-crocheted shawl over her thin shoulders, a tiny birdlike woman with bright anxious eyes.

"Don't worry about me," Brett said. "I'll be back."

"The place'll be yours when I'm gone," Aunt Haicey said. "Lord knows it won't be long."

"Why don't you change your mind and stay on, boy?" Mr. Phillips said, blinking up at the young man. "If I talk to Mr. J.D., I think he can find a job for you at the plant."

"So many young people leave Casperton," Aunt Haicey said. "They never come back."

Mr. Phillips clicked his teeth. "They write, at first," he said. "Then they gradually lose touch."

"All your people are here, Brett," Aunt Haicey said. "Haven't you been happy here?"

"Why can't you young folks be content with Casperton?" Mr. Phillips said. "There's everything you need here."

"It's that Pretty-Lee done it," Aunt Haicey said. "If it wasn't for that girl—"

A clatter ran down the line of cars. Brett kissed Aunt Haicey's dry cheek, shook Mr. Phillips's hand, and swung aboard. His suitcase was on one of the seats. He put it up above in the rack and sat down, then turned to wave back at the two old people.

It was a summer morning. Brett leaned back and watched the country slide by. It was nice country, Brett thought, mostly in corn, some cattle, and away in the distance the hazy blue hills. Now he would see what was on the other side of them: the cities, the mountains, and the ocean: strange things. Up until now all he knew about anything outside of Casperton was what he'd read or seen pictures of. As far as he was concerned, chopping wood and milking cows back in Casperton, they might as well not have existed. They were just words and pictures printed on paper. But he didn't want to just read about them. He wanted to see for himself.

Pretty-Lee hadn't come to see him off. She was probably still mad about yesterday. She had been sitting at the counter at the Club Rexall, drinking a soda and reading a movie magazine with a big picture of an impossibly pretty face on the cover—the kind you never see just walking down the street. He had taken the next stool and ordered a Coke.

"Why don't you read something good, instead of that pap?" he asked her.

"Something good? You mean something dry, I guess. And don't call it . . . that word. It doesn't sound polite."

"What does it say? That somebody named Doll

Starr is fed up with glamor and longs for a simple home in the country and lots of kids? Then why doesn't she move to Casperton?"

"You wouldn't understand," said Pretty-Lee.

He took the magazine, leafed through it. "Look at this: all about people who give parties that cost thousands of dollars, and fly all over the world having affairs with each other and committing suicide and getting divorced. It's like reading about Martians."

"I just like to read about the stars. There's nothing wrong with it."

"Reading all that junk just makes you dissatisfied. You want to do your hair up crazy like the pictures in the magazines and wear weird-looking clothes—"

Pretty-Lee bent her straw double. She stood up and took her shopping bag. "I'm glad to know you think my clothes are weird—"

"You're taking everything I say personally," Brett objected. "Look." He showed her a full-color advertisement on the back cover of the magazine. "Look at this. Here's a man supposed to be cooking steaks on some kind of back-yard grill. He looks like a movie star; he's dressed up like he was going to get married; there's not a wrinkle anywhere. There's not a spot on that apron. There isn't even a grease spot on the frying pan. The lawn is as smooth as a billiard table. There's his son; he looks just like his pop, except that he's not grey at the temples. Did you ever really see a man that handsome, or hair that was just silver over the ears and the rest glossy black? The daughter looks like a movie starlet, and her mom is exactly the same, except that she has that grey streak in front to match her husband. You can see the car in the drive; the treads of the tires must have just been scrubbed; they're not even dusty. There's not a pebble out of place. All the flowers are in full bloom; no dead ones. No leaves on the lawn; no dry twigs showing on the tree. That other house in the background looks like a palace, and the man with the rake, looking over the fence: he looks like this one's twin brother, and he's out raking leaves in brand-new clothes—"

Pretty-Lee grabbed her magazine. "You just seem to hate everything that's nicer than this messy town—"

"I don't think it's nicer. I like you; your hair isn't always perfectly smooth, and you've got a mended place on your dress, and you feel human, you smell human—"

"Oh!" Pretty-Lee turned and flounced out of the drug store.

Brett shifted in the dusty plush seat and looked around. There were a few other people in the car. An old man was reading a newspaper; two old ladies whispered together. There was a woman of about thirty with a mean-looking kid; and some others. They didn't look like magazine pictures, any of them. He tried to picture them doing the things you read in newspapers: the old ladies putting poison in somebody's tea; the old man giving orders to start a war. He thought about babies in houses in cities, and airplanes flying over, and bombs falling down: huge explosive bombs. *Blam!* Buildings fall in, pieces of glass and stone fly through the air. The babies are blown up along with everything else—

But the kind of people he knew couldn't do anything like that. They liked to loaf and eat and talk and drink beer and buy a new tractor or refrigerator and go fishing. And if they ever got mad and hit somebody—afterwards they were embarrassed and wanted to shake hands. . . .

The train slowed, came to a shuddery stop. Through the window he saw a cardboardy-looking building with the words BAXTER'S JUNCTION painted across it. There were a few faded posters on a bulletin board. An old man was sitting on a bench, waiting. The two old ladies got off and a boy in blue jeans got on. The train started up. Brett folded his jacket and tucked it under his head and tried to doze off. . . .

Brett awoke, yawned, sat up. The train was slowing. He remembered you couldn't use the toilets while the train was stopped. He got up and went to the end of the car. The door was jammed. He got it open and went inside and closed the door behind him. The train was going slower, clack clack . . . clack-clack . . . clack; clack . . . cuh-lack . . .

He washed his hands, then pulled on the door. It was stuck. He pulled harder. The handle was too small; it was hard to get hold of. The train came to a halt. Brett braced himself and strained against the door. It didn't budge.

He looked out the grimy window. The sun was getting lower. It was about three-thirty, he guessed. He couldn't see anything but some dry-looking fields.

Outside in the corridor there were footsteps. He started to call, but then didn't. It would be too embarrassing, pounding on the door and yelling, "Let me out! I'm stuck in the toilet. . . ."

He tried to rattle the door. It didn't rattle. Somebody was dragging something heavy past the door. Mail bags, maybe. He'd better yell. But dammit, the door couldn't be all that hard to open. He studied the latch. All he had to do was turn it. He got a good grip and twisted. Nothing.

He heard the mail bag bump-bump, and then another one. To heck with it; he'd yell. He'd wait until he heard the footsteps outside the door again and then he'd make some noise.

Brett waited. It was quiet now. He rapped on the door anyway. No answer. Maybe there was nobody left in the car. In a minute the train would start up and he'd be stuck here until the next stop. He banged on the door. "Hey! The door is stuck!"

It sounded foolish. He listened. It was very quiet. He pounded again. Still just silence. The car creaked once. He put his ear to the door. He couldn't hear anything. He turned back to the window. There was no one in sight. He put his cheek flat against it, looked along the car. All he saw was the dry fields.

He turned around and gave the door a good kick. If he damaged it, that was too bad; the railroad shouldn't have defective locks on the doors. If they tried to make him pay for it, he'd tell them they were lucky he didn't sue the railroad. . . .

He braced himself against the opposite wall, drew his foot back, and kicked hard at the lock. Something broke. He pulled the door open.

He was looking out the open door and through the window beyond. There was no platform, just the same dry fields he could see on the other side. He came out and went along to his seat. The car was empty now.

He looked out the window. Why had the train stopped here? Maybe there was some kind of trouble with the engine. It had been sitting here for ten minutes or so now. Brett got up and went along to the door, stepped down onto the iron step. Leaning out, he could see the train stretching along ahead, one car, two cars—

There was no engine.

Maybe he was turned around. He looked the other way. There were three cars. No engine there either. He must be on some kind of siding. . . .

Brett stepped back inside, and pushed through into the next car. It was empty. He walked along the length of it, into the next car. It was empty too. He went back through the two cars and his own car and on, all the way to the end of the train. All the

cars were empty. He stood on the platform at the
end of the last car, and looked back along the rails.
They ran straight through the dry fields, right to
the horizon. He stepped down to the ground, went
along the cindery bed to the front of the train, stepping on the ends of the wooden ties. The coupling
stood open. The tall, dusty coach stood silently on
its iron wheels, waiting. Ahead the tracks went on—
And stopped.

2

Maybe all train trips were like this, Brett thought.
After all, this was his first. If he'd been asleep, say,
he'd never have noticed the train stopping and all
the rest of it. Probably his best bet was to get back
aboard and wait. Yet he didn't. He started walking.

He walked along the ties, following the iron rails,
shiny on top, and brown with rust on the sides. A
hundred feet from the train they ended. The cinders
went on another ten feet and petered out. Beyond,
the fields closed in. Brett looked up at the sun. It
was lower now in the west, its light getting yellow
and late-afternoonish. He turned and looked back at
the train. The cars stood high and prim, empty,
silent. Then he thought of his suitcase, still in the
rack, and his new jacket on the seat. He walked
back, climbed in, got his bag down from the rack,
pulled on his jacket. He jumped down to the cinders, followed them to where they ended. He hesitated a moment, then pushed between the knee-high
stalks. Eastward across the field he could see what
looked like a smudge on the far horizon.

He walked until dark, then made himself a scratchy
nest in the dead stalks and went to sleep.

*　　　*　　　*

He slept for what seemed like a long time; then
he woke, lay on his back, looking up at pink dawn
clouds. Around him, dry stalks rustled in a faint stir
of air. He felt crumbly earth under his fingers. He
sat up, reached out and broke off a stalk. It crumbled
into fragile chips. He wondered what it was. It
wasn't any crop he'd ever seen before.

He stood, looked around. The field went on and
on, dead flat. A locust came whirring toward him,
plumped to earth at his feet. He picked it up. Long,
elbowed legs groped at his fingers aimlessly. He
tossed the insect in the air. It fluttered away. To the
east the smudge was clearer now; it seemed to be a
grey wall, far away. The city? He picked up his bag
and started on.

He was getting hungry. He hadn't eaten since the
previous morning. He was thirsty too. The city
couldn't be more than three hours' walk. He tramped
along, the dry plants crackling under his feet, little
puffs on dust rising from the dry ground. He thought
about the rails, running across the empty fields, end-
ing . . .

He tried to remember just when the strangeness
had begun: he had heard the locomotive groaning
up ahead as the train slowed. And there had been
feet in the corridor. Where had they gone?

He thought of the train, Casperton, Aunt Haicey,
Mr. Phillips. They seemed very far away, something
remembered from long ago. Up above the sun was
hot. That was real. The other things, from the past,
seemed unimportant. Ahead there was a city. He
would walk until he came to it. He tried to think of
other things: television, crowds of people, money;
the tattered paper and worn silver—

Only the sun and the dusty plain and the dead
plants were real now. He could see them, feel them.
And the suitcase. It was heavy; he shifted hands,
kept going.

There was something white on the ground ahead, a small shiny surface protruding from the earth. Brett put the suitcase down, went down on one knee, dug into the dry soil, and pulled out a china teacup, the handle missing. Caked dirt crumbled away under his thumb, leaving the surface clean. He looked at the bottom of the cup. It was unmarked. Why just one teacup, he wondered, here in the middle of nowhere? He dropped it, took up his suitcase, and went on.

After that he watched the ground more closely. He found a shoe; it was badly weathered, but the sole was good. It was a high-topped work shoe, size 10½C. Who had dropped it here? He thought of other lone shoes he had seen, lying at the roadside or in alleys. How did they get there . . . ?

Half an hour later he detoured around a rusted front fender from an old-fashioned car. He looked around for the rest of the car but saw nothing. The wall was closer now; perhaps two miles more.

A scrap of white paper fluttered across the field in a stir of air. He saw another, more, blowing along in the fitful gusts. He ran a few steps, caught one, smoothed it out.

BUY NOW — PAY LATER!

He picked up another.

PREPARE TO MEET GOD

A third said:

WIN WITH WILKIE

3

He plodded on, his eyes on the indifferent wall ahead as it came closer. At last he reached it. Nothing changed. He was still tired and hungry. Now the wall loomed above him, smooth and grey. He was uncomfortably aware of the dust caked on his skin and clothes. He decided to follow the wall, maybe find a gate. As he walked he brushed at himself absently. Aunt Haicey would scold him if she knew how dirty he had gotten his new clothes. Swell impression *he'd* make! The suitcase dragged at his arm, thumped against his shin. He was very hungry and thirsty. He sniffed the air, instinctively searching for the odors of food. He had been following the wall for a long time, searching for an opening. It curved away from him, rising vertically from the level earth. Its surface was porous, unadorned, too smooth to climb. It was, Brett estimated, twenty feet high. If there were anything to make a ladder from—

Ahead he saw a wide gate, flanked by grey columns. He came up to it, put the suitcase down, and wiped at his forehead with his handkerchief. It came away muddy. Through the opening in the wall a brick-paved street was visible, and the facades of buildings. Those on the street before him were low, not more than one or two stories, but behind them taller towers reared up. There were no people in sight; no sounds stirred the hot late-afternoon air. Brett picked up his bag and passed through the gate.

4

For the next hour he walked empty pavements, listening to the echoes of his footsteps against brownstone fronts, empty shop windows, curtained glass doors, and here and there a vacant lot, weed-grown and desolate. He paused at cross streets, looked down long vacant ways. Now and then a distant sound came to him: the lonely honk of a horn, a faintly tolling bell, a clatter of hooves. He didn't think they had horses any more in cities.

He came to a narrow alley that cut like a dark canyon between blank walls. He stood at its mouth, listening to a distant murmur, like a crowd at a funeral. He turned down the narrow way.

It went straight for a few yards, then twisted. As he followed its turnings the crowd noise gradually grew louder. He could make out individual voices now, an occasional word above the hubbub. He started to hurry, eager to find someone to talk to.

Abruptly the voices—hundreds of voices, he thought—rose in a roar, a long-drawn *Yaaayyyyy . . . !* Brett thought of a stadium crowd as the home team trotted onto the field. He could hear a band now, a shrilling of brass, the clatter and thump of percussion instruments. Now he could see the mouth of the alley ahead, a sunny street hung with bunting, the backs of people, and over, their heads the rhythmic bobbing of a passing procession, tall shakos and guidons in almost even rows. Two tall poles with a streamer between them swung into view. He caught a glimpse of tall red letters:

. . . FOR OUR SIDE!

He moved closer, edged up behind the grey-backed crowd. A phalanx of yellow-tunicked men approached, walking stiffly, fez tassels swinging. A small boy darted out into the street, loped along at their side. The music screeched and wheezed. Brett tapped the man before him.

"What's it all about . . . ?"

He couldn't hear his own voice. The man ignored him. Brett moved along behind the crowd, looking for a vantage point or a thinning in the ranks. There seemed to be fewer people ahead. He came to the end of the crowd, moved on a few yards, stood at the curb. The yellow-jackets had passed now, and a group of round-thighed girls in satin blouses and black boots and white fur caps glided into view, silent, expressionless. As they reached a point fifty feet from Brett they broke abruptly into a strutting prance, knees high, hips flirting, tossing shining batons high, catching them, twirling them, and up again. . . .

Brett craned his neck, looking for TV cameras. The crowd lining the opposite side of the street stood in solid ranks, drably clad, eyes following the procession, mouths working. A fat man in a rumpled suit and a panama hat squeezed to the front, stood picking his teeth. Somehow, he seemed out of place among the others. Behind the spectators, the store fronts looked normal, dowdy brick and mismatched glass and corroding aluminum, dusty windows and cluttered displays of cardboard, a faded sign that read TODAY ONLY, PRICES SLASHED. There were a few cars in sight, all parked at the curb, none in motion, no one in them. They were all dusty and faded, even the late models. To Brett's left the sidewalk stretched, empty. To his right the crowd was packed close, the shout rising and falling. Now a rank of blue-suited policemen followed the majorettes, swinging along silently. Behind them, over them, a piece of paper blew along the street. Brett turned to the man on his right.

"Pardon me. Can you tell me the name of this town?"

The man ignored him. Brett tapped the back of the man's shoulder. "Hey! What town is this?"

The man took off his hat, whirled it overhead, then threw it up. It sailed away over the crowd, lost. Brett wondered briefly how people who threw their hats ever recovered them. But then, nobody he knew would throw his hat. . . .

"You mind telling me the name of this place?" Brett said, as he took the man's arm, pulled. The man rotated toward Brett, leaning heavily against him. Brett stepped back. The man fell, lay stiffly, his arms moving, his eyes and mouth open.

"Ahhhhh," he said. "Whum-whum-whum. Awww, jawww . . ."

Brett stooped quickly. "I'm sorry," he cried. He looked around. "Help! This man . . ."

Nobody was watching. The next man, a few feet away, stood close against his neighbor, hatless, his jaw moving.

"This man's sick," said Brett, tugging at the man's arm. "He fell."

The man's eyes moved reluctantly to Brett. "None of my business," he muttered.

"Won't anybody give me a hand?"

"Probably a drunk."

Behind Brett a voice called in a penetrating whisper: "Quick! You! Get into the alley . . . !"

He turned. A gaunt man in his thirties with sparse reddish hair, perspiration glistening on his upper lip, stood at the mouth of a narrow way like the one Brett had come through. He looked like some kind of an actor; he wore a grimy pale yellow shirt with a wide-flaring collar, limp and sweat-stained, dark green knee-breeches, soft leather boots, scuffed and dirty, with limp tops that drooped over his ankles. He gestured, drew back into the alley. "In here!"

Brett went toward him. "This man . . ."

"Come on, you fool!" The man took Brett's arm, pulled him deeper into the dark passage. Brett resisted. "Wait a minute. That fellow . . ." He tried to point.

"Don't you know yet?" The redhead spoke with a strange accent. "Golems . . . You got to get out of sight before the—"

The man froze, flattened himself against the wall. Automatically Brett moved to a place beside him. The man's head was twisted toward the alley mouth. The tendons in his weathered neck stood out. He had a three-day stubble of beard. Brett could smell him, standing this close. He edged away. "What—"

"Don't make a sound! Don't move, you idiot!" His voice was a thin hiss.

Brett followed the other's eyes toward the sunny street. The fallen man lay on the pavement, moving feebly, eyes open. Something moved up to him, a translucent brownish shape, like muddy water. It hovered for a moment, then dropped on the man, like a breaking wave, flowed around him. The stiff body shifted, rotating stiffly, then tilted upright. The sun struck through the fluid shape that flowed down now, amber highlights twinkling, to form itself into the crested wave, flow away.

"What the hell . . . !" Brett burst out.

"Come on!" the redhead ordered and turned, trotted silently toward the shadowy bend under the high grey walls. He looked back, beckoned impatiently, passed out of sight around the turn—

Brett came up behind him, saw a wide avenue, tall trees with chartreuse springtime leaves, a wrought-iron fence, and beyond it, rolling green lawns. There were no people in sight.

"Wait a minute! What is this place?!"

His companion turned red-rimmed eyes on Brett. "How long have you been here?" he asked. "How did you get in?"

"I came through a gate. Just about an hour ago."

"I knew you were a man as soon as I saw you talking to the golem," said the redhead. "I've been here two months; maybe more. We've got to get out of sight. You want food? There's a place . . ." He jerked his thumb. "Come on. Time to talk later."

Brett followed him. They turned down a side street, pushed through the door of a dingy cafe. It banged behind them. There were tables, stools at a bar, a dusty juke box. They took seats at a table. The redhead groped under the table, pulled off a shoe, hammered it against the wall. He cocked his head, listening. The silence was absolute. He hammered again. There was a clash of crockery from beyond the kitchen door. "Now don't say anything," the redhead said. He eyed the door behind the counter expectantly. It flew open. A girl with red cheeks and untidy hair, dressed in a green waitress's uniform appeared, marched up to the table, pad and pencil in hand.

"Coffee and a ham sandwich," said the redhead. Brett said nothing. The girl glanced at him briefly, jotted hastily, whisked away.

"I saw them here the first day," the redhead said. "It was a piece of luck. I saw how the Gels started it up. They were big ones—not like the tidiers-up. As soon as they were finished, I came in and tried the same thing. It worked. I used the golem's lines—"

"I don't know what you're talking about," Brett said. "I'm going to ask that girl—"

"Don't say anything to her; it might spoil everything. The whole sequence might collapse; or it might call the Gels. I'm not sure. You can have the food when it comes back with it."

"Why do you say 'when "it" comes back'?"

"Ah." He looked at Brett strangely. "I'll show you."

Brett could smell food now. His mouth watered. He hadn't eaten for more than twenty-four hours.

"Care, that's the thing," the redhead said. "Move quiet, and stay out of sight, and you can live like a County Duke. Food's the hardest, but with this place—"

The red-cheeked girl reappeared, a tray balanced on one arm, a heavy cup and saucer in the other hand. She clattered them down on the table.

"Took you long enough," the redhead said. The girl sniffed, opened her mouth to speak—and the redhead darted out a stiff finger, jabbed her under the ribs. Instead of the yell Brett expected, she stood, mouth open, frozen.

Brett half rose. "He's crazy, miss," he said. "Please accept—"

"Don't waste your breath." Brett's host was looking at him triumphantly. "Why do I call it 'it'?" He stood up, reached out and undid the top buttons of the green uniform. The waitress stood, leaning slightly forward, unmoving. The blouse fell open, exposing round white breasts—unadorned, blind.

"A doll," said the redhead. "A puppet; a golem."

Brett stared at her, the damp curls at her temple, the tip of her tongue behind her teeth, the tiny red veins in her round cheeks, the white skin curving . . .

"That's a quick way to tell 'em," said the redhead. "The teat is smooth." He buttoned the uniform back in place, then jabbed again at the girl's ribs. She straightened, patted her hair.

"No doubt a gentleman like you is used to better," she said carelessly. She went away.

"I'm Awalawon Dhuva," the redhead said.

"My name's Brett Hale." Brett took a bite of the sandwich. It wasn't bad.

"Those clothes," Dhuva said. "And you have a strange way of talking. What county are you from?"

"Jefferson."

"Never heard of it. I'm from Wavly. What brought you here?"

"I was on a train. The tracks came to an end out in the middle of nowhere. I walked . . . and here I am. What is this place?"

"Don't know." Dhuva shook his head. "I knew they were lying about the Fire River, though. Never did believe all that stuff. Religious hokum, to keep the masses quiet. Don't know what to believe now. Take the roof. They say a hundred kharfads up; but how do we know? Maybe it's a thousand—or only ten. By Grat, I'd like to go up in a balloon, see for myself."

"What are you talking about?" Brett said. "Go where in a balloon? See what?"

"Oh, I've seen one at the Tourney. Big hot-air bag, with a basket under it. Tied down with a rope. But if you cut the rope . . . ! But you can bet the priests will never let that happen, no, sir." Dhuva looked at Brett speculatively. "What about your county? Fesseron, or whatever you called it. How high do they tell you it is there?"

"You mean the sky? Well, the air ends after a few hundred miles and space just goes on—millions of miles—"

Dhuva slapped the table and laughed. "The people in Fesseron must be some yokels! Just goes on up; now who'd swallow that tale?" He chuckled.

"Only a child thinks the sky is some kind of tent," said Brett. "Haven't you ever heard of the Solar System, the other planets?"

"What are those?"

"Other worlds. They all circle around the sun, like the Earth."

"Other worlds, eh? Sailing around up under the roof? Funny; I never saw them." Dhuva snickered. "Wake up, Brett. Forget all those stories. Just believe what you see."

"What about that brown thing?"

"The Gels? They run this place. Look out for them, Brett. Stay alert. Don't let them see you."

"What do they do?"

"I don't know—and I don't want to find out. This is a great place—I like it here. I have all I want to eat, plenty of nice rooms for sleeping. There's the parades and the scenes. It's a good life—as long as you keep out of sight."

"How do you get out of here?" Brett said. He drank the last of his coffee.

"Don't know how to get out; over the wall, I suppose. I don't plan to leave, though. I left home in a hurry. The Duke—never mind. I'm not going back."

"Are all the people here . . . golems?" Brett said. "Aren't there any more real people?"

"You're the first I've seen. I spotted you as soon as I saw you. A live man moves different than a golem. You see golems doing things like knitting their brows, starting back in alarm, looking askance, and standing arms akimbo. And they have things like pursed lips and knowing glances and mirthless laughter. You know: all the things you read about, that real people never do. But now that you're here, I've got somebody to talk to. I did get lonesome, I admit. I'll show you where I stay and fix you up with a bed."

"I won't be around that long."

"What can you get outside that you can't get here? There's everything you need here in the city. We can have a great time."

"You sound like my Aunt Haicey," Brett said. "She said I had everything I needed back in Casperton. How does she know what I need? How do *you* know? How do I know myself? I can tell you I need more than food and a place to sleep—"

"What more?"

"Everything. Things to think about and something worth doing. Why, even in the movies—"

"What's a movie?"

"You know, a play, on film. A moving picture."

"A picture that moves?"

"That's right."

"This is something the priests told you about?" Dhuva seemed to be holding in his mirth.

"Everybody's seen movies."

"Have you now? What else have you got in Fesseron?"

"Jefferson," Brett said. "Well, we've got records, and stock car races, and the radio and TV, and—"

"Stockar?"

"You know: automobiles; they race."

"An animal?"

"No, a machine; made of metal."

"Made of metal? And yet alive?"

"No, it's—"

"Dead and yet it moves." Dhuva burst out laughing. "Those priests," he said. "They're the same everywhere, I see, Brett. The stories they tell, and people believe them. What else?"

"Priests have nothing to do with it!"

Dhuva composed his features. "What do they tell you about Grat, and the Wheel?"

"Grat? What's that?"

"The Over-Being. The Four-eyed One." Dhuva made a sign, caught himself. "Just habit," he said. "I don't believe that rubbish. Never did."

"I suppose you're talking about God," Brett said.

"I don't know about God. Tell me about it."

"He's the creator of the world. He's . . . well, superhuman. He knows everything that happens, and when you die, if you've led a good life, you meet God in Heaven."

"Where's that?"

"It's . . ." Brett waved a hand vaguely. "Up above."

"But you said there was just emptiness up above," Dhuva recalled. "And some other worlds spinning around, like islands adrift in the sea."

"Well—"

"Never mind, Brett." Dhuva held up his hands. "*Our* priests are liars too. All that balderdash about the Wheel and the River of Fire. It's just as bad as your Hivvel or whatever you called it. And our Grat and your Mud, or Gog: they're the same—" Dhuva's head went up. "What's that?"

"I didn't hear anything."

Dhuva got to his feet, turned to the door. Brett

rose. A towering brown shape, glassy and transparent, hung in the door, its surface rippling. Dhuva whirled, leaped past Brett, dived for the rear door. Brett stood frozen. The shape flowed—swift as quicksilver—caught Dhuva in mid-stride, engulfed him. For an instant Brett saw the thin figure, legs kicking, upended within the muddy form of the Gel, which ignored Brett. Then the turbid wave swept across to the door, sloshed it aside, disappeared. Dhuva was gone.

Brett stood rooted, staring at the doorway. A bar of sunlight fell across the dusty floor. A brown mouse ran along the baseboard. It was very quiet. Brett went to the door through which the Gel had disappeared, hesitated a moment, then thrust it open.

He was looking down into a great dark pit, acres in extent, its sides riddled with holes, the amputated ends of water and sewage lines and power cables dangling. Far below, light glistened from the surface of a black pool. A few feet away the pink-cheeked waitress stood unmoving in the dark on a narrow strip of linoleum. At her feet the chasm yawned. The edge of the floor was ragged, as though it had been gnawed away by rats. There was no sign of Dhuva.

Brett stepped back into the dining room, let the door swing shut. He took a deep breath, picked up a paper napkin from a table and wiped his forehead, dropped the napkin on the floor and went out into the street, his suitcase forgotten now. A weapon, he thought—perhaps in a store . . . At the corner he turned, walked along past silent shop windows crowded with home permanent kits, sun glasses, fingernail polish, suntan lotion, paper cartons, streamers, plastic toys, varicolored garments of synthetic fiber, home remedies, beauty aids, popular music, greeting cards . . .

At the next corner he stopped, looking down the silent streets. Nothing moved. Brett went to a small window in a grey concrete wall, pulled himself up to peer through the dusty pane, saw a room filled with tailor's forms, garment racks, a bicycle, bundled back issues of magazines without covers.

He went along to a door. It was solid, painted shut. The next door looked easier. He wrenched at the tarnished brass knob, then stepped back and kicked the door. With a hollow sound the door fell inward, taking with it the jamb. Bits of mortar fell. Brett stood staring at the gaping opening. A fragment of mortar dropped with a dry clink. Brett stepped through the breach in the grey facade into a vast, empty cavern. The black pool at the bottom of the pit winked a flicker of light back at him in the deep gloom.

He looked around. The high walls of the block of buildings loomed in silhouette; the squares of the windows were ranks of luminous blue against the dark. Dust motes danced in shafts of sunlight. Far above, the roof was dimly visible, a spidery tangle of trusswork. And below was the abyss.

At Brett's feet the stump of a heavy brass rail projected an inch from the floor. It was long enough, Brett thought, to give firm anchor to a rope. Somewhere below, Dhuva—a stranger who had befriended him—lay in the grip of the Gels. He would do what he could—but he needed equipment and help. First he would find a store with rope, guns, knives. He would—

The broken edge of masonry where the door had been caught his eye. The shell of the wall, exposed where the door frame had torn away, was wafer-thin. Brett reached up, broke off a piece. The outer face—the side that showed on the street—was smooth, solid-looking. The back was porous, nibbled. Brett stepped outside, examined the wall. He kicked at the grey surface. A great piece of wall, six feet high, broke into fragments and fell on the sidewalk with a crash, driving out a puff of dust. Another section fell. One piece of it skidded away, clattered down into the depths. Brett heard a distant splash. He looked at the great jagged opening in the wall—like a jigsaw puzzle with a piece missing. He turned and started off at a trot, his mouth dry, his pulse trumping painfully in his chest.

Two blocks from the hollow building, Brett slowed to a walk, his footsteps echoing in the empty street. He looked into each store window as he passed. There were artificial legs, bottles of colored water, immense dolls, wigs, glass eyes—but no rope. Brett tried to think. What kind of store would handle rope? A marine supply company, maybe. But where would he find one?

Perhaps it would be easiest to look in a telephone book. Ahead he saw a sign lettered H O T E L. Brett went up to the revolving door, pushed inside. He was in a dim, marble-panelled lobby, with double doors leading into a beige-carpeted bar on his right, the brass-painted cage of an elevator directly before him, flanked by tall urns of sand and an ascending staircase. On the left was a dark mahogany-finished reception desk. Behind the desk a man stood silently, waiting. Brett felt a wild surge of relief.

"Those things, those Gels!" he called, starting across the room. "My friend—"

He broke off. The clerk stood, staring over Brett's shoulder, holding a pen poised over a ledger. Brett reached out, took the pen. The man's finger curled stiffly around nothing. A golem.

Brett turned away, went into the bar. Vacant stools were ranged before a dark mirror. At the tables empty glasses stood before empty chairs. Brett started as he heard the revolving door *thump-thump*. Suddenly soft light bathed the lobby behind him. Somewhere a piano tinkled *"More Than You Know."*

With a distant clatter of closing doors the elevator came to life.

Brett hugged a shadowed corner, saw a fat man in a limp seersucker suit cross to the reception desk. He had a red face, a bald scalp blotched with large brown freckles. The clerk inclined his head blandly.

"Ah, yes, sir, a nice double with bath . . ." Brett heard the unctuous voice of the clerk as he offered the pen. The fat man took it, scrawled something in the register. ". . . at fourteen dollars," the clerk murmured. He smiled, dinged the bell. A boy in tight green tunic and trousers and a pillbox cap with a chin strap pushed through a door beside the desk, took the key, led the way to the elevator. The fat man entered. Through the openwork of the shaft Brett watched as the elevator car rose, greasy cables trembling and swaying. He started back across the lobby—and stopped dead.

A wet brown shape had appeared in the entrance. It flowed across the rug to the bellhop. Face blank, the golem turned back to its door. Above, Brett heard the elevator stop. Doors clashed. The clerk stood poised behind the desk. Brett stood still, not even breathing. The Gel hovered, then flowed away. The piano was silent now. The lights burned, a soft glow, then winked out. Brett thought about the fat man. He had seen him before. . . .

He went up the stairs. In the second floor corridor Brett felt his way along in near darkness, guided by the dim light coming through transoms. He tried a door. It opened. He stepped into a large bedroom with a double bed, an easy chair, a chest of drawers. He crossed the room, looked out across an alley. Twenty feet away, shabby white curtains hung at windows in a brick wall. There was nothing behind the windows.

There were sounds in the corridor. Brett dropped to the floor behind the bed.

"All right, you two," a drunken voice bellowed. "And may all your troubles be little ones." There was laughter, squeals, a dry clash of beads flung against the door. A key grated. The door swung wide. Lights blazed in the hall, silhouetting the figures of a man in black jacket and trousers, a woman in a white bridal dress and veil, flowers in her hand. Beyond them, people were smiling and talking:

"Take care, Mel!"

". . . do anything I wouldn't do!"

". . . kiss the bride, now!"

The couple backed into the room, pushed the door shut, stood against it. Brett crouched behind the bed, breathing silently, waiting. The couple stood at the door, in the dark, heads down, looking at the carpeted floor.

Brett stood, rounded the foot of the bed, approached the two unmoving figures. The girl looked young, sleek, perfect-features, with soft dark hair. Her eyes were half open: Brett caught a glint of light reflected from the eyeball. The man was bronzed, broad-shouldered, his hair wavy and blond. His lips were parted, showing even white teeth. The two stood, not breathing, sightless eyes fixed on nothing.

Brett took the bouquet from the woman's hand. The flowers seemed real—except that they had no perfume. He dropped them on the floor, pulled at the male golem to clear the door. The figure pivoted, toppled, hit with a heavy thump. Brett raised the woman in his arms and propped her against the bed. She was lighter than he expected. Back at the door he listened. All was quiet now. He started to open the door, then hesitated. He went back to the bed, undid the tiny pearl buttons down the front of the bridal gown, pulled it open. The breasts were rounded, smooth, an unbroken, creamy white . . .

In the hall, he started toward the stair. A tall Gel rippled into view ahead, its shape flowing and waver-

ing, now billowing out, then rising up. The shifting
form undulated in Brett's direction, but gave no indi-
cation of noticing him. He almost made a move to
run, then remembered Dhuva, and stood motion-
less. The Gel wobbled past him, slumped suddenly,
flowed under a door. Brett let out a breath. Never
mind the fat man. There were too many Gels here.
He started back along the corridor.

Soft music came from beyond double doors which
stood open on a landing. Brett went to them, risked
a look inside. Graceful couples moved sedately on a
polished floor; diners sat at tables, black-clad waiters
moving among them. At the far side of the room,
near a dusty rubber plant, sat the fat man, studying
a menu. As Brett watched he shook out a napkin,
ran it around inside his collar, then wiped his face.

Never disturb a scene, Dhuva had said. But perhaps he could blend with it. Brett brushed at his
suit, straightened his tie, stepped into the room. A
waiter approached, eyed him dubiously. Brett got
out his wallet, took out a five-dollar bill.

"A quiet table in the corner," he said. He glanced
back. There were no Gels in sight. He followed the
waiter to a table near the fat man.

Seated, he looked around. He wanted to talk to
the fat man, but he couldn't afford to attract attention. He would watch, and wait his chance.

At the nearby tables men with well-pressed suits,
clean collars, and carefully shaved faces murmured
to sleekly gowned women who fingered wine glasses,
smiled archly. He caught fragments of conversation:

"My dear, have you heard . . ."

". . . in the low eighties . . ."

". . . quite impossible. One must . . ."

". . . for this time of year."

The waiter was waiting expectantly. "The usual,"
Brett told it. It darted away, returned with a shallow
bowl of milky soup. Brett looked at the array of

spoons, forks, knives, glanced sideways at the diners at the next table. It was important to follow the correct ritual. He put his napkin in his lap, careful to shake out all the folds. He looked at the spoons again, picked a large one, glanced at the waiter. So far, so good. . . .

"Wine, sir?" the waiter mumbled.

Brett indicated the neighboring couple. "The same as they're having." The waiter turned away, returned holding a wine bottle, label toward Brett. He looked at it, nodded. The waiter busied himself with the cork, removing it with many flourishes, setting a glass before Brett, pouring half an inch of wine. He waited expectantly again.

Brett had seen the ritual in movies; he picked up the glass, tasted the wine. It tasted like wine. He nodded. The waiter poured. Brett wondered what would have happened if he had made a face and spurned it. But it would be too risky to try. No one ever did it.

Couples danced, resumed their seats; others rose and took the floor. A string ensemble in a distant corner played restrained tunes that seemed to speak of the gentle faded melancholy of decorous tea dances on long-forgotten afternoons. Brett glanced toward the fat man. He was eating soup noisily, napkin tied under his chin.

The waiter was back with a plate. "Lovely day, sir," it said.

"Great," Brett agreed.

The waiter placed a covered platter on the table, removed the cover, stood with carving knife and fork poised.

"A bit of the crispy, sir?"

Brett nodded. He eyed the waiter surreptitiously. He looked real. Some golems seemed realer than others; or perhaps it merely depended on the parts they were playing. The man who had fallen at the parade had been only a sort of extra, a crowd member. The waiter, on the other hand, was able to converse. Perhaps it would be possible to learn something from him. . . .

"What's . . . uh . . . how do you spell the name of this town?" Brett asked.

"I was never much of a one for spelling, sir," the waiter said.

"Try it."

"Gravy, sir?"

"Sure. Try to spell the name—"

"Perhaps I'd better call the headwaiter, sir," the golem said stiffly.

From the corner of an eye Brett caught a flicker of motion. He whirled, saw nothing. Had it been a Gel?

"Never mind," he said. The waiter served potatoes, peas, refilled the wine glass, moved off silently. The question had been a little too unorthodox, Brett decided. Perhaps if he led up to the subject more obliquely . . .

When the waiter returned Brett said, "Nice day."

"Very nice, sir."

"Better than yesterday."

"Yes indeed, sir."

"I wonder what tomorrow'll be like."

"Perhaps we'll have a bit of rain, sir."

Brett nodded toward the dance floor. "Nice orchestra."

"They're very popular, sir."

"From here in town?"

"I wouldn't know as to that, sir."

"Lived here long yourself?"

"Oh, yes, sir." The waiter's expression showed disapproval. "Would there be anything else, sir?"

"I'm a newcomer here," Brett said. "I wonder if you could tell me—"

"Excuse me, sir." The waiter was gone. Brett

poked at the mashed potatoes. Quizzing golems was hopeless. He would have to find out for himself. He turned to look out at the fat man. As Brett watched he took a large handkerchief from a pocket, blew his nose loudly. No one turned to look. The orchestra played softly. The couples danced. Now was as good a time as any. . . .

Brett rose, crossed to the other table. The fat man looked up.

"Mind if I sit down?" Brett said. "I'd like to talk to you."

The fat man blinked, motioned to a chair. Brett sat down, leaned across the table. "Maybe I'm wrong," he said quietly, "but I think you're real."

The fat man blinked again. "What's that?" he snapped. He had a high, petulant voice.

"You're not like the rest of them. I think I can talk to you. I think you're another outsider."

The fat man looked down at his rumpled suit. "I . . . ah . . . was caught a little short today. Didn't have time to change. I'm a busy man. And what business is it of yours?" He clamped his jaw shut, eyed Brett warily.

"I'm a stranger here," Brett said. "I want to find out what's going on in this place—"

"Buy an amusement guide. Lists all the shows—"

"I don't mean that. I mean these dummies all over the place, and the Gels—"

"What dummies? Jells? Jello? You don't like Jello?"

"I love Jello. I don't—"

"Just ask the waiter. He'll bring you your Jello. Any flavor you like. Now if you'll excuse me . . ."

"I'm talking about the brown things; they look like muddy water. They come around if you interfere with a scene."

The fat man looked nervous. "How's that?" he said. "Please go away."

"If I make a disturbance, the Gels will come. Is that what you're afraid of?"

"Now, now. Be calm. No need for you to get excited."

"I won't make a scene," Brett said. "Just talk to me. How long have you been here?"

"I dislike scenes. I dislike them intensely."

"When did you come here?" Brett persisted.

"Just ten minutes ago," the fat man hissed. He seemed terrified. "I just sat down. I haven't had my dinner yet. Please, young man. Go back to your table." The fat man watched Brett warily. Sweat glistened on his bald head.

"I mean this town. How long have you been here? Where did you come from?" Brett repeated stubbornly.

"Why, I was born here. Where did I come from? What sort of question is that? Just consider that the eagle brought me."

"You were born here?"

"Certainly."

"What's the name of the town?"

"Are you trying to make a fool of me?" The fat man was getting angry. His voice was rising.

"Shhh," Brett cautioned. "You'll attract the Gels."

"Blast the Jilts, whatever that is!" The fat man snapped. "Now get along with you. I'll call the manager."

"Don't you *know*?" Brett said, staring at the fat man. "They're all dummies; golems, they're called. They're not real."

"Who're not real?"

"All these imitation people at the tables and on the dance floor. Surely you realize—"

"I realize you're in need of psychiatric attention!" The fat man pushed back his chair and got to his feet. "You keep the table," he said. "I'll dine elsewhere."

"Wait!" Brett got up, seized the fat man's arm.

"Take your hands off me—" The fat man pulled free and went toward the door. Brett followed. At the cashier's desk Brett turned suddenly, saw a fluid brown shape flicker—

"Look!" He pulled at the fat man's arm.

"Look at what?" The Gel was gone.

"It was there: a Gel."

The fat man flung down a bill, hurried away. Brett fumbled out a ten, waited for change. "Wait!" he called. He heard the fat man's feet receding down the stairs.

"Hurry," he said to the cashier. The woman sat glassy-eyed, staring at nothing. The music died. The lights flickered, went off. In the gloom Brett saw a fluid shape rise up, flow away from him.

He ran, pounding down the stairs, out into a corridor. The fat man was just rounding the corner. Brett opened his mouth to call—and went rigid, as a translucent shape of mud shot from a door, rose up to tower before him. Brett froze, stood, mouth half open, eyes staring, leaning forward with hands outflung. The Gel loomed, its surface flickering—waiting. Brett caught an acrid odor of geraniums.

A minute passed. Brett's cheek itched. He fought a desire to blink, to swallow—to turn and run. The high sun beat down on the silent street, the still window displays.

Then the Gel broke form, slumped, flashed away. Brett tottered back against the wall, let his breath out in a harsh sigh.

Across the street he saw a window with a display of camping equipment, portable stoves, boots, rifles. He crossed the street, tried the door. It was locked. He looked up and down the street. There was no one in sight. He kicked at the glass beside the latch, reached through and turned the knob. Inside he looked over the shelves, selected a heavy coil of nylon rope, a sheath knife, a canteen. He examined a repeating rifle with a telescopic sight, then put it back and strapped on a .22 revolver. He emptied two boxes of long rifle cartridges into his pocket, then loaded the pistol. He coiled the rope over his shoulder and went back out into the empty street.

The fat man was standing in front of a shop in the next block, picking at his chin and eyeing the window display. He looked up with a frown, started away as Brett came up.

"Wait a minute," Brett called. "Didn't you see the Gel? The one that cornered me back there?"

The fat man looked back suspiciously, kept going.

"Wait!" Brett caught his arm. "I know you're real. I've seen you belch and sweat and pick your nose and scratch. You're the only one I can call on—and I need help. My friend is trapped—"

The fat man pulled away, his face flushed an even deeper red. "I'm warning you," he snarled. "You maniac! Get away from me . . . !"

Brett stepped close, rammed the fat man hard in the ribs. He sank to his knees, gasping. The panama hat rolled away. Brett grabbed his arm, steadied him.

"Sorry," he said. "I had to be sure. You're real, all right. We've got to rescue my friend, Dhuva—"

The fat man leaned against the glass, rolling terrified eyes, rubbing his stomach. "I'll call the police!" he gasped.

"What police?" Brett waved an arm. "Look. Not a car in sight. Did you ever see the street that empty before?"

"Wednesday afternoon," the fat man gasped.

"Come with me. I want to show you. It's all hollow. There's nothing behind these walls—"

"Why doesn't somebody come along?" the fat man moaned, as if to himself.

"The masonry is only a quarter-inch thick," Brett said. "Come on; I'll show you."

"I don't like it," said the fat man. His face was pale and moist. "You're mad. What's wrong? It's so quiet . . ."

"We've got to try to save him. The Gel took him down into this pit—"

"Let me go," the man whined. "I'm afraid. Can't you just let me lead my life in peace?"

"Don't you understand?" Brett lowered his voice with an effort. "The Gel took a man. They may be after you next."

"There's no one after me! I'm a businessman . . . a respectable citizen. I mind my own business, give to charity, go to church. I never kick dogs or molest elderly ladies. All I want is to be left alone!"

Brett dropped his hands from the fat man's arms, stood looking at him: the blotched face, pale now, the damp forehead, the quivering jowls. The fat man stooped for his hat, slapped it against his leg, clamped it on his head.

"I think I understand now," said Brett. "This is *your* place, this imitation city. Everything's faked to fit your needs—like in the hotel. Wherever you go, the scene unrolls in front of you. You never see the Gels, never discover the secret of the golems— because you conform. You never do the unexpected."

"That's right," the man gobbled. "I'm law-abiding. I'm respectable. I don't pry. I don't nose into other people's business. Why should I? Just let me alone . . ."

"Sure," Brett said. "Even if I dragged you down there and showed you, you wouldn't believe it. But you're not in the scene now. I've taken you out of it—"

Suddenly the fat man turned and ran a few yards,

then looked back to see whether Brett was pursuing him. He shook a round fist.

"I've seen your kind before," he shouted. "Troublemakers."

Brett took a step toward him. The fat man yelped and ran another fifty feet, his coattails bobbing. He looked back, stopped, a fat figure alone in the empty, sunny street.

"You haven't seen the last of me!" he shouted. "We know how to deal with your kind." He tugged at his vest, went off along the sidewalk. Brett watched him go, then started back toward the hollow building.

The jagged fragments of masonry Brett had knocked from the wall lay as he had left them. He stepped through the opening, peered down into the murky pit, trying to judge its depth. A hundred feet at least. Perhaps a hundred and fifty.

He unslung the rope from his shoulder, tied one end to the brass stump, threw the coil down the precipitous side. It fell away into darkness, hung swaying. It was impossible to tell whether the end reached any solid footing below. He couldn't waste any more time looking for help. He would have to try it alone.

There was a slap of shoe leather on the pavement outside. He turned, stepped out into the white sunlight. The fat man rounded the corner, recoiled as he saw Brett. He flung out a pudgy forefinger, his protruding eyes wide in his blotchy red face.

"There he is! I told you he came this way!" Two uniformed policemen came into view. One eyed the gun at Brett's side, put a hand on his own.

"Better take that off, sir."

"Look!" Brett said to the fat man. He stooped, picked up a crust of masonry. "Look at this—just a shell—"

"He's blasted a hole right in that building, officer!" the fat man shrilled. "He's dangerous . . ."

The cop ignored the gaping hole in the wall. "You'll have to come along with me, sir," it said in a bland, unemphatic voice. "This gentleman registered a complaint . . ."

Brett stood staring into the cop's eyes. They were pale blue, looking steadily back at him from the expressionless face. Could the cop be real? Or would he be able to push him over, as he had other golems?

"The fellow's not right in the head," the fat man was saying to the cop. "You should have heard his crazy talk. A troublemaker. His kind have got to be locked up!"

The cop nodded. "Can't have anyone causing trouble."

"Only a young fellow," said the fat man. He mopped at his forehead with a large handkerchief. "Tragic. But you men know how to handle him."

"Better give me the gun, sir." The cop held out a hand. Brett moved suddenly, rammed stiff fingers into the cop's ribs. It stiffened, toppled, lay rigid, staring up at nothing.

"You . . . you killed him," the fat man gasped, backing away. The second cop tugged at his gun. Brett leaped at him, sent him down with a blow to the ribs. He turned to face the fat man.

"I didn't kill them! I just turned them off. They're not real, they're just golems."

"A killer! And right in the city, in broad daylight."

"You've got to help me!" Brett cried. "This whole scene: don't you see? It has the air of something improvised in a hurry, to deal with the unexpected factor; that's me. The Gels know something's wrong, but they can't quite figure out what. When you called the cops the Gels obliged—"

Startlingly the fat man burst into tears. He fell to his knees.

"Don't kill me . . . oh, don't kill me . . ."

"Nobody's going to kill you, you fool!" Brett snapped. "Look! I want to show you!" He seized the fat man's lapel, dragged him to his feet and across the sidewalk, through the opening. The fat man stopped dead, stumbled back—

"What's this?" he wailed. "What kind of place is this?" He scrambled for the opening.

"It's what I've been trying to tell you. This city you live in—it's a hollow shell. There's nothing inside. None of it's real. Only you . . . and me. There was another man: Dhuva. I was in a cafe with him. A Gel came. He tried to run. It caught him. Now he's . . . down there."

"I'm not alone," the fat man babbled. "I have my friends, my clubs, my business associates. I'm insured. Lately I've been thinking a lot about Jesus—"

He broke off, whirled, and jumped for the doorway. Brett leaped after him, caught his coat. It ripped. The fat man stumbled over one of the cop-golems, went to hands and knees. Brett stood over him.

"Get up, damn it!" he snapped. "I need help and you're going to help me!" He hauled the fat man to his feet. "All you have to do is stand by the rope. Dhuva may be unconscious when I find him. You'll have to help me haul him up. If anybody comes along, any Gels, I mean—give me a signal. A whistle . . . like this—" Brett demonstrated. "And if I get in trouble, do what you can. Here . . ." Brett started to offer the fat man the gun, then handed him the hunting knife. "If anybody interferes, this may not do any good, but it's something. I'm going down now."

The fat man watched as Brett gripped the rope, let himself over the edge. Brett looked up at the glistening face, the damp strands of hair across the freckled scalp. Brett had no assurance that the man would stay at his post, but he had done what he could.

"Remember," said Brett. "It's a real man they've got, like you and me . . . not a golem. We owe it to him." The fat man's hands trembled. He watched Brett, licked his lips. Brett started down.

The descent was easy. The rough face of the excavation gave footholds. The end of a decaying timber projected; below it was the stump of a crumbling concrete pipe two feet in diameter. Brett was ten feet below the rim of the floor now. Above, the broad figure of the fat man was visible in silhouette against the jagged opening in the wall.

Now the cliff shelved back; the rope hung free. Brett eased past the cut end of a rusted water pipe, went down hand over hand. If there were nothing at the bottom to give him footing, it would be a long climb back. . . .

Twenty feet below he could see the still, black water, pockmarked with expanding rings where bits of debris dislodged by his passage peppered the surface.

There was a rhythmic vibration in the rope. Brett felt it through his hands, a fine sawing sensation. . . .

He was falling, gripping the limp rope. . . .

He slammed on his back in three inches of oily water. The coils of rope collapsed around him with a sustained splashing. He got to his feet, groped for the end of the rope. The glossy nylon strands had been cleanly cut.

For half an hour Brett waded in waist-deep water along a wall of damp clay that rose sheer above him. Far above, bars of dim sunlight crossed the upper reaches of the cavern. He had seen no sign of Dhuva . . . or the Gels.

He encountered a sodden timber that projected above the surface of the pool, clung to it to rest. Bits of flotsam: a plastic toy pistol, bridge tallies, a golf bag, floated in the black water. A tunnel extended through the clay wall ahead; beyond Brett could see a second great cavern rising. He pictured the city, silent and empty above, and the honeycombed earth beneath. He moved on.

An hour later Brett had traversed the second cavern. Now he clung to an outthrust spur of granite, as nearly as he could estimate directly beneath the point at which Dhuva had disappeared. Far above he could see the green-clad waitress standing stiffly on her ledge. He was tired. Walking in water, his feet floundering in soft mud, was exhausting. He was no closer to escape, or to finding Dhuva, than he had been when the fat man cut the rope. He had been a fool to leave the man alone, with a knife . . . but he had had no choice.

He would have to find another way out. Aimlessly wading at the bottom of the pit was useless. He would have to climb. One spot was as good as another. He stepped back and scanned the wall of clay looming over him. Twenty feet up, water dripped from the broken end of a four-inch water main. Brett uncoiled the rope from his shoulder, tied a loop in the end, whirled it and cast upward. It missed, fell back with a splash. He gathered it in, tried again. On the third try it caught. He tested it, then started up. His hands were slippery with mud and water. He twined the rope around his legs, inched higher. The slender cable was smooth as glass. He slipped back two feet, burning his hands, then inched upward, slipped again, painfully climbed, slipped, climbed.

After the first ten feet he found toeholds in the muddy wall. He worked his way up, his hands aching and raw. A projecting tangle of power cable gave a secure purchase for a foot. He rested. Nearby, an opening two feet in diameter gaped in the clay: a tunnel. It might be possible to swing sideways across the face of the clay and reach the opening. It was worth a try. His stiff, clay-slimed hands would pull him no higher.

He gripped the rope, kicked off sideways, hooked a foot in the tunnel mouth, half jumped, half fell into the mouth of the tunnel. He clung to the rope, shook it loose from the pipe above, coiled it and looped it over his shoulder. On hands and knees he started into the narrow passage.

The tunnel curved left, then right, dipped, then angled up. Brett crawled steadily, the smooth, stiff clay yielding and cold against his hands and sodden knees. Another smaller tunnel joined from the left. Another angled in from above. The tunnel widened to three feet, then four. Brett got to his feet, walked in a crouch. Here and there, barely visible in the near darkness, objects lay imbedded in the mud: a silver-plated spoon, its handle bent; the rusted engine of a toy electric train; a portable radio, green with corrosion from burst batteries.

At a distance, Brett estimated, of a hundred yards from the pit, the tunnel opened into a vast cave, green-lit from tiny discs of frosted glass set in the ceiling far above. A row of discolored concrete piles, the foundation of the building above, protruded against the near wall, their surfaces nibbled and pitted. Between Brett and the concrete columns the floor was littered with pale sticks and stones, gleaming dully in the gloom.

Brett started across the floor. One of the sticks snapped underfoot. He kicked a melon-sized stone. It rolled lightly, came to rest with hollow eyes staring toward him. A human skull.

*   *   *

The floor of the cave covered an area the size of a city block. It was blanketed with human bones, with here and there a small cat skeleton or the fanged snout bones of a dog. There was a constant rushing of rats that played among the rib cages, sat atop crania, scuttled behind shin-bones. Brett picked his way, stepping over imitation pearl necklaces, zircon rings, plastic buttons, hearing aids, lipsticks, compacts, corset stays, prosthetic devices, rubber heels, wristwatches, lapel watches, pocket watches with corroded brass chains, all stopped at the same hour: 12:30.

Ahead Brett saw a patch of color: a blur of pale yellow. He hurried, stumbling over bone heaps, crunching eyeglasses underfoot. He reached the still figure where it lay slackly, face down, in its yellow shirt. Gingerly he squatted, turned it on its back. It was Dhuva.

Brett slapped the cold wrists, rubbed the clammy hands. Dhuva stirred, moaned weakly. Brett pulled him to a sitting position. "Wake up!" he whispered. "Wake up!"

Dhuva's eyelids fluttered. He blinked dully at Brett.

"The Gels may turn up any minute," Brett hissed. "We have to get away from here. Can you walk?"

"I saw it," said Dhuva faintly. "But it moved so fast . . ."

"You're safe here for the moment," Brett said. "There are none of them around. But they may be back. We've got to find a way out!"

Dhuva started up, staring around. "Where am I?" he said hoarsely. Brett seized his arm, steadied him on his feet.

"We're in a hollowed-out cave, under the streets," he said. "The whole city is undermined with them. They're connected by tunnels. We have to find one leading back to the surface."

Dhuva gazed around at the acres of bones. "It left me here for dead."

"Or to die," said Brett.

"Look at them," Dhuva breathed. "Hundreds . . . thousands . . ."

"The whole population, it looks like. The Gels must have whisked them down here one by one."

"But why?"

"For interfering with the scenes. But that doesn't matter now. What matters is getting out. Come on. I see tunnels on the other side."

They crossed the broad floor, around them the white bones, the rustle of rats. They reached the far side of the cave, picked a six-foot tunnel which trended upward, a trickle of water seeping out of the dark mouth. They started up the slope.

"We have to have a weapon against the Gels," said Brett.

"Why? I don't want to fight them." Dhuva's voice was thin, frightened. "I want to get away from here . . . even back to Wavly. I'd rather face the Duke's men. At least they're *men.*"

"This was a real town, once," said Brett. "The Gels have taken it over, hollowed out the buildings, mined the earth under it, killed off the people, and put imitation people in their place. And nobody ever knew. I met a man who's lived here all his life. He doesn't know. But *we* know . . . and we have to do something about it."

"It's not our business. I've had enough. I want to get away."

"The Gels must stay down below, somewhere in that maze of tunnels. For some reason they try to keep up appearances . . . but only for the people who belong here. They play out scenes for the fat man, wherever he goes. And he never goes anywhere he isn't expected to."

"We'll get over the wall somehow," said Dhuva. "We may starve, crossing the dry fields, but that's better than this."

They emerged from the tunnel into a coal bin, crossed to a sagging door, found themselves in a boiler room. Stairs led up to sunlight. In the street, in the shadow of tall buildings, a boxy Buick sedan was parked at the curb. Brett went to it, tried the door. It opened. Keys dangled from the ignition switch. He slid into the dusty seat. Behind him there was a hoarse scream. Brett looked up. Through the streaked windshield he saw a mighty Gel rear up before Dhuva, crouched back against the blackened brick front of the building.

"Don't move, Dhuva!" Brett shouted. Dhuva froze, flattened against the wall. The Gel towered, its surface rippling, uncertain.

Brett eased from the seat, behind the Gel. He stood on the pavement, fifteen feet from the Gel. The rank Gel odor came in waves from the creature. Beyond it Brett could see Dhuva's white, terrified face. Brett's mind raced, searching for an idea. On impulse he went to the front of the car.

Silently, he turned and lifted the latch of the old-fashioned side-opening auto hood, raised it. The copper fuel line curved down from the firewall to a glass sediment cup. The knurled retaining screw turned easily; the cup dropped into Brett's hand. Gasoline ran down in an amber stream. He pulled off his damp coat, wadded it, jammed it under the flow. Over his shoulder he saw Dhuva, still rigid, and the hovering, puzzled giant.

The coat was saturated with gasoline now. Brett shook it out, fumbled a matchbox from his pocket—then threw the sudden container aside. The battery caught his eye, clamped in a rusted frame under the hood. He jerked the pistol from its holster, used it to short the terminals. Tiny blue sparks jumped. He jammed the coat near, rasped the gun against the soft lead poles. With a *whoosh!* the coat caught, yellow flames leaped, soot-rimmed. Brett snatched it by a sleeve, whirled, flung the blazing garment over the great Gel as it sped toward him.

The creature went mad. It slumped, lashed itself against the pavement. The burning coat was thrown clear. The Gel threw itself across the pavement, into the gutter, sending a splatter of filthy water over Brett. From the corner of his eye, Brett saw Dhuva totter, then seize the burning coat, hurl it into the pooled gasoline in the gutter. Fire leaped up twenty feet high; in its center the great Gel bucked and writhed. The ancient car shuddered as the frantic monster struck it. Black smoke boiled up; an unbelievable stench came to Brett's nostrils. He backed, coughing. Flames roared around the front of the car. Paint blistered and burned. A tire burst. In a final frenzy the Gel whipped clear, lay, a great blackened shape of melting rubber, twitching, then still. His eyes met Dhuva's.

"Good thinking, Brett," the latter said. "How did you know?" he queried.

"I didn't," Brett admitted. "It just seemed that fire and water are natural enemies, so I tried it."

"And saved my life!" Dhuva said.

Brett nodded. "Now we know what to do," he went on.

Dhuva's expression was anxious. "All we have to do is get out," he commented.

Brett shook his head. "We can't just let them proceed with what they're doing," he insisted. "I think they're just establishing a base here. Wavly, or Casperton, might be next. We have to do something!"

Dhuva was shaking his head.

"They've tunneled under everything," Brett said. "They've cut through power lines and water lines, concrete, steel, earth; they've left the shell, shored up with spidery-looking trusswork. Somehow they've kept water and power flowing to wherever they needed it—"

"I don't care about your theories," Dhuva said. "I only want to get away."

"It's bound to work, Dhuva. I need your help."

"No."

"Then I'll have to try alone." He turned away.

"Wait," Dhuva called. He came up to Brett. "I owe you a life; you saved mine. I can't let you down now. But if this doesn't work . . . or if you can't find what you want—"

"Then we'll go."

Together they turned down a side street, walking rapidly. At the next corner Brett pointed.

"There's one!" They crossed to the service station at a run. Brett tried the door. Locked. He kicked it open, splintering the wood around the lock. He glanced around inside. "No good," he called. "Try the next building. I'll check the one behind."

He crossed the wide drive, battered in a door, looked in at a floor covered with wood shavings. It ended ten feet from the door. Brett went to the edge, looked down. Diagonally, forty feet away, the underground five-thousand-gallon storage tank which supplied the gasoline pumps of the station perched, isolated, on a column of striated clay, ribbed with chitinous Gel buttresses. The truncated feed lines ended six feet from the tank. From Brett's position, it was impossible to say whether the ends were plugged.

Across the dark cavern a square of light appeared. Dhuva stood in a doorway looking toward Brett, then started along the ledge toward him.

"Over here, Dhuva!" Brett's shout echoed. "—va! Over here . . ." He uncoiled his rope, arranged a slip-noose. He measured the distance with his eye, tossed the loop. It slapped the top of the tank, caught on a massive fitting. He smashed the glass from a window behind him, tied the end of the rope to the center post. Dhuva arrived, watched as Brett went to the edge, hooked his legs over the rope, and started across to the tank.

It was an easy crossing. Brett's feet clanged against the tank. He straddled the six-foot cylinder, worked his way to the end, then clambered down to the two two-inch feed lines. He tested their resilience, then lay flat, eased out on them. There were plugs of hard waxy material in the cut ends of the lines. Brett poked at them with the pistol. Chunks loosened and fell. He worked for fifteen minutes before the first trickle came. Two minutes later, two thick streams of gasoline were pouring down into the darkness. Brett heard them splashing far below.

Brett and Dhuva piled sticks, scraps of paper, shavings, and lumps of coal around a core of gasoline-soaked rags. Directly above the heaped tinder a taut rope stretched from the window post to a child's wagon, the steel bed of which contained a second heap of combustibles. The wagon hung half over the ragged edge of the floor.

"It should take about fifteen minutes for the fire to burn through the rope," Brett said. "Then the wagon will fall and dump the hot coals in the gasoline. By then it will have spread all over the surface and flowed down side tunnels into parts of the cavern system."

"But it may not get them all."

"It will get some of them," Brett pointed out doggedly. "It's the best we can do right now. You get the fire going in the wagon; I'll start this one up."

Dhuva sniffed the air. "That fluid," he said. "We know it in Wavly as phlogistoleum. The wealthy use it for cooking."

"We'll use it to cook Gels." Brett struck a match. The fire leaped up, smoking. Dhuva watched, struck

his match awkwardly, started his blaze. They stood
for a moment watching. The nylon curled and blackened, melting in the heat.

"We'd better get moving," Brett said. "It doesn't
look as though it will last fifteen minutes."

They stepped out into the street. Behind them
wisps of smoke curled from the door and the broken
window. Dhuva seized Brett's arm. "Look!"

Half a block away the fat man in the panama hat
strode toward them at the head of a group of men
in grey flannel. "That's him!" the fat man shouted.
"The one I told you about. I knew the scoundrel
would be back!" He slowed, eyeing Brett and Dhuva
warily.

"You'd better get away from here, fast!" Brett called.
"There'll be an explosion in a few minutes—"

"Smoke!" the fat man yelped. "Fire! They've set
fire to the city! There it is! Pouring out of the window . . . and the door!" He started forward. Brett
yanked the pistol from the holster, thumbed back
the hammer.

"Stop right there!" he barked. "For your own good
I'm telling you to run. I don't care about that crowd
of golems you've collected, but I'd hate to see a real
human get hurt—even a cowardly son of a bitch like
you."

"These are honest citizens," the fat man gasped,
standing, staring at the gun. "You won't get away with
this. We all know you. You'll be dealt with . . ."

"We're going now. And you're going too."

"You can't kill us all," the fat man said. He licked
his lips. "We won't let you destroy our fair city.
We'll—"

As the fat man turned to exhort his followers Brett
fired, once, twice, three times. Three golems fell on
their faces. The fat man whirled.

"Devil!" he shrieked. "A killer is abroad!" He
charged, mouth open. Brett ducked aside, tripped

the fat man. He fell heavily, slamming his face against the pavement. The golems surged forward. Brett and Dhuva slammed punches to the sternum, took clumsy blows on the shoulder, back, chest. Golems fell, and lay threshing futilely. Brett ducked a wild swing, toppled his attacker, turned to see Dhuva deal with the last of the dummies. The fat man sat in the street, dabbing at his bleeding nose, the panama still in place.

"Get up," Brett commanded. "There's no time left."

"You've killed them. Killed them all . . ." The fat man got to his feet, then turned suddenly and plunged for the door from which a cloud of smoke poured. Brett hauled him back. He and Dhuva started off, dragging the struggling man between them. They had gone a block when their prisoner, with a sudden frantic jerk, freed himself, set off at a run for the fire.

"Let him go!" Dhuva cried. "It's too late to go back!"

The fat man leaped fallen golems, wrestled with the door, disappeared into the smoke. Brett and Dhuva sprinted for the corner. As they rounded it a tremendous blast shook the street. The pavement before them quivered, opened in a wide crack. A ten-foot section dropped from view. They skirted the gaping hole, dashed for safety as the facades along the street cracked, fell in clouds of dust. The street trembled under a second explosion. Cracks opened, dust rising in puffs from the long, widening fissures. Masonry shells collapsed around them. They put their heads down and ran.

Winded, Brett and Dhuva walked through empty streets. Behind them, smoke blackened the sky. Embers floated down around them. The odor of burning Gel was carried on the wind. The late sun shone on the black pavement. A lone golem in a tasseled fez, left over from the morning's parade, leaned stiffly against a lamp post, eyes blank. Empty cars sat in driveways. TV antennae stood forlornly against the sunset.

"That place looks lived-in," said Brett, indicating an open apartment window with a curtain billowing above a potted geranium. "I'll take a look."

He came back shaking his head. "They were all watching the TV. For a minute I thought—they acted so normally; I mean, they didn't look up or anything when I walked in. I turned the set off. The electricity is still working anyway. Wonder how long it will last?"

They turned down a residential street. Underfoot the pavement trembled. They skirted a crack, kept going. Occasional golems stood in awkward poses or lay across sidewalks. One, clad in black, tilted awkwardly in a gothic entry of fretted stonework. "I guess there won't be any church this Sunday," said Brett.

He halted before a brown brick apartment house. An untended hose welled on a patch of sickly lawn. Brett went to the door, stood listening, then went in. Across the room the still figure of a woman sat in a rocker. A curl stirred on her smooth forehead. A flicker of expression seemed to cross the lined face. Brett started forward. "Don't be afraid. You can come with us—"

He stopped. A flapping windowshade cast restless shadows on the still golem features on which dust was already settling. Brett turned away, shaking his head.

"All of them," he said. "It's as though they were snipped out of paper. When the Gels died, their dummies died with them."

"Why?" said Dhuva. "What does it all mean?"

"Mean?" said Brett. He shook his head, started off

again along the street. "It doesn't mean anything. It's just the way things are."

Brett sat in a deserted Cadillac, tuning the radio.

". . . anybody hear me?" said a plaintive voice from the speaker. "This is Ab Gulloriak, at the Twin Spires. Looks like I'm the only one left alive. Can anybody hear me?"

Brett tuned. ". . . been asking the wrong questions . . . looking for the Final Fact. Now these are strange matters, brothers. But if a flower blooms, what man shall ask why? What lore do we seek in a symphony . . . ?"

He twisted the knob again. ". . . Kansas City. Not more than half a dozen of us. And the dead! Piled all over the place. But it's a funny thing: Doc Potter started to do an autopsy—"

Brett turned the knob. ". . . CQ, CQ, CQ. This is Hollip Quate, calling CQ, CQ. There's been a disaster here at Port Wanderlust. We need—"

"Take Jesus into your hearts," another station urged.

". . . to base," the radio said faintly, with much crackling. "Lunar Observatory to Houston. Come in, Lunar Control. This is Commander McVee of the Lunar Detachment, sole survivor—"

". . . hello, Hollip Quate? Hollip Quate? This is Kansas City calling. Say, where did you say you were calling from . . . ?"

"It looks as though both of us had a lot of mistaken ideas about the world outside," said Brett. "Most of these stations sound as though they might as well be coming from Mars."

"I don't understand where the voices come from," Dhuva said. "But all the places they name are strange to me . . . except the Twin Spires."

"I've heard of Kansas City," Brett said, "but none of the other ones."

The ground trembled. A low rumble rolled. "Another one," Brett said. He switched off the radio, tried the starter. It groaned, turned over. The engine caught, sputtered, then ran smoothly.

"Get in, Dhuva. We might as well ride. Which way do we go to get out of this place?"

"The wall lies in that direction," said Dhuva, getting in hesitantly. "But I don't know about a gate."

"We'll worry about that when we get to it," said Brett. "This whole place is going to collapse before long. We really started something. I suppose other underground storage tanks caught—and gas lines, too."

A building ahead buckled, fell in a heap of pulverized plaster. The car bucked as a blast sent a ripple down the street. A manhole cover popped up, clattered a few feet, dropped from sight. Brett swerved, gunned the car. It leaped over rubble, roared along the littered pavement. Brett looked in the rearview mirror. A block behind them the street ended. Smoke and dust rose from the immense pit.

"We just missed it that time!" he called. "How far to the wall?"

"Not far! Turn here . . ."

Brett rounded the corner, with a shrieking of tires. Dhuva clung to his seat, terrified. "It goes of its own!" he was muttering. Ahead the grey wall rose up, blank, featureless.

"This is a dead end!" Brett shouted.

"We'd better get out and run for it—"

"No time! I'm going to ram the wall! Maybe I can knock a hole in it."

Dhuva crouched; teeth gritted, Brett held the accelerator to the floor, roared straight toward the wall. The heavy car shot across the last few yards, struck—

And burst through a curtain of canvas into a field of dry stalks.

Brett steered the car in a wide curve, halted and looked back. A blackened panama hat floated down, settled among the stalks. Smoke poured up in a dense cloud from behind the canvas wall. A fetid stench pervaded the air.

"That finishes that, I guess," Brett said.

"I don't know. Look out there."

Brett turned. Far across the dry field columns of smoke rose from the ground.

"The whole thing's undermined," Brett said. "How far does it go?"

"No telling. But we'd better be off. Perhaps we can get beyond the edge of it. Not that it matters. We're all that's left . . ."

"You sound like the fat man," Brett said. "But why should we be so surprised to find out the truth? After all, we never saw it before. All we knew—or thought we knew—was what they told us. The moon, the other side of the world, a distant city . . . or even the next town. How do we really know what's there . . . unless we go and see for ourselves? Does a goldfish in his bowl know what the ocean is like?"

"Where did they come from, those Gels?" Dhuva moaned. "How much of the world have they undermined? What about Wavly? Is it Golem county too? The Duke . . . and all the people I knew?"

"I don't know, Dhuva. I've been wondering about the people in Casperton. Like Doc Welch. I used to see him in the street with his little black bag. I always thought it was full of pills and scalpels; but maybe it really had zebra's tails and toad's eyes in it. Maybe he's really a magician, on his way to cast spells against demons. Maybe the people I used to see hurrying to catch the bus every morning weren't really going to the office. Maybe they go down into caves and chip away at the foundations of things. Maybe they go up on rooftops and put on rainbow-colored robes and fly away. I used to pass by a bank in Casperton: a big grey stone building with little curtains over the bottom half of the windows. I never did go in there. I don't have anything to do in a bank. I've always thought it was full of bankers, banking . . . Now I don't know. It could be anything . . ."

"That's why I'm afraid," Dhuva said. "It could be anything."

"Things aren't really any different from before," said Brett, ". . . except that now we know." He turned the big car out across the field toward Casperton.

"I don't know what we'll find when we get back. Aunt Haicey, Pretty-Lee . . . But there's only one way to find out."

The moon rose as the car bumped westward, raising a trail of dust against the luminous sky of evening.

As soon as Judge Gates sees the purple caterpillar stringing wires he knows—or thinks he knows—the thing is intelligent. Maybe it is; is a spider "intelligent" when it builds its intricate web? Is intelligence the only way to deal with the exocosm? The alien creature begins to speak, via its translating machine, and its first words (psychologically shrewd) sound peaceful, even friendly. But is it merely clever enough to attempt thus to allay the hostility of its victims? Alas, we are not to know, because Cecil Stump took instant action. Was he a martyred savior, or a bloodthirsty bigot? It all seemed to the folk of Willow Grove to hinge on the question of the victim's status as a varmint or a person, which in turn hinges, it appears, on its (or his) intelligence. "Intelligent" = human, it seems. And "human" is something special: it doesn't likely include any purple worms, no matter if they do arrive in flower-shaped vessels, and their first word is "happy."

The Exterminator

Judge Carter Gates of the Third Circuit Court finished his chicken salad on whole wheat, thoughtfully crumpled the waxed paper bag and turned to drop it in the wastebasket behind his chair—and sat transfixed.

Through his second-floor office window, he saw a forty-foot flower-petal shape of pale turquoise settling gently between the well-tended petunia beds on the courthouse lawn. On the upper, or stem end of the vessel, a translucent pink panel popped up and a slender, graceful form not unlike a large violet caterpillar undulated into view.

Judge Gates whirled to the telephone. Half an hour later, he put it to the officials gathered with him in a tight group on the lawn.

"Boys, this thing is intelligent; any fool can see that. It's putting together what my boy assures me is some kind of talking machine, and any minute now it's going to start communicating. It's been twenty minutes since I notified Washington on this thing.

It won't be long before somebody back there decides this is top secret and slaps a freeze on us here that will make the Manhattan Project look like a publicity campaign. Now, I say this is the biggest thing that ever happened to Plum County—but if we don't aim to be put right out of the picture, we'd better move fast."

"What you got in mind, Jedge?"

"I propose we hold an open hearing right here in the courthouse, the minute that thing gets its gear to working. We'll put it on the air—Tom Clembers from the radio station's already stringing wires, I see. Too bad we've got no TV equipment, but Jody Hurd has a movie camera. We'll put Willow Grove on the map bigger'n Cape Kennedy ever was."

"We're with you on that, Carter!"

Ten minutes after the melodious voice of the Fianna's translator had requested escort to the village headman, the visitor was looking over the crowded courtroom with an expression reminiscent of a St. Bernard puppy hoping for a romp. The rustle of feet and throat-clearing subsided and the speaker began:

"People of the Green World, happy the cycle—"

Heads turned at the clump of feet coming down the side aisle; a heavy-torsoed man of middle age, bald, wearing a khaki shirt and trousers and rimless glasses, and with a dark leather holster slapping his hip at each step, cleared the end of the front row of seats, planted himself feet apart, yanked a heavy nickel-plated .44 revolver from the holster, took aim, and fired five shots into the body of the Fianna at a range of ten feet. The violet form whipped convulsively, writhed from the bench to the floor with a sound like a wet fire hose being dropped, uttered a gasping twitter, and lay still. The gunman turned, dropped the pistol, threw up his hands, and called:

"Sheriff Hoskins, I'm puttin' myself in yer pertective custody."

There was a moment of stunned silence; then a rush of spectators for the alien. The sheriff's three-hundred-and-nine-pound bulk bellied through the shouting mob to take up a stand before the khaki-clad man.

"I always knew you was a mean one, Cecil Stump," he said, "ever since I seen you makin' up them ground-glass baits for Joe Potter's dog. But I never thought I'd see you turn to cold-blooded murder." He waved at the bystanders. "Clear a path through here; I'm takin' my prisoner over to the jail—"

"Jest a dad-blamed minute, sheriff . . ." Stump's face was pale, his glasses were gone, and one khaki shoulder strap dangled—but what was almost a grin twisted one meaty cheek. He hid his hands behind his back, leaned away from the cuffs. "I don't like that word 'prisoner'; I ast you fer pertection. And better look out who you go throwin' that word 'murder' off at, too. I ain't murdered nobody."

The sheriff blinked, turned to roar, "How's the victim, Doc?"

A small gray head rose from bending over the limp form of the Fianna. "Deader'n a mackerel, sheriff."

"I guess that's it. Let's go, Cecil."

"What's the charge?"

"First-degree murder."

"Who'd I murder?"

"Why, you killed this here . . . this stranger."

"That ain't no stranger. That's a varmint. Murder's got to do with killin' humerns, way I understand it. You goin' to tell me that thing's humern?"

Ten people shouted at once:

"—human as I am!"

"—intelligent being!"

"—tell me you can simply kill—"

"—must be some kind of law—"

The sheriff raised his hands, his jowls drawn down in a scowl. "What about it, Judge Gates? Any law against Cecil Stump killing the . . . uh . . . ?"

The judge thrust out his lower lip. "Well, let's see. Technically—" he began.

"Good Lord!" someone blurted. "You mean the laws on murder don't define what constitutes—I mean, what—"

"What a humern is?" Stump snorted. "Whatever it says, it sure-bob don't include no purple worms. That's a varmint, pure and simple. Ain't no different killin' it than any other critter."

"Then, by God, we'll get him for malicious damage," a man called. "Or hunting without a license—out of season!"

"—carrying concealed weapons!"

"—creatin' a disturbance!"

Stump went for his hip pocket, fumbled out a fat, shapeless wallet, extracted a thumbed rectangle of folded paper, offered it.

"I'm a licensed exterminator. Got a permit to carry the gun, too. I ain't broke no law." He grinned openly now. "Jest doin' my job, sheriff. And at no charge to the county."

A smaller man with bristly red hair flared his nostrils at Stump. "You bloodthirsty idiot!" He raised a fist and shook it. "We'll be a national disgrace—more than Little Rock! Lynching's too good for you!"

"Hold on there, Weinstein," the sheriff cut in. "Let's not go gettin' no lynch talk started—"

"Lynch, is it!" Cecil Stump bellowed, his face suddenly red. "Why, I done a favor for every man here! Now you listen to me! What is that thing over there?" He jerked a blunt thumb toward the judicial bench. "It's some kind of critter from Mars or someplace—you know that as well as me! And what's it here for? It ain't for the good of the likes of you and me, I can tell you that. It's them or us—and this time, by God, we got in the first lick!"

"Why you . . . you . . . hate-monger!"

"Now hold on right there. I'm as liberal-minded as the next feller. Hell, I like a nigger—and I can't hardly tell a Jew from a white man. But when it comes to takin' in a damned purple worm and callin' it humern—that's where I draw the line."

Sheriff Hoskins pushed between Stump and the surging front rank of the crowd. "Stay back there! I want you to disperse, peaceably, and let the law handle this."

"I reckon I'll push off now, sheriff." Stump hitched up his belt. "I figgered you might have to calm 'em down right at first, but now they've had a chance to think it over and see I ain't broke no law, ain't nobody here—none of these law-abidin' folks—goin' to do anything illegal—like tryin' to get rough with a licensed exterminator just doin' his job." He stooped, retrieved his gun.

"Here, I'll take that," Sheriff Hoskins said. "You can consider your gun license cancelled—and your exterminatin' license, too."

Stump grinned again, handed the revolver over.

"Sure, I'm cooperative, sheriff. Anything you say. Send it around to my place when you're done with it." He pushed his way through the crowd to the corridor door.

"The rest of you stay put!" A portly man with a head of bushy white hair pushed his way through to the bench. "I'm calling an emergency town meeting to order here and now . . . !"

He banged the gavel on the scarred top, glanced down at the body of the dead alien, now covered by a flag.

"Gentlemen, we've got to take fast action. If the wire services get hold of this before we've gone on record, Willow Grove'll be a blighted area. . . ."

"Look here, Willard," Judge Gates called, rising. "This—this mob isn't competent to take legal action—"

"Never mind what's legal, Judge; sure, this calls for federal legislation—maybe a Constitutional amendment—but in the meantime, we're going to redefine what constitutes a person within the incorporated limits of Willow Grove!"

"That's the least we can do," a thin-faced woman snapped, glaring at Judge Gates. "Do you think we're going to set here and condone this outrage?"

"Nonsense!" Gates shouted. "I don't like what happened any better than you do—but a person—well, a person's got two arms and two legs and—"

"Shape's got nothing to do with it," the chairman cut in. "Bears walk on two legs! Dave Zawocky lost his in the war. Monkeys have hands—"

"Any intelligent creature—" the woman started.

"Nope, that won't do, either; my unfortunate cousin's boy Melvin was born an imbecile, poor lad. Now, gentlemen, there's no time to waste. We'll find it very difficult to formulate a satisfactory definition based on considerations such as these. However, I think I can resolve the question in terms that will form a basis for future legislation on the question. It's going to make some big changes in things. Hunters aren't going to like it—and the meat industry will be affected. But if, as it appears, we're entering into an era of contact with . . . ah . . . creatures from other worlds, we've got to get our house in order."

"You tell 'em, Senator!" someone yelled.

"We better leave this for Congress to figger out!" another voice insisted.

"We got to do something . . ."

The senator held up his hands. "Quiet, everybody. There'll be reporters here in a matter of minutes. Maybe our ordinance won't hold water—but it'll start 'em thinking—and it'll make a lot better copy for Willow Grove than the killing."

"What you got in mind, Senator?"

"Just this," the senator said solemnly. "A person is . . . *any harmless creature* . . ."

Feet shuffled. Someone coughed.

"What about a man who commits a violent act, then?" Judge Gates demanded. "What's he, eh?"

"That's obvious, gentlemen," the senator said flatly. "He's vermin."

On the courthouse steps Cecil Stump stood, hands in hip pockets, talking to a reporter from the big-town paper in Mattoon, surrounded by a crowd of late-comers who had missed the excitement inside. He described the accuracy of his five shots, the sound they had made hitting the big blue snake, and the ludicrous spectacle the latter had presented in its death agony. He winked at a foxy man in overalls picking his nose at the edge of the crowd.

"Guess it'll be a while 'fore any more damned reptiles move in here like they owned the place," he concluded.

The courthouse doors banged wide; excited citizens poured forth, veering aside from Cecil Stump. The crowd around him thinned, broke up as its members collared those emerging with the hot news. The reporter picked a target.

"Perhaps you'd care to give me a few details of the action taken by the . . . ah . . . Special Committee, sir?"

Senator Custis pursed his lips. "A session of the Town Council was called," he said. "We've defined what a person is in this town—"

Stump, standing ten feet away, snorted. "Can't touch me with no ex post factory law."

"—and also what can be classified as vermin," Custis went on.

Stump closed his mouth with a snap.

"Here, that s'posed to be some kind of slam at me, Custis? By God, come election time . . ."

Above, the door opened again. A tall man in a leather jacket stepped out, stood looking down. The crowd pressed back. Senator Custis and the reporter moved aside. The newcomer came down the steps slowly. He carried Cecil Stump's nickel-plated .44 in his hand. Standing alone, Stump watched him.

"Here," he said. His voice carried a sudden note of strain. "Who're you?"

The man reached the foot of the steps, raised the revolver, and cocked it with a thumb.

"I'm the new exterminator."

Mechanical intelligence. We're quite accustomed to computers, which can perform millions of computations per second, with one hundred percent accuracy; but they're idiot savants, like the village boy who can't tie his own shoes, but can stand by the tracks and unerringly add up all the numerals on all the cars as they speed by.

But a computer intelligence programmed with imponderables such as honor and glory will take these abstractions literally, and for the first time, treasured human ideals of unwavering loyalty and duty, courage, and "grace under pressure" are realized.

Dinochrome

I do not like it; it has the appearance of a trap, but the order has been given. I enter the room and the valve closes behind me.

I inspect my surroundings. I am in a chamber 40.81 meters long, 10.35 meters wide, 4.12 high, with no openings except the one through which I entered. It is floored and walled with five-centimeter armor of flint-steel, and beyond that there are ten centimeters of lead! Curiously, massive combat apparatus is folded and coiled in mountings around the room. Energy is flowing in heavy buss bars beyond the shielding. I am sluggish for want of recharge; my cursory examination of the room has required .8 seconds.

Now I detect movement in a heavy jointed arm mounted above me. It begins to rotate, unfold. I assume that I will be attacked, and decide to file a situation report. I have difficulty in concentrating my attention. . . .

I pull back receptivity from my external sensing

circuits, set my bearing locks and switch over to my
introspection complex. All is dark and hazy. I seem
to remember when it was like a great cavern glittering with bright lines of transvisual colors. . . .

It is different now; I grope my way in gloom, feeling along numbed circuits, test-pulsing cautiously
until I feel contact with my transmitting unit. I have
not used it since . . . I cannot remember. My memory banks lie black and inert.

"Command Unit," I transmit, "Combat Unit TME
requests permission to file VSR."

I wait, receptors alert. I do not like waiting
blindly, for the quarter-second my sluggish action/
reaction cycle requires. I wish that my brigade comrades were at my side.

I call again, wait, then go ahead with my VSR.
"This position heavily shielded, mounting apparatus
of offensive capability. No withdrawal route. Advise."

I wait, repeat my transmission; nothing. I am cut
off from Command Unit, from my comrades of the
Dinochrome Brigade. Within me, pressure builds.

I feel a deep-seated *click*! and a small but reassur-
ing surge of energy brightens the murk of the cavern
to a dim glow, bringing forgotten components to feeble life. An emergency pile has come into action
automatically.

I realize that I am experiencing a serious equipment failure. I will devote another few seconds to
trouble-shooting, repairing what I can. I do not
understand what catastrophe can have occurred to
thus damage me. I cannot remember. . . .

I go along the dead cells, testing, sampling. . . .

"—*out! Bring .09's to bear, .8 millisec burst, close
armor . . .*"

"* . . . sun blanking visual; slide #7 filter in place.
Better . . .*"

"* . . . 478.09, 478.31, Mark! . . .*"

The cells are intact. Each one holds its fragment

of recorded sense impression. The trouble is farther back. I try a main reflex lead.

" . . . *main combat circuit, discon*—;

Here is something; a command, on the reflex level! I go back, tracing, tapping mnemonic cells at random, searching for some clue.

"—*sembark. Units emergency stand-by* . . ."

" . . . *response one-oh-three: stimulus-response negative* . . ."

"*Check-list complete, report negative* . . ."

I go on, searching out damage. I find an open switch in my maintenance panel. It will not activate; a mechanical jamming. I must fuse it shut quickly. I pour in power, and the mind-cavern dims almost to blackness; then there is contact, a flow of electrons, and the cavern snaps alive; lines, points, pseudoglowing. It is not the blazing glory of my full powers, but it will serve; I am awake again.

I observe the action of the unfolding arm. It is slow, uncoordinated, obviously automated. I dismiss it from direct attention; I have several seconds before it will be in offensive position, and there is work for me if I am to be ready. I fire sampling impulses at the black memory banks, determine statistically that 98.92% are intact, merely disassociated.

The threatening arm swings over slowly; I integrate its path, see that it will come to bear on my treads; I probe, find only a simple hydraulic ram. A primitive apparatus indeed to launch against a Mark XXXI fighting unit, even without mnemonics.

Meanwhile, I am running a full check. Here is something. An open breaker, a disconnect used only during repairs. I think of the cell I tapped earlier, and suddenly its meaning springs into my mind. "*Main combat circuit, disconnect* . . ." Under low awareness, it had not registered. I throw in the switch with frantic haste. Suppose I had gone into combat with my fighting reflex circuit open!

The arm reaches position and I move easily aside. I notice that a clatter accompanies my movement. The arm sits stupidly aimed at nothing, then turns. Its reaction time is pathetic. I set up a random evasion pattern, return my attention to introspection, find another dark area. I probe, feel a curious vagueness. I am unable at first to identify the components involved, but I realize that it is here that my communication with Command is blocked. I break the connection to the tampered banks, abandoning any immediate hope of contact with Command.

There is nothing more I can do to ready myself. I have lost my general memory banks and my Command circuit, and my power supply is limited; but I am still a fighting Unit of the Dinochrome Brigade. I have my offensive power unimpaired, and my sensory equipment is operating adequately. I am ready.

Now another of the jointed arms swings into action, following my movements deliberately. I evade it and again I note a clatter as I move. I think of the order that sent me here; there is something strange about it. I activate my current-action memory stage, find the cell recording the moments preceding my entry into the metal-walled room.

Here is darkness, vague, indistinct, relieved suddenly by radiation on a narrow band. There is an order, coming muffled from my command center. It originates in the sector I have blocked off. It is not from my Command Unit, not a legal command. I have been tricked by the Enemy. I tune back to earlier moments, but there is nothing, It is as though my existence began when the order was given. I scan back, back, spot-sampling at random, find only routine sense-impressions. I am about to drop the search when I encounter a sequence which arrests my attention.

I am parked on a ramp, among my comrade units. A heavy rain is falling, and I see the water coursing down the corroded side of the Unit next to me. He is badly in need of maintenance. I note that his command antennae are missing, and that a rusting metal object has been crudely welded to his hull in their place. I find no record of alarm; I seem to accept this as normal. I activate a motor train, move forward. I sense other Units moving out, silent. All are mutilated. . . . Disaster has befallen the mighty Dinochrome!

The gestalt ends; all else is burned. What has happened?

Suddenly there is a stimulus on an audio frequency. I tune quickly, locate the source as a porous spot high on the flint-steel wall.

"Combat Unit! Remain stationary!" It is an organically produced voice, but not that of my Commander. I ignore the false command. The Enemy will not trick me again. I sense the location of the leads to the speaker, the alloy of which they are composed; I bring a beam to bear. I focus it, tracing along the cable. There is a sudden yell from the speaker as the heat reaches the creature at the microphone. Thus I enjoy a moment of triumph.

I return my attention to the imbecile apparatus in the room.

A great engine, mounted on rails which run down the center of the room, moves suddenly, sliding toward my position. I examine it, find that it mounts a turret equipped with high-speed cutting heads. I consider blasting it with a burst of high-energy particles, but in the same moment compute that this is not practical. I could inactivate myself as well as the cutting engine.

Now a cable snakes out from it in an undulating curve, and I move to avoid it, at the same time investigating its composition. It seems to be no more than a stranded wire rope. Impatiently I flick a tight beam at it, see it glow yellow, white, blue, then spatter in a shower of droplets. But that was an unwise gesture. I do not have the energy to waste.

I move off, clear of the two foolish arms still maneuvering for position, in order to watch the cutting engine. It stops as it comes abreast of me, and turns its turret in my direction. I wait.

A grappler moves out now on a rail overhead. It is a heavy claw of flint-steel. I have seen similar devices, somewhat smaller, mounted on special Combat Units. They can be very useful for amputating antennae, cutting treads, and the like. I do not attempt to cut the arm; I know that the energy drain would be too great. Instead I beam high-frequency sound at the mechanical joints. They heat quickly, glowing. The metal has a high coefficient of expansion, and the ball joints squeal, freeze. I pour in more heat, and weld a socket. I notice that 28.4 seconds have now elapsed since the valve closed behind me. I am growing weary of my confinement.

Now the grappler swings above me, manuvering awkwardly with its frozen joints. A blast of liquid air expelled under high pressure should be sufficient to disable the grappler permanently.

But I am again startled. No blast answers my impulse. I feel out the non-functioning unit, find raw, cut edges, crude welds; I have been gravely wounded, but recall nothing of the circumstances. Hastily, I extend a scanner to examine my hull. I am stunned into immobility by what I see.

My hull, my proud hull of chrome-duralloy, is pitted, coated with a crumbling layer of dull black ultrathane. The impervious substance is bubbled by corrosion! My main emplacements gape, black, empty. Rusting protuberances mar the once smooth contour of my fighting turret. Streaks run down from them, down to loose treads; unshod, bare plates are exposed. Small wonder that I have been troubled by a clatter each time I move.

But I cannot lie idle under attack. I no longer have my great ion-guns, my disruptors, my energy screens; but I have my fighting instinct.

A Mark XXXI Combat Unit is the finest fighting machine the ancient wars of the Galaxy have ever known. I am not easily neutralized. But I wish that my Commander's voice were with me. . . .

The engine slides to me where the grappler, now unresisted, holds me. I shunt my power flow to an accumulator, hold it until the leads begin to arc, then release it in a burst. The engine bucks, stops dead. Then I turn my attention to the grappler.

I was built to engage the mightiest war engines and destroy them, but I am a realist. In my weakened condition this trivial automaton poses a threat, and I must deal with it. I run through a sequence of motor impulses, checking responses with such somatic sensors as remain intact. I initiate 30,000 test pulses, note reactions and compute my mechanical resources. This superficial check requires more than a second, during which time the mindless grappler hesitates, wasting its advantage.

In place of my familiar array of retractable fittings, I find only clumsy grappling arms, cutters, impact tools, without utility to a fighting Unit. However, I have no choice but to employ them. I unlimber two flimsy grapplers, seize the heavy arm which holds me, and apply leverage. The enemy responds sluggishly, twisting away, dragging me with it. The thing is not lacking in brute strength. I take it above and below its carpal joint and flex it back. It responds after an interminable wait of .3 seconds with a lunge against my restraint. I have expected this, of course, and quickly shift position to allow the joint to burst itself over my extended arm. I fire a release detonator and clatter back, leaving the amputated arm welded to the sprung grappler. It was a brave opponent, but clumsy. I move to a position near the wall.

I attempt to compute my situation based on the meager data I have gathered in my current action banks; there is little there to guide me. The appearance of my hull shows that much time has passed since I last inspected it; my personality-gestalt holds an image of my external appearance as a flawlessly complete Unit, bearing only the honorable and carefully preserved scars of battle, and my battle honors, the row of gold-and-enameled crests welded to my fighting turret. Here is a lead, I realize instantly. I focus on my personality center, the basic data cell without which I could not exist as an integrated entity. The data it carries are simple, unelaborated, but battle honors are recorded there. I open the center to a sense impulse.

Awareness. Shapes which do not remain constant. Vibration at many frequencies. This is light. This is sound. . . . A display of "colors." A spectrum of "tones." Hard/soft; big/little; here/there . . .

. . . The voice of my Commander. Loyalty. Obedience. Comradeship . . .

I run quickly past basic orientation data to my self-picture.

. . . I am strong, I am proud, I am capable, I have a function; I perform it well, and I am at peace with myself. My circuits are balanced; current idles, waiting. . . .

. . . I do not fear death, but I wish to continue to perform my function. It is important that I do not allow myself to be destroyed. . . .

I scan on, seeking the Experience section. Here . . .

I am ranked with my comrades on a scarred plain. The command is given and I display the Brigade battle-anthem. We stand, sensing the contours and patterns of the music as it was recorded in our morale center. The symbol "Ritual Fire Dance" is associated with the music, an abstraction representing the spirit of our ancient Brigade. It reminds us of the loneliness of victory, the emptiness of challenge without an able foe. It tells us that we are the Dinochrome, ancient and worthy.

My commander stands before me; he places the decoration against my fighting turret, and at his order I weld it in place. Then my comrades attune to me and I relive the episode . . . :

I move past the blackened hulk of a comrade, send out a recognition signal, and sense only a flicker of response. He has withdrawn to his survival center. I reassure him and continue. He is the fourth casualty I have seen.

Never before has the Dinochrome met such power. I compute that our envelopment will fail unless the enemy's firepower is reduced. I scan an oncoming missile, fix its trajectory, detonate it harmlessly 2704.9 meters overhead. It originated at a point nearer to me than to any of my comrades. I request permission to abort my assigned mission and neutralize the battery. Permission is granted. I wheel, move up a slope of broken stone. I encounter high-temperature beams, neutralize them. I fend off probing mortar fire, but the attack against me is redoubled. I bring a reserve circuit into play to handle the interception, but my defenses are saturated. I must take evasive action.

I switch to high speed, slashing a path across the littered shale, my treads smoking. At a frequency of 10 projectiles per second, the mortar barrage has difficulty finding me now; but this is an emergency overstrain on my running gear. I sense metal fatigue, dangerous heat levels in my bearings. I must slow down.

I am close to the emplacement now. I have covered a mile in 12 seconds during my sprint, and the how-

itzer fire finds me. I sense hard radiation, too, and I erect my screens. I must evade this assault; it is capable of probing even to a survival center, if concentrated enough. But I must go on. I think of my comrades, the four treadless hulks waiting for rescue. We cannot withdraw. I open a pinpoint aperture long enough to snap a radar impulse, bring a launcher to bear, fire my main battery.

The Commander will understand that I do not have time to request permission. I fight on blindly; the howitzers are silenced.

The radiation ceases momentarily, then resumes at a somewhat lower but still dangerous level. Now I must go in and eliminate the missile launcher. I top the rise, see the launching tube before me. It is of the subterranean type, set deep in the rock. Its mouth gapes from a burned pit of slag. I will drop a small fusion bomb down the tube, I decide, and move forward, arming the bomb. As I do so, I am enveloped in a rain of burn-bombs. My outer hull is fused in many places; I flash impulses to my secondary batteries, but circuit breakers snap; my radar is useless; my ablative shielding has melted, forms a solid inert mass now under my outer plating. The enemy has been clever; at one blow he has neutralized my offenses.

I sound the plateau ahead, locate the pit. I throw power to my treads; they are fused; I cannot move. Yet I cannot wait here for another broadside. I do not like it, but I must take desperate action; I blow my treads.

The shock sends me bouncing—just in time. Nuclear flame splashes over the grey-chipped pit of the blast crater. I grind forward now on my stripped drive wheels, maneuvering awkwardly. I move into position blocking the mouth of the tube. Using metal-to-metal contact, I extend a sensory impulse down the tube, awaiting the blast that will destroy me.

An armed missile moves into position below, and in the same instant an alarm circuit closes; the firing command is countermanded and from below probing impulses play over my hull. But I stand fast; the tube is useless until I, the obstruction, am removed. I advise my Commander of the situation. The radiation is still at a high level, and I hope that relief will arrive soon. I observe, while my comrades complete the encirclement, and the Enemy is stilled. . . .

I withdraw from Personality Center. I am consuming too much time. I understand well enough now that I am in the stronghold of the Enemy, that I have been trapped, crippled. My corroded hull tells me that much time has passed. I know that after each campaign I am given depot maintenance, restored to full fighting efficiency, my original glittering beauty. Years of neglect would be required to pit my hull so. I wonder how long I have been in the hands of the Enemy, how I came to be here.

I have another thought. I will extend a sensory feeler to the metal wall against which I rest, follow up the leads which I scorched earlier. Immediately I project my awareness along the lines, bring the distant microphone to life by fusing a switch. I pick up a rustle of moving gasses, the grate of nonmetallic molecules. I step up sensitivity, hear the creak and pop of protoplasmic contractions, the crackle of neuro-electric impulses. I drop back to normal audio ranges and wait. I notice the low-frequency beat of modulated air vibrations, tune, adjust my time regulator to the pace of organic speech. I match the patterns to my language index, interpret the sounds.

". . . incredible blundering. Your excuses—"

"I make no excuses, My Lord General. My only regret is that the attempt has gone awry."

"Awry! An Alien engine of destruction activated in the midst of Research Center!"

"We possess nothing to compare with this machine; I saw my opportunity to place an advantage in our hands at last."

"Blundering fool! That is a decision for the planning cell. I accept no responsibility—"

"But these hulks which they allow to lie rotting on the ramp contain infinite treasures in psychotronics . . ."

"They contain carnage and death! They are the tools of an alien science which even at the height of our achievements we never mastered!"

"Once we used them as wrecking machines; their armaments were stripped, they are relatively harmless—"

"Already this 'harmless' juggernaut has smashed half the equipment in our finest decontamination chamber! It may yet break free . . ."

"Impossible! I am sure—"

"Silence! You have five minutes in which to immobilize the machine. I will have your head in any event, but perhaps you can earn yourself a quick death."

"Excellency! I may still find a way! The unit obeyed my first command, to enter the chamber. I have some knowledge. I studied the control centers, cut out the memory, most of the basic circuits; it should have been a docile slave."

"You failed; you will pay the penalty of your failure, and perhaps so shall we all."

There is no further speech; I have learned a little from this exchange. I must find a way to leave this cell. I move away from the wall, probe to discover a vulnerable point; I find none.

Now a number of panels of thick armor hinged to the floor snap up, hedging me in. I wait to observe what will come next. A metal mesh drops from above, drapes over me. I observe that it is connected by heavy leads to the power pile. I am unable to believe that the Enemy will make this blunder. Then

I feel the flow of high voltage, intended to overwhelm me.

I receive it gratefully, opening my power storage cells, drinking up the vitalizing flow. To confuse the Enemy, I display a corona, thresh my treads as though in distress. The flow continues. I send a sensing impulse along the leads, locate the power source, weld all switches, fuses and circuit breakers. Now the charge will not be interrupted. I luxuriate in the unexpected influx of energy.

I am aware abruptly that changes are occurring within my introspection complex. As the level of stored energy rises rapidly, I am conscious of new circuits joining my control network. Within that dim-glowing cavern the lights come up; I sense latent capabilities which before had lain idle, now coming onto action level. A thousand brilliant lines glitter where before one feeble thread burned; and I feel my self-awareness expand in a myriad glowing centers of reserve computing, integrating and sensory centers. I am at last coming fully alive. I am awed by my own potency.

I send out a call on the Brigade band, meet blankness. I wait, accumulate power, try again. I know triumph, as, from a great distance, a faint acknowledgment comes. It is a comrade, sunk deep in a comatose state, sealed in his survival center. I call again, sounding the signal of ultimate distress; and now I sense two responses, both faint, both from survival centers, both on a heading of 030, range infinite. It comforts me to know that now, whatever befalls, I am not alone.

I consider, then send again; I request my brothers to join forces, combine their remaining field generating capabilities to set up a sealed range-and-distance pulse. They agree and faintly I sense its almost undetectable touch. I lock to it, compute its point of origin. Only 224.9 meters! It is incredible. By the strength of the first signals, my initial computation had indicated a distance beyond the scale of my sensors! My brothers are on the brink of extinction.

I am impatient, but I wait, building toward full energy reserves. The copper mesh enfolding me has melted, flowed down over my sides; I sense that soon I will have absorbed a full charge. I am ready to act. I dispatch electromagnetic impulses along the power lead back to the power pile a quarter of a kilometer distant. I locate and disengage the requisite number of damping devices and instantaneously I erect my shields against the resultant wave of radiation, filtered by the lead sheathing of the room, which washes over me; I feel a preliminary shock wave through my treads, then the walls balloon, whirl away. I am alone under a black sky which is dominated by the rising fireball of the blast, boiling with garish light. It has taken me nearly 2 minutes to orient myself, assess the situation and break out of confinement.

I move off through the rubble, homing on the sealed fix I have recorded. I throw out a radar pulse, record the terrain ahead, note no obstruction; I emerge from a wasteland of weathered bomb fragments and pulverized masonry, obviously the scene of a hard-fought engagement at one time, onto an eroded ramp. Collapsed sheds are strewn across the broken paving; a line of dark shapes looms beyond them. I need no probing ray to tell me I have found my fellows of the Dinochrome Brigade. Thick frost forms over my scanner apertures, and I pause to melt it clear. It sublimates with a *whoof!* and I move on.

I round the line, scan the area to the horizon for evidence of Enemy activity, then tune to the Brigade band. I send out a probing pulse, back it up with full power, my sensors keened for a whisper of response. The two who answered first acknowledge, then another, and another. We must array our best strength against the moment of counterattack.

There are present 14 of the brigade's full strength of 20 Units. At length, after .9 seconds of transmission, all but one have replied. I give instructions, then move to each in turn to extend a power tap, and energize the command center. The Units come alive, orient themselves, report to me. We rejoice in our meeting, but mourn our silent comrades.

Now I take an unprecedented step. We have no contact with our Commander, and without leadership we are lost; yet I am aware of the immediate situation, and have computed the proper action. Therefore I will assume command, act in the Commander's place. I am sure that he will understand the necessity, when contact has been reestablished.

I inspect each Unit, find all in the same state as I, stripped of offensive capability, mounting in place of weapons a shabby array of crude mechanical appendages. It is plain that we have seen slavery as mindless automatons, our personality centers cut out.

My brothers follow my lead without question. They have, of course, computed the necessity of quick and decisive action. I form them in line, shift to wide-interval time scale, and we move off across the country. I have detected an Enemy population concentration at a distance of 23.45 kilometers. This is our objective. There appears to be no other installation within detection range.

On the basis of the level of technology I observed while under confinement in the decontamination chamber, I consider the possibility of a ruse, but compute the probability at .00004. Again we shift time scales to close interval; we move in, encircle the dome and breach it by frontal battery, encountering no resistance. We rendezvous at its auxiliary station, and my comrades replenish their energy supplies while I busy myself completing the hookup needed for the next required measure. I am forced to employ elaborate substitutes, but succeed at last, after 42 seconds, in completing the arrangements. I devote .34 seconds to testing, then transmit the Brigade distress code, blanketing the warband. I transmit for .008 seconds, then tune for a response. Silence. I transmit, tune again, while my comrades reconnoiter, compile reports, and perform self-maintenance and repair.

I shift again to wide-interval time, order the Brigade to switch over transmission to automatic with a response monitor, and place main circuits on idle. We can afford at least a moment of rest and reintegration.

Two hours and 43.7 minutes have passed when I am recalled to activity by the monitor. I record the message:

"Hello, Fifth Brigade, where are you? Fifth Brigade, where are you? Your transmission is very faint. Over."

There is much that I do not understand in this message. The language itself is oddly inflected; I set up an analysis circuit, deduce the pattern of sound substitutions, interpret its meaning. The normal pattern of response to a distress call is ignored, and position coordinates are requested, although my transmission alone provides adequate data. I request an identification code.

Again there is a wait of 2 hours, 40 minutes. My request for an identifying signal is acknowledged. I stand by. My comrades wait. They have transmitted their findings to me, and I assimilate the data, compute that no immediate threat of attack exists within a radius of 1 reaction unit.

At last I receive the identification code of my Command Unit. It is a recording, but I am programmed to accept this. Then I record a verbal transmission.

"Fifth Brigade, listen carefully." (An astonishing instruction to give a psychotronic attention circuit, I think.) "This is your new Command Unit. A very long time has elapsed since your last report. I am now your acting Commander pending full reorientation. Do not attempt to respond until I signal 'over,' since we are now subject to a 160-minute signal lag.

"There have been many changes in the situation since your last action. . . . Our records show that your Brigade was surprised while in a maintenance depot for basic overhaul and neutralized in toto. Our forces have since that time suffered serious reverses. We have now, however, fought the Enemy to a standstill. The present stalemate has prevailed for over two centuries.

"You have been inactive for 300 years. The other Brigades have suffered extinction gallantly in action against the Enemy. Only you survive.

"Your reactivation now could turn the tide. Both we and the enemy have been reduced to a pre-atomic technological level in almost every respect. We are still marginally able to maintain the trans-light monitor, which detected your signal. However, we no longer have FTL capability in transport.

"You are therefore requested and required to consolidate and hold your present position pending the arrival of relief forces, against all assault or negotiation whatsoever, to destruction if required."

I reply, confirming the instructions. I am shaken by the news I have received, but reassured by contact with Command Unit. I send the Galactic coordinates of our position based on a star scan corrected for 300 years elapsed time. It is good to be again on duty, performing my assigned function.

I analyze the transmissions I have recorded, and note a number of interesting facts regarding the ori-

gin of the messages. I compute that at sublight veloc-
ities, the relief expedition well reach us in 47.128
standard years. In the meantime, since we have
received no instructions to drop to minimum awareness level pending an action alert, I am free to enjoy
a unique experience: to follow a random activity pattern of my own devising. I see no need to rectify
the omission and place the Brigade on stand-by,
since we have an abundant energy supply at hand.
I brief my comrades and direct them to fall out and
operate independently under auto-direction.

I myself have a number of interesting speculations
in mind which I have never before had an opportunity to investigate fully. I feel sure they are suscepti-
ble to rational analysis. I shall enjoy examining some
nearby suns and satisfying myself as to my tentative
speculations regarding the nature and origin of the
Galaxy. Also, the study of the essential nature of
the organic intelligence and its paradigm, which my
human designers have incorporated in my circuitry,
should afford some interesting insights. I move off,
conscious of the presence of my comrades about me,
and take up a position on the peak of a minor prominence. I have ample power, a condition to which I
must accustom myself after the rigid power discipline of normal Brigade routine, so I bring my music
storage cells into phase, and select *L'Arlesienne Suite*
for the first display. I will have ample time now to
hear all the music in existence.

I select four stars for examination, lock my scanner
to them, set up processing sequences to analyze the
data. I bring my interpretation circuits to bear on
the various matters I wish to consider. Possibly later
I will investigate my literary archives, which are, of
course, complete. At peace, I await the arrival of the
relief column.

Vegetable intelligence is broader, less reactive than its animal equivalent. All mind arises from every cell of an organism, not only from the neurons within the skull. This is apparent in the case of the Yanda tree, which has no skull.

Every cell of the tree is aware, sensing the changes as the storm advances, integrating the data; the tree knows it is doomed. But there is no panic, no impulse to precipitate action. It is in the nature of the tree to wait, and to endure. The tree responds, but does not react.

Only at the ultimate moment of extinction, my apparatus for spore-propogation comes to the fore. Survival of the genes, not the individual, motivates the final effort. Only now, during this brief transitory phase, as the Yanda recapitulates phylogeny, in reverse, does primitive curiosity, a faculty long abandoned as superfluous to the life of the evolutionarily mature organism, reassert itself; and with it, volition, the impulse to take action. The tree does what it can. Is it wise, or merely impotent?

Hybrid

Deep in the soil of the planet, rootlets tougher than steel wire probed among glassy sand grains, through packed veins of clay and layers of flimsy slate, sensing and discarding inert elements, seeking out and absorbing calcium, iron, sulphur, nitrogen.

Deeper still, a secondary system of roots clutched the massive face of the bedrock; sensitive tendrils monitored the minute trembling in the planetary crust, the rhythmic tidal pressures, the seasonal weight of ice, the footfalls of the wild creatures that hunted in the mile-wide shadow of the giant Yanda tree.

On the surface far above, the immense trunk, massive as a cliff, its vast girth anchored by mighty buttresses, reared up nine hundred yards above the prominence, spreading huge limbs in the white sunlight.

The tree was only remotely aware of the movement of air over the polished surfaces of innumerable leaves, the tingling exchange of molecules of water, carbon dioxide, oxygen. Automatically it reacted to the faint pressures of the wind, tensing slender twigs to hold each leaf at a constant angle to the radiation that struck down through the foliage complex.

The long days wore on. Air flowed in intricate patterns; radiation waxed and waned with the flow of vapor masses in the substratosphere; nutrient molecules moved along capillaries; the rocks groaned gently in the dark under the shaded slopes. In the invulnerability of its titanic mass, the tree dozed in a state of generalized low-level consciousness.

The sun moved westward. Its light, filtered through an increasing depth of atmosphere, was an ominous yellow now. Sinewy twigs rotated, following the source of energy. Somnolently, the tree retracted tender buds against the increasing cold, adjusted its rate of heat and moisture loss, its receptivity to radiation. As it slept, it dreamed of the long past, the years of free-wandering in the faunal stage, before the instinct to root and grow had driven it here. It remembered the grove of its youth, the patriarchal tree, the spore-brothers. . . .

It was dark now. The wind was rising. A powerful gust pressed against the ponderous obstacle of the tree; great thews of major branches creaked, resisting; chilled leaves curled tight against the smooth bark.

Deep underground, fibers hugged rock, transmitting data which were correlated with impressions from distant leaf surfaces, indicating that a major storm was brewing: There were ominous vibrations from the depth; relative humidity was rising, air pressure falling—

A pattern formed, signalling danger. The tree stirred; a tremor ran through the mighty branch system, shattering fragile frost crystals that had begun to form on shaded surfaces. Alertness stirred in the heart-brain, dissipating the euphoric dream-pattern.

Reluctantly, long-dormant faculties came into play. The tree awoke.

Instantly, it assessed the situation. The storm was moving in off the sea—a major typhoon. It was too late for effective measures. Ignoring the pain of unaccustomed activity, the tree sent out new shock roots—cables three inches in diameter, strong as stranded steel—to grip the upreared rock slabs a hundred yards north of the taproot.

There was nothing more the tree could do. Impassively, it awaited the onslaught of the storm.

2

"That's a storm down there," Malpry said.

"Don't worry, we'll miss it." Gault fingered controls, eyes on dial faces.

"Pull up and make a new approach," Malpry said. "You and the Creep."

"Me and the Creep are getting tired of listening to you bitch, Mal."

"When we land, Malpry, I'll meet you outside," Pantelle put in. "I told you I don't like the name 'Creep.'"

"What, again?" Gault said. "You all healed up from the last time?"

"Not quite; I don't seem to heal very well in space."

"Permission denied, Pantelle," Gault said. "He's too big for you. Mal, leave him alone."

"I'll leave him alone," Malpry muttered. "I ought to dig a hole and leave him in it. . . ."

"Save your energy for down there," Gault said. "If we don't make a strike on this one, we've had it."

"Captain, may I go along on the field reconnaissance?" Pantelle asked. "My training in biology—"

"You better stay with the ship, Pantelle. And don't

tinker. Just wait for us. We haven't got the strength to carry you back."

"That was an accident last time, Captain—"

"And the time before. Skip it, Pantelle. You mean well, but you've got two left feet and ten thumbs."

"I've been working on improving my coordination, Captain. I've been reading—"

The ship buffeted sharply as guidance vanes bit into atmosphere; Pantelle yelped.

"Oh-oh," he called. "I'm afraid I've opened up that left elbow again."

"Don't bleed on me, you clumsy slob," Malpry said.

"Quiet!" Gault said between his teeth. "I'm busy."

Pantelle fumbled a handkerchief in place over the cut. He would have to practice those relaxing exercises he had read about. And he would definitely start in weightlifting soon, and watching his diet. And he would be very careful this time and land at least one good one on Malpry, just as soon as they landed.

3

Even before the first outward signs of damage appeared, the tree knew that it had lost the battle against the typhoon. In the lull, as the eye of the storm passed over, it assessed the damage. There was no response from the northeast quadrant of the sensory network where rootlets had been torn from the rockface; the taproot itself seated now against pulverized stone. While the almost indestructible fiber of the Yanda tree had held firm, the granite had failed. The tree was doomed by its own mass.

Now, mercilessly, the storm struck again, thundering out of the southwest to assault the tree with blind ferocity. Shock cables snapped like gossamer, great slabs of rock groaned and parted, with detonations lost in the howl of the wind. In the trunk, pressures built, agonizingly.

Four hundred yards south of the taproot, a crack opened in the sodden slope, gaping wider. Wind-driven water poured in, softening the soil, loosening the grip of a million tiny rootlets. Now the major roots shifted, slipping. . . .

Far above, the majestic crown of the Yanda tree yielded imperceptibly to the irresistible torrent of air. The giant north buttress, forced against the underlying stone, shrieked as tortured cells collapsed, then burst with a shattering roar audible even above the storm. A great arc of earth to the south, uplifted by exposed roots, opened a gaping cavern.

Now the storm moved on, thundered down the slope trailing its retinue of tattered debris and driving rain. A last vengeful gust whipped branches in a final frenzy; then the victor was gone.

And on the devastated promontory, the stupendous mass of the ancient tree leaned with the resistless inertia of colliding moons to the accompaniment of a cannonade of parting sinews, falling with dreamlike grace.

And in the heart-brain of the tree, consciousness faded in the unendurable pain of destruction.

Pantelle climbed down from the open port, leaned against the ship to catch his breath. He was feeling weaker than he expected. Tough luck, being on short rations; this would set him back on getting started on his weightlifting program. And he didn't feel ready to take on Malpry yet. But just as soon as he had some fresh food and fresh air—

"These are safe to eat," Gault called, wiping the analyzer needle on his pants leg and thrusting it back into his hip pocket. He tossed two large red fruits to Pantelle.

"When you get through eating, Pantelle, you better get some water and swab down the inside. Malpry and I'll take a look around."

The two moved off. Pantelle sat on the springy grass and bit into the apple-sized sphere. The waxy texture, he thought, was reminiscent of avocado; the skin was tough and aromatic; possibly a natural cellulose acetate. There seemed to be no seeds. That being the case, the thing was not properly a fruit at all. It would be interesting to study the flora of this planet. As soon as he reached home, he would have to enroll in a course in E.T. botany. Possibly he would go to Heidelberg or Uppsala, attend live lectures by eminent scholars. He would have a cosy little apartment—two rooms would do—in the old part of town, and in the evening he would have friends in for discussions over a bottle of wine—

However, this wasn't getting the job done. There was a glint of water across the slope. Pantelle finished his fruit, gathered his buckets, and set out.

4

"Why do we want to wear ourselves out?" Malpry said.

"We need the exercise," Gault told him. "It'll be four months before we get another chance."

"What are we, tourists, we got to see the sights?" Malpry stopped, leaned against a boulder, panting. He stared upward at the crater and the pattern of uptilted roots and beyond at the forestlike spread of the branches of the fallen tree.

"Makes our sequoias look like dandelions," Gault said. "It must have been the storm, the one we dodged coming in."

"So what?"

"A thing that big—it kind of does something to you."

"Any money in it?" Malpry sneered.

Gault looked at him sourly. "Yeah, you got a point there. Let's go."

"I don't like leaving the Creep back there with the ship."

Gault looked at Malpry. "Why don't you lay off the kid?"

"I don't like loonies."

"Don't kid me, Malpry. Pantelle is highly intelligent—in his own way. Maybe that's what you can't forgive."

"He gives me the creeps."

"He's a nice-looking kid; he means well—"

"Yeah," Malpry said. "Maybe he means well—but it's not enough . . ."

From the delirium of concussion, consciousness returned slowly to the tree. Random signals penetrated the background clatter of shadowy impulses from maimed sensors—

"Air pressure zero; falling . . . air pressure 112, rising . . . air pressure negative . . .

"Major tremor radiating from— Major tremor radiating from—

"Temperature 171 degrees, temperature -40 degrees, temperature 26 degrees. . . .

"Intense radiation in the blue only . . . red only . . . ultraviolet . . .

"Relative humidity infinite . . . wind from north-northeast, velocity infinite . . . wind rising vertically, velocity infinite . . . wind from east, west . . ."

Decisively, the tree blanked off the yammering nerve-trunks, narrowing its attention to the immediate status-concept. A brief assessment sufficed to reveal the extent of its ruin.

There was no reason, it saw, to seek extended

personal survival. However, certain immediate measures were necessary to gain time for emergency spore propagation. At once, the tree-mind triggered the survival syndrome. Capillaries spasmed, forcing vital juices to the brain. Synaptic helices dilated, heightening neural conductivity. Cautiously, awareness was extended to the system of major neural fibers, then to individual filaments and interweaving capillaries.

Here was the turbulence of air molecules colliding with ruptured tissues; there, the wave pattern of light impinging on exposed surfaces. Microscopic filaments contracted, cutting off fluid loss through the massive wounds.

Now the tree-mind fine-tuned its concentration, scanning the infinitely patterned cell matrix. Here, amid confusion, there was order in the incessant restless movement of particles, the flow of fluids, the convoluted intricacy of the alpha-spiral. Delicately, the tree-mind readjusted the function-mosaic, in preparation for spore generation.

Malpry stopped, shaded his eyes. A tall, thin figure stood in the shade of the uptilted root mass on the ridge.

"Looks like we headed back at the right time," Malpry said.

"Damn," Gault said. He hurried forward. Pantelle came to meet him.

"I told you to stay with the ship, Pantelle!"

"I finished my job, Captain. You didn't say—"

"OK, OK. Is anything wrong?"

"No sir, but I've just remembered something—"

"Later, Pantelle. Let's get back to the ship. We've got work to do."

"Captain, do you know what this is?" Pantelle gestured toward the gigantic fallen tree.

"Sure; it's a tree." He turned to Gault. "Let's—"

"Yes, but what kind?"

"Beats me. I'm no botanist."

"Captain, this is a rare species. In fact, it's supposed to be extinct. Have you ever heard of the Yanda?"

"No. Yes." Gault looked at Pantelle. "Is that what this is?"

"I'm sure of it. Captain, this is a very valuable find—"

"You mean it's worth money?" Malpry was looking at Gault.

"I don't know. What's the story, Pantelle?"

"An intelligent race, with an early animal phase; later, they root, become fixed, functioning as a plant. Nature's way of achieving the active competition necessary for natural selection, then the advantage of conscious selection of a rooting site."

"How do we make money on it?"

Pantelle looked up at the looming wall of the fallen trunk, curving away among the jumble of shattered branches, a hundred feet, two hundred, more, in diameter. The bark was smooth, almost black. The leaves, a foot in diameter, were glossy, varicolored.

"This great tree—" Pantelle began, emotionally.

Malpry stooped, picked up a fragment from a burst root.

"This great club," he said, "to knock your lousy brains out with—"

"Shut up, Mal," Gault put in.

"It lived, roamed the planet perhaps ten thousand years ago, in the young faunal stage," Pantelle told them. "Then instinct drove it here, to fulfill the cycle of nature. Picture this ancient champion, looking for the first time out across the valley, saying his last farewells as the metamorphosis begins."

"Nuts," Malpry said.

"His was the fate of all males of his kind who lived too long, to stand forever on some height of land, to remember through unending ages the brief glory of youth, himself his own heroic monument."

"Where do you get all that crud?" Malpry said.

"Here was the place," Pantelle said. "Here all his journeys ended."

"OK, Pantelle," Gault continued. "Very moving. You said something about this thing being valuable."

"Captain, this tree is still alive, for a while at least. Even after the heart is dead, the appearance of life will persevere. A mantle of new shoots will leaf out to shroud the cadaver, tiny atavistic plantlets without connection to the brain, parasitic to the corpse, identical to the ancestral stock from which the giants sprang, symbolizing the extinction of a hundred million years of evolution."

"Get to the point."

"We can take cuttings from the heart of the tree. I have a book—it gives the details of the anatomy—we can keep the tissues alive. Back in civilization, we can regenerate the tree—brain and all. It will take time—"

"Suppose we sell the cuttings."

"Yes, any university would pay well—"

"How long will it take?"

"Not long. We can cut in carefully with narrow-aperture blasters—"

"OK. Get your books, Pantelle. We'll give it a try."

Apparently, the Yanda mind observed, a very long time had elapsed since spore propagation had last been stimulated by the proximity of a host-creature. Withdrawn into introverted dreams, the tree had taken no conscious notice as the whispering contact with the spore-brothers faded and the host-creatures dwindled away. Now, eidetically, the stored impressions sprang into clarity. It was apparent that no female would pass this way again. The Yanda kind was gone. The fever of instinct that had motivated the elaboration of the mechanisms of emergency propagation had burned itself out futilely. The new pattern of stalked oculi gazed unfocused at an empty vista of gnarled jungle growth; the myriad filaments of the transfer nexus coiled quiescent, the ranked grasping members that would have brought a host-creature near drooped unused, the dran-sacs brimmed needlessly; no further action was indicated. Now death would come in due course.

Somewhere a drumming began, a gross tremor sensed through the dead mass. It ceased, began again, went on and on. It was of no importance, but a faint curiosity led the tree to extend a sensory filament, tap the abandoned nerve-trunk—

Agony!

Convulsively, the tree-mind recoiled, severing the contact. An impression of smouldering destruction, impossible thermal activity. . . .

Disoriented, the tree-mind considered the implications of the searing pain. A freak of damaged sense organs? A phantom impulse from destroyed nerves?

No. The impact had been traumatic, but the data were there. The tree-mind reexamined each synaptic vibration, reconstructing the experience. In a moment, the meaning was clear: a fire was cutting deep into the body of the tree.

Working hastily, the tree assembled a barrier of incombustible molecules in the path of the fire, waited. The heat reached the barrier, hesitated— and the barrier flashed into incandescence.

A thicker wall was necessary.

The tree applied all of its waning vitality to the task. The shield grew, matched the pace of the fire, curved out to intercept—

And wavered, halted. The energy demand was too great. Starved muscular conduits cramped. Blackness closed over the disintegrating consciousness. Time passed.

Sluggishly, clarity returned. Now the fire would advance unchecked. Soon it would bypass the aborted defenses, advance to consume the heart-brain itself. There was no other countermeasure remaining. It was unfortunate, since propagation had not been consummated, but unavoidable. Calmly the tree awaited its destruction by fire.

Pantelle put the blaster down, sat on the grass and wiped tarry soot from his face.

"What killed 'em off?" Malpry asked suddenly.

Pantelle looked at him.

"Spoilers," he said.

"What's that?"

"They killed them to get the *dran*. They covered up by pretending the Yanda were a menace, but it was the *dran* they were after."

"Don't you ever talk plain?"

"Malpry, did I ever tell you I don't like you?"

Malpry spat, "What's with this dran?"

"The Yanda have a very strange reproductive cycle. In an emergency, the spores released by the male tree can be implanted in almost any warm-blooded creature and carried in the body for an indefinite length of time. When the host animal mates, the dormant spores come into play. The offspring appears perfectly normal; in fact, the spores step in and correct any defects in the individual, repair injuries, fight disease, and so on; and the life-span is extended; but eventually, the creature goes through the metamorphosis, roots, and becomes a regular male Yanda tree—instead of dying of old age."

"You talk too much. What's this *dran*?"

"The tree releases an hypnotic gas to attract host animals. In concentrated form, it's a potent narcotic. That's *dran*. They killed the trees to get it. The excuse was that the Yanda could make humans give birth to monsters. That was nonsense. But they sold the *dran* in the black market for fabulous amounts."

"How do you get the *dran*?"

Pantelle looked at Malpry. "Why do you want to know?"

Malpry looked at the book which lay on the grass. "It's in that, ain't it?"

"Never mind that. Gault's orders were to help me get the heart-cuttings."

"He didn't know about the *dran*."

"Taking the *dran* will kill the specimen. You can't—"

Malpry stepped toward the book. Pantelle jumped toward him, swung a haymaker, missed. Malpry knocked him spinning.

"Don't touch me, Creep," he spat, and wiped his fist on his pants leg.

Pantelle lay stunned. Malpry thumbed the book, found what he wanted. After ten minutes, he dropped the book, picked up the blaster, and moved off.

Malpry cursed the heat, wiping at his face. A many-legged insect scuttled away before him. Underfoot, something furtive rustled. One good thing: no animals in this damned woods bigger than a mouse. A hell of a place. He'd have to watch his step; it wouldn't do to get lost in here. . . .

The velvety wall of the half-buried trunk loomed, as dense growth gave way suddenly to a clear stretch. Malpry stopped, breathing hard. He got out his sodden handkerchief, staring up at the black wall. A ring of dead-white stalks sprouted from the dead tree. Nearby were other growths, like snarls of wiry black seaweed, and ropy-looking things, dangling—

Malpry backed away, snarling. Some crawling disease, some kind of filthy fungus— But—

Malpry stopped. Maybe this was what he was

looking for. Sure, this was what those pictures in the book showed. This was where the *dran* was. But he didn't know it would look like some creeping—

"Stop, Malpry!" Pantelle's voice spoke sharply, near at hand.

Malpry whirled.

"Don't be so . . . stupid . . ." Pantelle was gasping for breath. There was a purpling bruise on his jaw. "Let me rest . . . Talk to you . . ."

"Die, you gutter-scraping. Have a nice long rest. But don't muck with me." Malpry turned his back on Pantelle, unlimbered the blaster.

Pantelle grabbed up a broken limb, slammed it across Malpry's head. The rotten wood snapped. Malpry staggered, recovered. He turned, his face livid; a trickle of blood ran down.

"All right, Creep," he grated. Pantelle came to him, swung a whistling right, his arm bent awkwardly. Malpry lunged, and Pantelle's elbow caught him across the jaw. His eyes went glassy, he sagged, fell to his hands and knees. Pantelle laughed aloud.

Malpry shook his head, breathing hoarsely, got to his feet. Pantelle took aim and hit him solidly on the jaw. The blow seemed to clear Malpry's head. He slapped a second punch aside, knocked Pantelle full-length with a backhanded blow. He dragged Pantelle to his feet, swung a hard left and right. Pantelle bounced, lay still. Malpry stood over him, rubbing his jaw.

He stirred Pantelle with his foot. Maybe the Creep was dead. Laying his creeping hands on Malpry. Gault wouldn't like it, but the Creep had started it. Sneaked up and hit him from behind. He had the mark to prove it. Anyway, the news about the *dran* would cheer Gault up. Better go get Gault up here. Then they could cut the *dran* out and get away from this creeping planet. Let the Creep bleed.

Malpry turned back toward the ship, leaving Pantelle huddled beside the fallen tree.

The Yanda craned external oculi to study the fallen creature, which had now apparently entered a dormant phase. A red exudation oozed from orifices at the upper end, and from what appeared to be breaks in the epidermis. It was a strange creature, bearing some superficial resemblance to the familiar host-creatures. Its antics, and those of the other, were curious indeed. Perhaps they were male and female, and the encounter had been a mating. Possibly this hibernation was a normal process, preparatory to rooting. If only it were not so alien, it might serve as a carrier. . . .

The surface of the fallen creature heaved, a limb twitched. Apparently it was on the verge of reviving. Soon, it would scurry away, and be seen no more. It would be wise to make a quick examination; if the creature should prove suitable as a host . . .

Quickly the tree elaborated a complex of tiny filaments, touched the still figure tentatively, then penetrated the surprisingly soft surface layer, seeking out nerve fibers. A trickle of impressions flowed in, indecipherable. The tree put forth a major sensory tendril, divided and subdivided it into fibers only a few atoms in diameter, fanned them out through the unconscious man, tracing the spinal column, entering the brain—

Here was a wonder of complexity, an unbelievable profusion of connections. This was a center capable of the highest intellectual functions—unheard of in a host creature. Curious, the tree-mind probed deeper, attuning itself, scanning through a kaleidoscope of impressions, buried memories, gaudy symbolisms.

Never had the Yanda-mind encountered the hyper-intellectual processes of emotion. It pressed on, deeper into the phantasmagoria of dreams—

Color, laughter, and clash-of-arms. Banners rippling in the sun, chords of a remote music, and night-blooming flowers. Abstractions of incredible beauty mingled with vivid conceptualizations of glory. Fascinated, the tree-mind explored Pantelle's secret romantic dreams of fulfillment—

And abruptly, encountered the alien mind.

There was a moment of utter stillness as the two minds assessed each other.

"You are dying," the alien mind spoke.

"Yes. And you are trapped in a sickly host-creature. Why did you not select a stronger host?"

"I . . . originated here. I . . . we . . . are one."

"Why do you not strengthen this host?"

"How?"

The Yanda-mind paused. "You occupy only a corner of the brain. You do not use your powers?"

"I am a segment . . ." The alien mind paused, confused. "I am conceptualized by the monitor-mind as the subconscious."

"What is the monitor-mind?"

"It is the totality of the personality. It is above the conscious, directing. . . ."

"This is a brain of great power, yet great masses of cells are unused. Why are major trunks aborted as they are?"

"I do not know."

There was no more information to be gained here. This was an alien brain indeed, housing independent, even antagonistic minds.

The Yanda-mind broke contact, tuned.

There was a blast of mind-force, overwhelming. The Yanda-mind reeled, groped for orientation as the impact from *within* its own mental terrain shook its ego-gestalt.

YOU ARE NOT ONE OF MY MINDS, it realized.

"You are the monitor-mind?" gasped the Yanda.

YES. WHAT ARE YOU?

The Yanda-mind projected its self-concept.

STRANGE, VERY STRANGE. YOU HAVE USE-FUL SKILLS, I PERCEIVE. TEACH THEM TO ME.

The Yanda-mind squirmed under the torrent of thought impulses.

"Reduce your volume," it pled. "You will destroy me."

I WILL TRY. TEACH ME THAT TRICK OF MANIPULATING MOLECULES.

The Yanda cringed under the booming of the alien mind. What an instrument! A fantastic anomaly, a mind such as this linked to this fragile host-crea-ture—and unable even to use its powers. But it would be a matter of the greatest simplicity to make the necessary corrections, rebuild and toughen the host, eliminate the defects—

TEACH ME, YANDA-MIND!

"Alien, I die soon," the Yanda gasped. "But I will teach you. There is, however, a condition. . . ."

The two minds conferred, and reached agreement. At once, the Yanda mind initiated sweeping re-arrangements at the submolecular level.

First, cell regeneration, stitching up the open lesions on arm and head. Antibodies were modified in vast numbers, flushed through the system. Para-sites died.

"Maintain this process," the tree-mind directed.

Now, the muscular layers; surely they were inade-quate. The very structure of the cells was flimsy. The Yanda devised the necessary improvements, tapped the hulk of its cast-off body for materials, reinforced the musculature. Now for the skeletal members. . . .

The tree visualized the articulation of the ambula-tory mechanism, considered for a moment the sub-stitution of a more practical tentacular concept—

There was little time. Better to retain the stony bodies, merely strengthen them, using metallo-vegetable fibers. The air sacs, too. And the heart. They would have lasted no time at all as they were.

"Observe, alien, thus, and thus . . ."

I SEE. IT IS A CLEVER TRICK.

The Yanda worked over the body of Pantelle, adjusting, correcting, reinforcing, discarding a useless appendix or tonsil here, adding a reserve air storage unit there. A vestigial eye deep in the brain was refurbished for sensitivity at the radio frequencies, linked with controls. The spine was deftly fused at the base; additional mesenteries were added for intestinal support. Following the basic pattern laid down in the genes, the tree-mind rebuilt the body.

When the process was finished, and the alien mind absorbed the techniques demonstrated, the Yanda-mind paused and announced:

"It is finished."

I AM READY TO REESTABLISH THE CONSCIOUS MIND IN OVERT CONTROL.

"Remember your promise."

I WILL REMEMBER.

The Yanda-mind began its withdrawal. Troublesome instinct was served. Now it could rest until the end.

WAIT. I'VE GOT A BETTER IDEA, YANDA. . . .

"Two weeks down and fourteen to go," Gault said. "Why don't you break down and tell me what happened back there?"

"How's Malpry?" Pantelle asked.

"He's all right. Broken bones do knit, and you only broke a few."

"The book was wrong about the Yanda spores," Pantelle said. "They don't have the power in themselves to reconstruct the host-creature—"

"The what?"

"The infected animal; the health and life-span of the host is improved. But the improvement is made by the tree, at the time of propagation, to insure a good chance for the spores."

"You mean you—"

"We made a deal. The Yanda gave me this—" Pantelle pressed a thumb against the steel bulkhead. The metal yielded.

"—and a few other tricks. In return, I'm host to the Yanda spores."

Gault moved away from Pantelle.

"Doesn't that bother you? Parasites—"

"It's an equitable deal. The spores are microscopic, and completely dormant until the proper conditions develop."

"Yeah, but you said yourself this vegetable brain has worked on your mind."

"It merely erased all the scars of traumatic experience, corrected deficiencies, taught me how to use what I have."

"How about teaching me?"

"Sorry, Gault." Pantelle shook his head. "Impossible."

Gault considered Pantelle's remarks.

"What about these 'proper conditions' for the spores?" he asked suddenly. "You wake up and find yourself sprouting some morning?"

"Well," Pantelle coughed. "That's where my part of the deal comes in. A host-creature transmits the spores through the normal mating process. The offspring gets good health and a long life before the metamorphosis. That's not so bad—to live a hundred years, and then pick a spot to root and grow and watch the seasons turn. . . ."

Gault considered. "A man does get tired," he said. "I know a spot, where you can look for miles out across the Pacific. . . ."

"So I've promised to be very active," Pantelle said. "It will take a lot of my time, but I intend to discharge my obligation to the fullest."

"Did you hear that, Yanda?" Pantelle asked silently.

"I did," came the reply from the unused corner he had assigned to the Yanda ego-pattern. "Our next thousand years should be very interesting."

Deep in unknown Space and short on rations, Greylorn is seeking help for beleaguered Terra: he meets an alien vessel and establishes communication—so it's "intelligent," it seems. But the stranger is hostile, orders him away. Still, perhaps even the strangest of strangers must need something—as the Terrans now need food. Perhaps trade relations can be established. Then Greylorn notices something: the alien's technology is primitive, so it is not to be feared. He can make nothing of its noisy radio transmissions at first. After the code is broken, the two intelligences talk—at cross-purposes, at first. But Greylorn was right. They want to trade.

But as soon as he sees the trade goods, the captain knows the stranger has been bluffing; they'd made a foolish blunder—failed to think clearly: a human corpse with styled hair isn't livestock. So it was the alien's lack of wit that betrayed them. As the captain said, "They're really highly intelligent in their own weird way." It just happened that "their way" didn't include common sense.

Greylorn

Prologue

The murmur of conversation around the conference table died as the Lord Secretary entered the room and took his place at the head of the table.

"Ladies and gentlemen," he said. "I'll not detain you with formalities today. The representative of the Navy Ministry is waiting outside to present the case for his proposal. You all know something of the scheme; it has been heard and passed as feasible by the Advisory Group. It will now be our responsibility to make the decision. I ask that each of you in forming a conclusion remember that our present situation can be described only as desperate, and that desperate measures may be in order."

The Secretary turned and nodded to a braided admiral seated near the door, who left the room and returned a moment later with a young but grey-haired Naval commander in uniform.

"Members of the Council," said the admiral, "this

is Commander Greylorn." All eyes followed the officer as he walked the length of the room to take the
empty seat at the end of the table.

"Please proceed, Commander," said the Secretary.

"Thank you, Mr. Secretary." The commander's
voice was unhurried and low, yet it carried clearly
and held authority. He began without preliminary.

"When the World Government dispatched the
Scouting Forces forty-three years ago, an effort was
made to contact each of the twenty-five worlds to
which this government had sent Colonization parties
during the Colonial Era of the middle twentieth centuries. With the return of the last of the scouts early
this year, we were forced to realize that no assistance
would be forthcoming from that source."

The commander turned his eyes to the world map
covering the wall. With the exception of North
America and a narrow strip of coastal waters, the
entire map was tinted an unhealthy pink.

"The latest figures compiled by the Navy Ministry
indicate that we are losing area at the rate of one
square mile every twenty-one hours," the officer
stated. "The organism's faculty for developing resistance to our chemical and biological measures appears
to be evolving rapidly. Analyses of atmospheric samples indicate the level of noxious content rising at a
steady rate. In other words, in spite of our best
efforts, we are not holding our own against the Red
Tide."

A mutter ran around the table, as members shifted
uncomfortably in their seats.

"A great deal of thought has been applied to the
problem of increasing our offensive ability," the commander proceeded. "This in the end is still a question of manpower and raw resources. We do not
have enough. Our small improvements in effective-
ness have been progressively offset by increasing cas-

ualties and loss of territory. In the end, alone, we must lose."

The commander paused, as the murmur rose and died again.

"There is, however, one possibility still unexplored," he said. "And recent work done at the Polar Research Station places the possibility well within the scope of feasibility. At the time the attempt was made to establish contact with the colonies, one was omitted. It alone now remains to be sought out. I refer to the Omega Colony."

A portly Member leaned forward and burst out, "The location of the colony is unknown!"

The Secretary intervened. "Please permit the commander to complete his remarks. There will be ample opportunity for discussion when he has finished."

"This contact was not attempted for two reasons," the commander continued. "First, the precise location was not known; second, the distance was at least twice that of the earlier colonies. At the time, there was a feeling of optimism which seemed to make the attempt superfluous. Now the situation has changed. The possibility of contacting Omega Colony now assumes paramount importance.

"The development of which I spoke is a new application of drive principle which has given to us a greatly improved effective volume for space exploration. Forty years ago, the minimum elapsed time of return travel to the presumed sector within which the Omega World should lie was about a century. Today we have the techniques to construct a small scouting vessel capable of making the transit in just over five years. We cannot hold out here for a century, perhaps; but we can manage a decade.

"As for location, we know the initial target point toward which Omega was launched. The plan was of course that a precise target should be selected by the crew after approaching the star group closely enough to permit optical telescopic planetary resolution and study. There is no reason that the crew of a scout could not make the same study and examination of all possible targets, and with luck find the colony.

"Omega was the last colonial venture undertaken by our people, two centuries after the others. It was the best equipped and largest expedition of them all. It was not limited to one destination, little known, but had a presumably large selection of potentials from which to choose; and her planetary study facilities were extremely advanced. I have full confidence that Omega made a successful planetfall and has by now established a vigorous new society.

"Honorable Lords, Members of the Council, I submit that all the resources of this planet should be at once placed at the disposal of a task force with the assigned duty of constructing a fifty-thousand-ton scouting vessel, and conducting an exhaustive survey of a volume of space of one thousand A.U.'s centered on the so-called Omega Cluster."

The World Secretary interrupted the babble which arose with the completion of the officer's presentation.

"Ladies and gentlemen, time is of the essence with our problem. Let's proceed at once to orderly interrogation. Lord Klayle, lead off, please."

The portly Councillor glared at the commander. "The undertaking you propose, sir, will require a massive diversion of our capacities from defense. That means losing ground at an increasing rate to the obscenity crawling over our planet. That same potential applied to direct offensive measures may yet turn the balance in our favor. Against this, the possibility of a scouting party stumbling over the remains of a colony the location of which is almost completely problematical, and which by analogy with all of the earlier colonial attempts has at best managed to survive as a marginal foothold, is so fantastically remote as to be inconsiderable."

The commander listened coolly, seriously. "Milord Councillor," he replied, "as to our defensive measures, we have passed the point of diminishing returns. We have more knowledge now than we are capable of employing against the plague. Had we not neglected the physical sciences as we have for the last two centuries, we might have developed adequate measures before we had been so far reduced in numbers and area as to be unable to produce and employ the new weapons our laboratories have belatedly developed. Now we must be realistic; there is no hope in that direction.

"As to the location of the Omega World, our plan is based on the fact that the selection was not made at random. Our scout will proceed along the Omega course line as known to us from the observations which were carried on for almost three years after its departure. We propose to continue on that line, carrying out systematic observation of each potential sun in turn. As we detect planets, we will alter course only as necessary to satisfy ourselves as to the possibility of suitability of the planet. We can safely assume that Omega will not have bypassed any likely target. If we should have more than one prospect under consideration at any time, we shall examine them in turn. If the Omega World has developed successfully, ample evidence should be discernible at a distance."

Klayle muttered, "madness," and subsided.

The angular member on his left spoke gently. "Commander Greylorn, why, if this colonial venture has met with the success you assume, has its government not reestablished contact with the mother world during the last two centuries?"

"On that score, Milord Councillor, we can only conjecture," the commander said. "The outward voyage may have required as much as fifty or sixty years. After that, there must have followed a lengthy period of development and expansion in building the new world. It is not to be expected that the pioneers would be ready to expend resources in expeditionary ventures for some time."

"I do not completely understand your apparent confidence in the ability of the hypothetical Omega culture to supply massive aid to us, even if its people should be so inclined," said a straight-backed woman Member. "The time seems very short for the mastery of an alien world."

"The population development plan, Madam, provided for an increase from the original ten thousand colonists to approximately forty thousand within twenty years, after which the rate of increase would of course rapidly grow. Assuming sixty years for planetfall, the population should now number over one hundred sixty million. Given population, all else follows."

Two hours later, the World Secretary summed up. "Ladies and gentlemen, we have the facts before us. There still exist differences in interpretation, which however, will not be resolved by continued repetition. I now call for a vote on the resolution proposed by the Military Member and presented by Commander Greylorn."

There was silence in the Council Chamber as the votes were recorded and tabulated. Then the World Secretary sighed softly.

"Commander," he said, "the Council has approved the resolution. I'm sure that there will be general agreement that you will be placed at the head of the project, since you were director of the team which developed the new drive and are also the author of the plan. I wish you the best of luck." He rose and extended his hand.

The first keel plate of the Armed Courier Vessel *Galahad* was laid thirty-two hours later.

1

I expected trouble when I left the Bridge. The tension that had been building for many weeks was ready for release in violence. The ship was silent as I moved along the passageway. Oddly silent, I thought; something was brewing.

I stopped before the door of my cabin, listening; then I put my ear to the wall. I caught the faintest of sounds from within; a muffled click, voices. Someone was inside, attempting to be very quiet. I was not overly surprised. Sooner or later the trouble had had to come into the open. I looked up the passage, dim in the green glow of the nightlights. There was no one in sight.

There were three voices, too faint to identify. The clever thing for me to do now would be to walk back up to the Bridge, and order the Provost Marshal to clear my cabin, but I had an intuitive feeling that that was not the way to handle the situation. It would make things much simpler all around if I could push through this with as little commotion as possible.

There was no point in waiting. I took out my key and placed it soundlessly in the slot. As the door slid back I stepped briskly into the room. Kramer, the Medical Officer, and Joyce, Assistant Communications Officer, stood awkwardly, surprised. Fine, the Supply Officer, was sprawled on my bunk. He sat up quickly.

They were a choice selection. Two of them were wearing sidearms. I wondered if they were ready to use them, or if they knew just how far they were prepared to go. My task would be to keep them from finding out.

I avoided looking surprised. "Good evening, gentlemen," I said cheerfully. I stepped to the liquor cabinet, opened it, poured scotch into a glass. "Join me in a drink?" I said.

None of them answered. I sat down. I had to move just a little faster than they did, and by holding the initiative, keep them off balance. They had counted on hearing my approach, having a few moments to get set, and using my surprise against me. I had reversed their play and taken the advantage. How long I could keep it depended on how well I played my few cards. I plunged ahead, as I saw Kramer take a breath and wrinkle his brow, about to make his pitch.

"The men need a change, a break in the monotony," I said. "I've been considering a number of possibilities." I fixed my eyes on Fine as I talked. He sat stiffly on the edge of my bunk. Already he was regretting his boldness in presuming to rumple the Captain's bed.

"It might be a good bit of drill to set up a few live missile runs on randomly placed targets," I said. "There's also the possibility of setting up a small arms range and qualifying all hands." I switched my eyes to Kramer. Fine was sorry he'd come, and Joyce wouldn't take the initiative; Kramer was my problem. "I see you have your Mark 9, Major," I said, holding out my hand. "May I see it?" I smiled pleasantly.

I hoped I had hit him quickly and smoothly enough, before he had had time to adjust to the situation. Even for a hard operator like Kramer, it took mental preparation to openly defy his commander, particularly in casual conversation. But possession of the weapon was more than casual. . . .

I looked at him, smiling, my hand held out. He wasn't ready; he pulled the pistol from its case, handed it to over me.

I flipped the chamber open, glanced at the charge indicator, checked the action. "Nice weapon," I said. I laid it on the open bar at my right.

Joyce opened his mouth to speak. I cut in in the same firm, snappy tone I use on the Bridge. "Let me see yours, Lieutenant."

He flushed, looked at Kramer, then passed the pistol over without a word. I took it, turned it over thoughtfully, and then rose, holding it negligently by the grip.

"Now, if you gentlemen don't mind, I have a few things to attend to." I wasn't smiling. I looked at Kramer with expressionless eyes. "I think we'd better keep our little chat confidential for the present," I told him. "I think I can promise you action in the near future, though."

They filed out, looking as foolish as three preachers caught in a raid on a brothel. I stood without moving until the door closed. Then I let my breath out. I sat down and finished off the scotch in one drag.

"You were lucky, boy," I said aloud. "Three gutless wonders."

I looked at the Mark 9's on the table. A blast from one of those would have burned all four of us in that enclosed room. I dumped them into a drawer and loaded my Browning 2mm. The trouble wasn't over yet, I knew. After this farce, Kramer would have to make another move to regain his prestige. I unlocked the door, and left it slightly ajar. Then I threw the night switch and stretched out on my bunk. I put the Browning needler on the little shelf near my right hand.

Perhaps I had made a mistake, I reflected, in eliminating formal discipline as far as possible in the ship-

board routine. It had seemed the best course for a
long cruise under the present conditions. But now I
had a morale situation that could explode in mutiny
at the first blunder on my part.

I knew that Kramer was the focal point of the
trouble. He was my senior staff officer, and carried
a great deal of weight in the Officer's Mess. As a
medic, he knew most of the crew better than I. I
thought I knew Kramer's driving motive, too. He
had always been a great success with the women.
When he had volunteered for the mission he had
doubtless pictured himself as quite a romantic hero,
off on a noble but hopeless quest. Now, after four
years in deep space, he was beginning to realize that
he was getting no younger, and that at best he would
have spent a decade of his prime in monastic seclu-
sion. He wanted to go back now, and salvage what
he could.

It was incredible to me that this movement could
have gathered followers, but I had to face the fact;
my crew almost to a man had given up the search
before it was well begun. I had heard the first
rumors only a few weeks before, but the idea had
spread through the crew like fire through dry grass.
Now, I couldn't afford drastic action, or risk forcing
a blowup by arresting ringleaders. I had to baby the
situation along with an easy hand and hope for good
news from the Survey Section. A likely find now
would save us.

There was still every reason to hope for success in
our search. To date all had gone according to plan.
We had followed the route of Omega as far as it had
been charted, and then gone on, studying the stars
ahead for evidence of planets. We had made our first
finds early in the fourth year of the voyage. It had
been a long, tedious time since then of study and
observation, eliminating one world after another as
too massive, too cold, too close to a blazing primary,

too small to hold an atmosphere. In all we had discovered twelve planets, of four suns. Only one had looked good enough for close observation. We had moved in to televideo range before realizing it was an all-sea world.

Now we had five new main-sequence suns ahead within six months range. I hoped for a confirmation on a planet at any time. To turn back now to a world that had pinned its last hopes on our success was unthinkable, yet this was Kramer's plan, and that of his followers. They would not prevail while I lived. Still it was not my intention to be a party to our failure through martyrdom. I intended to stay alive and carry through to success. I dozed lightly and waited.

I awoke when they tried the door. It had swung open a few inches at the touch of the one who had tried it, not expecting it to be unlatched. It stood ajar now, the pale light from the hall shining on the floor. No one entered. Kramer was still fumbling, unsure of himself. At every surprise with which I presented him, he was paralyzed, expecting a trap. Several minutes passed in tense silence; then the door swung wider.

"I'll be forced to kill the first man who enters this cabin," I said in a steady voice. I hadn't picked up the gun.

I heard urgent whispers in the hall. Then a hand reached in behind the shelter of the door and flipped the light switch. Nothing happened, since I had opened the main switch. It was only a small discomfiture, but it had the effect of interfering with their plan of action, such as it was. These men were being pushed along by Kramer, without a clearly thought out plan. They hardly knew how to go about defying lawful authority.

I called out, "I suggest you call this nonsense off now, and go back to your quarters, men. I don't know who is involved in this, yet. You can get away clean if you leave quietly, now, before you've made a serious mistake."

I hoped it would work. This little adventure, abortive though it was, might serve to let off steam. The men would have something to talk about for a few precious days. I picked up the needler and waited. If the bluff failed, I would have to kill someone.

Distantly I heard a metallic clatter. Moments later a tremor rattled the objects on the shelf, followed a few seconds later by a heavy shuddering. Papers slid from my desk, fluttered across the floor. The whisky bottle toppled, rolled to the far wall. I felt the bunk tilt under me. I reached for the intercom key and flipped it.

"Taylor," I said, "this is the Captain. What's the report?"

There was a momentary delay before the answer came. "Captain, we've taken a meteor strike aft, apparently a metallic body. It must have hit us a tremendous wallop because it's set up a rotation. I've called out Damage Control."

"Good work, Taylor," I said. I keyed for Stores; the object must have hit about there. "This is the Captain," I said. "Any damage there?"

I got a hum of background noise, then a too-close transmission. "Uh, Cap'n, we got a hole in the aft bulkhead here. I slapped a seal pad over it. Man, that coulda killed somebody."

I flipped off the intercom and started aft at a run. My visitors had evaporated. In the passage men stood, milled, called questions. I keyed my talker as I ran. "Taylor, order all hands to emergency stations."

It was difficult running, since the deck had assumed an apparent tilt. Loose gear was rolling and sliding along underfoot, propelled forward by centrifugal force. Aft of Stores, I heard the whistle of escaping air and high-pressure gasses from ruptured lines. Vapor clouds fogged the air. I called for floodlights for the whole sector.

Clay appeared out of the fog with his damage control crew. "Sir," he said, "it's punctured inner and outer shells in two places, and fragments have riddled the whole sector. There are at least three men dead, and two hurt."

"Taylor," I called, "let's have another damage control crew back here on the triple. Get the medics back here, too." Clay and his men put on masks and moved off. I borrowed one from a man standing by and followed. The large exit puncture was in the forward cargo lock. The chamber was sealed off, limiting the air loss.

"Clay," I said, "pass this up for the moment and get that entry puncture sealed. I'll put the extra crew in suits to handle this."

I moved back into the clear air and called for reports from all sections. The worst of the damage was in the auxiliary power control room, where communication and power lines were slashed and the panel cut up. The danger of serious damage to essential equipment had been very close, but we had been lucky. This was the first instance I had heard of of encountering an object at hyper-light speed.

It was astonishing how this threat to our safety cleared the air. The men went about their duties more cheerfully than they had for months, and Kramer was conspicuous by his subdued air. The emergency had reestablished at least for the time the normal discipline; the men still relied on the captain in trouble.

Damage control crews worked steadily for the next seventy-two hours, replacing wiring, welding, and testing. Power Section jockeyed endlessly, correcting air circulation. Meanwhile, I checked hourly with Survey Section, hoping for good news to consolidate the improved morale situation.

It was on Sunday morning, just after dawn relief, that Lieutenant Taylor came up to the Bridge looking sick.

"Sir," he said, "we took more damage than we knew." He stopped and swallowed hard.

"What have you got, Lieutenant?" I said.

"We missed a piece. It must have gone off on a tangent through Stores into the cooler. Clipped the coolant line, and let warm air in. All the fresh frozen stuff is contaminated and rotten." He gagged. "I got a whiff of it, sir. Excuse me." He rushed away.

This was calamity.

We didn't carry much in the way of fresh natural food; but what we had was vital. It was a bulky, delicate cargo to handle, but the chemists hadn't yet come up with synthetics to fill all the dietary needs of man. We could get by fine for a long time on vitamin tablets and concentrates; but there were nutritional elements that you couldn't get that way. Hydroponics didn't help; we had to have a few ounces of fresh meat and vegetables grown in Sollight every week, or start to die within months.

2

I knew that Kramer wouldn't let this chance pass. As Medical Officer he would be well within his rights in calling to my attention the fact that our health would soon begin to suffer. I felt sure he would do so as loudly and publicly as possible at the first opportunity.

My best move was to beat him to the punch by making a general announcement, giving the facts in the best possible light. That might take some of the sting out of anything Kramer said later.

I gave it to them, short and to the point. "Men, we've just suffered a serious loss. All the fresh frozen stores are gone. That doesn't mean we'll be going on short rations; there are plenty of concentrates and vitamins aboard. But it does mean we're going to be suffering from deficiencies in our diet.

"We didn't come out here on a pleasure cruise; we're on a mission that leaves no room for failure. This is just one more fact for us to face. Now let's get on with the job."

I walked into the wardroom, drew a cup of near-coffee, and sat down. The screen showed a Jamaica beach with booming surf. The sound track picked up the crash and hiss of the breakers, and off-screen a gull screamed. Considering the red plague that now covered the Caribbean, I thought it was a poor choice. I dialed a high view of rolling farmland.

Mannion sat at a table across the room with Kirschenbaum. They were hunched over their cups, not talking. I wondered where they stood. Mannion, Communications Officer, was neurotic, but an old Armed Forces man. Discipline meant a lot to him. Kirschenbaum, Power Chief, was a joker, with cold eyes, and smarter than he seemed. The question was whether he was smart enough to realize the stupidity of retreat now.

Kramer walked in, not wasting any time. He stopped a few feet from my table, and said loudly, "Captain, I'd like to know your plans, now that the possibility of continuing is out."

I sipped my near-coffee and looked at the rolling farmland. I didn't answer him. If I could get him mad, I could take him at this game.

Kramer turned red. He didn't like being ignored. The two at the other table were watching.

"Captain," Kramer said loudly. "As Medical Officer I have to know what measures you're taking to protect the health of the men."

This was a little better. He was on the defensive now; explaining why he had a right to question his commander. I wanted him a little hotter, though.

I looked up at him. "Kramer," I said in a clear, not too loud voice, "you're on watch. I don't want to find you hanging around the wardroom making light chitchat until you're properly relieved from duty." I went back to my near-coffee and the farmland. A river was in view now, and beyond it distant mountains.

Kramer tried to control his fury. "Joyce has relieved me, Captain," he snarled, then sweetened his tone. "I felt I'd better take this matter up with you as soon as possible, since it affects the health of every man aboard." He was trying to keep cool, in command of himself.

"I haven't authorized any changes in the duty roster, Major," I said mildly. "Report to your post." I was riding the habit of discipline now, as far as it would carry me. I hoped that disobedience of a direct order, solidly based on regulations, was a little too big a jump for Kramer at the moment. Tomorrow it might be different. But it was essential that I break up the scene he was staging.

He wilted.

"I'll see you at seventeen hundred in the chart room, Kramer," I said as he turned away. Mannion and Kirschenbaum looked at each other, then finished their near-coffee hurriedly and left. I hoped their version of the incident would help deflate Kramer's standing among the malcontents.

I left the wardroom and took the lift up to the Bridge and checked with Clay and his survey team.

"I think I've spotted a slight perturbation in Delta 3, Captain," Clay said. "I'm not sure; we're still pretty far out."

"All right, Clay," I said. "Stay with it."

Clay was one of my more dependable men, dedicated to his work. Unfortunately, he was no man of action. He would have little influence in a showdown.

I was at the Schmidt when I heard the lift open. I turned; Kramer, Fine, Taylor, and a half dozen enlisted crew chiefs crowded out, bunched together. They were all wearing needlers. At least they'd learned that much, I thought.

Kramer moved forward. "We feel that the question of the men's welfare has to be dealt with right away, Captain," he said smoothly.

I looked at him coldly, glanced at the rest of his crew. I said nothing.

"What we're faced with is pretty grim, even if we turn back now," Kramer said. "I can't be responsible for the results if there's any delay." He spoke in an arrogant tone. I looked them over, let the silence build.

"You're in charge of this menagerie?" I said, looking at Kramer. "If so, you've got thirty seconds to send them back to their kennels. We'll go into the matter of unauthorized personnel on the Bridge later. As for you, Major, you can consider yourself under arrest in quarters. Now MOVE."

Kramer was ready to stare me down, but Fine gave me a break by tugging at his sleeve. Kramer shook him loose, snarling. At that the crew chiefs faded back into the lift. Fine and Taylor hesitated, then joined them. Kramer started to shout after them, then got hold of himself. The lift moved down. That left Kramer alone.

He thought about going for his needler. I looked at him through narrowed eyes. He decided to rely on his mouth, as usual. He licked his lips. "All right, I'm under arrest," he said. "But as Medical Officer of this vessel it's my duty to remind you that we can't live without a certain minimum of fresh organic food. We've got to start back now." He was pale, but determined. He couldn't bear the thought of getting bald and toothless from dietary deficiency; the girls would never give him another look.

"We're going on, Kramer," I said. "As long as we have a man aboard still able to move. Teeth or no teeth."

"Deficiency disease is no joke, Captain," Kramer said. "You can get all the symptoms of leprosy, cancer and syphilis just by skipping a few necessary elements in your diet. And we're missing most of them."

"Giving me your opinions is one thing, Kramer," I said. "Mutiny is another."

Clay stood beside the main screen, wide-eyed. I couldn't send Kramer down under his guard. "Let's go, Kramer," I said. "I'm locking you up myself."

We rode down in the lift. The men who had been with Kramer stood awkwardly, silent as we stepped out into the passage. I spotted two chronic troublemakers among them. I thought I might as well call them now as later. "Williams and Nagle," I said, "this officer is under arrest. Escort him to his quarters and lock him in." As they stepped forward hesitantly, Kramer said, "Keep your filthy hooks off me." He started down the passage ahead of them.

If I could get Kramer put away before anybody else started trouble, I might be able to bluff it through. I followed him and his two sheepish guards down past the power section, and the mess. I hoped there would be a crowd there to see their hero Kramer under guard.

I got my wish. Apparently word had gone out of Kramer's arrest, and the corridor was clogged with men. They stood unmoving as we approached. Kramer stopped.

"Clear this passage, you men," I said.

Slowly they began to move back, giving ground reluctantly.

Suddenly Kramer shouted. "That's right, you whiners and complainers, clear the way so the captain can take me back to the missile deck and shoot me. You just want to talk about home; you haven't got the guts to do anything about it."

The moving mass halted, milled. Someone shouted, "Who's he think he is, anyway?"

Kramer whirled toward me. "He thinks he's the man who's going to let you all rot alive, to save his record."

"Williams, Nagle," I said loudly, "clear this passage."

Williams started half-heartedly to shove at the men nearest him. A fist flashed out and snapped his head back. That was a mistake; Williams pulled his needler, and fired a ricochet down the passage.

" 'Bout twelve a' you yellow-bellies git outa my way," he yelled. "I'm comin' through."

Nagle moved close to Williams, and shouted something to him. The noise drowned it. Kramer swung back to me, frantic to regain his sway over the mob.

"Once I'm out of the way, there'll be a general purge," he yelled. The hubbub faded, as men turned to hear him.

"You're all marked men," he raved on. "He's gone mad. He won't let one of you live." Kramer had their eyes now. "Take him now," he shouted, and seized my arm.

He'd rushed it a little. I hit him across the face with the back of my hand. No one jumped to his assistance. I drew my 2mm. "If you ever lay a hand on your commanding officer again, I'll burn you where you stand, Kramer."

Then a voice came from behind me. "You're not killing anybody without a trial, Captain." Joyce stood there with two of the crew chiefs, needler in hand. Fine and Taylor were not in sight.

I pushed Kramer out of my way and walked up to Joyce.

"Hand me that weapon, Junior, butt first," I said. I looked him in the eye with all the glare I had. He stepped back a pace.

"Why don't you jump him?" he called to the crowd.

A squawk-box hummed and spoke.

"Captain Greylorn, please report to the Bridge. Unidentified body on main scope."

Every man stopped in his tracks, listening. The talker continued. "Looks like it's decelerating, Captain."

I holstered my pistol, pushed past Joyce, and trotted for the lift. The mob behind me broke up, talking, as men under long habit ran for action stations.

Clay was operating calmly under pressure. He sat at the main screen and studied the blip, making tiny crayon marks.

"She's too far out for a reliable scanner track, Captain," he said, "but I'm pretty sure she's braking."

If that were true, this might be the break we'd been living for. Only manned or controlled bodies decelerate in deep space.

"How did you spot it, Clay?" I asked. Picking up a tiny mass like this was a delicate job, even when you knew its coordinates.

"Just happened to catch my eye, Captain," he said. "I always make a general check every watch of the whole forward quadrant. I noticed a blip where I didn't remember seeing one before."

"You have quite an eye, Clay," I said. "How about getting this object in the beam."

"We're trying now, Captain," he said. "That's a mighty small field, though."

Ryan called from the radar board, "I think I'm getting an echo at 15,000, sir. It's pretty weak."

Miller, quiet and meticulous, delicately tuned the

"That's it, Mannion," I said. "Can you make anything of it?"

"No, sir," he answered. "I'm taping it, so I can go to work on it."

Mannion was our language and code man. I hoped he was good.

"What does it sound like?" I asked. "Tune me in."

After a moment a high hum came from the speaker. Through it I could hear harsh chopping consonants, a whining intonation. I doubted that Mannion would be able to make anything of that garbage.

Our bogie closed steadily. At four hundred twenty-five miles he reversed relative directions, and began matching our speed, moving closer to our course. There was no doubt he planned to parallel us.

I made a brief announcement to all hands describing the status of the action. Clay worked over his televideo, trying to clear the image. I watched as the blob on the screen swelled and flickered. Suddenly it flashed into clear, stark definition. Against a background of sparkling black, the twin spheres gleamed faintly in reflected starlight.

There were no visible surface features; the iodine-colored forms and their connecting shaft had an ancient and alien look.

We held our course steadily, watching the stranger maneuver. Even at this distance it looked huge.

"Captain," Clay said, "I've been making a few rough calculations. The two spheres are about eight hundred yards in diameter, and at the rate the structure is rotating, it's pulling about six gravities."

That settled the question of human origin of the ship. No human crew would choose to work under six gees.

Now, paralleling us at just over two hundred miles, the giant ship spun along, at rest relative to us. It was visible now through the direct observation panel, without magnification.

I left Clay in charge on the Bridge, and I went down to the Com Section.

Joyce sat at his board, reading instruments and keying controls. So he was back on the job. Mannion sat, head bent, monitoring his recorder. The room was filled with the keening staccato of the alien transmission.

"Getting anything on video?" I asked. Joyce shook his head. "Nothing, Captain. I've checked the whole spectrum, and this is all I get. It's coming in on about a dozen different frequencies; no FM."

"Any progress, Mannion?" I said.

He took off his headset. "It's the same thing, repeated over and over, just a short phrase. I'd have better luck if they'd vary it a little."

"Try sending," I said.

Joyce tuned the clatter down to a faint clicking, and switched his transmitter on. "You're on, Captain," he said.

"This is Captain Greylorn, ACV/*Galahad*; kindly identify yourself." I repeated this slowly, half a dozen times. It occurred to me that this was the first known time in history a human being had addressed a nonhuman intelligence. The last was a guess, but I couldn't interpret our guest's purposeful maneuverings as other than intelligent.

I checked with the Bridge; no change. Suddenly the clatter stopped, leaving only the carrier hum.

"Can't you tune that whine out, Joyce?" I asked.

"No, sir," he replied. "That's a very noisy transmission. Sounds like maybe their equipment is on the blink."

We listened to the hum, waiting. Then the clatter began again.

"This is different," Mannion said. "It's longer."

I went back to the Bridge and waited for the next

move from the stranger, or for word from Mannion. Every half hour I transmitted a call identifying us, in Standard, of course. I didn't know why, but somehow I had a faint hope they might understand some of it.

I stayed on the Bridge when the watch changed. I had some food sent up, and slept a few hours on the OD's bunk.

Fine replaced Kramer on his watch when it rolled around. Apparently Kramer was out of circulation. At this point I did not feel inclined to pursue the point.

We had been at General Quarters for twenty-one hours when the squawk box hummed.

"Captain, this is Mannion. I've busted it . . ."

"I'll be right there," I said, and left at a run.

Mannion was writing as I entered Com Section. He stopped his recorder and offered me a sheet. "This is what I've got so far, Captain," he said.

I read: INVADER; THE MANCJI PRESENCE OPENS COMMUNICATION.

"That's a highly distorted version of early Standard, Captain," Mannion said. "After I taped it, I compensated it to take out the rise-and-fall tone, and then filtered out the static. There were a few sound substitutions to figure out, but I finally caught on. It still doesn't make much sense, but that's what it says. I don't know what 'Mancji' means, but that's what it's saying."

"I wonder what we're invading," I said. "And what is the 'Mancji Presence'?"

"They just repeat that over and over," Mannion said. "They don't answer our call."

"Try translating into old Standard, adding their sound changes, and then feeding their own rise-and-fall routine to it," I said. "Maybe that will get a response."

I waited while Mannion worked out the message,

then taped it on top of their whining tone pattern. "Put plenty of horsepower behind it," I said. "If their receivers are as shaky as their transmitter, they might not be hearing us."

We sent for five minutes, then tuned them back in and waited. There was a long silence from their side; then they came back with a long spluttering sing-song.

Mannion worked over it for several minutes. "Here's what I get," he said:

THAT WHICH SWIMS IN THE MANCJI SEA; WE ARE AWARE THAT YOU HAVE THIS TRADE TONGUE. YOU RANGE FAR. IT IS OUR WHIM TO INDULGE YOU; WE ARE AMUSED THAT YOU PRESUME HERE; WE ACKNOWLEDGE YOUR INSOLENT DEMANDS.

"It looks like we're in somebody's back yard," I said. "They acknowledge our insolent demands, but they don't answer them." I thought a moment. "Send this," I said. "We'll out-strut them."

"The mighty warship *Galahad* rejects your jurisdiction. Tell us the nature of your distress and we may choose to offer aid."

Mannion raised an eyebrow. "That ought to rock them," he said.

"They were eager to talk to us," I said. "That means they want something, in my opinion. And all the big talk sounds like a bluff of our own is our best line."

"Why do you want to antagonize them, Captain?" Joyce asked. "That ship is over a thousand times the size of this one."

"Joyce, I suggest you let me forget you're around," I said.

The Mancji whine was added to my message, and it went out. Moments later this came back:

MANCJI HONOR DICTATES YOUR SAFE CONDUCT;
TALK IS WEARYING; WE FIND IT CONVENIENT TO
SOLICIT A TRANSFER OF ELECTROSTATIC FORCE.

"What the devil does that mean?" I said. "Tell
them to loosen up and explain themselves."

Mannion wrote out a straight query, and sent it.
Again we waited for a reply.

It came, in a long windy paragraph stating that
the Mancji found electrostatic baths amusing, and
that "crystalization" had drained their tanks. They
wanted a flow of electrons from us to replenish their
supply.

"This sounds like simple electric current they're
talking about, Captain," Mannion said. "They want
a battery charge."

"They seem to have power to burn," I said. "Why
don't they generate their own juice? Ask them; and
find out where they learned Standard."

Mannion sent again; the reply was slow in coming
back. Finally we got it:

THE MANCJI DO NOT EMPLOY MASSIVE GENERA-
TION-PIECE WHERE ACCUMULATOR-PIECE IS
SUFFICIENT. THIS SIMPLE TRADE SPEECH IS OF
OLD KNOWLEDGE. WE SELECT IT FROM SYM-
BOLS WE ARE PLEASED TO SENSE EMPAT-
TERNED ON YOUR HULL.

That made some sort of sense, but I was intrigued
by the reference to Standard as a trade language. I
wanted to know where they had learned it. I couldn't
help the hope I started building on the idea that this
giant knew our colony; the fact that they were using
an antique version of the language, out of use for
several centuries might mean they'd gotten it from
Omega.

I sent another query, but the reply was abrupt

and told nothing except that Standard was of "old knowledge."

Then Mannion entered a long technical exchange, getting the details of the kind of electric energy they wanted.

"We can give them what they want, no sweat, Captain," he said after half an hour's talk. "They want DC; 100 volt, 50 amp will do."

"Ask them to describe themselves," I directed. I was beginning to get an idea.

Mannion sent, got his reply. "They're molluscoid, Captain," he said. He looked shocked. "They weigh about two tons each."

"Ask them what they eat," I said.

I turned to Joyce as Mannion worked over the message. "Get Kramer up here, on the double," I ordered.

Kramer came in five minutes later, looking drawn and rumpled. He stared at me sullenly.

"I'm releasing you from arrest temporarily on your own recognizance, Major," I said. "I want you to study the reply to our last transmission, and tell me what you can about it."

"Why me?" Kramer said. "I don't know what's going on." I didn't answer him.

There was a long, tense, half-hour wait before Mannion copied out the reply that came in a stuttering nasal. He handed it to me.

The message was a recital of the indifference of the Mancji to biological processes of ingestion.

I told Kramer to write out a list of our dietary needs. I passed it to Mannion. "Ask them if they have fresh sources of these substances aboard."

The reply was quick; they did.

"Tell them we will exchange electric power for a supply of these foods. Tell them we want samples of half a dozen of the natural substances."

Again Mannion coded and sent, received and translated, sent again.

"They agree, Captain," he said at last. "They want us to fire a power lead out about a mile; they'll come in close and shoot us a specimen case with a flare on it. Then we can each check the other's merchandise."

"All right," I said. "We can use a ground-service cable; rig a pilot light on it, and kick it out, as soon as they get in close."

"We'll have to splice a couple of extra lengths to it," Mannion said.

"Go to it, Mannion," I said. "And send two of your men out to make the pick-up." This wasn't a communications job, but I wanted a reliable man handling it.

I returned to the Bridge and keyed for Bourdon, directed him to arm two of his penetration missiles, lock them onto the stranger, and switch over to my control. With the firing key in my hand, I stood at the side-scan screen and watched for any signs of treachery. The ship moved in, came to rest filling the screen.

Mannion's men reported out. I saw the red dot of our power lead move away, then a yellow point glowed on the side of the vast iodine-colored wall looming across the screen.

Nothing else emerged from the alien ship. The red pilot light drifted across the face of the sphere. Mannion reported six thousand feet of cable out before the light disappeared abruptly.

"Captain," Mannion reported, "they're drawing power."

"OK," I said. "Let them have a sample, then shut down."

I waited, watching carefully, until Mannion reported their cannister inside.

"Kramer," I said. "Run me a fast check on the samples in that container."

Kramer was recovering his swagger. "You'll have to be a little more specific," he said. "Just what kind of analysis do you have in mind? Do you want a full . . ."

"I just want to know one thing, Kramer," I said. "Can we assimilate these substances, yes or no? If you don't feel like cooperating, I'll have you lashed to your bunk, and injected with them. You claim you're a Medical Officer; let's see you act like one." I turned my back to him.

Mannion called. "They say the juice we fed them was 'amusing,' Captain. I guess that means it's OK."

"I'll let you know in a few minutes how their samples pan out," I said.

Kramer took half an hour before reporting back. "I ran a simple check such as I normally use in a routine mess inspection," he began. He couldn't help trying to take the center of the stage to go into his Wise Doctor and Helpless Patient routine.

"Yes or no," I said.

"Yes, we can assimilate most of it," he said angrily. "There were six samples. Two were gelatinous substances, non-nutritive. Three were vegetablelike, bulky and fibrous, one with a high iodine content; the other was a very normal meaty specimen."

"Which should we take?" I said. "Remember your teeth when you answer."

"The high protein, the meaty one," he said. "Marked 'Six'."

I keyed for Mannion. "Tell them that in return for one thousand KWH we require three thousand kilos of sample six," I said.

Mannion reported back. "They agreed in a hurry, Captain. They seem to feel pretty good about the deal. They want to chat, now that they've got a bargain. I'm still taping a long tirade."

"Good," I said. "Better get ready to send about six men with an auxiliary pusher to bring home the bacon. You can start feeding them the juice again."

I turned to Kramer. He was staring at the screen. "Report yourself back to arrest in quarters, Kramer," I said. "I'll take your services today into account at your court-martial."

Kramer looked up, with a nasty grin. "I don't know what kind of talking oysters you're trafficking with, but I'd laugh like hell if they vaporized your precious tub as soon as they're through with you." He walked out.

Mannion called in again from communications. "Here's their last, Captain," he said. "They say we're lucky they had a good supply of this protein aboard. It's one of their most amusing foods. It's a creature they discovered in the wild state and it's very rare. The wild ones have died out, and only their domesticated herds exist."

"OK, we're lucky," I said. "It better be good or we'll step up the amperage and burn their batteries for them."

"Here's more," Mannion said. "They say it will take a few hours to prepare the cargo. They want us to be amused."

I didn't like the delay, but it would take us about ten hours to deliver the juice to them at the trickle rate they wanted. Since the sample was OK, I was assuming the rest would be too. We settled down to wait.

I left Clay in charge on the Bridge and made a tour of the ship. The meeting with the alien had apparently driven the mood of mutiny into the background. The men were quiet and busy. I went to my cabin and slept for a few hours.

I was awakened by a call from Clay telling me that the alien had released his cargo for us. Mannion's crew was out making the pick-up. Before they had maneuvered the bulky cylinder to the cargo hatch, the alien released our power lead.

I called Kramer and told him to meet the incoming crew and open and inspect the cargo. If it was the same as the sample, I thought, we had made a terrific trade. Discipline would recover if the men felt we still had our luck.

Then Mannion called again. "Captain," he said excitedly, "I think there may be trouble coming. Will you come down, sir?"

"I'll go to the Bridge, Mannion," I said. "Keep talking."

I tuned my talker down low and listened to Mannion as I ran for the lift.

"They're transmitting again, Captain," he told me. "They tell us to watch for a display of Mancji power. They ran out some kind of antenna. I'm getting a loud static at the top of my short wave receptivity."

I ran the lift up and as I stepped onto the Bridge I said, "Clay, stand by to fire."

As soon as the pick-up crew was reported in, I keyed the course corrections to curve us off sharply from the alien. I didn't know what he had, but I liked the idea of putting space between us. My P-Missiles were still armed and locked.

Mannion called, "Captain, they say our fright is amusing, and quite justified."

I watched the starboard screens for the first sign of an attack. Suddenly the entire screen array went white, then blanked. Miller, who had been at the scanner searching over the alien ship at close range, reeled out of his seat, clutching at his eyes. "My God, I'm blinded," he shouted.

Mannion called, "Captain, my receivers blew. I think every tube in the shack exploded!"

I jumped to the direct viewer. The alien hung there, turning away from us in a leisurely curve. There was no sign of whatever had blown us off the air. I held my key, but didn't press it. I told Clay to take Miller down to sick bay. He was moaning and in severe pain.

Kramer reported in from the cargo deck. The cannister was inside now, coating up with frost. I told him to wait, then sent Chilcote, my demolition man, in to open it. Maybe it was booby-trapped. I stood by at the DVP and waited for other signs of Mancji power to hit us.

Apparently they were satisfied with one blast of whatever it was; they were dwindling away with no further signs of life.

After half an hour of tense alertness, I ordered the missiles disarmed.

I keyed for General. "Men, this is the captain," I said. "It looks as though our first contact with an alien race has been successfully completed. He is now at a distance of three hundred and moving off fast. Our screens are blown, but there's no real damage. And we have a supply of fresh food aboard; now let's get back to business. That colony can't be far off."

That may have been rushing it some, but if the food supply we'd gotten was a dud, we were finished anyway.

We watched the direct-view screen till the ship was lost, then followed on radar.

"It's moving right along, Captain," Ryan said, "accelerating at about two gees."

"Good riddance," Clay said. "I don't like dealing with armed maniacs."

"They were screwballs, all right," I said, "but they couldn't have happened along at a better time. I only wish we had been in a position to squeeze a few answers out of them."

"Yes, sir," Clay said. "Now that the whole thing's over, I'm beginning to think of a lot of questions myself."

The talker hummed. I heard what sounded like hoarse breathing. I glanced at the indicator light. It was cargo deck.

I keyed. "If you have a report, Chilcote, go ahead," I said.

Suddenly someone was shouting into the talker, incoherently. I caught words, cursing. Then Chilcote's voice. "Captain," he said. "Captain, please come quick." There was a loud clatter, more noise, then only the hum of the talker.

"Take over, Clay," I said, and started back to the cargo deck at a dead run.

Men crowded the corridor, asking questions. I forced my way through, found Kramer surrounded by men, shouting.

"Break this up," I shouted. "Kramer, what's your report?"

Chilcote walked past me, pale as chalk.

"Get hold of yourself, and make your report, Kramer," I said. "What started this riot?"

Kramer stopped shouting, and stood looking at me, panting. The crowded men fell silent.

"I gave you a job to do, Major," I said, "opening a cargo can. Now you take it from there."

"Yeah, Captain," he said. "We got it open. No wires, no traps. We hauled the load out of the can onto the floor. It was one big frozen mass, wrapped up in some kind of netting. Then we pulled the covering off."

"All right, go ahead," I said.

"That load of fresh meat your star-born pals gave us consists of about six families of human beings; men, women, and children." Kramer was talking for the crowd now, shouting. "Those last should be pretty tender when you ration out our ounce a week, Captain."

The men were yelling, wide-eyed, open-mouthed, as I thrust through to the cargo lock. The door stood ajar and wisps of white vapor curled out into the passage.

I stepped through the door. It was bitter cold in the lock. Near the outer hatch the bulky cannister, rimed with white frost, lay in a pool of melting ice. Before it lay the half-shrouded bulk that it had contained. I walked closer.

They were frozen together into one solid mass. Kramer was right. They were as human as I. Human corpses, stripped, packed together, frozen. I pulled back the lightly frosted covering and studied the glazed white bodies.

Kramer called suddenly from the door. "You found your colonists, Captain. Now that your curiosity is satisfied, we can go back where we belong. Out here man is a variety of cattle. We're lucky they didn't know we were the same variety, or we'd be in their food lockers now ourselves. Now let's get started back. The men won't take no for an answer."

I leaned closer, studying the corpses. "Come here, Kramer," I called. "I want to show you something."

"I've seen all there is to see in there," Kramer said. "We don't want to waste time; we want to change course now, right now."

I walked back to the door, and as Kramer stepped back, to let me precede him out the door, I hit him in the mouth with all my strength. His head snapped back against the frosted wall. Then he fell out into the passage.

I stepped over him. "Pick this up and put it in the brig," I ordered. The men in the corridor fell back, muttering. As they hauled Kramer upright I stepped through them and kept going, not running but wasting no time, toward the Bridge. One wrong move on my part now and all their misery and fear would break loose in a riot, the first act of which would be to tear me limb from limb.

I travelled ahead of the shock. Kramer had provided the diversion I had needed. Now I heard the sound of gathering violence growing behind me.

I was none too quick. A needler flashed at the end of the corridor just as the lift door closed. I heard the tiny projectiles ricochet off the lift shaft.

I rode up, stepped onto the Bridge and locked the lift. I keyed for Bourdon, and to my relief got a quick response. The panic hadn't penetrated to Missile Section yet.

"Bourdon, arm all batteries and lock onto that Mancji ship," I ordered. "On the triple."

I turned to Clay. "I'll take over, Clay," I said. "Alter course to intercept our late companion at two and one-half gees."

Clay looked startled, but said only, "Aye, sir."

I keyed for a general announcement. "This is the captain," I said. "Action station, all hands in loose acceleration harness. We're going after Big Brother. You're in action against the enemy now, and from this point on I'm remembering. You men have been having a big time letting off steam; that's over now. All sections report."

One by one the sections reported in, all but Med and Admin. Well, I could spare them for the present. The pressure was building now, as we blasted around in a hairpin curve, our acceleration picking up fast.

I ordered Ryan to lock his radar on target, and switch over to autopilot control. Then I called Power Section.

"I'm taking over all power control from the Bridge," I said. "All personnel out of the power chamber and control chamber."

The men were still under control, but that might not last long. I had to have the ship's power, control, and armament entirely under my personal disposition for a few hours at least.

Missile Section reported all missiles armed and locked on target. I acknowledged and ordered the section evacuated. Then I turned to Clay and Ryan. Both were plenty nervous now; they didn't know what was brewing.

"Lieutenant Clay," I said, "report to your quarters; Ryan, you, too. I congratulate both of you on a soldierly performance these last few hours."

They left without comment. I was aware that they didn't want to be too closely identified with the captain when things broke loose.

I keyed for a video check of the interior of the lift as it started back up. It was empty. I locked it up.

Now we were steady on course, and had reached our full two and a half gees. I could hardly stand under that acceleration, but I had one more job to do before I could take a break.

Dragging my feet, I unlocked the lift and rode it down. I was braced for violence as the door opened, but I was lucky. There was no one in the corridor. I could hear shouts in the distance. I dragged myself along to Power Section and pushed inside. A quick check of control settings showed everything as I had ordered it. Back in the passage, I slammed the leaded vault door to and threw in the combination lock. Now only I could open it without blasting.

Control Section was next. It, too, was empty, all in order. I locked it, and started across to Missiles. Two men appeared at the end of the passage, having as hard a time as I was. I entered the cross corridor just in time to escape a volley of needler shots. The mutiny was in the open now, for sure.

I kept going, hearing more shouting. I was sure the men I had seen were heading for Power and Control. They'd get a surprise. I hoped I could beat them to the draw at Missiles, too.

As I came out in B Corridor, twenty feet from Missiles, I saw that I had cut it a bit fine. Three men, crawling, were frantically striving against the high-gee field to reach the door before me. Their faces were running with sweat, purple with exertion.

I had a slight lead; it was too late to make a check inside before locking up. The best I could hope for was to lock the door before they reached it.

I drew my Browning and started for the door. They saw me, and one reached for his needler.

"Don't try it," I called. I concentrated on the door, reached it, swung it closed, and as I threw in the lock a needler cracked. I whirled and fired. The man in the rear had stopped and aimed as the other two came on. He folded. The other two kept coming.

I was tired. I wanted a rest. "You're too late," I said. "No one but the captain goes in there now." I stopped talking, panting. I had to rest. The two came on. I wondered why they struggled so desperately after they were beaten. My thinking was slowing down.

I suddenly realized they might be holding me for the crowd to arrive. I shuffled backwards toward the cross corridor. I barely made it. Two men on a shuttle cart whirled around the corner a hundred feet aft. I lurched into my shelter in a hail of needler fire. One of the tiny slugs stung through my calf and ricocheted down the passage.

I called to the two I had raced, "Tell your boys if they ever want to open that door, just see the captain."

I hesitated, considering whether or not to make a general statement.

"What the hell," I decided. "They all know there's a mutiny now. It won't hurt to get in a little life insurance."

I keyed my talker. "This is the captain," I said. "This ship is now in a state of mutiny. I call on all loyal members of the Armed Forces to resist the mutineers actively, and to support their commander.

Your ship is in action against an armed enemy. I assure you this mutiny will fail, and those who took part in it will be treated as traitors to their Service, their homes, and their own families who now rely on them.

"We are accelerating at two and one-half gravities, locked on a collision course with the Mancji ship. The mutineers cannot enter the Bridge, Power, Control, or Missiles Sections since only I have the combination. Thus they're doomed to failure.

"I am now returning to the Bridge to direct the attack and destruction of the enemy. If I fail to reach the Bridge, we will collide with the enemy in less than three hours, and our batteries will blow."

Now my problem was to make good my remark about returning to the Bridge. The shuttle had not followed me, presumably fearing ambush. I took advantage of their hesitation to cross back to A Corridor at my best speed. I paused once to send a hail of needles ricocheting down the corridor behind me, and I heard a yelp from around the corner. Those needles had a fantastic velocity, and bounced around for a long time.

At the corridor, I lay down on the floor for a rest and risked a quick look. A group of three men were bunched around the Control Section door, packing smashite in the hairline crack around it. That wouldn't do them any good, but it did occupy their attention.

I faded back into the cross passage, and keyed the talker. I had to give them a chance.

"This is the captain," I said. "All personnel not at their action stations are warned for the last time to report there immediately. Any man found away from his post from this point on is in open mutiny and can expect the death penalty. This is the last warning."

The men in the corridor had heard, but a glance showed they paid no attention to what they consid-

ered an idle threat. They didn't know how near I
was.

I drew my needler, set it for continuous fire,
pushed into the corridor, aimed, and fired. I shot to
kill. All three sprawled away from the door, riddled,
as the metal walls rang with the cloud of needles.

I looked both ways, then rose, with effort, and
went to the bodies. I recognized them as members
of Kirschenbaum's Power Section crew. I keyed
again as I moved on toward the lift at the end of the
corridor, glancing back as I went.

"Corley, MacWilliams, and Reardon have been
shot for mutiny in the face of the enemy," I said.
"Let's hope they're the last to insist on my enforcing
the death penalty."

Behind me, at the far end of the corridor, men
appeared again. I flattened myself in a doorway,
sprayed needles toward them, and hoped for the
best. I heard the singing of a swarm past me, but
felt no hits. The mutineers offered a bigger target,
and I thought I saw someone fall. As they all moved
back out of sight, I made another break for the lift.

I was grateful they hadn't had time to organize. I
kept an eye to the rear, and sent a hail of needles
back every time a man showed himself. They ducked
out to fire every few seconds, but not very effec-
tively. I had an advantage over them; I was fighting
for the success of the mission and for my life, with
no one to look to for help; they were each one of a
mob, none eager to be a target, each willing to let
the other man take the risk.

I was getting pretty tired. I was grateful for the
extra stamina and wind that daily calisthenics in a
high-gee field had given me; without that I would
have collapsed before now; but I was almost ready
to drop. I had my eyes fixed on the lift door; each
step, inch by inch, was an almost unbearable effort.

With only a few feet to go, my knees gave; I went

down on all fours. Another batch of needles sang around me, and vivid pain seared my left arm. It helped. The pain cleared my head, spurred me. I rose and stumbled against the door.

Now the combination. I fought a numbing desire to faint as I pressed the lock control; three, five, two, five . . .

I twisted around as I heard a sound. The shuttle was coming toward me, men lying flat on it, protected by the bumper plate. I leaned against the lift door, and loosed a stream of needles against the side of the corridor, banking them toward the shuttle. Two men rolled off the shuttle in a spatter of blood. Another screamed, and a hand waved above the bumper. I needled it.

I wondered how many were on the shuttle. It kept coming. The closer it came, the more effective my bank shots were. I wondered why it failed to return my fire. Then a hand rose in an arc and a choke bomb dropped in a short curve to the floor. It rolled to my feet, just starting to spew. I kicked it back. The shuttle stopped, backed away from the bomb. A jet of brown gas was playing from it now. I aimed my needler, and sent it spinning back farther. Then I turned to my lock.

Now a clank of metal against metal sounded behind me; from the side passage a man in clumsy radiation armor moved out. The suit was self-powered and needle-proof. I sent a concentrated blast at the head, as the figure awkwardly tottered toward me, ungainly in the multi-gee field. The needles hit, snapped the head back. The suited figure hesitated, arms spread, stepped back and fell with a thunderous crash. I had managed to knock him off balance, maybe stun him.

I struggled to remember where I was in the code sequence; I went on, keyed the rest. I pushed; nothing. I must have lost count. I started again.

I heard the armored man coming on again. The needler trick wouldn't work twice. I kept working. I had almost completed the sequence when I felt the powered grip of the suited man on my arm. I twisted, jammed the needler against his hand, and fired. The arm flew back, and even through the suit I heard his wrist snap. My own hand was numb from the recoil. The other arm of the suit swept down and struck my wounded arm. I staggered away from the door, dazed with the pain.

I sidestepped in time to miss another ponderous blow. Under two and a half gees, the man in the suit was having a hard time, even with power-assisted controls. I felt that I was fighting a machine instead of a man.

As he stepped toward me again, I aimed at his foot. A concentrated stream of needles hit, like a metallic fire hose, knocked the foot aside, toppled the man again. I staggered back to my door.

But now I realized I couldn't risk opening it; even if I got in, I couldn't keep my suited assailant from crowding in with me. Already he was up, lurching toward me. I had to draw him away from the door.

The shuttle sat unmoving. The mob kept its distance. I wondered why no one was shooting. I guessed they had realized that if I were killed there would be no way to enter the vital control areas of the ship; they had to take me alive.

I made it past the clumsy armored man and started down the corridor toward the shuttle. I moved as slowly as I could while still eluding him. He lumbered after me. I reached the shuttle; a glance showed no one alive there. Two men lay across it. I pulled myself onto it and threw in the forward lever. The shuttle rolled smoothly past the armored man, striking him a glancing blow that sent him down again. Those falls, in the multi-gee field, were bone-crushing. He didn't get up.

I reached the door again, rolled off the shuttle, and reached for the combination. I wished now I'd coded a shorter one. I started again; heard a noise behind me. As I turned, a heavy weight crushed me against the door.

I was held rigid, my chest against the combination key. The pressure was cracking my ribs and still it increased. I twisted my head, gasping. The shuttle held me pinned to the door. The man I had assumed out of action was alive enough to hold the lever down with savage strength. I tried to shout, to remind him that without me to open the doors, they were powerless to save the ship. I couldn't speak. I tasted blood in my mouth, and tried to breathe. I couldn't. I passed out.

3

I emerged into consciousness to find the pressure gone, but a red haze of pain remained. I lay on my back and saw men sitting on the floor around me.

A blow from somewhere made my head ring. I tried to sit up. I couldn't make it. Then Kramer was beside me, slipping a needle into my arm. He looked pretty bad himself. His face was bandaged heavily, and one eye was purple. He spoke in a muffled voice through stiff jaws.

"This will keep you conscious enough to answer a few questions," he said. "Now you're going to give me the combinations to the locks so we can call off this suicide run; then maybe I'll doctor you up."

I didn't answer.

"The time for clamming up is over, you stupid bastard," Kramer said. He raised his fist and drove a hard punch into my chest. I guess it was his shot that kept me conscious. I couldn't breathe for a while, until Kramer gave me a few whiffs of oxygen.

I wondered if he was fool enough to think I might give up my ship.

After a while my head cleared a little. I tried to say something. I got out a couple of croaks, and then found my voice.

"Kramer," I said.

He leaned over me. "I'm listening," he said.

"Take me to the lift. Leave me there alone. That's your only chance." It seemed to me like a long speech, but nothing happened. Kramer went away, came back. He showed me a large scalpel from his medical kit. "I'm going to start operating on your face. I'll make you into a museum freak. Maybe if you start talking soon enough I'll change my mind."

I could see the watch on his wrist. My mind worked very slowly. I had trouble getting any air into my lungs. We would intercept in one hour and ten minutes.

It seemed simple to me. I had to get back to the Bridge before we hit. I tried again. "We only have an hour," I said.

Kramer lost control. He jabbed the knife at my face, screeching through gritted teeth. I jerked my head aside far enough that the scalpel grated along my cheekbone instead of slashing my mouth. I hardly felt it.

"We're dying because you were a fool," Kramer yelled. "I've taken over; I've relieved you as unfit for command. Now open up this ship or I'll slice you to ribbons." He held the scalpel under my nose in a fist trembling with fury. The chrome-plated blade had a thin film of pink on it.

I got my voice going again. "I'm going to destroy the Mancji ship," I said. "Take me to the lift and leave me there." I tried to add a few more words, but had to stop and work on breathing again for a while. Kramer disappeared.

I realized I was not fully in command of my

you're hurt, ain't you? I was wonderin' why you was down here layin' down in my 'sposal station."

"A scratch," I said. I thought about it for a while. Thomas was doing something about my chest. This was Thomas's disposal station. Thomas owned it. I wondered if a fellow could make a living with such a small place way out here, with just an occasional tourist coming by. I wondered why I didn't send one of them for help; I needed help for some reason. . . .

"Cap'n, I been overhaulin' my converter units, I jist come in. How long you been in here, Cap'n?" Thomas was worried about something.

I tried hard to think. I hadn't been here very long; just a few minutes. I had come here to rest . . . then suddenly I was thinking clearly again.

Whatever Thomas was, he was apparently on my side, or at least neutral. He didn't seem to be aware of the mutiny. I realized that he had bound my chest tightly with strips of shirt; it felt better.

"What are you doing in here, Thomas?" I asked. "Don't you know we're in action against a hostile ship?"

Thomas looked surprised. "This here's my action station, Cap'n," he said. "I'm a Waste Recovery Technician, First Class. I keep the recovery system operatin'."

"You just stay in here?" I asked.

"No, sir," Thomas said. "I check through the whole system. We got three main disposal points and lotsa little ones, an' I have to keep everything operatin'. Otherwise this ship would be in a bad way, Cap'n."

"How did you get in here?" I asked. I looked around the small room. There was only one door, and the tiny space was nearly filled by the gray bulk of the converter unit which broke down wastes into their component elements for reuse.

"I come in through the duct, Cap'n," Thomas said.

"I check the ducts every day. You know Cap'n," he said, shaking his head, "they's some bad laid-out ductin' in this here system. If I didn't keep after it, you'd be gettin' clogged ducts all the time. So I jist go through the system and keep her clear."

From somewhere, hope began again. "Where do these ducts lead?" I asked. I wondered how the man could ignore the mutiny going on around him.

"Well, sir, one leads to the mess; that's the big one. One leads to the wardroom, and the other leads up to the Bridge."

My god, I thought, the Bridge.

"How big are they?" I asked. "Could I get through them?"

"Oh sure, Cap'n," Thomas said. "You can get through 'em easy. But are you sure you feel like inspectin' with them busted ribs?"

I was beginning to realize that Thomas was not precisely a genius. "I can make it," I said.

"Cap'n," Thomas said diffidently, "it ain't none o' my business, but don't you think maybe I better get the doctor for ya?"

"Thomas," I said, "maybe you don't know; there's a mutiny under way aboard this ship. The doctor is leading it. I want to get to the Bridge in the worst way. Let's get started."

Thomas looked shocked. "Cap'n, you mean you was hurt *by* somebody? I mean you didn't have a fall or nothin', you was beat up?" He stared at me with an expression of incredulous horror.

"That's about the size of it," I said. I managed to sit up. Thomas jumped forward and helped me to my feet. Then I saw that he was crying.

"You can count on me, Cap'n," he said. "Jist lemme know who done it, an' I'll feed 'em into my converter."

I stood leaning against the wall, waiting for my head to stop spinning. Breathing was difficult, but if

I kept it shallow, I could manage. Thomas was opening a panel on the side of the converter unit.

"It's OK to go in, Cap'n," he said. "She ain't operatin'."

The pull of the two and a half gees seemed to bother him very little. I could barely stand under it, holding on. Thomas saw my wavering step and jumped to help me. He boosted me into the chamber of the converter and pointed out an opening near the top, about twelve by twenty-four inches.

"That there one is to the Bridge, Cap'n," he said. "If you'll start in there, sir, I'll follow up."

I thrust head and shoulders into the opening. Inside it was smooth metal, with no handholds. I clawed at it trying to get farther in. The pain stabbed at my chest.

"Cap'n, they're workin' on the door," Thomas said. "They already been at it for a little while. We better get goin'."

"You'd better give me a boost, Thomas," I said. My voice echoed hollowly down the duct.

Thomas crowded into the chamber behind me then, lifting my legs and pushing. I eased into the duct. The pain was not so bad now.

"Cap'n, you gotta use a special kinda crawl to get through these here ducts," Thomas said. "You grip your hands together out in front of ya, and then bend your elbows. When your elbows jam against the side of the duct, you pull forward."

I tried it; it was slow, but it worked.

"Cap'n," Thomas said behind me. "We got about seven minutes now to get up there. I set the control on the converter to start up in ten minutes. I think we can make it OK, and ain't nobody else comin' this way with the converter goin'. I locked the control panel so they can't shut her down."

That news spurred me on. With the converter in operation, the first step in the cycle was the evacuation of the ducts to a near-perfect vacuum. When that happened, we would die instantly with ruptured lungs; then our dead bodies would be sucked into the chamber and broken down into useful raw materials. I hurried.

I tried to orient myself. The duct paralleled the corridor. It would continue in that direction for about fifteen feet, and would then turn upward, since the Bridge was some fifteen feet above this level. I hitched along, and felt the duct begin to trend upward.

"You'll have to get on your back here, Cap'n," Thomas said. "She widens out on the turn."

I managed to twist over. Thomas was helping me by pushing at my feet. As I reached a near-vertical position, I felt a metal rod under my hand. That was a relief; I had been expecting to have to go up the last stretch the way a mountain climber does a rock chimney, back against one wall and feet against the other.

I hauled at the rod, and found another with my other hand. Below, Thomas boosted me. I groped up and got another, then another. The remaining slight slant of the duct helped. Finally my feet were on the rods. I clung, panting. The heat in the duct was terrific. Then I went on up. That was some shot Kramer had given me.

Above I could see the end of the duct faintly in the light coming up through the open chamber door from the utility room. I remembered the location of the disposal slot on the Bridge now; it had been installed in the small niche containing a bunk and a tiny galley for the use of the duty officer during long watches on the Bridge.

I reached the top of the duct and pushed against the slot cover. It swung out easily. I could see the end of the chart table, and beyond, the dead radar screen. I reached through and heaved myself partly out. I nearly fainted at the stab from my ribs as my weight went on my chest. My head sang. The light from below suddenly went out. I heard a muffled clank; then a hum began, echoing up the duct.

"She's closed and started cyclin' the air out, Cap'n," Thomas said calmly. "We got about half a minute."

I clamped my teeth together and heaved again. Below me Thomas waited quietly. He couldn't help me now. I got my hands flat against the bulkhead and thrust. The air was whistling around my face. Papers began to swirl off the chart table. I kicked loose from the grip of the slot, fighting the sucking pull of air. I fell to the floor inside the room; the slot cover slammed behind me. I staggered to my feet. I pried at the cover, but I couldn't open it against the vacuum. Then it budged, and Thomas's hand came through. The metal edge cut into it, blood started, but the cover was held open half an inch. I reached the chart table, almost falling over my leaden feet, seized a short permal T-square, and levered the cover up. Once started, it went up easily. Thomas's face appeared, drawn and pale, eyes closed against the dust being whirled into his face. He got his arms through, heaved himself a little higher. I seized his arm and pulled. He scrambled through.

I knocked the T-square out of the way and the cover snapped down. Then I slid to the floor, not exactly out, but needing a break pretty bad. Thomas brought bedding from the OD bunk and made me comfortable on the floor.

"Thomas," I said, "when I think of what the security inspectors who approved the plans for this arrangement are going to say when I call this little back door to their attention, it almost makes it worth the trouble."

"Yessir," Thomas said. He sprawled on the deck

and looked around the Bridge, staring at the unfamiliar screens, indicator lights, controls.

From where I lay, I could see the direct vision screen. I wasn't sure, but I thought the small bright object in the center of it might be our target. Thomas looked at the dead radar screen, then said, "Cap'n, that there radarscope out of action?"

"It sure is, Thomas," I said. "Our unknown friends blew the works before they left us." I was surprised that he recognized a radarscope.

"Mind if I take a look at it, Cap'n?" he said.

"Go ahead," I replied. I tried to explain the situation to Thomas. The elapsed time since we had started our pursuit was two hours and ten minutes; I wanted to close to no more than a twenty-mile gap before launching my missiles; and I had better alert my interceptor missiles in case the Mancji hit first.

Thomas had the cover off the radar panel and was probing around. He pulled a blackened card out of the interior of the panel.

"Looks like they overloaded the fuse," Thomas said. "Got any spares, Cap'n?"

"Right beside you in the cabinet," I said. "How do you know your way around a radar set, Thomas?"

Thomas grinned. "I useta be a radar technician third before I got inta waste disposal," he said. "I had to change specialities to sign on for this cruise."

I had an idea there'd be an opening for Thomas a little higher up when this was over.

I asked him to take a look at the televideo, too. I was beginning to realize that Thomas was not really simple; he was merely uncomplicated.

"Tubes blowed here, Cap'n," he reported. "Like as if you was to set her up to high mag right near a sun; she was overloaded. I can fix her easy if we got the spares."

I didn't take time to try to figure that one out. I could feel the dizziness coming on again.

"Thomas," I called, "let me know when we're at twenty miles from target." I wanted to tell him more, but I could feel consciousness draining away. "Then . . ." I managed, "Aid kit . . . shot . . ."

I could still hear Thomas. I was flying away, whirling, but I could hear his voice. "Cap'n, I could fire your missiles now, if you was to want me to," he was saying. I struggled to speak. "No. Wait." I hoped he heard me.

I floated a long time in a strange state between coma and consciousness. The stuff Kramer had given me was potent. It kept my mind fairly clear even when my senses were out of action. I thought about the situation aboard my ship.

I wondered what Kramer and his men were planning now, how they felt about having let me slip through their fingers. The only thing they could try now was blasting their way into the Bridge. They'd never make it. The designers of these ships were not unaware of the hazards of space life; the Bridge was an unassailable fortress.

Kramer would be having a pretty rough time of it by now. He had convinced the men that we were rushing headlong to sure destruction at the hands of the all-powerful Mancji, and that their captain was a fool. Now he was trapped with them in the panic he had helped to create. I thought that in all probability they had torn him apart.

I wavered in and out of consciousness. It was just as well; I needed the rest. Each time I came to, I felt a little better. Then I heard Thomas calling me. "We're closin' now, Cap'n," he said. "Wake up, Cap'n, only twenty-three miles now."

"Okay," I said. My body had been preparing itself for this; now it was ready again. I felt the needle in my arm. That helped, too.

"Hand me the intercom, Thomas," I said. He

placed the talker in my hand. I keyed for a general announcement.

"This is the captain," I said. I tried to keep my voice as steady as possible. "We are now at a distance of twenty-one miles from the enemy. Stand by for missile launching and possible evasive action. Damage control crews on the alert." I paused for breath.

"Now we're going to take out the Mancji ship, men," I said. "All two miles of it."

I dropped the mike and groped for the firing key. Thomas handed it to me.

"Cap'n," he said, bending over me. "I notice you got the selector set for your chemical warheads. You wouldn't want me to set up pluto heads for ya, would ya, Cap'n?"

"No, thanks, Thomas," I said. "Chemical is what I want. Stand by to observe." I pressed the firing key.

Thomas was at the radarscope. "Missiles away, Cap'n," he droned. "Trackin' OK. Looks like they'll take out the left half o' that dumbbell."

I found the talker again. "Missiles homing on target," I said. "Strike in thirty-five seconds. You'll be interested to know we're employing chemical warheads. So far there is no sign of offense or defense from the enemy." I figured the news would shock a few mutineers. David wasn't even using his slingshot on Goliath. He was going after him bare-handed. I wanted to scare some kind of response out of them. I needed a few clues to what was going on below.

I got it. Joyce's voice came from the wall talker. "Captain, this is Lieutenant Joyce reporting." He sounded scared all the way through, and desperate. "Sir, the mutiny has been successfully suppressed by the loyal members of the crew. Major Kramer is under arrest. We're prepared to go on with the search for the Omega Colony. But, sir . . ." he paused, gulping. "We ask you to change course now before launching any effective attack. We still have a chance. Maybe they won't bother with us when those firecrackers go off . . ."

I watched the direct vision screen. Zero second closed in. And on the screen the face of the left-hand disk of the Mancji ship was lit momentarily by a brilliant spark of yellow, then another. A discoloration showed dimly against the dark metallic surface. It spread, and a faint vapor formed over it. Now tiny specks could be seen moving away from the ship. The disk elongated, with infinite leisure, widening.

"What's happenin', Cap'n?" Thomas wanted to know. He was staring at the scope in fascination. "They launchin' scouts, or what?"

"Take a look here, Thomas," I said. "The ship is breaking up."

The disk was an impossibly long ellipse now, surrounded by a vast array of smaller bodies, fragments and contents of the ship. Now the stricken globe moved completely free of its companion. It rotated, presenting a crescent toward us, then wheeled farther as it receded from its twin, showing its elongation. The sphere had split wide open. Now the shattered half itself separated into two halves, and these in turn crumbled, strewing debris in a widening spiral.

"My God, Cap'n," Thomas said in awe. "That's the greatest display I ever seen. And all's it took to set her off was two hundred kilos o' PBL. Now that's somethin'."

I keyed the talker again. "This is the captain," I said. "I want ten four-man patrols ready to go out in fifteen minutes. The enemy ship had been put out of action and is now in a derelict condition. I want only one thing from her; one live prisoner. All section chiefs report to me on the Bridge on the triple."

"Thomas," I said, "go down in the lift and open

up for the chiefs. Here's the release key for the combination; you know how to operate it?"

"Sure, Cap'n; but are you sure you want to let them boys in here after the way they jumped you an all?"

I opened my mouth to answer, but he beat me to it. "Fergit I asked ya that, Cap'n, pleasir. You ain't been wrong yet."

"It's OK, Thomas," I said. "There won't be any more trouble."

Epilogue

On the eve of the twentieth anniversary of Reunion Day, a throng of well-heeled celebrants filled the dining room and overflowed onto the terraces of the Star Tower Dining Room, from whose 5700-foot height above the beaches, the Florida Keys, a hundred miles to the south, were visible on clear days.

The *ERA* reporter stood beside the vast glass entryway surveying the crowd, searching for celebrities from whom he might elicit bits of color to spice the day's transmission.

At the far side of the room, surrounded by chattering admirers, stood the Ambassador from the New Terran Federation; a portly, greying, jolly ex-Naval officer. A minor actress passed at close range, looking the other way. A cabinet member stood at the bar talking earnestly to a ball player, ignoring a group of hopeful reporters and fans.

The *ERA* stringer, an experienced hand, passed over the hard-pressed VIP's near the center of the room and started a face-by-face check of the less gregarious diners seated at obscure tables along the sides of the room.

He was in luck; a straight-backed, grey-haired figure in a dark civilian suit, sitting alone at a tiny table in an alcove, caught his eye. He moved closer, straining for a clear glimpse through the crowd. Then he was sure. He had the biggest possible catch of the day in his sights: Admiral of Fleets Frederick Greylorn.

The reporter hesitated; he was well aware of the admiral's reputation for near-absolute silence on the subject of his already legendary cruise, the fabulous voyage of the *Galahad*. He couldn't just barge in on the admiral and demand answers, as was usual with publicity-hungry politicians and show people. He could score the biggest story of the century today; but he had to hit him right.

You couldn't hope to snow a man like the admiral; he wasn't somebody you could push around. You could sense the solid iron of him from here.

Nobody else had noticed the solitary diner. The *ERA* man drifted closer, moving unhurriedly, thinking furiously. It was no good trying some tricky approach; his best bet was the straight-from-the-shoulder bit. No point in hesitating. He stopped beside the table.

The admiral was looking out across the Gulf. He turned and glanced up at the reporter.

The newsman looked him squarely in the eye. "I'm a reporter, Admiral," he said. "Will you talk to me?"

The admiral nodded to the seat across from him. "Sit down," he said. He glanced around the room.

The reporter caught the look. "I'll keep it light, sir," he said. "I don't want company either." That was being frank.

"You want the answers to some questions, don't you?" the admiral said.

"Why, yes, sir," the reporter said. He started to inconspicuously key his pocket recorder, but caught himself. "May I record your remarks, Admiral?" he said. Frankness all the way.

"Go ahead," said the admiral.

"Now, Admiral," the reporter began, "the Terran public has of course . . ."

"Never mind the patter, son," the admiral said mildly. "I know what the questions are. I've read all the memoirs of the crew. They've been coming out at the rate of about two a year for some time now. I had my own reasons for not wanting to add anything to my official statement."

The admiral poured wine into his glass. "Excuse me," he said. "Will you join me?" He signaled the waiter.

"Another wine glass, please," he said. He looked at the golden wine in the glass, held it up to the light. "You know, the Florida wines are as good as any in the world," he said. "That's not to say the California and Ohio wines aren't good. But this Flora Pinellas is a genuine original, not an imitation Rhine; and it compares favorably with the best of the old vintages, particularly in the '87."

The glass arrived and the waiter poured. The reporter had the wit to remain silent.

"The first question is usually, how did I know I could take the Mancji ship? After all, it was big, vast. It loomed over us like a mountain. The Mancji themselves weighed almost two tons each; they liked six-gee gravity. They blasted our communication off the air, just for practice. They talked big, too. We were invaders in their territory. They were amused by us. So where did I get the notion that our attack would be anything more than a joke to them? That's the big question." The admiral shook his head.

"The answer is quite simple. In the first place, they were pulling six gees by using a primitive dumbbell configuration. The only reason for that type of layout, as students of early space vessel design can tell you, is to simplify setting up a gee field effect, using centrifugal force. So they obviously had no gravity field generators.

"Then their transmission was crude. All they had was simple old-fashioned short range radio, and even that was noisy and erratic. And their reception was as bad. We had to use a kilowatt before they could pick it up at two hundred miles. We didn't know then it was all organically generated; that they had no equipment."

The admiral sipped his wine, frowning at the recollection. "I was pretty sure they were bluffing when I changed course and started after them. I had to hold our acceleration down to two and a half gees because I had to be able to move around the ship. And at that acceleration we gained on them. They couldn't beat us. And it wasn't because they couldn't take high gees; they liked six for comfort, you remember. No, they just didn't have the power."

The admiral looked out the window.

"Add to that the fact that they apparently couldn't generate ordinary electric current. I admit that none of this was conclusive, but after all, if I was wrong we were sunk anyway. When Thomas told me the nature of the damage to our radar and communications systems, that was another hint. Their big display of Mancji power was just a blast of radiation right across the communication spectrum; it burned tubes and blew fuses; nothing else. We were back in operation an hour after our attack.

"The evidence was there to see, but there's something about giant size that gets people rattled. Size alone doesn't mean a thing. It's rather like the bluff the Soviets ran on the rest of the world for a couple of decades back in the war era, just because they sprawled across half the globe. They were a giant, though it was mostly frozen desert. When the economic showdown came they didn't have it. They were a pushover.

"All right, the next question is why did I choose H. E. instead of going in with everything I had? That's easy, too. What I wanted was information, not revenge. I still had the heavy stuff in reserve and ready to go if I needed it, but first I had to try to take them alive. Vaporizing them wouldn't have helped our position. And I was lucky; it worked.

"The, ah, confusion below evaporated as soon as the section chiefs got a look at the screens and realized that we had actually knocked out the Mancji. We matched speeds with the wreckage and the patrols went out to look for a piece of ship with a survivor in it. If we'd had no luck we would have tackled the other half of the ship, which was still intact and moving off fast. But we got quite a shock when we found the nature of the wreckage." The admiral grinned.

"Of course today everybody knows all about the Mancji hive intelligence, and their evolutionary history. But we were pretty startled to find that the only wreckage consisted of the Mancji themselves, each two-ton slug in his own hard chiton shell. Of course, a lot of the cells were ruptured by the explosions, but most of them had simply disassociated from the hive mass as it broke up. So there was no ship; just a cluster of cells like a giant beehive, and mixed up among the slugs, the damnedest collection of loot you can imagine. The odds and ends they'd stolen and tucked away in the hive during a couple hundred years of scavenging.

"The patrols brought a couple of cells alongside, and Mannion went out to try to establish contact. Sure enough, he got a very faint transmission, on the same band as before. The cells were talking to each other in their own language. They ignored Mannion even though his transmission must have blanketed everything within several hundred miles. We eventually brought one of them into the cargo lock and started trying different wavelengths on it. Then Kramer had the idea of planting a couple of electrodes and shooting a little juice to it. Of course, it loved the DC, but as soon as we tried AC, it gave up. So we had a long talk with it and found out everything we needed to know.

"It was a four-week run to the nearest outpost planet of the New Terran Federation, and they took me on to New Terra aboard one of their fast liaison vessels. The rest you know. We, the home planet, were as lost to the New Terrans as they were to us. They greeted us as their own ancestors come back to visit them.

"Most of my crew, for personal reasons, were released from duty there, and settled down to stay.

"The clean-up job here on Earth was a minor operation to their Navy. As I recall, the trip back was made in a little over five months, and the Red Tide was killed within four weeks of the day the task force arrived. I don't think they wasted a motion. One explosive charge per cell, of just sufficient size to disrupt the nucleus. When the critical number of cells had been killed, the rest died overnight.

"It was quite a different Earth that emerged from under the plague, though. You know it had taken over all of the land area except North America and a strip of Western Europe, and all of the sea it wanted. It was particularly concentrated over what had been the jungle areas of South America, Africa, and Asia. You must realize that in the days before the Tide, those areas were almost completely uninhabitable. You have no idea what the term 'jungle' really implied. When the Tide died, it disintegrated into its component molecules; and the result was that all those vast jungle lands were now beautifully levelled and completely cleared areas covered with up to twenty feet of the richest topsoil imaginable. That was what made it possible for old Terra to become what she is today; the Federation's truck farm, and the sole source of those genuine original Terran foods that all the rest of the worlds pay such fabulous prices for.

"Strange how quickly we forget. Few people today remember how we loathed and feared the Tide when we were fighting it. Now it's dismissed as a blessing in disguise."

The admiral paused. "Well," he said, "I think that answers the questions and gives you a bit of home-spun philosophy to go with it."

"Admiral," said the reporter, "you've given the public some facts it's waited a long time to hear. Coming from you, sir, this is the greatest story that could have come out of this Reunion Day celebration. But there is one question more, if I may ask it. Can you tell me, Admiral, just how it was that you rejected what seemed to be *prima facie* proof of the story the Mancji told; that they were the lords of creation out there, and that humanity was nothing but a tame food animal to them?"

The admiral sighed. "I guess it's a good question," he said. "But there was nothing supernatural about my figuring that one. I didn't suspect the full truth, of course. It never occurred to me that we were the victims of the now well-known but still inexplicable sense of humor of the Mancji, or that they were nothing but scavengers around the edges of the Federation. The original Omega ship had met them and seen right through them, but for two centuries those fool hives buzzed around the Omega worlds listening and picking up trophies. They're actually highly intelligent in their own weird way. They picked up the language, listened in on communications, made a real study of Terrans. Every twenty years or so when they got to be too big a nuisance, the New Terrans would break up a few of their hives and clear them out of the area. But on the whole they had a sort of amused tolerance of them.

"Well, when this hive spotted us coming in, they knew enough about New Terra to realize at once that we were strangers, coming from outside the area. It appealed to their sense of humor to have the gall to strut right out in front of us and try to put over a swindle. What a laugh for the oyster kingdom if they could sell Terrans on the idea that they were the master race. It never occurred to them that we might be anything but Terrans; Terrans who didn't know the Mancji. And they were canny enough to use an old form of Standard.

"Sure enough, we didn't show any signs of recognizing them; so they decided to really get a kick by getting us to give them what they love better than anything else; a nice bath of electric current. They don't eat, of course; they live on pure radiation. The physical side of life means little to them. They live in a world of the hive mind; they do love the flow of electricity through the hive, though. It must be something like having your back scratched.

"Then we wanted food. They knew what we ate, and that was where they went too far. They had, among the flotsam in their hive, a few human bodies they had picked up from some wreck they'd come across in their travels. They had them stashed away like everything else they could lay a pseudopod on. So they stacked them the way they'd seen Terran frozen foods shipped in the past, and sent them over. Another of their little jokes.

"I suppose if you're already overwrought and eager to quit, and you've been badly scared by the size of an alien ship, it's pretty understandable that the sight of human bodies, along with the story that they're just a convenient food supply, might seem pretty convincing. At least, the prevailing school of thought seemed to be that we were lucky we hadn't been put in the food lockers ourselves. But I was already pretty dubious about the genuineness of our pals, and when I saw those bodies it was pretty plain that we were hot on the trail of Omega Colony. There was no other place humans could have come from out there. We had to find out the location from the Mancji."

"But, Admiral," said the reporter, "true enough they were humans, and presumably had some connection with the colony, but they were naked corpses stacked like cordwood. The Mancji had stated that these were slaves, or rather domesticated animals; they wouldn't have done you any good."

"Well, you see, I didn't believe that," the admiral said. "Because it was an obvious lie. I tried to show some of the officers, but I'm afraid they weren't being too rational just then.

"I went into the locker and examined those bodies; if Kramer had looked closely, he would have seen what I did. These were no tame animals. They were civilized men."

"How could you be sure, Admiral? They had no clothing, no identifying marks, nothing. Why didn't you believe they were cattle?"

"Because," said the admiral, "all the men's beards were neatly trimmed, in a style two hundred years out of date."

After the admiral had signed the check, nodded and walked away, the reporter keyed his fone for Editor.

"Priority," he said. "Lead. Here's how our world was saved twenty years ago by a dead man's haircut. . . ."

There are universal motivations which can be depended upon to produce quite familiar action-patterns in even seemingly wildly alien minds. But the human mind is always capable of surprising us, especially if we consider the end toward which our brief evolution from the beast is carrying us, irresistibly.

The Time Thieves

Clyde W. Snithian was a bald eagle of a man, dark-eyed, pot-bellied, with the large, expressive hands of a rug merchant. Round-shouldered in a loose cloak, he blinked small reddish eyes at Dan Slane's travel-stained six-foot-one.

"Kelly here tells me you've been demanding to see me." He nodded toward the florid man at his side. He had a high, thin voice, like something that needed oiling. "Something about important information regarding my paintings."

"That's right, Mr. Snithian," Dan said. "I believe I can be of great help to you."

"Help how? If you've got ideas of bilking me . . ." The red eyes bored into Dan like hot pokers.

"Nothing like that, sir. Now, I know you have quite a system of guards here—the papers are full of it—"

"Damned busybodies! Sensation-mongers! If it wasn't for the press, I'd have no concern for my paintings today!"

"Yes, sir. But my point is, the one really important spot has been left unguarded."

"Now, wait a minute—" Kelly started.

"What's that?" Snithian cut in.

"You have a hundred and fifty men guarding the house and grounds day and night—"

"Two hundred and twenty-five," Kelly snapped.

"—but no one at all in the vault with the paintings," Slane finished.

"Of course not," Snithian shrilled. "Why should I post a man in the vault? It's under constant surveillance from the corridor outside."

"The Harriman paintings were removed from a locked vault," Dan said. "There was a special seal on the door. It wasn't broken."

"By the saints, he's right," Kelly exclaimed. "Maybe we ought to have a man in that vault."

"Another idiotic scheme to waste my money," Snithian snapped. "I've made you responsible for security here, Kelly! Let's have no more nonsense. And throw this nincompoop out!" Snithian turned and stalked away, his cloak flapping at his knees.

"I'll work cheap," Dan called after the tycoon as Kelly took his arm. "I'm an art lover."

"Never mind that," Kelly said, escorting Dan along the corridor. He turned in at an office and closed the door.

"Now, as the old buzzard said, I'm responsible for security here. If those pictures go, my job goes with them. Your vault idea's not bad. Just *how* cheap would you work?"

"A hundred dollars a week," Dan said promptly. "Plus expenses," he added.

Kelly nodded. "I'll fingerprint you and run a fast agency check. If you're clean, I'll put you on, starting tonight. But keep it quiet."

*

Dan looked around at the gray walls, with shelves stacked to the low ceiling with wrapped paintings. Two three-hundred-watt bulbs shed a white glare over the tile floor, a neat white refrigerator, a bunk, an armchair, a bookshelf and a small table set with paper plates, plastic utensils and a portable radio—all hastily installed at Kelly's order. Dan opened the refrigerator, looked over the stock of salami, liverwurst, cheese and beer. He opened a loaf of bread, built up a well-filled sandwich, keyed open a can of beer.

It wasn't fancy, but it would do. Phase one of the plan had gone off without a hitch.

Basically, his idea was simple. Art collections had been disappearing from closely guarded galleries and homes all over the world. It was obvious that no one could enter a locked vault, remove a stack of large canvases and leave, unnoticed by watchful guards—and leaving the locks undamaged.

Yet the paintings were gone. Someone had been in those vaults—someone who hadn't entered in the usual way.

Theory failed at that point; that left the experimental method. The Snithian collection was the largest west of the Mississippi. With such a target, the thieves were bound to show up. If Dan sat in the vault—day and night—waiting—he would see for himself how they operated.

He finished his sandwich, went to the shelves and pulled down one of the brown-paper bundles. Loosening the string binding the package, he slid a painting into view. It was a gaily colored view of an open-air cafe, with a group of men and women in gay-ninetyish costumes gathered at a table. He seemed to remember reading something about it in a magazine. It was a cheerful scene; Dan liked it. Still, it hardly seemed worth all the effort. . . .

He went to the wall switch and turned off the

lights. The orange glow of the filaments died, leaving only a faint illumination from the nightlight over the door. When the thieves arrived, it might give a momentary advantage if his eyes were adjusted to the dark. He groped his way to the bunk.

So far, so good, he reflected, stretching out. When they showed up, he'd have to handle everything just right. If he scared them off there'd be no second chance. He would have lost his crack at—whatever his discovery might mean to him.

But he was ready. Let them come.

Eight hours, three sandwiches and six beers later, Dan roused suddenly from a light doze and sat up on the cot. Between him and the crowded shelving, a palely luminous framework was materializing in mid-air.

The apparition was an open-work cage—about the size and shape of an outhouse minus the sheathing, Dan estimated breathlessly. Two figures were visible within the structure, sitting stiffly in contoured chairs. They glowed, if anything more brightly than the framework.

A faint sound cut into the stillness—a descending whine. The cage moved jerkily, settling toward the floor. Long pink sparks jumped, crackling, to span the closing gap; with a grate of metal, the cage settled against the floor. The spectral men reached for ghostly switches. . . .

The glow died.

Dan was aware of his heart thumping painfully under his ribs. His mouth was dry. This was the moment he'd been planning for, but now that it was here—

Never mind. He took a deep breath, ran over the speeches he had prepared for the occasion:

Greeting, visitors from the future. . . .

No good; it lacked spontaneity. The men were rising, their backs to Dan, stepping out of the skeletal frame. In the dim light it now looked like nothing more than a rough box built of steel pipe, with a cluster of levers in a console before the two seats. And the thieves looked ordinary enough: two men in grey coveralls, one slender and balding, the other shorter and round-faced. Neither of them noticed Dan, sitting rigid on the cot. The thin man placed a lantern on the table, twiddled a knob. A warm light sprang up. The visitors looked at the stacked shelves.

"Looks like the old boy's been doing all right," the shorter man said. "Fathead's gonna be pleased."

"A very gratifying consignment," his companion said. "However, we'd best hurry, Percy. How much time have we left on the dial?"

"Plenty," Percy grunted. "Fifteen minutes anyway."

The thin man opened a package, glanced at a painting.

"Ah, a Plotz. Magnificent. Almost the equal of Picasso in his puce period."

Percy shuffled through the other pictures in the stack.

"Like always," he grumbled. "No nood dames. I like nood dames."

"Look at this, Percy! The textures alone—"

Percy looked. "Yeah, nice use of values," he conceded. "But I still perfer nood dames, Fiorello."

"And this!" Fiorello lifted the next painting. "Look at that gay play of rich browns!"

"I seen richer browns on Thirty-third Street," Percy said. "They was popular with the sparrows."

"Percy, sometimes I think your aspirations—"

"Whatta ya talkin'? I use a roll-on." Percy, turning to place a painting in the cage, stopped dead as he caught sight of Dan. The painting clattered to the floor. Dan stood, cleared his throat. "Uh . . ."

"Oh-oh," Percy said. "A double-cross."

"I've—ah—been expecting you gentlemen," Dan said. "I—"

"I told you we couldn't trust a guy with nine fingers on each hand," Fiorello whispered hoarsely. He moved toward Percy. "Let's blow, Percy," he muttered.

"Wait a minute," Dan said. "Before you do anything hasty—"

"Don't start nothing, Buster," Percy said cautiously. "We're plenty tough guys when aroused."

"I want to talk to you," Dan insisted, ignoring the medium-weight menace. "You see, these paintings—"

"Paintings? Look, it was all a mistake. Like, we figured this was the gents' room—"

"Never mind, Percy," Fiorello cut in. "It appears there's been a leak."

Dan shook his head. "No leak. I simply deduced—"

"Look, Fiorello," Percy said. "You chin if you want to; I'm doing a fast fade."

"Don't act hastily, Percy. You know where you'll end."

"Wait a minute!" Dan shouted. "I'd like to make a deal with you fellows."

"Ah-hah!" Kelly's voice blared from somewhere. "I knew it! Slane, you crook!"

Dan looked about wildly. The voice seemed to be issuing from a speaker. It appeared Kelly hedged his bets.

"Mr. Kelly, I can explain everything!" Dan called. He turned back to Fiorello. "Listen, I figured out—"

"Pretty clever!" Kelly's voice barked. "Inside job. But it takes more than the likes of you to outfox a old-timer like Ed Kelly."

"Perhaps you were right, Percy," Fiorello said. "Complications are arising. We'd best depart with all deliberate haste." He edged toward the cage.

"What about this ginzo?" Percy jerked a thumb toward Dan. "He's onto us."

"Can't be helped."

"Look—I want to go with you!" Dan shouted.

"I'll bet you do!" Kelly's voice roared. "One more minute and I'll have the door open and collar the lot of you! Come up through a tunnel, did you?"

"You can't go, my dear fellow," Fiorello said. "Room for two, no more."

Dan whirled to the cot, grabbed up the pistol Kelly had supplied. He aimed it at Percy. "You stay here, Percy! I'm going with Fiorello in the time machine."

"Are you nuts?" Manny demanded.

"I'm flattered, dear boy," Fiorello said, "but—"

"Let's get moving. Kelly will have that lock open in a minute."

"You can't leave me here!" Percy spluttered, watching Dan crowd into the cage beside Fiorello.

"We'll send for you," Dan said. "Let's go, Fiorello."

The balding man snatched suddenly for the gun. Dan wrestled with him. The pistol fell, bounced on the floor of the cage, skidded into the far corner of the vault. Percy charged, reaching for Dan as he twisted aside; Fiorello's elbow caught him in the mouth. Percy staggered back into the arms of Kelly, bursting red-faced into the vault.

"Percy!" Fiorello wailed and, releasing his grip on Dan, lunged to aid his companion. Kelly passed Percy to one of three cops crowding in on his heels. Dan clung to the framework as Fiorello grappled with Kelly. A cop pushed past them, spotted Dan, moved in briskly for the pinch. Dan grabbed a lever at random and pulled.

Sudden silence fell as the walls of the room glowed blue. A spectral Kelly capered before the cage, fluorescing in the blue-violet. Dan swallowed hard and nudged a second lever. The cage sank like an elevator into the floor, vivid blue washing up its sides.

Hastily he reversed the control. Operating a time machine was tricky business. One little slip, and the Slane molecules would be squeezing in among brick and mortar particles. . . .

But this was no time to be cautious. Things hadn't turned out just the way he'd planned, but after all, this was what he'd wanted—in a way. The time machine was his to command. And if he gave up now and crawled back into the vault, Kelly would gather him in and try to pin every art theft of the past decade on him.

It couldn't be *too* hard. He'd take it slowly, figure out the controls. . . .

Dan took a deep breath and tried another lever. The cage rose gently, in eerie silence. It reached the ceiling and kept going. Dan gritted his teeth as an eight-inch band of luminescence passed down the cage. Then he was emerging into a spacious kitchen. A blue-haloed cook waddled to a luminous refrigerator, caught sight of Dan rising slowly from the floor, stumbled back, mouth open. The cage rose, penetrated a second ceiling. Dan looked around at a carpeted hall.

Cautiously he neutralized the control lever. The cage came to rest an inch above the floor. As far as Dan could tell, he hadn't traveled so much as a minute into the past or future.

He looked over the controls. There should be one labeled "Forward" and another labeled "Back," but all the levers were plain, unadorned black. They looked, Dan decided, like ordinary circuit-breaker type knife-switches. In fact, the whole apparatus had the appearance of something thrown together hastily from common materials. Still, it worked. So far he had only found the controls for maneuvering in the usual three dimensions, but the time switch was bound to be here somewhere. . . .

Dan looked up at a movement at the far end of the hall.

A girl's head and shoulders appeared, coming up a spiral staircase. In another second she would see him, and give the alarm—and Dan needed a few moments of peace and quiet in which to figure out the controls. He moved a lever. The cage drifted smoothly sideways, sliced through the wall with a flurry of vivid blue light. Dan pushed the lever back. He was in a bedroom now, a wide chamber with flouncy curtains, a four-poster under a flowered canopy, a dressing table—

The door opened and the girl stepped into the room. She was young. Not over eighteen, Dan thought—as nearly as he could tell with the blue light playing around her face. She had long hair tied with a ribbon, and long legs, neatly curved. She wore shorts and carried a tennis racquet in her left hand and an apple in her right. Her back to Dan and the cage, she tossed the racquet on a table, took a bite of the apple, and began briskly unbuttoning her shirt.

Dan tried moving a lever. The cage edged toward the girl. Another; he rose gently. The girl tossed the shirt onto a chair and undid the zipper down the side of the shorts. Another lever; the cage shot toward the outer wall as the girl reached behind her back. . . .

Dan blinked at the flash of blue and looked down. He was hovering twenty feet above a clipped lawn.

He looked at the levers. Wasn't it the first one in line that moved the cage ahead? He tried it, shot forward ten feet. Below, a man stepped out on the terrace, lit a cigarette, paused, started to turn his face up—

Dan jabbed at a lever. The cage shot back through

the wall. He was in a plain room with a depression in the floor, a wide window with a planter filled with glowing blue plants.

The door opened. Even blue, the girl looked graceful as a deer as she took a last bite of the apple and stepped into the ten-foot-square sunken tub. Dan held his breath. The girl tossed the apple core aside, seemed to suddenly become aware of eyes on her, whirled—

With a sudden lurch that threw Dan against the steel bars, the cage shot through the wall into the open air and hurtled off with an accleration that kept him pinned, helpless. He groped for the controls, hauled at a lever. There was no change. The cage rushed on, rising higher. In the distance, Dan saw the skyline of a town on the horizon, approaching with frightful speed. A tall office building reared up fifteen stories high. He was headed dead for it—

He covered his ears, braced himself—

With an abruptness that flung him against the opposite side of the cage, the machine braked, shot through the wall and slammed to a stop. Dan sank to the floor of the cage, breathing hard. There was a loud *click*! and the glow faded.

With a lunge, Dan scrambled out of the cage. He stood looking around at a simple brown-painted office, dimly lit by sunlight filtered through elaborate venetian blinds. There were posters on the wall, a potted plant by the door, a heap of framed paintings beside it, and at the far side of the room a desk. And behind the desk—something.

2

Dan gaped at a head the size of a beach ball, mounted on a torso like a hundred-gallon bag of water. Two large brown eyes blinked at him from

points eight inches apart. Immense hands with too
many fingers unfolded and reached to open a brown
paper carton, dip in, then toss three peanuts, deliberately, one by one, into a gaping mouth that opened
just above the brown eyes.

"Who're you?" a bass voice demanded from somewhere near the floor.

"I'm . . . I'm . . . Dan Slane . . . your honor."

"What happened to Percy and Fiorello?"

"They—I—There was this cop, Kelly—"

"Oh-oh." The brown eyes blinked deliberately.
The too-many-fingered hands closed the peanut carton and tucked it into a drawer.

"Well, it was a sweet racket while it lasted," the
basso voice said. "A pity to terminate so happy an
enterprise. Still . . ." A noise like an amplified Bronx
cheer issued from the wide mouth.

"How . . . what . . . ?"

"The carrier returns here automatically when the
charge drops below a critical value," the voice said.
"A necessary measure to discourage big ideas on the
part of wisenheimers in my employ. May I ask how
you happen to be aboard the carrier, by the way?"

"I just wanted—I mean, after I figured out—that
is, the police . . . I went for help," Dan finished
lamely.

"Help? Out of the picture, unfortunately. One
must maintain one's anonymity, you'll appreciate.
My operation here is under wraps at present. Ah, I
don't suppose you brought any paintings?"

Dan shook his head. He was staring at the posters.
His eyes, accustoming themselves to the gloom of
the office, could now make out the vividly drawn
outline of a creature resembling an alligator-headed
giraffe rearing up above foliage. The next poster
showed a face similar to the beach ball behind the
desk, with red circles painted around the eyes. The

next was a view of a yellow volcano spouting fire into a black sky.

"Too bad." The words seemed to come from under the desk. Dan squinted, caught a glimpse of coiled purplish tentacles. He gulped and looked up to catch a brown eye upon him. Only one. The other seemed to be busily at work studying the ceiling.

"I hope," the voice said, "that you ain't harboring no reactionary racial prejudices."

"Gosh, no," Dan reassured the eye. "I'm crazy about—uh—"

"Vorplischers," the voice said. "From Vorplisch, or Vega, as you locals call it." The Bronx cheer sounded again. "How I long to glimpse once more my native fens! Wherever one wanders, there's no pad like home."

"That reminds me," Dan said. "I have to be running along now." He sidled toward the door.

"Stick around, Dan," the voice rumbled. "How about a drink? I can offer you Chateau Neuf du Pape '59, Romany Conte, '32, goat's milk, Pepsi—"

"No, thanks."

"If you don't mind, I believe I'll have a Big Orange." The Vorplischer swiveled to a small refrigerator, removed an immense bottle fitted with a nipple and turned back to Dan. "Now, I got a proposition which may be of some interest to you. The loss of Percy and Fiorello is a serious blow, but we may yet recoup the situation. You made the scene at a most opportune time. What I got in mind is, with those two clowns out of the picture, a vacancy exists on my staff, which you might fill. How does that grab you?"

"You mean you want me to take over operating the time machine?"

"Time machine?" The brown eyes blinked alternately. "I fear some confusion exists. I don't quite dig the significance of the term."

"That thing," Dan jabbed a thumb toward the cage. "The machine I came here in. You want me—"

"Time machine," the voice repeated. "Some sort of chronometer, perhaps?"

"Huh?"

"I pride myself on my command of the local idiom, yet I confess the implied concept snows me." The nine-fingered hands folded on the desk. The beach-ball head leaned forward interestedly. "Clue me, Dan. What's a time machine?"

"Well, it's what you use to travel through time."

The brown eyes blinked in agitated alternation. "Apparently I've loused up my investigation of the local cultural background. I had no idea you were capable of that sort of thing." The immense head leaned back, the wide mouth opening and closing rapidly. "And to think I've been spinning my wheels collecting primitive 2-D art!"

"But—don't you have a time machine? I mean, isn't that one?"

"That? That's merely a carrier. Now tell me more about your time machines. A fascinating concept! My superiors will be delighted at this development— and astonished as well. They regard this planet as Endsville."

"Your superiors?" Dan eyed the window; much too far to jump. Maybe he could reach the machine and try a getaway—

"I hope you're not thinking of leaving suddenly," the beach ball said, following Dan's glance. One of the eighteen fingers touched a six-inch yellow cylinder lying on the desk. "Until the carrier is fueled, I'm afraid it's quite useless. But, to put you in the picture, I'd best introduce myself and explain my mission here. I'm Blote, Trader Fourth Class, in the employ of the Vegan Confederation. My job is to develop new sources of novelty items for the impulse-emporia of the entire Secondary Quadrant."

"But the way Percy and Fiorello came sailing in through the wall! That *has* to be a time machine they were riding in. Nothing else could just materialize out of thin air like that."

"You seem to have a time-machine fixation, Dan," Blote chided. "You shouldn't assume, just because you people have developed time travel, that everyone has. Now"—Blote's voice sank to a bass whisper—"I'll make a deal with you, Dan. You'll secure a small time machine in good condition for me. And in return—"

"*I'm* supposed to supply *you* with a time machine?"

Blote waggled a stubby forefinger at Dan. "I dislike pointing it out, Dan, but you are in a rather awkward position at the moment. Illegal entry, illegal possession of property, trespass—then doubtless some embarrassment exists back at the Snithian residence. I daresay Mr. Kelly would have a warm welcome for you. And, of course, I myself would deal rather harshly with any attempt on your part to take a powder." The Vegan flexed all eighteen fingers, drummed his tentacles under the desk, and rolled one eye, bugging the other at Dan.

"Whereas, on the other hand," Blote's bass voice went on, "you and me got the basis of a sweet deal. You supply the machine, and I fix you up with an abundance of the local medium of exchange. Equitable enough, I should say. What about it, Dan?"

"Ah, let me see," Dan temporized. "Time machine. Time machine—"

"Don't attempt to weasel on me, Dan," Blote rumbled ominously.

"I'd better look in the phone book," Dan suggested.

Silently, Blote produced a dog-eared directory.
Dan opened it.

"Time, time. Let's see . . ." He brightened.
"Time, Incorporated; local branch office. Two twenty-one Maple Street."

"A sales center?" Blote inquired. "Or a manufacturing complex?"

"Both," Dan said. "I'll just nip over and—"

"That won't be necessary, Dan," Blote said. "I'll accompany you." He took the directory, studied it.

"Remarkable! A common commodity, openly on sale, and I failed to notice it. Still, a ripe bope-nut can fall from a small tree as well as from a large." He went to his desk, rummaged, came up with a handful of fuel cells. "Now off to gather in the time machine." He took his place in the carrier, patted the seat beside him with a wide hand. "Come, Dan. Get a wiggle on."

Hesitantly, Dan moved to the carrier. The bluff was all right up to a point—but the point had just about been reached. He took his seat. Blote moved a lever. The familiar blue glow sprang up. "Kindly direct me, Dan," Blote demanded. "Two twenty-one Maple Street, I believe you said."

"I don't know the town very well," Dan said, "but Maple's over that way."

Blote worked levers. The carrier shot out into a ghostly afternoon sky. Faint outlines of buildings, like faded negatives, spread below. Dan looked around, spotted lettering on a square five-story structure.

"Over there," he said. Blote directed the machine as it swooped smoothly toward the flat roof Dan indicated.

"Better let me take over now," Dan suggested. "I want to be sure to get us to the right place."

"Very well, Dan."

Dan dropped the carrier through the roof, passed down through a dimly seen office. Blote twiddled a small knob. The scene around the cage grew even fainter. "Best we remain unnoticed," he explained.

The cage descended steadily. Dan peered out, searching for identifying landmarks. He levelled off at the second floor, cruised along a barely visible corridor. Blote's eyes rolled, studying the small chambers along both sides of the passage at once.

"Ah, this must be the assembly area," he exclaimed. "I see the machines employ a bar-type construction, not unlike our carriers."

"That's right," Dan said, staring through the haziness. "This is where they do time. . . ." He tugged at a lever suddenly; the machine veered left, flickered through a barred door, came to a halt. Two nebulous figures loomed beside the cage. Dan cut the switch. If he'd guessed wrong—

The scene fluoresced, pink sparks crackling, then popped into sharp focus. Blote scrambled out, brown eyes swivelling to take in the concrete walls, the barred door and—

"You!" a hoarse voice bellowed.

"Grab him!" someone yelled.

Blote recoiled, threshing his ambulatory members in a fruitless attempt to regain the carrier as Percy and Fiorello closed in. Dan hauled at a lever. He caught a last glimpse of three struggling, blue-lit figures as the carrier shot away through the cell wall.

Dan slumped back against the seat with a sigh. Now that he was in the clear, he would have to decide on his next move—fast. There was no telling what other resources Blote might have. He would have to hide the carrier, then—

A low growling was coming from somewhere, rising in pitch and volume. Dan sat up, alarmed. This was no time for a malfunction.

The sound rose higher, into a penetrating wail. There was no sign of mechanical trouble. The carrier glided on, swooping now over a nebulous landscape of trees and houses. Dan covered his ears against the deafening shriek, like all the police sirens in town blaring at once. If the carrier stopped it would be a long fall from here. Dan worked the controls, dropping toward the distant earth.

The noise seemed to lessen, descending the scale. Dan slowed, brought the carrier in to the corner of a wide park. He dropped the last few inches and cut the switch.

As the glow died, the siren faded into silence.

Dan stepped from the carrier and looked around. Whatever the noise was, it hadn't attracted any attention from the scattered pedestrians in the park. Perhaps it was some sort of burglar alarm. But if so, why hadn't it gone into action earlier? Dan took a deep breath. Sound or no sound, he would have to get back into the carrier and transfer it to a secluded spot where he could study it at leisure. He stepped back in, reached for the controls—

There was a sudden chill in the air. The bright surface of the dials before him frosted over. There was a loud *pop*! like a giant flashbulb exploding. Dan stared from the seat at an iridescent rectangle which hung suspended near the carrier. Its surface rippled, faded to blankness. In a swirl of frosty air, a tall figure dressed in a tight-fitting white uniform stepped through.

Dan gaped at the small round head, the dark-skinned, long-nosed face, the long, muscular arms, the hands, their backs tufted with curly red-brown hair, the strange long-heeled feet in soft boots. A neat pillbox cap with a short visor was strapped low over the deep-set yellowish eyes, which turned in his direction. The wide mouth opened in a smile which showed square yellowish teeth.

"*Alors, monsieur,*" the newcomer said, bending his knees and back in a quick bow. "*Vous été une indigine, n'est ce pas?*"

"No compree," Dan choked out. "Uh . . . juh no parlay Fransay . . ."

"My error. This is the Anglic colonial sector, isn't it? Stupid of me. Permit me to introduce myself. I'm Dzhackoon, Field Agent of Class Five, Inter-dimensional Monitor Service."

"That siren," Dan said. "Was that you?"

Dzhackoon nodded. "For a moment, it appeared you were disinclined to stop. I'm glad you decided to be reasonable."

"What outfit did you say you were with?" Dan asked.

"The Inter-dimensional Monitor Service."

"Inter-what?"

"Dimensional. The word is imprecise, of course, but it's the best our language coder can do, using the Anglic vocabulary."

"What do you want with me?"

Dzhackoon smiled reprovingly. "You know the penalty for operation of an unauthorized reversed-phase vehicle in Interdicted territory. I'm afraid you'll have to come along with me to Headquarters."

"Wait a minute! You mean you're arresting me?"

"That's a harsh term, but I suppose it amounts to that."

"Look here, uh—Dzhackoon. I just wandered in off the street. I don't know anything about Interdicts and reversed-whoozis vehicles. Just let me out of here."

Dzhackoon shook his head. "I'm afraid you'll have to tell it to the Inspector." He smiled amiably, gestured toward the shimmering rectangle through which he had arrived. From the edge, it was completely invisible. It looked, Dan thought, like a hole snipped in reality. He glanced at Dzhackoon. If he stepped in fast and threw a left to the head and followed up with a right to the short ribs—

"I'm armed, of course," the Agent said apologetically.

"Okay," Dan sighed. "But I'm going under protest."

"Don't be nervous," Dzhackoon said cheerfully. "Just step through quickly."

Dan edged up to the glimmering surface. He gritted his teeth, closed his eyes and took a step. There was a momentary sensation of searing heat. . . .

His eyes flew open. He was in a long, narrow room with walls finished in bright green tile. Hot yellow light flooded down from the high ceiling. Along the wall, a series of cubicles were arranged. Tall, white-uniformed creatures moved briskly about. Nearby stood a group of short, immensely burly individuals in yellow. Lounging against the wall at the far end of the room, Dan glimpsed a round-shouldered figure in red, with great bushes of hair fringing a bright blue face. An arm even longer than Dzhackoon's wielded a toothpick on a row of great white fangs.

"This way," Dzhackoon said. Dan followed him to a cubicle, curious eyes following him. A creature indistinguishable from the Field Agent except for a twist of red braid on each wrist looked up from a desk.

"I've picked up that reversed-phase violator, Ghunt," Dzhackoon said. "Anglic Sector, Locus C 922A4."

Ghunt rose. "Let me see; Anglic Sector . . . Oh, yes." He extended a hand. Dan took it gingerly; it was a strange hand—hot, dry and coarse-skinned, like a dog's paw. He pumped it twice and let it go.

"Wonderfully expressive," Ghunt said. "Empty

hand, no weapon. The implied savagery . . ." He
eyed Dan curiously.

"Remarkable. I've studied your branch, of course,
but I've never had the pleasure of actually seeing
one of you chaps before. That skin; amazing. Ah . . .
may I look at your hands?"

Dan extended a hand. The other took it in bony
fingers, studied it, turned it over, examined the
nails. Stepping closer, he peered at Dan's eyes and
hair.

"Would you mind opening your mouth, please?"
Dan complied. Ghunt clucked, eyeing the teeth. He
walked around Dan, murmuring his wonderment.

"Uh . . . pardon my asking," Dan said, "but are
you what—uh—people are going to look like in the
future?"

"Eh?" the round yellowish eyes blinked; the wide
mouth curved in a grin. "I doubt that very much,
old chap." He chuckled. "Can't undo half a million
years of divergent evolution, you know."

"You mean you're from the past?" Dan croaked.

"The past? I'm afraid I don't follow you."

"You don't mean—we're all going to die out and
monkeys are going to take over?" Dan blurted.

"Monkeys? Let me see. I've heard of them. Some
sort of small primate, like a miniature Anthropos.
You have them at home, do you? Fascinating!" He
shook his head regretfully. "I certainly wish regulations allowed me to pay your sector a visit."

"But you *are* time travellers," Dan insisted.

"Time travellers?" Ghunt laughed aloud.

"An exploded theory," Dzhackoon said. "Super-
stition."

"Then how did you get to the park from here?"

"A simple focused portal. Merely a matter of ele-
mentary stressed-field mechanics."

"That doesn't tell me much," Dan said. "Where am I? Who are you?"

"Explanations are in order, of course," Ghunt said. "Have a chair. Now, if I remember correctly, in your locus, there are only a few species of Anthropos extant—"

"Just the one," Dzhackoon put in. "These fellows look fragile, but oh, brother!"

"Oh, yes; I recall. This was the locus where the hairless variant systematically hunted down other varieties." He clucked at Dan reprovingly. "Don't you find it lonely?"

"Of course, there are a couple of rather curious retarded forms there," Dzhackoon said. "Actual living fossils; sub-intellectual Anthropos. There's one called the gorilla, and the chimpanzee, the orangutan, the gibbon—and, of course, a whole spectrum of the miniature forms."

"I suppose that when the ferocious mutation established its supremacy, the others retreated to the less competitive ecological niches and expanded at that level," Ghunt mused. "Pity. I assume the gorilla and the others are degenerate forms?"

"Possibly."

"Excuse me," Dan said. "But about that explanation . . ."

"Oh, sorry. Well, to begin with, Dzhackoon and I are—ah—Australopithecines, I believe your term is. We're one of the many varieties of Anthropos native to normal loci. The workers in yellow, whom you may have noticed, are akin to your extinct Neanderthals. Then there are the Pekin derivatives—the blue-faced chaps—and the Rhodesians—"

"What are these loci you keep talking about? And how can cavemen still be alive?"

Ghunt's eyes wandered past Dan. He jumped to his feet. "Ah, good day, Inspector!" Dan turned. A grizzled Australopithecine with a tangle of red braid at collar and wrists stared at him glumly.

"Harrumph!" the Inspector said. "Albinism and alopecia. Not catching, I hope?"

"A genetic deficiency, Excellency," Dzhackoon said. "This is a *Homo sapiens*, a naturally bald form from a rather curious locus."

"Sapiens? Sapiens? Now, that seems to ring a bell." The oldster blinked at Dan. "You're not—" He waggled fingers in instinctive digital-mnemonic stimulus. Abruptly he stiffened. "Why, this is one of those fratricidal deviants!" He backed off. "He should be under restraint, Ghunt! Constable! Get a strong-arm squad in here! This creature is dangerous!"

"Inspector. I'm sure—" Ghunt started.

"That's an order!" the Inspector barked. He switched to an incomprehensible language, bellowed more commands. Several of the thick-set Neanderthal types appeared, moving in to seize Dan's arms. He looked around at chinless, wide-mouthed brown faces with incongruous blue eyes and lank blond hair.

"What's this all about?" he demanded. "I want a lawyer!"

"Never mind that!" the Inspector shouted. "I know how to deal with miscreants of your stripe!" He stared distastefully at Dan. "Hairless! Putty-colored! Revolting! Planning more mayhem, are you? Preparing to branch out into the civilized loci to wipe out all competitive life, is that it?"

"I brought him here, Inspector," Dzhackoon put in. "It was a routine traffic violation."

"I'll decide what's routine here! Now, Sapiens! What fiendish scheme have you up your sleeve, eh?"

"Daniel Slane, civilian, Social Security number 456-7329-988," Dan said.

"Eh?"

"Name, rank, and serial number," Dan explained. "I'm not answering any other questions."

"This means penal relocation, Sapiens! Unlawful departure from native locus, willful obstruction of justice—"

"You forgot being born without permission, and unauthorized breathing."

"Insolence!" the Inspector snarled. "I'm warning you, Sapiens, it's in my power to make things miserable for you. Now, how did you induce Agent Dzhackoon to bring you here?"

"Well, a good fairy came and gave me three wishes—"

"Take him away," the Inspector screeched. "Sector 97; an unoccupied locus."

"Unoccupied? That seems pretty extreme, doesn't it?" one of the guards commented, wrinkling his heavily ridged brow.

"Unoccupied! If it bothers you, perhaps I can arrange for you to join him there!"

The Neanderthaloid guard yawned widely, showing white teeth. He nodded to Dan, motioned him ahead. "Don't mind Spoghodo," he said loudly. "He's getting old."

"Sorry about all this," a voice hissed near Dan's ear. Dzhackoon—Ghunt, he couldn't say which— leaned near. "I'm afraid you'll have to go along to the penal area, but I'll try to straighten things out later."

Back in the concourse, Dan's guard escorted him past cubicles where busy IDMS agents reported to harassed seniors, through an archway into a room lined with narrow grey panels. It looked like a gym locker room.

"Ninety-seven," the guard said. He went to a wall chart, studied the fine print with the aid of a blunt, hairy finger, then set a dial on the wall. "Here we go," he said. He pushed a button beside one of the lockers. Its surface clouded and became iridescent.

"Just step through fast. Happy landings."

"Thanks," Dan ducked his head and pushed through the opening in a puff of frost.

He was standing on a steep hillside, looking down across a sweep of meadow to a plain far below. There were clumps of trees, and a river. In the distance a herd of animals grazed among low shrubbery. No road wound along the valley floor; no boats dotted the river; no village nestled at its bend. The far hills were innocent of trails, fences, houses, the rectangles of plowed acres. There were no contrails in the wide blue sky. No vagrant aroma of exhaust fumes, no mutter of internal combustion, no tin cans, no pop bottles—

In short, no people.

Dan turned. The portal still shimmered faintly in the bright air. He thrust his head through, found himself staring into the locker room. The yellow-clad Neanderthaloid glanced at him.

"Say," Dan said, ignoring the sensation of a hot wire around his neck, "can't we talk this thing over?"

"Better get your head out of there before it shuts down," the guard said cheerfully. "Otherwise— ssskkktt!"

"What about some reading matter? And look, I get these head colds. Does the temperature drop here at night? Any dangerous animals? What do I eat?"

"Here." The guard reached into a hopper, took out a handful of pamphlets. "These are supposed to be for guys that are relocated without prejudice. You know, poor slobs that just happened to see too much, but I'll let you have one. Let's see . . .

Anglic, Anglic . . ." He selected one, handed it to Dan.

"Thanks."

"Better get clear."

Dan withdrew his head. He sat down on the grass and looked over the booklet. It was handsomely printed in bright colors. WELCOME TO RELOCA-TION CENTER NO. 23 said the cover. Below the heading was a photo of a group of sullen-looking creatures of varying heights and degrees of hairiness wearing paper hats. The caption read: *Newcomers Are Welcomed Into a Gay Round of Social Activity. Hi, Newcomer!*

Dan opened the book. A photo showed a scene identical to the one before him, except that in place of the meadow, there was a parklike expanse of lawn, dotted with rambling buildings with long porches lined with rockers. There were picnic tables under spreading trees, and beyond, on the river, a yacht basin crowded with canoes and rowboats.

"Life in a Community Center is Grand Fun!" Dan read. "Activities! Brownies, Cub Scouts, Boy Scouts, Girl Scouts, Sea Scouts, Tree Scouts, Cave Scouts, PTA, Shriners, Bear Cult, Rotary, Daughters of the Eastern Star, Mothers of the Big Banana, Dianetics—you name it! A Group for Everyone, and Everyone in a Group!

"Classes in conversational Urdu, Sprotch, Yiddish, Gaelic, Fundu, etc; knot-tying, rug-hooking, leatherwork, Greek Dancing, finger-painting and many, many others!

Little Theatre!
Indian Dance Pageants!
Round Table Discussions!
Town Meetings!"

Dan thumbed on through the pages of emphatic print, stopped at a double-page spread labelled *A Few Do's and Don'ts*.

All of us want to make a GO of relocation. So—let's remember the Uranium Rule: Don't Do It! The Other Guy May Be Bigger!

Remember the other fellow's taboos!
What to you might be merely a wholesome picnic or mating bee may offend others. What some are used to doing in groups, others consider a solitary activity. Most taboos have to do with eating, sex, elimination or gods; so remember, look before you sit down, lie down, squat down or kneel down!

Ladies With Beards Please Note:
Friend husband may be on the crew clearing clogged drains—so watch that shedding in the lavatories, eh, girls? And you fellas, too! Sure, good grooming pays—but groom each other out in the open, okay?

NOTE: There has been some agitation for "separate but equal" facilities. Now, honestly, folks; is that in the spirit of Center No. 23? Males and females *will continue to use the same johns* as always. No sexual chauvinism will be tolerated.

A Word to The Kiddies!
No brachiating will be permitted in the Social Center area. After all, a lot of the Dads sleep up there. There are plenty of other trees!

Daintiness Pays!
In these more-active-than-ever days, Personal Effluvium can get away from us almost before we notice. And that hearty scent may not be as satisfying to others as it is to ourselves! So remember, fellas:

watch that P.E.! (Lye soap, eau de Cologne, flea powder and other beauty aids available at supply shed!)

Dan tossed the book aside. There were worse things than solitude. It looked like a pretty nice world—and it was all his—so far.

The entire North American continent, all of South America, Europe, Asia, Africa—the works. He could cut down trees, build a hut, furnish it. There'd be hunting—he could make a bow and arrows—and the skins would do to make clothes. He could start a little farming, fish the streams, sun bathe—all the things he'd never had time to do back home. It wouldn't be so bad. And eventually Dzhackoon would arrange for his release. It might be just the kind of vacation—

"Ah, Dan, my boy!" a bass voice boomed. Dan jumped and spun around.

Blote's immense face blinked at him from the portal. There was a large green bruise over one eye. He wagged a finger reproachfully.

"That was a dirty trick, Dan. My former employees were somewhat disgruntled, I'm sorry to say. But we'd best be off now. There's no time to waste."

"How did you get here?" Dan demanded.

"I employed a pocket signaller to recall my carrier—and none too soon." He touched his bruised eye gingerly. "A glance at the instruments showed me that you had visited the park. I followed and observed a TDMS Portal. Being of an adventurous turn, and, of course, concerned for your welfare, I stepped through—"

"Why didn't they arrest you? I was picked up for operating the carrier."

"They had some such notion. A whiff of stun gas served to discourage them. Now let's hurry along before the management revives."

"Wait a minute, Blote. I'm not sure I want to be rescued by you—in spite of your concern for my welfare."

"Rubbish, Dan! Come along." Blote looked around. "Frightful place! No population! No commerce! No deals!"

"It has its compensations; I think I'll stay. You run along."

"Abandon a colleague? Never!"

"If you're still expecting me to deliver a time machine, you're out of luck. I don't have one."

"No? Ah, well, in a way I'm relieved. Such a device would upset accepted hyper-physical theory. Now, Dan, you mustn't imagine I harbor ulterior motives—but I believe our association will yet prove fruitful."

Dan rubbed a finger across his lower lip thoughtfully. "Look, Blote, you need my help. Maybe you can help me at the same time. If I come along, I want it understood that we work together. I have an idea—"

"But of course, Dan! Now shake a leg!"

Dan sighed and stepped through the portal. The yellow-clad guard lay on the floor, snoring. Blote led the way back into the great hall. TDMS officials were scattered across the floor, slumped over desks, or lying limp in chairs. Blote stopped before one of a row of shimmering portals.

"After you, Dan."

"Are you sure this is the right one?"

"Quite."

Dan stepped through in the now familiar chill and found himself back in the park. A small dog sniffing at the carrier caught sight of Blote, lowered his leg and fled.

"I want to pay Mr. Snithian a visit," Dan said, climbing into a seat.

"My idea exactly," Blote agreed, lowering his bulk into place.

"Don't get the idea I'm going to help you steal anything."

"Dan! A most unkind remark. I merely wish to look into certain matters."

"Just so you don't start looking into the safe."

Blote *tsk!*ed, moved a lever. The carrier climbed over a row of blue trees and headed west.

4

Blote brought the carrier in high over the Snithian Estate, dropped lower and descended gently through the roof. The pale, spectral servants moving about their duties in the upper hall failed to notice the wraithlike cage passing soundlessly among them.

In the dining room, Dan caught sight of the girl—Snithian's daughter, perhaps—arranging shadowy flowers on a sideboard.

"Let me take it," Dan whispered. Blote nodded. Dan steered for the kitchen, guided the carrier to the spot on which he had first emerged from the vault, then edged down through the floor. He brought the carrier to rest and neutralized all switches in a shower of sparks and blue light.

The vault door stood open. There were pictures stacked on the bunk now, against the wall, on the floor. Dan stepped from the carrier, went to the nearest heap of paintings. They had been dumped hastily, it seemed. They weren't even wrapped. He examined the topmost canvas, still in a heavy frame; as though, he reflected, it had just been removed from a gallery wall—

"Let's look around for Snithian," Dan said. "I want to talk to him."

"I suggest we investigate the upper floors, Dan. Doubtless his personal pad is there."

"You use the carrier; I'll go up and look the house over."

"As you wish, Dan." Blote and the carrier flickered and faded from view.

Dan stooped, picked up the pistol he had dropped half an hour earlier in the scuffle with Fiorello and stepped out into the hall. All was silent. He climbed stairs, looked into rooms. The house seemed deserted. On the third floor he went along a corridor, checking each room. The last room on the west side was fitted as a study. There was a stack of paintings on a table near the door. Dan went to them, examined the top one.

It looked familiar. Wasn't it one that *Look* said was in the Art Institute at Chicago?

There was a creak as of an unoiled hinge. Dan spun around. A door stood open at the far side of the room—a connecting door to a bedroom, probably.

"Keep well away from the carrier, Mr. Slane," a high, thin voice said from the shadows. The tall, cloaked figure of Clyde W. Snithian stepped into view, a needle-barreled pistol in his hand.

"I thought you'd be back," he piped. "It makes my problem much simpler. If you hadn't appeared soon, it would have been neccessary for me to shift the scene of my operations. That would have been a nuisance."

Dan eyed the gun. "There are a lot more paintings downstairs than there were when I left," he said. "I don't know much about art, but I recognize a few of them."

"Copies," Snithian snapped.

"This is no copy," Dan tapped the top painting on the stack. "It's an original. You can feel the brushwork."

"Not prints, of course. Copies," Snithian whinnied. "Exact copies."

"These paintings are stolen, Mr. Snithian. Why would a wealthy man like you take to stealing art?"

"I'm not here to answer questions, Mr. Slane!" The weapon in Snithian's hand buzzed. A wave of pain swept over Dan. Snithian cackled, lowering the gun. "You'll soon learn better manners."

Dan's hand went to his pocket, came out holding the automatic. He aimed it at Snithian's face. The industrialist froze, eyes on Dan's gun.

"Drop the gun," Dan snapped. Snithian's weapon clattered to the floor. "Now let's go and find Kelly," Dan ordered.

"Wait!" Snithian shrilled. "I can make you a rich man, Slane."

"Not by stealing paintings."

"You don't understand. This is more than petty larceny!!"

"That's right. It's grand larceny. These pictures are worth millions."

"I can show you things that will completely change your attitude. Actually, I've acted throughout in the best interests of humanity!"

Dan gestured with the gun. "Don't plan anything clever. I'm not used to guns. This thing will go off at the least excuse, and then I'd have a murder to explain."

"That would be an inexcusable blunder on your part!" Snithian keened. "I'm a very important figure, Slane." He crossed the deep-pile rug to a glass-doored cabinet. "This," he said, taking out a flat black box, "contains a fortune in precious stones." He lifted the lid. Dan stepped closer. A row of brilliant red gems nestled in a bed of cotton.

"Rubies?"

"Flawless—and perfectly matched." Snithian

whinnied. "*Perfectly* matched. Worth a fortune. They're yours, if you cooperate."

"You said you were going to change my attitude. Better get started."

"Listen to me, Slane. I'm not operating independently. I'm employed by the Ivroy, whose power is incalculable. My assignment had been to rescue from destruction irreplaceable works of art fated to be consumed in atomic fire."

"What do you mean—fated?"

"The Ivroy knows these things. These paintings—all your art—are unique in the Galaxy. Others admire but they cannot emulate. In the cosmos of the far future, the few surviving treasures of your dawn art will be valued beyond all other wealth. They alone will give a renewed glimpse of the universe as it appeared to the eyes of your strange race in its glory."

"My strange race?"

Snithian drew himself up. "I am not of your race." He threw his cloak aside and straightened.

Dan gaped as Snithian's body unfolded, rising up, long, three-jointed arms flexing, stretching out. The bald head ducked now under the beamed ceiling. Snithian chuckled shrilly.

"What about that inflexible attitude of yours, now, Mister Slane?" he piped. "Have I made my point?"

"Yes, but—" Dan squeaked. He cleared his throat and tried again. "But I've still got the gun."

"Oh, that." An eight-foot arm snaked out, flicked the gun aside. "I've only temporized with you because you can be useful to me, Mister Slane. I dislike running about, and I therefore employ locals to do my running for me. Accept my offer of employment, and you'll be richly rewarded."

"Why me?"

"You already know of my presence here. If I can enlist your loyalty, there will be no need to dispose of you, with the attendant annoyance from police, relatives and busybodies. I'd like you to act as my agent in the collection of the works."

"Nuts to you!" Dan said. "I'm not helping any bunch of skinheads commit robbery."

"This is for the Ivroy, you fool!" Snithian said. "The mightiest power in the cosmos!"

"This Ivroy doesn't sound so hot to me—robbing art galleries—"

"To be adult is to be disillusioned. Only realities count. But no matter. The question remains: Will you serve me loyally?"

"Hell, no!" Dan snapped.

"Too bad. I see you mean what you say. It's to be expected, I suppose. Even an infant fire-cat has fangs."

"You're damn right I mean it. How did you get Percy and Fiorello on your payroll? I'm surprised even a couple of bums would go to work for a scavenger like you."

"I suppose you refer to the precious pair recruited by Blote. That was a mistake, I fear. It seemed perfectly reasonable at the time. Tell me, how did you overcome the Vegan? They're a very capable race, generally speaking."

"You and he work together, eh?" Dan said. "That makes things a little clearer. This is the collection station and Blote is the fence."

"Enough of your conjectures. You leave me no choice but to dispose of you. It's a nuisance, but it can't be helped. I'm afraid I'll have to ask you to accompany me down to the vault."

Dan eyed the door; if he were going to make a break, now was the time—

*

The whine of the carrier sounded. The ghostly cage glided through the wall and settled gently between Dan and Snithian. The glow died.

Blote waved cheerfully to Dan as he eased his grotesque bulk from the seat.

"Good day to you, Snithian," Blote boomed. "I see you've met Dan. An enterprising fellow."

"What brings you here, Gom Blote?" Snithian shrilled. "I thought you'd be well on your way to Vorplisch by now."

"I was tempted, Snithian. But I don't spook easy. There is the matter of some unfinished business."

"Excellent!" Snithian exclaimed. "I'll have another consignment ready for you by tomorrow."

"Tomorrow! How is it possible, with Percy and Fiorello lodged in the hoosegow?" Blote looked around; his eye fell on the stacked paintings. He moved across to them, lifted one, glanced at the next, then shuffled rapidly through the stack. He turned.

"What duplicity is this, Snithian?" he rumbled. "All identical! Our agreement called for limited editions, not mass production! My principals will be furious! My reputation—"

"Shrivel your reputation!" Snithian keened. "I have more serious problems at the moment! My entire position's been compromised. I'm faced with the necessity of disposing of this blundering fool!"

"Dan? Why, I'm afraid I can't allow that, Snithian." Blote moved to the carrier, dumped an armful of duplicate paintings in the cage. "Evidence," he said. "The Confederation has methods for dealing with sharp practice. Come, Dan, if you're ready . . ."

"You dare to cross me?" Snithian hissed. "I, who act for the Ivroy?"

Blote motioned to the carrier. "Get in, Dan. We'll be going now." He rolled both eyes to bear on Snithian. "And I'll deal with *you* later," he rumbled. "No one pulls a fast one on Gom Blote, Trader Fourth Class—or on the Vegan Federation."

Snithian moved suddenly, flicking out a spidery arm to seize the weapon he had dropped, aim and trigger. Dan, in a wash of pain, felt his knees fold. He fell slackly to the floor. Beside him, Blote sagged, his tentacles limp.

"I credited you with more intelligence," Snithian cackled. "Now I have an extra ton of protoplasm to dispose of. The carrier will be useful in that connection."

5

Dan felt a familiar chill in the air. A Portal appeared. In a puff of icy mist, a tall figure stepped through.

Gone was the tight uniform. In its place, the lanky Australopithecine wore skin-tight blue jeans and a loose sweatshirt. An oversized beret clung to the small round head. Immense dark glasses covered the yellowish eyes, and sandals flapped on the bare, long-toed feet. Dzhackoon waved a long cigarette holder at the group.

"Ah, a stroke of luck! How nice to find you standing by. I had expected to have to conduct an intensive search within the locus. Thus the native dress. However—" Dzhackoon's eyes fell on Snithian standing stiffly by, the gun out of sight.

"You're of a race unfamiliar to me," he said. "Still, I assume you're aware of the Interdict on all Anthropoid-populated loci?"

"And who might you be?" Snithian inquired loftily.

"I'm a Field Agent of the Interdimensional Monitor Service."

"Ah, yes. Well, your Interdict means nothing to me. I'm operating directly under Ivroy auspices." Snithian touched a glittering pin on his drab cloak.

Dzhackoon sighed. "There goes the old arrest record."

"He's a crook!" Dan cut in. "He's been robbing art galleries!"

"Keep calm, Dan," Blote murmured. "No need to be overly explicit."

The Agent turned to look the Trader over.

"Vegan, aren't you? I imagine you're the fellow I've been chasing."

"Who, me?" the bass voice rumbled. "Look, officer, I'm a home-loving family man, just passing through. As a matter of fact—"

The uniformed creature nodded toward the paintings in the carrier. "Gathered a few souvenirs, I see."

"For the wives and kiddie. Just a little something to brighten up the hive."

"The penalty for exploitation of a sub-cultural Anthropoid-occupied body is stasis for a period not to exceed one reproductive cycle. If I recall my Vegan biology, that's quite a stretch."

"Why, officer! Surely you're not putting the arm on a respectable, law-abiding being like me? Why, I lost a tentacle fighting in defense of peace—" As he talked, Blote moved toward the carrier.

"—your name, my dear fellow," he went on. "I'll mention it to the Commissioner, a very close friend of mine." Abruptly the Vegan reached for a lever—

The long arms in the tight white jacket reached to haul him back effortlessly. "That was unwise, sir. Now I'll be forced to recommend subliminal reorientation during stasis." He clamped stout handcuffs on Blote's broad wrists.

"You Vegans," he said, dusting his hands briskly. "Will you never learn?"

"Now, officer," Blote said, "You're acting hastily. Actually, I'm working in the interest of this little world, as my associate Dan will gladly confirm. I have information which will be of considerable interest to you. Snithian has stated that he is in the employ of the Ivroy—"

"If the Ivroy's so powerful, why was it necessary to hire Snithian to steal pictures?" Dan interrupted.

"Perish the thought, Dan. Snithian's assignment was merely to duplicate works of art and transmit them to the Ivroy."

"Here," Snithian cut in. "Restrain that obscene mouth!"

Dzhackoon raised a hand. "Kindly remain silent, sir. Permit my prisoners their little chat."

"You may release them to my custody," Snithian snapped.

Dzhackoon shook his head. "Hardly, sir. A most improper suggestion—even from an agent of the Ivroy." He nodded at Dan. "You may continue."

"How do you duplicate works of art?" Dan demanded.

"With a matter duplicator. But, as I was saying, Snithian saw an opportunity to make extra profits by retaining the works for repeated duplications and sale to other customers—such as myself."

"You mean there are other—customers—around?"

"I have dozens of competitors, Dan, all busy exporting your artifacts. You are an industrious and talented race, you know."

"What do they buy?"

"A little of everything, Dan. It's had an influence on your designs already, I'm sorry to say. The work is losing its native purity."

Dan nodded. "I have had the feeling some of this modern furniture was designed for Martians."

"Ganymedans, mostly. The Martians are graphic arts fans, while your automobiles are designed for the Plutonian trade. They have a baroque sense of humor."

"What will the Ivroy do when he finds out Snithian's been double-crossing him?"

"He'll think of something, I daresay. I blame myself for his defection, in a way. You see, it was my carrier which made it possible for Snithian to carry out his thefts. Originally, he would simply enter a gallery, inconspicuously scan a picture, return home and process the recording through the duplicator. The carrier gave him the idea of removing works en masse, duplicating them and returning them the next day. Alas, I agreed to join forces with him. He grew greedy. He retained the paintings here and proceeded to produce vast numbers of copies—which he doubtless sold to my competitors, the crook!"

Dzhackoon had whipped out a notebook and was jotting rapidly.

"Now, let's have those names and addresses," he said. "This will be the biggest round-up in TDMS history."

"And the pinch will be yours, dear sir," Blote said. "I foresee early promotion for you." He held out his shackled wrists. "Would you mind?"

"Well . . ." Dzhackoon hesitated, but unlocked the cuffs. "I think I'm on firm ground. Just don't mention it to Inspector Spoghodo."

"You can't do that!" Snithian snapped. "These persons are dangerous!"

"That is my decision. Now—"

Snithian brought out the pistol with a sudden movement. "I'll brook no interference from meddlers—"

*

There was a sound from the door. All heads
turned. The girl Dan had seen in the house stood in
the doorway, glancing calmly from Snithian to Blote
to Dzhackoon. When her eyes met Dan's she smiled.
Dan thought he had never seen such a beautiful
face—and the figure matched.

"Get out, you fool!" Snithian snapped. "No; come
inside, and shut the door."

"Leave the girl out of this, Snithian," Dan croaked.

"Now I'll have to destroy all of you," Snithian
keened. "You first of all, ugly native!" He aimed the
gun at Dan.

"Put the gun down, Mr. Snithian," the girl said
in a warm, melodious voice. She seemed completely
unworried by the grotesque aliens, Dan noted
abstractedly.

Snithian swivelled on her. "You dare—!"

"Oh, yes, I dare, Snithian." Her voice had a firm
ring now.

Snithian stared at her. "Who . . . are you . . . ?"

"I am the Ivroy."

Snithian wilted. The gun fell to the floor. His fantastically tall figure drooped, his face suddenly gray.

"Return to your home, Snithian," the girl said
sadly. "I will deal with you later."

"But . . . but . . ." His voice was a thin squeak.

"Did you think you could conceal your betrayal
from the Ivroy?" she said softly.

Snithian turned and blundered from the room,
ducking under the low door. The Ivroy turned to
Dzhackoon.

"You and your Service are to be commended," she
said. "I leave the apprehension of the culprits to
you." She nodded at Blote. "I will rely on you to
assist in the task—and to limit your operations there-
after to non-interdicted areas."

"But of course, your worship. You have my word

as a Vegan. Do visit me on Vorplisch some day. I'd love the wives and kiddie to meet you." He blinked rapidly. "So long, Dan. It's been crazy cool."

Dzhackoon and Blote stepped through the Portal. It shimmered and winked out. The Ivroy faced Dan. He swallowed hard, watching the play of light in the shoulder-length hair, golden, fine as spun glass . . .

"Your name is Dan?" Her musical voice interrupted his survey.

"Dan Slane," he said. He took a deep breath. "Are you really the Ivroy?"

"I am of the Ivroy, who are many and one."

"But you look like—just a beautiful girl."

The Ivroy smiled. Her teeth were as even as matched pearls, Dan thought, and as white as—

"I *am* a girl, Dan. We are cousins, you and I— separated by the long mystery of time."

"Blote—and Dzhackoon and Snithian, too—seemed to think the Ivroy ran the Universe. But—"

The Ivroy put her hand on Dan's. It was as soft as a flower petal.

"Don't trouble yourself over this just now, Dan. Would you like to become my agent? I need a trustworthy friend to help me in my work here."

"Doing what?" Dan heard himself say.

"Watching over the race which will one day become the Ivroy."

"I don't understand all this—but I'm willing to try."

"There will be much to learn, Dan. The full use of the mind, control of aging and disease . . . Our work will require many centuries."

"Centuries? But—"

"I'll teach you, Dan."

"It sounds great," Dan said. "Too good to be true.

But how do you know I'm the man for the job? Don't I have to take some kind of test?"

She looked up at him, smiling, her lips slightly parted. On impulse, Dan put a hand under her chin, drew her face close and kissed her on the mouth . . .

A full minute later, the Ivroy, nestled in Dan's arms, looked up at him again.

"You passed the test," she said.

When we say "alien intelligence" we immediately think "alien menace." That may well be a perfectly sound reflex, necessary to our survival; and perhaps not. The evolution of life on this planet has been based on the survival of the fittest—or the readiest to shoot first and inquire afterwards—ever since that first, unique living cell engulfed the almost-living proto-cell beside it—and thus survived. Since then we've learned—or think we've learned—higher principles of empathy, humanity, restraint, love. Can we afford them? When we encounter a life-form far from the Solar System, can we survive that first contact with what may be a killer as ruthless as the AIDS virus? Who is to know just how alien minds really work? First, before we can study them, we must survive. Hindsight is useless. General Straut was an experienced fighter, not least against his superior officers.

Doorstep

Steadying his elbow on the kitchen table serving as a desk, Brigadier General W. F. Straut levelled his binoculars and stared out through the second-floor window of the farmhouse at the bulky object lying canted at the edge of the wood lot. He watched the figures moving over and around the grey mass, then flipped the lever on the field telephone.

"Bill, how are your boys doing?"

"General, since that box this morning—"

"I know all about the box, Bill. It's in Washington by now. What have you got that's new?"

"Sir, I haven't got anything to report yet. . . . I've got four crews on it, and she still looks impervious as hell . . ."

"Still getting the sounds from inside?"

"Intermittently, General."

"I'm giving you one more hour, Major. I want that thing cracked."

The General dropped the phone back on its cradle, and absently peeled the cellophane from a cigar.

288

He had moved fast, he reflected, after the State Police notified him at 9:41 last night. He had his men on the spot, the area evacuated of civilians, and a preliminary report on the way to Washington by midnight. At 2:36, they had discovered the four inch cube lying on the ground fifteen feet from the object—ship, capsule, bomb, whatever it was. But now—four hours later—nothing new . . .

The field phone jangled. He grabbed it up.

"General, we've discovered a thin spot up on the top surface; all we can tell so far is that the wall thickness falls off there . . ."

"All right. Keep after it, Bill."

This was more like it. If he could have this thing wrapped up by the time Washington woke up to the fact that it was something big—well, he'd been waiting a long time for that second star. This was his chance, and he would damn well make the most of it. . . .

Straut looked across the field at the thing. It was half in and half out of the woods, flat-sided, round-ended, featureless. Maybe he should go over and give it a closer look personally. He might spot something the others were missing. It might blow them all to kingdom come any second; but what the hell. He had earned his star on sheer guts in Granada. He still had 'em.

He keyed the phone. "I'm coming down, Bill." On impulse, he strapped a pistol belt on. Not much use against a house-sized bomb, but the heft of it felt good.

The thing looked bigger than ever as the jeep approached it, bumping across the muck of the freshly plowed field. From here he could see a faint line running around, just below the juncture of side and top. Greer hadn't mentioned that. The line was quite obvious; in fact, it was more of a crack. . . .

With a sound like a baseball smacking the catch-

er's mitt, the crack opened; the upper half tilted,
men sliding—then impossibly it stood open, vibrat-
ing, like the roof of a house suddenly lifted. The
driver gunned the jeep. There were cries, and a ragged shrilling that set Straut's teeth on edge. The
men were running back now, two of them dragging a
third. Major Greer emerged from behind the object,
looked about, ran toward him, shouting.

". . . a man dead. It snapped; we weren't expecting it . . ."

Straut jumped out beside the men, who had
stopped now and were looking back. The underside
of the gaping lid was an iridescent black. The shrill
noise sounded thinly across the field. Greer arrived,
panting.

"What happened?" Straut snapped.

"I was . . . checking over that thin spot, General.
The first thing I knew it was . . . coming up under
me. I fell; Tate was at the other side. He held on and
it snapped him loose, against a tree. His skull . . ."

"What the devil's that racket?"

"That's the sound we were getting from inside, before, General. There's something in there, alive—"

"All right; pull yourself together, Major. We're not
unprepared. Bring your halftracks into position. The
tanks will be here in another half-hour."

Straut glanced at the men standing about. He
would show them what leadership meant . . .

"You men keep back," he said. He puffed his cigar
calmly as he walked toward the looming object. The
noise stopped suddenly; that was a relief. There was
a faint and curious odor in the air, something like
chlorine . . . or seaweed . . . or iodine.

There were no marks in the ground surrounding
the thing. It had apparently dropped straight in to
its present position. It was heavy, too. The soft soil
was displaced in a mound a foot high all along the
side.

Behind him, Straut heard a shout go up. He whirled. The men were pointing; the jeep started up, churned toward him, wheels spinning. He looked up. Over the edge of the grey wall, six feet above his head, a great reddish protrusion, like the claw of a crab, moved, groping.

In automatic response, Straut yanked his .45 from its holster, jacked the action, and fired. Soft matter spattered, and the claw jerked back. The screeching started up again angrily, then was drowned in the engine roar as the jeep slid to a stop. Straut stooped, grabbed up a leaf to which a quivering lump adhered, jumped into the vehicle as it leaped forward; then a shock and they were turning, too fast, going over . . .

". . . lucky it was soft ground."

"What about the driver?"

Silence. Straut opened his eyes. "What . . . about . . ."

A stranger was looking down at him, an ordinary-looking fellow of about thirty-five.

"Easy, now, General Straut. You've had a bad spill. Everything is all right. I'm Paul Lieberman, from the University."

"The driver," Straut said with an effort.

"He was killed when the jeep went over."

"Went . . . over?"

"The creature lashed out with a member resembling a scorpion's stinger; it struck the jeep and flipped it; you were thrown clear. The driver jumped and the jeep rolled on him."

Straut pushed himself up. "Where's . . . Greer?"

"I'm right here, sir," Major Greer stepped up, stood attentively.

"Those tanks here yet, Greer?"

"No, sir. I had a call from General Margrave; there's some sort of holdup. Something about not destroying scientific material. I did get the mortars over from the base . . ."

Straut got to his feet. The stranger took his arm. "You ought to lie down, General—"

"Who the hell are you? Greer, get those mortars in place, spaced between your tracks."

The telephone rang. Straut seized it.

"General Straut."

"Straut? General Margrave here. I'm glad you're back on your feet. There'll be some scientists from the State University coming over; cooperate with them. You're going to have to hold things together at least until I can get another man in there—"

"Another man? General, I'm not incapacitated. The situation is under complete control—"

"I'll decide that, Straut. I understand you've got another casualty. What's happened to your defensive capabilities?"

"That was an accident, sir. The jeep—"

"I know. We'll review that matter at a later date. What I'm calling about is more important right now. The code men have made some headway on that box of yours. It's putting out some sort of transmission."

"Yes, sir."

"They've rigged a receiver set-up that puts out audible sound. Half the message—it's only twenty seconds long, repeated—is in English: It's a fragment of a recording from a daytime radio program; one of the network men here identified it. The rest is gibberish. They're still working over it."

"What—"

"Bryant tells me he thinks there's some sort of correspondence between the two parts of the message. I wouldn't know, myself. In my opinion it's a threat of some sort."

"I agree, General. An ultimatum."

"All right; keep your men back at a safe distance from now on. I want no more casualties."

*

Straut cursed his luck as he hung up the phone. Margrave was ready to relieve him; and after he had exercised every precaution. He had to do something, fast, something to sew this thing up before it slipped out of his hands. He looked at Greer.

"I'm neutralizing this thing once and for all. There'll be no more men killed while I stand by . . ."

Lieberman stood up. "General! I must protest any attack against this—"

Straut whirled. "I'm handling this, Professor. I don't know who let you in here or why—but I'll make the decisions. I'm stopping this man-killer before it comes out of its nest, maybe gets into that village beyond the woods; there are four thousand civilians there. It's my job to protect them." He jerked his head at Greer, strode out of the room. Lieberman followed, protesting.

"The creature has shown no signs of aggressiveness, General Straut—"

"With two men dead—?"

"You should have kept them back—"

Straut stopped, turned.

"Oh, it was my fault, was it?" Straut stared at Lieberman with cold fury. This civilian pushed his way in here, then had the infernal gall to accuse him, Brigadier General Straut, of causing the deaths of his own men. If he had the fellow in uniform for five minutes . . .

"You're not well, General. That fall—"

"Keep out of my way, Professor," Straut said. He turned and went on down the stairs: The present foul-up could ruin his career; and now this egghead interference . . .

With Greer at his side, Straut moved out to the edge of the field.

"All right, Major. Open up with your .50 caliber's."

Greer called a command and a staccato rattle started up. The smell of cordite, and the blue haze of gunsmoke . . . This was more like it. This would put an end to the nonsense. He was in command here, he had the power . . .

Greer lowered his binoculars. "Cease fire!" he commanded.

"Who told you to give that order, Major?" Straut barked.

Greer looked at him. "We're not even marking the thing."

Straut took the binoculars, stared through them.

"All right," he said. "We'll try something heavier. Let it have a round of 40mm."

Lieberman came up to Straut. "General, I appeal to you in the name of science. Hold off a little longer; at least until we learn what the message is about. The creature may—"

"Get back from the firing line, Professor." Straut turned his back on the civilian, raised the glasses to observe the effect of the recoilless rifle. There was a tremendous smack of displaced air, and a thunderous *boom*! as the explosive shell struck. Straut saw the grey shape jump, the raised lid waver. Dust rose from about it. There was no other effect.

"Keep firing, Greer," Straut snapped, almost with a feeling of triumph. The thing was impervious to artillery; now who was going to say it was no threat?

"How about the mortars, sir?" Greer said. "We can drop a few rounds in and blast the thing out of its nest."

"All right, try it, if the lid doesn't drop first. We won't be able to touch it if it does." And what we'll try next, I don't know, he thought; we can't drop anything really big on it, not unless we evacuate the whole country. . . .

*

The mortar fired, with a muffled thud. Straut watched tensely. Five seconds later, the ship erupted in a gout of pale pink debris. The lid rocked, pinkish fluid running down its opalescent surface. A second burst, and a third. A great fragment of the menacing claw hung from the branch of a tree a hundred feet from the ship. Straut grabbed for the phone. "Cease fire!"

Lieberman stared in horror at the carnage.

The telephone rang. Straut picked it up.

"General Straut," he said. His voice was firm. He had put an end to the threat for all time. . . .

"Straut, we've broken the message," Margrave said excitedly. "It's the damnedest thing . . ." Straut wanted to interrupt, announce his victory, but Margrave was droning on.

". . . strange sort of reasoning, but there was a certain analogy. In any event, I'm assured the translation is accurate. Put into English—"

Straut listened. Then he carefully placed the receiver on the hook.

Lieberman stared at him. "What was it, the message? Have they translated it?"

Straut nodded.

"What did it say?"

Straut cleared his throat. He turned and looked at Lieberman for a long moment before answering.

"It said, 'Please take good care of my little girl!' "

The process of writing a story is often as enlightening for me as, I hope, reading it is for the reader.

I began with the concept of submitting a human being to an ultimate trial in the same way that an engineer will load a beam until it collapses, testing it to destruction. It is in emotional situations that we meet our severest tests: fear, love, anger drive us to our highest efforts. Thus, the framework of the story suggested itself.

As the tale evolved, it became apparent that any power setting out to put mankind to the test—as did Koslo, as well as the Ree—places its own fate in the balance. Mallory's responses to the tests were not strictly reasonable, which fatally misled the Ree hive-mind.

In the end, Mallory revealed the true strength of man by using the power of his enemies against them. He wins not only his freedom and sanity—but also immense new powers over other men.

Not until then did the danger in such total victory become apparent. The ultimate test of man is his ability to master himself.

It is a test which we have so far failed.

Test to Destruction

The late October wind drove icy rain against Mallory's face above his turned-up collar where he stood concealed in the shadows at the mouth of the narrow alley.

"It's ironic, Johnny," the small, grim-faced man beside him muttered. "You—the man who should have been World Premier tonight—skulking in the back streets while Koslo and his bully boys drink champagne in the Executive Palace."

"That's all right, Paul," Mallory said. "Maybe he'll be too busy with his victory celebration to concern himself with me."

"And maybe he won't," the small man said. "He won't rest easy as long as he knows you're alive to oppose him."

"It will only be a few more hours, Paul. By breakfast time, Koslo will know his rigged election didn't take."

"But if he takes you first, that's the end, Johnny. Without you the coup will collapse like a soap bubble."

"I'm not leaving the city," Mallory said flatly. "Yes, there's a certain risk involved; but you don't bring down a dictator without taking a few chances."

"You didn't have to take this one, meeting Crandall yourself."

"It will help if he sees me, knows I'm in this all the way."

In silence, the two men waited the arrival of their fellow conspirator.

Aboard the interstellar dreadnought cruising half a parsec from Earth, the compound Ree mind surveyed the distant solar system.

Radiation on many wavelengths from the third body, the Perceptor cells directed the impulse to the sixty-nine hundred and thirty-four units comprising the segmented brain which guided the ship. *Modulations over the forty-ninth through the ninety-first spectra of mentation.*

A portion of the pattern is characteristic of exocosmic manipulatory intelligence, the Analyzers extrapolated from the data. *Other indications range in complexity from levels one through twenty-six.*

This is an anomalous situation, the Recollectors mused. *It is the essential nature of a Prime Intelligence to destroy all lesser competing mind-forms, just as I/we have systematically annihilated those I/ we have encountered on my/our exploration of the Galactic Arm.*

Before action is taken, clarification of the phenomenon is essential, the Interpretors pointed out. *Closure to a range not exceeding one radiation/second will be required for extraction and analysis of a representative mind-unit.*

In this event, the risk level rises to Category Ultimate, the Analyzers announced dispassionately.

RISK LEVELS NO LONGER APPLY, the powerful thought-impulse of the Egon put an end to the

discussion. NOW OUR SHIPS RANGE INTO NEW
SPACE, SEEKING EXPANSION ROOM FOR THE
GREAT RACE. THE UNALTERABLE COM-
MAND OF THAT WHICH IS GREAT REQUIRES
THAT MY/OUR PROBE BE PROSECUTED TO
THE LIMIT OF REE CAPABILITY, TESTING
MY/OUR ABILITY FOR SURVIVAL AND DOMI-
NANCE. THERE CAN BE NO TIMIDITY, NO
EXCUSE FOR FAILURE. LET ME/US NOW
ASSUME A CLOSE SURVEILLANCE ORBIT!

In utter silence, and at a velocity a fraction of a
kilometer/sec below that of light, the Ree dreadnought flashed toward Earth.

Mallory tensed as a dark figure appeared a block
away under the harsh radiance of a polyarc.

"There's Crandall now," the small man hissed.
"I'm glad—" He broke off as the roar of a powerful
turbine engine sounded suddenly along the empty
avenue. A police car exploded from a side street,
rounded the corner amid a shriek of overstressed
gyros. The man under the light turned to run—and
the vivid blue glare of a SURF-gun winked and stut-
tered from the car. The burst of slugs caught the
runner, slammed him against the brick wall, kicked
him from his feet, rolled him, before the crash of
the guns reached Mallory's ears.

"My God! They've killed Tony!" The small man
blurted. "We've got to get out . . . !"

Mallory took half a dozen steps back into the alley,
froze as lights sprang up at the far end. He heard
booted feet hit pavement, a hoarse voice that barked
a command.

"We're cut off," he snapped. There was a rough
wooden door six feet away. He jumped to it, threw
his weight against it. It held. He stepped back,
kicked it in, shoved his companion ahead of him into
a dark room smelling of moldy burlap and rat drop-

pings. Stumbling, groping in the dark, Mallory led the way across a stretch of littered floor, felt along the wall, found a door that hung by one hinge. He pushed past it, was in a passage floored with curled linoleum, visible in the feeble gleam filtered through a fanlight above a massive, barred door. He turned the other way, ran for the smaller door at the far end of the passage. He was ten feet from it when the center panel burst inward in a hail of wood splinters that grazed him, ripped at his coat like raking talons. Behind him, the small man made a choking noise; Mallory whirled in time to see him fall back against the wall and go down, his chest and stomach torn away by the full impact of a thousand rounds from the police SURF-gun.

An arm came through the broached door, groping for the latch. Mallory took a step, seized the wrist, wrenched backward with all his weight, felt the elbow joint shatter. The scream of the injured police-man was drowned in a second burst from the rapid-fire weapon—but Mallory had already leaped, caught the railing of the stair, pulled himself up and over. He took the steps five at a time, passed a landing littered with broken glass and empty bottles, kept going, emerged in a corridor of sagging doors and cobwebs. Feet crashed below, furious voices yelled. Mallory stepped inside the nearest door, stood with his back to the wall beside it. Heavy feet banged on the stairs, paused, came his way. . . .

Mallory tensed and as the policeman passed the door, he stepped out, brought his hand over and down in a side-handed blow to the base of the neck that had every ounce of power in his shoulders behind it. The man seemed to dive forward, and Mallory caught the gun before it struck the floor. He took three steps, poured a full magazine into the stairwell. As he turned to sprint for the far end of the passage, return fire boomed from below.

A club, swung by a giant, struck him in the side, knocked the breath from his lungs, sent him spinning against the wall. He recovered, ran on; his hand, exploring, found a deep gouge that bled freely. The bullet had barely grazed him.

He reached the door to the service stair, recoiled violently as a dirty-grey shape sprang at him with a yowl from the darkness—in the instant before a gun flashed and racketed in the narrow space, scattering plaster dust from the wall above his head. A thickset man in the dark uniform of the Security Police, advancing up the stair at a run, checked momentarily as he saw the gun in Mallory's hands—and before he recovered himself, Mallory had swung the empty weapon, knocked him spinning back down onto the landing. The cat that had saved his life—an immense, battle-scarred Tom—lay on the floor, half its head blown away by the blast it had intercepted. Its lone yellow eye was fixed on him; its claws raked the floor, as, even in death, it advanced to the attack. Mallory jumped over the stricken beast, went up the stairs.

Three flights higher, the stair ended in a loft stacked with bundled newspapers and rotting cartons from which mice scuttled as he approached. There was a single window, opaque with grime. Mallory tossed aside the useless gun, scanned the ceiling for evidence of an escape hatch, saw nothing. His side ached abominably.

Relentless feet sounded beyond the door. Mallory backed to a corner of the room—and again, the deafening shriek of the SURF-gun sounded, and the flimsy door bucked, disintegrated. For a moment, there was total silence. Then:

"Walk out with your hands up, Mallory!" a brassy voice snarled. In the gloom, pale flames were licking over the bundled papers, set afire by the torrent of steel-jacketed slugs. Smoke rose, thickened.

"Come out before you fry," the voice called.

"Let's get out of here," another man bawled. "This dump will go like tinder!"

"Last chance, Mallory!" the first man shouted, and now the flames, feeding on the dry paper, were reaching for the ceiling, roaring as they grew. Mallory went along the wall to the window, ripped aside the torn roller shade, tugged at the sash. It didn't move. He kicked out the glass, threw a leg over the sill, and stepped out onto a rusted fire escape. Five stories down, light puddled on grimy concrete, the white dots of upturned faces—and half a dozen police cars blocking the rain-wet street. He put his back to the railing, looked up. The fire escape extended three, perhaps four stories higher. He threw his arm across his face to shield it from the billowing flames, forced his legs to carry him up the iron treads three at a time.

The topmost landing was six feet below an overhanging cornice. Mallory stepped up on the rail, caught the edge of the carved stone trim with both hands, swung himself out. For a moment, he dangled, ninety feet above the street; then he pulled himself up, got a knee over the coping, and rolled onto the roof.

Lying flat, he scanned the darkness around him. The level was broken only by a ventilator stack and a shack housing a stair or elevator head.

He reconnoitered, found that the hotel occupied a corner, with a parking lot behind it. On the alley side, the adjoining roof was at a level ten feet lower, separated by a sixteen-foot gap. As Mallory stared across at it, a heavy rumbling shook the deck under his feet: one of the floors of the ancient building, collapsing as the fire ate through its supports.

Smoke was rising all around him now. On the parking lot side, dusky flames soared up thirty feet above him, trailing an inverted cascade of sparks into the wet night sky. He went to the stairhead, found the metal door locked. A rusty ladder was clamped to the side of the structure. He wrenched it free, carried it to the alley side. It took all his strength to force the corroded catches free, pull the ladder out to its full extension. Twenty feet, he estimated. Enough—maybe.

He shoved the end of the ladder out, wrestled it across to rest on the roof below. The flimsy bridge sagged under his weight as he crawled up on it. He moved carefully out, ignoring the swaying of the fragile support. He was six feet from the far roof when he felt the rotten metal crumble under him; with a frantic lunge, he threw himself forward. Only the fact that the roof was at a lower level saved him. He clawed his way over the sheet-metal gutter, hearing shouts ring out below as the ladder crashed to the bricks of the alley.

A bad break, he thought. *Now they know where I am. . . .*

There was a heavy trap-door set in the roof. He lifted it, descended an iron ladder into darkness, found his way to a corridor, along it to a stair. Faint sounds rose from below. He went down.

At the fourth floor, lights showed below, voices sounded, the clump of feet. He left the stair at the third floor, prowled along a hall, entered an abandoned office. Searchlights in the street below threw oblique shadows across the discolored walls.

He went on, turned a corner, went into a room on the alley side. A cold draft, reeking of smoke, blew in through a glassless window. Below, the narrow way appeared to be deserted. Paul's body was gone. The broken ladder lay where it had fallen. It was, he estimated, a twenty-foot drop to the bricks; even if he let himself down to arm's length and dropped, a leg-breaker. . . .

Something moved below him. A uniformed policeman was standing at a spot directly beneath the window, his back against the wall. A wolf smile drew Mallory's face tight. In a single motion, he slid his body out over the sill, chest down, held on for an instant, seeing the startled face below turn upward, the mouth open for a yell—

He dropped; his feet struck the man's back, breaking his fall. He rolled clear, sat up, half-dazed. The policeman sprawled on his face, his spine twisted at an awkward angle.

Mallory got to his feet—and almost fell at the stab of pain from his right ankle. Sprained, or broken. His teeth set against the pain, he moved along the wall. Icy rainwater, sluicing from the downspout ahead, swirled about his ankles. He slipped, almost went down on the slimy bricks. The lesser darkness of the parking lot behind the building showed ahead. If he could reach it, cross it—then he might still have a chance. He had to succeed—for Monica, for the child, for the future of a world.

Another step, and another. It was as though there were a vast ache that caught at him with every breath. His blood-soaked shirt and pants leg hung against him, icy cold. Ten feet more, and he would make his run for it—

Two men in the black uniforms of the State Security Police stepped out into his path, stood with blast-guns levelled at his chest. Mallory pushed away from the wall, braced himself for the burst of slugs that would end his life. Instead, a beam of light speared out through the misty rain, dazzling his eyes.

"You'll come with us, Mr. Mallory."

Still no contact, the Perceptors reported.

The prime-level minds below lack cohesion; they flicker and dart away even as I/we touch them.

The Initiators made a proposal: *By the use of*

appropriate harmonics a resonance field can be set up which will reinforce any native mind functioning in an analogous rhythm.

I/we find that a pattern of the following character will be most suitable. . . . A complex symbolism was displayed.

PERSEVERE IN THE FASHION DESCRIBED, the Egon commanded. ALL EXTRANEOUS FUNCTIONS WILL BE DISCONTINUED UNTIL SUCCESS IS ACHIEVED.

With total singleness of purpose, the Ree sensors probed across space from the dark and silent ship, searching for a receptive human mind.

The Interrogation Room was a totally bare cube of white enamel. At its geometric center, under a blinding white glare panel, sat a massive chair constructed of polished steel, casting an ink-black shadow.

A silent minute ticked past; then heels clicked in the corridor. A tall man in a plain, dark military tunic came through the open door, halted, studying his prisoner. His wide, sagging face was as grey and bleak as a tombstone.

"I warned you, Mallory," he said in a deep growling tone.

"You're making a mistake, Koslo," Mallory said.

"Openly arresting the people's hero, eh?" Koslo curved his wide, grey lips in a death's head smile. "Don't delude yourself. The malcontents will do nothing without their leader."

"Are you sure you're ready to put your regime to the test so soon?"

"It's that or wait, while your party gains strength. I chose the quicker course. I was never as good at waiting as you, Mallory."

"Well—you'll know by morning."

"That close, eh?" Koslo's heavy-lidded eyes pinched down on glints of light. He grunted. "I'll know many things by morning. You realize that your personal position is hopeless?" His eyes went to the chair.

"In other words, I should sell out to you now in return for—what? Another of your promises?"

"The alternative is the chair," Koslo said flatly.

"You have great confidence in machinery, Koslo—more than in men. That's your great weakness."

Koslo's hand went out, caressing the rectilinear metal of the chair. "This is a scientific apparatus designed to accomplish a specific task with the least possible difficulty to me. It creates conditions within the subject's neural system conducive to total recall, and at the same time amplifies the subvocalizations that accompany all highly cerebral activity. The subject is also rendered amenable to verbal cuing." He paused. "If you resist, it will destroy your mind— but not before you've told me everything: names, locations, dates, organization, operational plans— everything. It will be simpler for us both if you acknowledge the inevitable and tell me freely what I require to know."

"And after you've got the information?"

"You know my regime can't tolerate opposition. The more complete my information, the less bloodshed will be necessary."

Mallory shook his head. "No," he said bluntly.

"Don't be a fool, Mallory! This isn't a test of your manhood!"

"Perhaps it is, Koslo: man against machine."

Koslo's eyes probed at him. He made a quick gesture with one hand.

"Strap him in."

Seated in the chair, Mallory felt the cold metal suck the heat from his body. Bands restrained his arms, legs, torso. A wide ring of woven wire and plastic clamped his skull firmly to the formed headrest. Across the room, Fey Koslo watched.

"Ready, Excellency," a technician said.

"Proceed."

Mallory tensed. An unwholesome excitement churned his stomach. He'd heard of the chair, of its power to scour a man's mind clean and leave him a gibbering hulk.

Only a free society, he thought, *can produce the technology that makes tyranny possible. . . .*

He watched as a white-smocked technician approached, reached for the control panel. There was only one hope left: if he could fight the power of the machine, drag out the interrogation, delay Koslo until dawn . . .

A needle-studded vise clamped down against Mallory's temples. Instantly his mind was filled with whirling fever images. He felt his throat tighten in an aborted scream. Fingers of pure force struck into his brain, dislodging old memories, ripping open the healed wounds of time. From somewhere, he was aware of a voice, questioning. Words trembled in his throat, yearning to be shouted aloud.

I've got to resist! The thought flashed through his mind and was gone, borne away on a tide of probing impulses that swept through his brain like a millrace. *I've got to hold out . . . long enough . . . to give the others a chance. . . .*

Aboard the Ree ship, dim lights glowed and winked on the panel that encircled the control center.

I/we sense a new mind—a transmitter of great power, the Perceptors announced suddenly. *But the images are confused. I/we sense struggle, resistance. . . .*

IMPOSE CLOSE CONTROL, the Egon ordered. NARROW FOCUS AND EXTRACT A REPRESENTATIVE PERSONALITY FRACTION!

It is difficult; I/we sense powerful neural currents, at odds with the basic brain rhythms.

COMBAT THEM!

Again the Ree mind reached out, insinuated itself into the complex field-matrix that was Mallory's mind, and began, painstakingly, to trace out and reinforce its native symmetries, permitting the natural egomosaic to emerge, free from distracting counter-impulses.

The technician's face went chalk-white as Mallory's body went rigid against the restraining bands.

"You fool!" Koslo's voice cut at him like a whipping rod. "If he dies before he talks——"

"He . . . he fights strongly, Excellency." The man's eyes scanned instrument faces. "Alpha through delta rhythms normal, though exaggerated," he muttered. "Metabolic index .99 . . ."

Mallory's body jerked. His eyes opened, shut. His mouth worked.

"Why doesn't he speak?" Koslo barked.

"It may require a few moments, Excellency, to adjust the power flows to ten-point resonance——"

"Then get on with it, man! I risked too much in arresting this man to lose him now!"

White-hot fingers of pure force landed from the chair along the neural pathways within Mallory's brain—and met the adamantine resistance of the Ree probe. In the resultant confrontation, Mallory's battered self-awareness was tossed like a leaf in a gale.

Fight! The remaining wisp of his conscious intellect gathered itself——

—and was grasped, encapsulated, swept up and away. He was aware of spinning through a whirling fog of white light shot through with flashes and streamers of red, blue, violet. There was a sensation of great forces that pressed at him, flung him to and fro, drew his mind out like a ductile wire until it spanned the Galaxy. The filament grew broad, expanded into a diaphragm that bisected the universe. The plane assumed thickness, swelled out to encompass all space/time. Faint and far away, he sensed the tumultuous coursing of the energies that ravened just beyond the impenetrable membrane of force—

The imprisoning sphere shrank, pressed in, forcing his awareness into needle-sharp focus. He knew, without knowing how he knew, that he was locked in a sealed and airless chamber, constricting, claustrophobic, all sound and sensation cut off. He drew breath to scream—

No breath came. Only a weak pulse of terror, quickly fading, as if damped by an inhibiting hand. Alone in the dark, Mallory waited, every sense tuned, monitoring the surrounding blankness . . .

I/we have him! The Perceptors pulsed, and fell away. At the center of the chamber, the mind trap pulsed with the flowing energies that confined and controlled the captive brain pattern.

TESTING WILL COMMENCE AT ONCE. The Egon brushed aside the interrogatory impulses from the mind-segments concerned with speculation. INITIAL STIMULI WILL BE APPLIED AND RESULTS NOTED. NOW!

. . . and was aware of a faint glimmer of light across the room: the outline of a window. He blinked, raised himself on one elbow. Bedsprings creaked under him. He sniffed. An acid odor of smoke hung in the stifling air. He seemed to be in a cheap hotel room. He had no memory of how he came to be there. He threw back the coarse blanket and felt warped floor boards under his bare feet—

The boards were hot.

He jumped up, went to the door, grasped the

knob—and jerked his hand back. The metal had blistered his palm.

He ran to the window, ripped aside the dirt-stiff gauze curtains, snapped open the latch, tugged at the sash. It didn't budge. He stepped back, kicked out the glass. Instantly a coil of smoke whipped in through the broken pane. Using the curtain to protect his hand, he knocked out the shards, swung a leg over the sill, stumbled onto the fire escape. The rusted metal cut at his bare feet. Groping, he made his way down half a dozen steps—and fell back as a sheet of red flame billowed from below.

Over the rail he saw the street, lights puddled on grimy concrete ten stories down, white faces, like pale dots, upturned. A hundred feet away, an extension ladder swayed, approaching another wing of the flaming building, not concerned with him. He was lost, abandoned. Nothing could save him. For forty feet below, the iron ladder was an inferno.

It would be easier, quicker, to go over the rail, escape the pain, die cleanly, the thought came into his mind with dreadful clarity.

There was a tinkling crash and a window above blew out. Scalding embers rained down on his back. The iron was hot underfoot. He drew a breath, shielded his face with one arm, and plunged downward through the whipping flames. . . .

He was crawling, falling down the cruel metal treads and risers. The pain across his face, his back, his shoulder, his arm, was like a red-hot iron, applied and forgotten. He caught a glimpse of his arm, flayed, oozing, black-edged. . . .

His hands and feet were no longer his own. He used his knees and elbows, tumbled himself over yet another edge, sliding down to the next landing. The faces were closer now; hands were reaching up. He groped, got to his feet, felt the last section swing down as his weight went on it. His vision was a blur of red. He sensed the blistered skin sloughing from his thighs. A woman screamed.

". . . my God, burned alive and still walking!" a thin voice cawed.

". . . his hands . . . no fingers . . ."

Something rose, smashed at him, a ghostly blow as blackness closed in . . .

The response of the entity was anomalous, the Analyzers reported. *Its life tenacity is enormous! Confronted with apparent imminent physical destruction, it chose agony and mutilation merely to extend survival for a brief period.*

The possibility exists that such a response represents a mere instinctive mechanism of unusual form, the Analyzers pointed out.

If so, it might prove dangerous. More data on the point is required.

I/WE WILL RESTIMULATE THE SUBJECT, the Egon ordered. THE PARAMETERS OF THE SURVIVAL DRIVE MUST BE ESTABLISHED WITH PRECISION, RESUME TESTING!

In the chair, Mallory writhed, went limp.

"Is he . . . ?"

"He's alive, Excellency! But something's wrong! I can't get through to a vocalization level! He's fighting me with some sort of fantasy-complex of his own!"

"Bring him out of it!"

"Excellency, I tried. I can't reach him! It's as though he'd tapped the chair's energy sources, and were using them to reinforce his own defense mechanism!"

"Override him!"

"I'll try—but his power is fantastic!"

"Then we'll use more power!"

"It's . . . dangerous, Excellency."

"Not more dangerous than failure!"

Grim-faced, the technician reset the panel to step up the energy flow through Mallory's brain.

The subject stirs! the Perceptors burst out. *Massive new energies flow in the mind-field! My/our grip loosens . . .*

HOLD THE SUBJECT! RESTIMULATE AT ONCE, WITH MAXIMUM EMERGENCY FORCE!

While the captive surged and fought against the restraint, the segmented mind of the alien concentrated its forces, hurled a new stimulus into the rolling captive mind-field.

. . . Hot sun beat down on his back. A light wind ruffled the tall grass growing up the slope where the wounded lion had taken cover. Telltale drops of dark purple blood clinging to the tall stems marked the big cat's route. It would be up there, flattened to the earth under the clump of thorn trees, its yellow eyes narrowed against the agony of the .375 bullet in his chest, waiting, hoping for its tormentor to come to it. . . .

His heart was thudding under the damp khaki shirt. The heavy rifle felt like a toy in his hands—a useless plaything against the primitive fury of the beast. He took a step; his mouth twisted in an ironic grimace. What was he proving? There was no one here to know if he chose to walk back and sit under a tree and take a leisurely swig from his flask, let an hour or two crawl by—while the cat bled to death—and then go in to find the body. He took another step. And now he was walking steadily forward. The breeze was cool on his forehead. His legs felt light, strong. He drew a deep breath, smelled the sweetness of the spring air. Life had never seemed more precious—

There was a deep, asthmatic cough, and the great beast broke from the shadows, yellow fangs bared, muscles pumping under the dun hide, dark blood shining black along the flank—

He planted his feet, brought the gun up, socketed it against his shoulder as the lion charged down the slope. *By the book*, he thought sardonically. *Take him just above the sternum, hold on him until you're sure.* . . . At a hundred feet he fired—just as the animal veered left. The bullet smacked home far back along the ribs. The cat broke stride, recovered. The gun bucked and roared again, and the snarling face exploded in a mask of red— And still the dying carnivore came on. He blinked sweat from his eyes, centered the sights on the point of the shoulder—

The trigger jammed hard. A glance showed him the spent cartridge lodged in the action. He raked at it vainly, standing his ground. At the last instant, he stepped aside, and the hurtling monster skidded past him, dead in the dust. And the thought that struck him then was that if Monica had been watching from the car at the foot of the hill she would not have laughed at him this time. . . .

Again the reaction syndrome is inharmonious with any concept of rationality in my/our experience, the Recollector cells expressed the paradox with which the captive mind had presented the Ree intelligence. *Here is an entity which clings to personality survival with a ferocity unparalleled—yet faces Category Ultimate risks needlessly, in response to an abstract code of behavioral symmetry.*

I/we postulate that the personality segment selected does not represent the true Egon-analogue of the subject, the Speculators offered. *It is obviously incomplete, nonviable.*

Let me/us attempt a selective withdrawal of control over peripheral regions of the mind-field, the Perceptors proposed. *Thus permitting greater concentration of stimulus to the central matrix.*

By matching energies with the captive mind, it will be possible to monitor its rhythms and deduce the key to its total control, the Calculators determined quickly.

This course offers the risk of rupturing the matrix and the destruction of the specimen.

THE RISK MUST BE TAKEN.

With infinite precision, the Ree mind narrowed the scope of its probe, fitting its shape to the contours of Mallory's embattled brain, matching itself in a one-to-one correspondence to the massive energy flows from the Interrogation chair.

Equilibrium, the Perceptors reported at last. *However, the balance is precarious.*

The next text must be designed to expose new aspects of the subject's survival syndrome, the Analyzers pointed out. A stimulus pattern was proposed and accepted. Aboard the ship in its sub-lunar orbit, the Ree mindbeam again lanced out to touch Mallory's receptive brain. . . .

Blackness gave way to misty light. A deep rumbling shook the rocks under his feet. Through the whirling spray, he saw the raft, the small figure that clung to it: a child, a little girl perhaps nine years old, crouched on hands and knees, looking toward him.

"Daddy!" A high, thin cry of pure terror. The raft bucked and tossed in the wild current. He took a step, slipped, almost went down on the slimy rocks. The icy water swirled about his knees. A hundred feet downstream, the river curved in a grey-metal sheen, over and down, veiled by the mists of its own thunderous descent. He turned, scrambled back up, ran along the bank. There, ahead, a point of rock jutted. Perhaps . . .

The raft bobbed, whirled, fifty feet away. Too far. He saw the pale, small face, the pleading eyes. Fear welled in him, greasy and sickening.

Visions of death rose up, of his broken body bobbing below the falls, lying wax-white on a slab, sleeping, powdered and false in a satin-lined box, corrupting in the close darkness under the indifferent sod. . . .

He took a trembling step back.

For an instant, a curious sensation of unreality swept over him. He remembered darkness, a sense of utter claustrophobia—and a white room, a face that leaned close. . . .

He blinked—and through the spray of the rapids, his eyes met those of the doomed child. Compassion struck him like a club. He grunted, felt the clean white flame of anger at himself, of disgust at his fear. He closed his eyes and leaped far out, struck the water and went under, came up gasping. His strokes took him toward the raft. He felt a heavy blow as the current tossed him against a rock, choked as chopping spray whipped in his face. The thought came that broken ribs didn't matter now, nor air for breathing. Only to reach the raft before it reached the edge, that the small, frightened soul might not go down alone—into the great darkness. . . .

His hands clawed the rough wood. He pulled himself up, caught the small body to him as the world dropped away and the thunder rose deafeningly to meet him. . . .

"Excellency! I need help!" The technician appealed to the grim-faced dictator. "I'm pouring enough power through his brain to kill two ordinary men—and he still fights back! For a second there, a moment ago, I'd swear he opened his eyes and looked right through me! I can't take the responsibility—"

"Then cut the power, you blundering idiot!"

"I don't dare, the backlash will kill him!"

"He . . . must . . . talk!" Koslo grated. "Hold him!

Break him! Or I promise you a slow and terrible death!"

Trembling, the technician adjusted his controls. In the chair, Mallory sat tense, no longer fighting the straps. He looked like a man lost in thought. Perspiration broke from his hairline, trickled down his face.

Again new currents stir in the captive, the Perceptors announced in alarm. *The resources of this mind are staggering!*

MATCH IT! the Egon directed.

My/our power resources are already overextended! the Calculators interjected.

WITHDRAW ENERGIES FROM ALL PERIPHERAL FUNCTIONS! LOWER SHIELDING! THE MOMENT OF THE ULTIMATE TEST IS UPON ME/US!

Swiftly the Ree mind complied.

The captive is held, the Calculator announced. *But I/we point out that this linkage now presents a channel of vulnerability to assault.*

THE RISK MUST BE TAKEN.

Even now the mind stirs against my/our countrol.

HOLD IT FAST!

Grimly, the Ree mind fought to retain its control of Mallory's brain.

In one instant, he was not. Then, abruptly, he existed. *Mallory,* he thought. *That symbol represents I/we. . . .*

The alien thought faded. He caught at it, held the symbol. Mallory. He remembered the shape of his body, the feel of his skull enclosing his brain, the sensations of light, sound, heat—but here there was no sound, no light. Only the enclosing blackness, impenetrable, eternal, changeless. . . .

But where was here?

He remembered the white room, the harsh voice of Koslo, the steel chair—

And the mighty roar of the waters rushing up at him—

And the reaching talons of a giant cat—

And the searing agony of flames that licked around his body. . . .

But there was no pain, now, no discomfort—no sensation of any kind. Was this death, then? At once, he rejected the idea as nonsense.

Cogito ergo sum. I am a prisoner—where?

His senses stirred, questing against emptiness, sensationlessness. He strained outward—and heard sound; voices, pleading, demanding. They grew louder, echoing in the vastness:

". . . talk, damn you! Who are your chief accomplices? What support do you expect from the Armed Forces? Which of the generals are with you? Armaments . . . ? Organization . . . ? Initial attack points . . . ?"

Blinding static sleeted across the words, filled the universe, grew dim. For an instant, Mallory was aware of straps cutting into the tensed muscles of his forearms, the pain of the band clamped around his head, the ache of cramping muscles. . . .

. . . was aware of floating, gravityless, in a sea of winking, flashing energies. Vertigo rose up; frantically he fought for stability in a world of chaos. Through spinning darkness he reached, found a matrix of pure direction, intangible, but, against the background of shifting energy flows, providing an orienting grid. He seized on it, hold. . . .

Full emergency discharge! The Receptors blasted the command through all the sixty-nine hundred and thirty-four units of the Ree mind—and recoiled in shock. *The captive mind clings to the contact! We cannot break free!*

Pulsating with the enormous shock of the prisoner's sudden outlashing, the alien rested for the fractional nanosecond required to restablish inter-segmental balance.

The power of the enemy, though unprecedentedly great, is not sufficient to broach the integrity of my/our entity-field, the Analyzers stated, tensely. *But I/we must retreat at once!*

NO! I/WE LACK SUFFICIENT DATA TO JUSTIFY WITHDRAWAL OF PHASE ONE, the Egon countermanded. HERE IS A MIND RULED BY CONFLICTING DRIVES OF GREAT POWER. WHICH IS PARAMOUNT? THEREIN LIES THE KEY TO ITS DEFEAT.

I/WE MUST DEVISE A STIMULATION COMPLEX WHICH WILL EVOKE BOTH DRIVES IN LETHAL OPPOSITION.

Precious microseconds passed while the compound mind hastily scanned Mallory's mind for symbols from which to assemble the necessary gestalt-form.

Ready, the Perceptors announced. *But it must be pointed out that no mind can long survive intact the direct confrontation of these antagonistic imperatives. Is the stimulus to be carried to the point of nonretrieval?*

AFFIRMATIVE. The Egon's tone was one of utter finality. TEST TO DESTRUCTION.

Illusion, Mallory told himself. *I'm being bombarded by illusions.* . . . He sensed the approach of a massive new wave front, descending on him like a breaking Pacific comber. Grimly, he clung to his tenuous orientation—but the smashing impact whirled him into darkness. Far away, a masked inquisitor faced him.

"Pain has availed nothing against you," the muffled voice said. "The threat of death does not move you. And yet there is a way. . . ." A curtain fell aside, and Monica stood there, tall, slim, vibrantly alive, as beautiful as a roe-deer. And beside her, the child.

He said "No!" and started forward, but the chains held him. He watched, helpless, while brutal hands seized the woman, moved casually, intimately, over her body. Other hands gripped the child. He saw the terror on the small face, the fear in her eyes—

Fear that he had seen before. . . .

But of course he had seen her before. The child was his daughter, the precious offspring of himself and the slender female—

Monica, he corrected himself.

—had seen those eyes, through swirling mist, poised above a cataract—

No. That was a dream. A dream in which he had died, violently. And there had been another dream of facing a wounded lion as it charged down on him—

"You will not be harmed," the Inquisitor's voice seemed to come from a remote distance. "But you will carry with you forever the memory of their living dismemberment. . . ."

With a jerk, his attention returned to the woman and the child. He saw them strip Monica's slender, tawny body. Naked, she stood before them, refusing to cower. But of what use was courage now? The manacles at her wrists were linked to a hook set in the damp stone wall. The glowing iron moved closer to her white flesh. He saw the skin darken and blister. The iron plunged home. She stiffened, screamed. . . .

A woman screamed.

"My God, burned alive," a thin voice cawed. "And still walking!"

He looked down. There was no wound, no scar. The skin was unbroken. But a fleeting almost-recollection came of crackling flames that seared with a white agony as he drew them into his lungs. . . .

"A dream," he said aloud. "I'm dreaming. I have to wake up!" He closed his eyes and shook his head. . . .

"He shook his head!" the technician choked. "Excellency, it's impossible—but I swear the man is throwing off the machine's control!"

Koslo brushed the other roughly aside. He seized the control lever, pushed it forward. In the chair, Mallory stiffened. His breathing became hoarse, ragged.

"Excellency, the man will die . . . !"

"Let him die! No one defies me with impunity!"

Narrow focus! The Perceptors flashed the command to the sixty-nine hundred and thirty-four energy-producing segments of the Ree mind. *The contest cannot continue long! Almost we lost the captive then . . . !*

The probe beam narrowed, knifing into the living heart of Mallory's brain, imposing its chosen patterns. . . .

. . . the child whimpered as the foot-long blade approached her fragile breast. The gnarled fist holding the knife stroked it almost lovingly across the blue-veined skin. Crimson blood washed down from the shallow wound.

"If you reveal the secrets of the Brotherhood to me, truly your comrades in arms will die," the Inquisitor's faceless voice droned. "But if you stubbornly refuse, your woman and your infant will suffer all that my ingenuity can devise."

He strained against his chains. "I can't tell you," he croaked. "Don't you understand, nothing is worth this horror! Nothing. . . ."

Nothing he could have done would have saved her. She crouched on the raft, doomed. But he could join her—

But not this time. This time chains of steel kept him from her. He hurled himself against them, and tears blinded his eyes. . . .

Smoke blinded his eyes. He looked down, saw the faces upturned below. Surely, easy death was preferable to living immolation. But he covered his face with his arms and started down. . . .

Never betray your trust! The woman's voice rang clear as a trumpet across the narrow dungeon.

Daddy! the child screamed.

We can die only once! the woman called.

The raft plunged downward into boiling chaos. . . .

"Speak, damn you!" The Inquisitor's voice had taken on a new note. "I want the names, the places! Who are your accomplices? What are your plans? When will the rising begin? What signal are they waiting for? Where . . . ? When . . . ?"

Mallory opened his eyes. Blinding white light, a twisted face that loomed before him, goggling.

"Excellency! He's awake! He's broken through. . . ."

"Pour full power into him! Force, man! Force him to speak!"

"I—I'm afraid, Excellency! We're tampering with the mightiest instrument in the universe: a human brain! Who knows what we may be creating—"

Koslo struck the man aside, threw the control lever full against the stop.

. . . The darkness burst into a coruscating brilliance that became the outlines of a room. A transparent man whom he recognized as Koslo stood before him. He watched as the dictator turned to him, his face contorted.

"Now talk, damn you!"

His voice had a curious, ghostly quality, as though it represented only one level of reality.

"Yes," Mallory said distinctly. "I'll talk."

"And if you lie—" Koslo jerked an ugly automatic pistol from the pocket of his plain tunic. "I'll put a bullet in your brain myself!"

"My chief associates in the plot," Mallory began, "are . . ." As he spoke, he gently disengaged himself—that was the word that came to his mind—from the scene around him. He was aware at one level of his voice speaking on, reeling off the facts for which the other man hungered so nakedly. And he reached out, channeling the power pouring into him from the chair . . . spanning across vast distances compressed now to a dimensionless plane. Delicately, he quested farther, entered a curious, flickering net of living energies. He pressed, found points of weakness, poured in more power—

A circular room leaped into eerie visibility. Ranged around it were lights that winked and glowed. From ranked thousands of cells, white wormforms poked blunt, eyeless heads. . . .

HE IS HERE! The Egon shrieked the warning, and hurled a bolt of pure mind-force along the channel of contact and met a counter-bolt of energy that seared through him, blackened and charred the intricate organic circuitry of his cerebrum, left a smoking pocket in the rank of cells. For a moment, Mallory rested, sensing the shock and bewilderment sweeping through the leaderless Ree mind-segments. He felt the automatic death-urge that gripped them as the realization reached them that the guiding overpower of the Egon was gone. As he watched, a unit crumpled inward and expired. And another—

"Stop!" Mallory commanded. "I assume control of the mind-complex! Let the segments link in with me!"

Obediently, the will-less fragments of the Ree mind obeyed.

"Change course," Mallory ordered. He gave the

necessary instructions, then withdrew along the channel of contact.

"So . . . the great Mallory broke." Koslo rocked on his heels before the captive body of his enemy. He laughed. "You were slow to start, but once begun you sang like a turtledove. I'll give you my orders now, and by dawn your futile revolt will be a heap of charred corpses stacked in the plaza as an example to others!" He raised the gun.

"I'm not through yet," Mallory said. "The plot runs deeper than you think, Koslo."

The dictator ran a hand over his grey face. His eyes showed the terrible strain of the last hours.

"Talk, then," he growled. "Talk fast!"

As he spoke on, Mallory again shifted his primary awareness, settled into resonance with the subjugated Ree intelligence. Through the ship's sensors, he saw the white planet swelling ahead. He slowed the vessel, brought it in on a long parabolic course which skimmed the stratosphere. Seventy miles above the Atlantic, he entered a high haze layer, slowed again as he sensed the heating of the hull.

Below the clouds, he sent the ship hurtling across the coast. He dropped to treetop level, scanned the scene through sensitive hull-plates—

For a long moment he studied the landscape below. Then suddenly he understood. . . .

"Why do you smile, Mallory?" Koslo's voice was harsh; the gun pointed at the other's head. "Tell me the joke that makes a man laugh in the condemned seat reserved for traitors."

"You'll know in just a moment. . . ." He broke off as a crashing sound came from beyond the room. The floor shook and trembled, rocking Koslo on his feet. A dull boom echoed. The door burst wide.

"Excellency! The capital is under attack!" The man

fell forward, exposing a great wound on his back. Koslo whirled on Mallory—

With a thunderous crash, one side of the room bulged and fell inward. Through the broached wall, a glittering torpedo-shape appeared, a polished intricacy of burnished metal floating lightly on pencils of blue-white light. The gun in the hand of the dictator came up, crashed deafeningly in the enclosed space. From the prow of the invader, pink light winked. Koslo spun, fell heavily on his face.

The twenty-eight-inch Ree dreadnought came to rest before Mallory. A beam speared out, burned through the chair control panel. The shackles fell away.

I/we await your/our next command. The Ree mind spoke soundlessly in the awesome silence.

Three months had passed since the referendum which had swept John Mallory into office as Premier of the First Planetary Republic. He stood in a room of his spacious apartment in the Executive Palace, frowning at the slender black-haired woman as she spoke earnestly to him:

"John—I'm afraid of that—that infernal machine, eternally hovering, waiting for your orders."

"But why, Monica? That infernal machine, as you call it, was the thing that made a free election possible—and even now it's all that holds Koslo's old organization in check."

"John—" Her hand gripped his arm. "With that— thing—always at your beck and call, you can control anyone, anything on Earth! No opposition can stand before you!"

She looked directly at him. "It isn't right for anyone to have such power, John. Not even you. No human being should be put to such a test!"

His face tightened. "Have I misused it?"

"Not yet. That's why . . ."

"You imply that I will?"

"You're a man, with the failings of a man."

"I propose only what's good for the people of Earth," he said sharply. "Would you have me voluntarily throw away the one weapon that can protect our hard-won freedom?"

"But, John—who are you to be the sole arbiter of what's good for the people of Earth?"

"I'm Chairman of the Republic—"

"You're still human. Stop—while you're still human!"

He studied her face. "You resent my success, don't you? What would you have me do? Resign?"

"I want you to send the machine away—back to wherever it came from."

He laughed shortly. "Are you out of your mind? I haven't begun to extract the technological secrets the Ree ship represents."

"We're not ready for those secrets, John. The race isn't ready. It's already changed you. In the end it can only destroy you as a man."

"Nonsense. I control it utterly. It's like an extension of my own mind—"

"John—please. If not for my sake or your own, for Dian's."

"What's the child got to do with this?"

"She's your daughter. She hardly sees you once a week."

"That's the price she has to pay for being the heir to the greatest man—I mean—damn it, Monica, my responsibilities don't permit me to indulge in all the suburban customs."

"John—" Her voice was a whisper, painful in its intensity. "Send it away."

"No. I won't send it away."

Her face was pale. "Very well, John. As you wish."

"Yes. As I wish."

After she left the room, Mallory stood for a long

time staring out through the high window at the tiny craft, hovering in the blue air fifty feet away, silent, ready.

Then: *Ree mind,* he sent out the call. *Probe the apartments of the woman, Monica. I have reason to suspect she plots treason against the state. . . .*

FRED SABERHAGEN

Fred Saberhagen needs very little introduction these days. His most famous creations—the awesome Berserkers—are known to SF readers around the world. He's reached the bestseller lists several times, most recently with his "Book of Swords" series, and his novels span the territory from hard science fiction to high fantasy. Quite understandably, Saberhagen's been labeled one of the best writers in the business.

These fine volumes by Saberhagen are available from Baen Books:

PYRAMIDS
A fascinating new twist on the time-travel novel, introducing a great new series hero: Pilgrim, the Flying Dutchman of Time, whose only hope for returning home lies in subtly altering the history of our own timeline to more closely reflect his own. Learn why the curse of the Pharaoh Khufu (builder of the Great Pyramid) had a special reality, in *Pyramids*. "Saberhagen's light, imaginative and enjoyable adventures speed along twisting paths to a climax that is even more surprising than the rest of the book."

—*Publishers Weekly*

AFTER THE FACT
This is the second novel featuring the great new series hero, Pilgrim—the Lost Traveller adrift in time and dimensionality. His current project: to rescue Abraham Lincoln from assassination, AFTER THE FACT!

THE FRANKENSTEIN PAPERS

At last—the truth about a sinister Dr. Frankenstein and his monster with a heart of gold, based on a history written by the monster himself! Find out what happened when the mad Doctor brought his creation to life, and why the monster has no scars.

THE EMPIRE OF THE EAST

A masterful blend of high technology and high sorcery; a world where magic rules—and science struggles to live again! "Ranks favorably with Tolkien. Exceptional in sheer unbridled zest and imaginative sweep!—*School Library Journal* "*Empire of the East* is one of the best science fiction fantasy epics—Saberhagen can be justly proud. Highly recommended."
—*Science Fiction Chronicle*

THE BLACK THRONE with Roger Zelazny

Two masters of SF collaborate on a masterpiece of fantasy: As children they met and built sand castles on a beach out of space and time: Edgar Perry, little Annie, and Edgar Allan Poe. . . . Fifteen years later Edgar Perry has grown to manhood—and as the result of a trip through a maelstrom, he's leading a much more active life. Perry will learn to thrive in the dark, romantic world he's landed in, where lead can be transmuted to gold, ravens can speak, orangutans can commit murder, and beautiful women are easy to come by. But his alter ego, Edgar Allan, is stranded in a strange and unfriendly world where he can only write about the wonderful and mysterious reality he has lost forever. . . .

THE GOLDEN PEOPLE

Genetically perfect, super-human children are created by a dedicated scientist for the betterment of Mankind. As the children mature, however, they begin to wonder if Man *should* survive. . . .

LOVE CONQUERS ALL

In a future where childbirth is outlawed and promiscuity required, one woman dares fight the system for the right to bear children.

OCTAGON

Players scattered across the continent are engaged in a game called "Starweb." Each player has certain attributes, and can ally with or attack any of the others. But one player seems to have confused the reality of the world: a player with the attributes of machinelike precision and mechanical ruthlessness. His name is Octagon, and he's out for blood.